CW00864279

TEMPORARILY INSANE

Carl Borgen

Acknowledgements

1st edition
Written by C.P.H. Borgen
Senior editor: Aurora Woods
Proof reading: Aurora Woods, Simone van Dijk
Interior design: Sandor Weijn
Cover design: Palamedes PR
Photo backcover: Adrienne Korzilius

www.carlborgen.com

This novel is based on a true story that took place between 1975
and 2021. Some of the characters and events portrayed have
been altered for the purpose of dramatisation and to protect
anonymity where appropriate.

Also by Carl Borgen

Cliff Barber and the Flower of Life
Available on request

The Bock Saga
Published on www.amazon.co.uk , www.amazon.com

Die Bock Saga
Published on www.amazon.de

Sa = "to get"; Ga = "to give"

Casper

The sun peered between the mountain peaks, and I saw the wind snapping at the dust as it tried to settle. It was six o'clock in the morning on the 24th of February 1975 in a freezing desert in Baluchistan, Pakistan. I stood by a rock that acted as a signpost, just outside the Quetta bus terminal. On it was written the distance to Amsterdam: 7,000 kilometres.

I had no idea that my life was about to change completely right here in this place and time, and that the man walking toward me would be the catalyst for everything that was to come. Out of seemingly nowhere, Ior walked up to the signpost. We both looked at it in silence and headed for the bus terminal in tandem. We happened to be travelling on the same bus. As there were no other Westerners around, we decided to stick together out of convenience.

We had a lot of time to talk and listen to each other. The bus brought us to Teheran. The signpost had mentioned it was 1,575 kilometres away. We'd both been in Goa, the hippie refuge in India, and he'd seen me there, dancing at the 1974 Christmas party. I hadn't noticed him.

From Goa, I'd hitchhiked several thousand kilometres through the south of India into the north. In the holy city of Benares, on the river Ganges, all my money had been stolen. From there on, I'd made my way without money and had ended up in Quetta. Ior was broke too. He'd been smart enough to leave his train ticket to Helsinki in Teheran in the safe hands of the Swedish/Finnish embassy when passing through seven months earlier. If he reached Teheran, he'd be ok.

The trip from Quetta to Teheran took a few weeks and there was always someone who offered to pay for our tickets and food in exchange for stories from other parts of the world. Most of the time, we sat with a sheep on our lap or on the roof of a bus with large families and chickens. It was an easy time, and the atmosphere was good. In those days, Pakistan and Iran were friendly places for travellers like us.

Ior had a lot to tell. He was an expert in 18th century European history. I listened carefully for hours to his stories and explanations of what had happened during that century, a time in which so much had changed for mankind. The diminishing power of the church, the flourishing of science, the technological revolution that this brought and all its implications. Ior came from an old and influential family who'd been part of the global action in the last few centuries.

I didn't have a lot to tell in exchange. I told Ior that I came from a suburb next to a run-down steel factory near Amsterdam, Holland. I told him that my parents loved chinchilla dogs and that we had a rabbit in the garden with droopy ears. As a street kid, I loved to kick balls. I was in primary school and then in secondary school and then in a teacher training course. After one year working as a teacher, I realised that I'd spent all my life in school and knew nothing of the real world.

My world was limited to a horizon of smoking chimneys and the perpetual smell of burning coal. I was fed up and wanted more from life, for myself and for the kids I taught. I didn't want to teach kids to become like me and to accept the world as it was. Shouldn't there be something more to life than that?

Of course, I knew more about the world than what I saw around me. The TV and radio saw to this. I knew that we belonged to the Free West and that the Russians were our enemies because they were communists that wanted to steal everything from us. There were wars all around the planet between us and them. The communists were very poor because everything they did was wrong. We were not only free, but rich as well. Although the latter was hard to see from where I lived.

They told us that the Russian women had to work hard in heavy industries, steering enormous machines. This made them ugly and manly. Everyone else in the world didn't matter; they were from different races and hadn't yet reached our level of development. They believed in all kinds of gods and usually died at a young age from terrible diseases.

One day, a letter arrived. It was a letter that all boys in Holland received sooner or later, and it summoned me to enrol in the army for 18 months. I decided to leave. To run away.

The bus pulled into the chaos of the main transport centre of Teheran. As far as the eye could see were buses, camels and donkeys pulling carts, each loaded with bales of produce on their way to feed the city. The roar of engines, the sound of animals and the crash of shouting mixed with a myriad of smells. It was busier than a distressed ant nest. We bumped our way through the flock of foreign bodies towards one of the exits and found a teashop where we sat down, our senses reeling from overstimulation.

"What are your plans then? Apart from picking up your train ticket to Helsinki, of course," I asked, eyeing up the golden pile of honey sweets a turbaned kid had just set on our table.

"I want to meet a friend. Or more of a client, I should say."

"Client?"

"I did a guided tour for him in Helsinki."

"Ah... so a tourist or something?"

"Not quite. He was on business in Finland and the government asked me to entertain him by giving him a tour. We got on really well, and he asked me to drop by if I ever came to Persia."

"Oh, so he's a businessman?"

"No, not really. He's a Shah."

"Shah? As in *the* Shah, ruler of Persia?"

"Yes."

After checking in at a hotel in the old marketplace, Ior went to the palace to ask for an audience. This was granted for the next day, which gave us twenty-four hours to make Ior presentable. We'd been broke for a long time and it showed. Ior managed to wash his travelling clothes in a well, shave and then smear his hair to one side. The look he was going for was that of a seasoned traveller, and this he truly was.

The next afternoon, I was drinking tea with the hotel receptionist when Ior came bursting in.

"We had a great time. The Shah insisted on being my personal guide, just as I'd been for him in Helsinki. He showed me the oldest parts of the palace; it's extremely beautiful. He knows a lot about the architecture and what all the mysterious mathematical symbols mean. Of course, much knowledge has been lost, but mathematics always stays the same. That's the beauty of it."

I was amazed that my dusty friend was received so well in high places.

"After the tour, we had lunch together in a saloon decorated with the most intricate adornments I've ever seen. The Shah is an interesting man. He both lives within ancient traditions and is fascinated by modern Western living and technology."

"What did you eat?" asked the receptionist.

"The table was full of little snacks. It was actually not hugely different from what you see here in the market."

"Our Shah is from a modest background. That's the food he grew up with."

"Was there no lobster and caviar?" I smirked.

"No, just pastries and fruit. Delicious ones, but nothing fancy."

"The Shah is like us. He loves his people, but not everyone loves him back. It must be sad for him. Thank God he is very strong and wise."

"He donated this book to me."

Ior took an enormous book from his bag. It was leather-bound with golden inscriptions.

"It's about his palace. Look, it's full of colourful handmade drawings."

We all focussed on the book and its content.

"That's the most beautiful thing I've ever seen," the receptionist told us solemnly.

"Out of this world," I mumbled back, without taking my eyes off the intricate illustrations in front of me.

The receptionist looked at us in awe. "This is a very expensive gift."

"Ior, if this book is really that expensive, then you realise what's happened, don't you? You're no longer a poor man!" I joked, eyes glinting in the afternoon sun.

"Right. Well, I should sell it then, so I can pay the hotel bill."

"What's this about the hotel bill?" the receptionist asked sharply.

"Not to worry, my friend," smiled Ior. "Can you tell us where we could get the best price for it?"

"Hmph. I do happen to know a place, but are you sure? This is a gift from the Shah. If you do decide to sell it, don't go yourself. Teheran is full of spies."

Ior turned to me, and I remember a slight sense of uneasiness crawl down my back. "Casper, please go and sell this book for me."

Although the uneasiness still lingered, it didn't change the fact that my friend had asked me a favour, so I set off with heavy shoes. The receptionist found a boy who guided me through the maze of the market to the prospective buyer. I entered the antique book shop through a side door. It was both light and dark simultaneously. Rays of light squeezed through little windows of different shapes and colours, illuminating the dusty air. It was more of a museum than a shop, filled with gold-leafed, leather-bound tomes looking down from their towering shelves. The book I carried was similar, albeit not yet antique. The shopkeeper looked up as I entered his shop. Like his books, his skin was leathery, and he balanced a pair of gold-rimmed glasses on his nose. I showed him my treasure.

"This is a masterpiece of art and handicraft," he told me, gently turning over each page. "Why have you brought this to me?"

"I want to sell it."

"When?"

"Now, of course."

"Its value is about 750 *abassi*. I'll give you half, due to the circumstances."

Haggling for a better price led to nothing. It was take it or leave it, and I decided to take it. Half of a lot of money is still a lot of money, especially when you're poor. I left with a bounce in my step.

When I arrived back at the hotel, I was welcomed by the receptionist and Ior in great agitation.

"A special envoy was sent by the Shah to tell me that I must go back to the palace with the book. The Shah wants to write a dedication in it for me. Do you still have it?"

"No... I just sold it. That's what you asked me to do! Here's the money," I handed him the notes and coins I'd crumpled into my pocket.

The receptionist shook his head slowly, a horrified look in his eyes.

"Go back to the bookshop and reverse the deal. Don't come back without the book," Ior commanded.

"Is it really that bad?" I asked, feeling slightly betrayed.

"I told you, the Shah is strong and wise. He will cut off your head with that strength and wisdom if you don't get that book back right now and bring it to the palace," the receptionist howled. "And he might come for my head too!"

I raced back through the market and found the shopkeeper still amongst the leather and dust of his shop. It took some persuasion, but in the end, I managed to convince him to relinquish the book. (Surely, he couldn't risk owning the very book the Shah had requested?) However, it cost me all of the notes and coins, as well as my last pair of shoes.

Ior returned to the palace, this time with a large book under his arm. The Shah scribbled some nice words inside its front cover and Ior walked back to the hotel relieved. We realised now that we couldn't sell it. There was no privacy in Teheran, and it would be too dangerous to risk displeasing and misusing the trust of the Shah. It was too traceable, especially for a second attempt. I was nineteen years old, and I learned a lesson in life.

We stayed another month in this city of fairy tales, villains and heroes; a city whose magic is ingrained in its architecture. I started to feel at home there, as if somehow, I belonged in one of those fairy tales.

The moment came to part ways. Before he boarded his train to Helsinki, Ior gave me a business card. It was the first such card I'd ever received. I glanced at it and tossed it in my bag.

His name written on it in black ink: Ior Svedlin. It was his step-father's family name. I didn't know then that written on that card was one of the richest and most dominant family names in Finland. Ior, the moneyless hippie I met at a dusty bus terminal in Baluchistan, surely didn't have this sort of gold shining on him. It was only later in life that he changed his name to what he considered to be his real one: Ior Bock.

Somewhere outside of Teheran, I stumbled across a group of hippie travellers heading to Istanbul in a couple of Mercedes 508 vans, the hippie workhorse of that time. Some months later, I ended up in London. There, I befriended a Dutch guy called Seppo. This is the same name that belongs to a mythological character in the Bock Saga, the king of the world to be more specific. This irony only dawned on me much later as I had not yet heard of the Bock Saga.

Seppo worked as a carpenter in a fairground. He was so inspired by my stories of travels through Asia that he decided he would follow me to India. However, the start of this new journey required some funding, and neither of us had much in that department. Seppo had a plan though; he had some connections at a fairground in Amsterdam where we could both work for a while. There was just one problem. I'd left Holland in a hurry after ditching the army and it wouldn't end well if the Dutch authorities found me.

"No problem at all," Seppo laughed. "I can smuggle you in the trunk of my car onto the ferry from England to Holland. Once we're on the boat, you'll be free to come out and walk around. Then, when we arrive in Holland, you can just hide again. Easy."

And so it was. I lived secretly in Seppo's flat, owned by a guy called Ilmarinen. Which, by the way, is yet another name that crops up in the Bock Saga! I tell you, I'd never before, and have never again, met anyone called Seppo and Ilmarinen. Maybe they were omens of things to come; if they were, I was oblivious to this at the time.

We worked for cash at the fairground. It turned out that Seppo had a real talent for carpentry and painting, and he taught me everything he knew. We worked day and night, with the help of coffee and cigarettes, and we made good money. Come the middle of the summer, we decided we had enough to go hitching to India. I dropped in to say goodbye to my parents. They tried their best to convince me to join the army and defend our country against the Russians and Chinese, or at least to return to my studies; all the usual wishes parents have for their children.

"No, I want to travel and see the world."

We soon found ourselves on the entry to highway A1 in Amsterdam, thumbs pointing towards the sky, ready to hitchhike our way to India. The air was filled with the promise of adventure. One day later, we were at the Kamener Kreuz interchange near Dortmund, Germany. We planned to go from there to Munich, Istanbul and further south and east in the direction of South-East Asia. Our thumbs were lifted high.

"Hey guys, jump in the back!" shouted a hairy head out of the driver's window. The side door of the van squeaked open, and we jumped inside. Deep in a cloud of hashish smoke, I could make out the outline of heads. Happy hippie heads.

"Hi, my name's Flower. Want a puff?"

"A puff from Flower, that's a dream come true," replied Seppo. "Compliments to your mother for giving you such a beautiful name."

"It was mother nature."

"Well, we're heading to visit Mother India, and thanks to you, it doesn't seem so far anymore. Where are you lot heading?"

"We just came from Amsterdam where we bought some mother nature to spread lovingly through Christiania in Copenhagen, where we're from. You're smoking some of it now."

"Oh. So, you're not actually driving in the direction of India, but to the north?" I asked, exhaling, adding to the cloud.

"Hey, groovy guy, you're pretty sharp, aren't you?" Flower laughed.

"What a coincidence!" exclaimed Seppo. "My landlord Ilmarinen is from Scandinavia. He's always busy with mother nature. He's got an organic farm up in the north of Finland. Maybe we should trust in coincidence and just head there. I've always wanted to visit that mysterious country."

"Wait... what's coincidental with what exactly?" I asked, but my question was lost in smoke and laughter.

"The only mystery I see is why anyone would visit that mosquito-infested country in the first place." But these words too went unnoticed.

And that's how we ended up going to Finland instead of India.

It was an enormous deviation from our original plan, but what the hell. We were free, and I liked to say yes to everything. After various meanderings through Sweden, we arrived in Turku, Finland, via ferry. We slept outside and were welcomed by the multitude of mosquitoes that plague Finland in the summertime. The next day, we went on to Houho, near Hämeenlinna, our provisional end destination. There we found an 'Opisto', a community of free-minded people that put all kinds of hippie idealisms into practice. They owned some forest and farming land, where they produced organic food. There was a lake full of fish. About forty local individuals ran the place and it attracted lots of people from all over the world, who came to share their visions for a better lifestyle.

"Who would have thought to see you guys here at the end of the world!" Ilmarinen uttered in disbelief when we appeared through the door of an old wooden farmhouse. "Is this a coincidence?"

"Yeah, it's all a coincidence," Seppo grinned.

"No, it's only a coincidence for me. We were on our way to India and then Seppo took a left turn unexpectedly," I explained.

"Coincidence or not, you're here now. Are you thinking of staying?" asked Ilmarinen, motioning us to follow him.

"If you'll have us..." Seppo replied.

"Oh, yes! The potatoes have been waiting, snug in the ground, for the likes of you to dig them up. And you wouldn't want their cousins the onions and carrots to feel left out now, would you?" Ilmarinen joked as he led us out to a field of crops.

"Great, we're in!" Seppo answered, looking around us enthusiastically.

They chatted on about the climate and other farming things like that.

"Sorry guys, I'm a city dweller, I'll leave you to it." I excused myself and went for a wander.

"Well, Casper," I thought to myself, "You were a hippie on your way to India, and now suddenly you're a farmer in Finland doing hard labour. We'll see what'll come of this."

After the harvest was finished, Seppo and I received more and more little jobs around the place. Sometimes we worked in the kitchen, catering for more than a hundred guests. Sometimes we used our carpenting skills and worked on the wooden houses and their interiors, painting them and so on.

One night, as we sat exhausted in front of the unintelligible television, an energetic washing powder advert suddenly appeared on the screen. It showed a man and a woman happily dancing with magically changing outfits.[1] For a second, I couldn't believe it. What in the world was my friend Ior doing in a wash-

---

[1] *If you fancy having a look, here's the YouTube link for the Coral Steppi advert: https://www.youtube.com/watch?v=a-qoKf87UHQ*

ing powder commercial?! My excitement must have been visible as Seppo looked up at me in surprise.

"Do you know that guy?"

"Yeah, I travelled with him from Quetta in Baluchistan to Teheran last year."

"Was it some kind of washing powder road trip?" Seppo laughed.

I remembered that Ior had given me his business card and I dug it up from the bottom of my bag. I called him immediately.

"Hi Ior, it's me, Casper, the guy from Teheran. Do you remember me? I'm in Finland at the moment and just saw you on TV."

"What a surprise! Is it just a coincidence you're here?"

"You know, I'm not quite sure anymore," I confessed. I explained that I was with Seppo and Ilmarinen in a farm and that we were working our asses off.

"Tell me about it all later, come to Helsinki, and bring your friends. I'm working as a tour guide in the seven islands; you're welcome to join. Then we can go to my family estate in Gumbostrand and spend the weekend there."

I said yes. Finally, a break from farm labour. And so, Ior took us to the locations of the ancient Valhalla and the Lemminkäinen Temple, although he did not mention any of these ancient names or the story behind them while we were there.

Ior must have been surprised, from a Bock Saga perspective, that the random guy he met in the middle of nowhere in Quetta was brought to Finland by someone called Seppo. Not only this, but that he had stayed with another guy called Ilmarinen and that we were now all together on the seven islands and Gumbostrand. I was totally ignorant of these coincidences at the time. It would be another nine years before Ior decided to begin telling the story of the Bock Saga. We just enjoyed a pleasant weekend with Ior and his friends in Gumbostrand.

Later that year I noticed:

"Look, the leaves, they're turning brown."

"Yep, I guess summer's over."

"What comes next?"

"Autumn, I guess."

"And then winter. Let's get the hell out of here."

"We didn't save any money. Turns out it's more expensive in Finland than in Monaco."

"The choice is clear: either we buy a winter coat from our savings, or a train ticket towards the sun. The second option is cheaper by the way."

"If we leave, what're we going to live from?"

"It's the same either way: from whatever comes our way."

We bought train tickets to St. Petersburg, Moscow, Kiev, Bucharest and Sophia, and these destinations took us South and then East.

"I hope you know what you're doing," Seppo sighed, head hanging low, as we boarded the long train marked for Moscow. "We'll be crossing the territories of the formidable and dangerous communists."

"They're just normal people like us."

"They're not like us."

"Yeah, they are. They eat, sleep and party, just like us."

"Hmm. If you say so. But I think it's more likely that the commies end up stealing our belongings and sending us to work camps in Siberia where we'll have to work the rest of our miserable lives in steel factories with monstrous women."

I opened the cabin door and three pairs of beautiful eyes looked up at us.

"You were saying?" I asked, turning to Seppo with a glint in my eye.

We spent over a month travelling in trains and exploring the beautiful cities in which they stopped. An unknown world opened up for us; it was still European, but subtly different. As we approached our train's final destination, Athens, I asked Seppo:

"Athens is the dead end for all trains. So, what's next?"

"Boats," he replied, staring up at a collection of signs, each pointing in a different direction. "Why are all these signs in Russian?"

"They're not. It's Greek, it just looks similar."

"Huh. Well, this is the only thing that looks familiar to me," Seppo said pointing at a large circled 'I'. "It must mean information."

We followed the sign and knocked on the little rusty door of the office. We were welcomed by the proverbial Greek man. From behind a big, black moustache came a single question:

"What?"

"We need a boat"

He lit a cigarette that smelled like a cigar.

"Where to?"

"As far south or east as possible in the direction of India."

The man poured himself a small coffee, which had the physical properties of lead mixed with mercury, and stamped, signed and scribbled all over our two tickets. When he finally handed them over, they were marinated with coffee, ash and the general dirt of the office.

Two days later, when our ship arrived in Crete, we discovered the dead end for all ships. Or at least a dead end for us, as we didn't have enough money to get to India and back. We had to adjust our plans. We were doing jobs here and there, but mainly we hung out on the various beaches, and any money we made, we spent in the restaurants and bars. We realised we would never reach India in this way.

Seppo proposed going back to Holland in spring and working once more in the fairgrounds. I was reluctant, because I knew that at any moment I could be asked for my ID and be put in jail for desertion. When winter came to an end, Seppo returned home with a fresh girlfriend and was absorbed into the social life and economics of Holland at that time. He never made it to India. I worked here and there in Germany and Belgium for a while and then decided to accept Ior's invitation and visit him in Helsinki.

Over the next few years, I spent all my summers in Scandinavia. I sometimes worked in Denmark and hung out in Christiania, while other times I found myself in Sweden. Every 4th of October, Ior left on a train to St. Petersburg, then to Moscow, then to Teheran. Next, he would travel, either by bus or train, all the way to Goa and sometimes further. Every 4th of October, I joined him for this lengthy trip. Each spring, we would begin the opposite trip, all the way back to Finland.

Ior always carried lots of historical books with him. He used these, along with the knowledge he had gained through his family, to prepare his guided tours of Finland for the next season.

During the long train journeys and the many hours spent on dusty platforms waiting for trains that sometimes never came, Ior would study these books. He peered with one eye through a large magnifying glass, a finger tracing each word he tried to decipher. It took him ages to get through a single page. When crossing borders, we often had to fill out lengthy forms for visas and permissions to pass. Ior didn't seem capable of reading and filling these out, and I usually ended up doing it for him. I was never sure whether he was dyslectic or whether he could read at all.

In any case, he always told great stories about how the 18th century was a tipping point in European culture. Europe went from being a largely feudal and agricultural society, to being one that was driven by technical inventions. The values of the church and the God-given aristocracy were transformed into a system where everything had a monetary value.

We spent countless hours together, talking about all kinds of things, except for the one thing that I learned later occupied such a large part of his mind: the Bock Saga. I had no notion that this existed at the time, he didn't reference it once. The focus of his guided tours and the 18th century were the seven islands in front of Helsinki. I realised later, that these were also the focal point in the lives of his prehistoric forebears.

As the years went on, Ior and I became good friends. My memories with him are filled with words and laughter. I think I was easy to be around, being a talkative, mellow guy, so different from the sturdy Finnish people. Ior introduced me to the Finnish social scenes of the time. We visited many clubs and got invited to chique dinner parties with the Helsinki elite. We felt at home with the poor artists that formed an international crew of vagabonds. We met intellectuals in all directions.

Wherever Ior wanted to go, or wherever he wanted to take me, I always said yes. I don't remember exactly when, but it was at a certain point during this period that Cecile came into the picture. She was Ior's new girlfriend, and she clearly belonged with the people around us. In a way, she was remarkably similar to Ior: she came from a wealthy background, she was arty, bohemian, intellectual and worked as a tour guide in the seven islands.

"I need your advice Casper." I could see that he was worried, I recognised that look.

"Lay it out for me."

"Cecile wants to come with us to Goa this winter."

"That's brave of her."

"It's a long and dangerous trip, especially for someone like her, you know what I mean?"

"I do, yes. In certain countries she's worth her weight in gold."

"Exactly. And on top of that, her father's one of the richest and most influential men in Finland. And when I say 'influential' I mean through his raw political power."

"Maybe let's not mention that too loudly while we're on the road. It certainly wouldn't help the situation. But I guess it's really up to her."

"Her father would kill me if anything happened to her."

"He'd kill you anyway if he found out you're seeing her."

"Maybe not actually, our families are connected through history."

"Just make sure she doesn't end up in some harem."

"I'm also not sure she can handle the hardships of travelling."

"Nobody's ever died from a hard mattress."

"So that's your advice?"

"If she wants to come, she's welcome. We'll manage somehow. Don't underestimate the girl."

Cecile was offered a plane ticket by both her family and by Ior. She refused and insisted to come with us instead. And that's exactly what she did. And guess what? She managed just fine.

There were five of us that morning: two Finnish guys (Aatos and Mikko), Cecile, Ior and I. The morning sun warmed our faces as we walked along the beach. The waves rolled in on our left and the palm trees waved in the gentle wind. We were floating back home after having danced for hours at a full-moon party in south-Anjuna, Goa, India.

Our home, Apolina house, sat at the foot of the mountain on top of which stood an old Portuguese fort called Chapora fort. We were still entranced from the party; immersed in the happy after-buzz only loud psychedelic music, dancing stars and a full moon could bring. We climbed the steps to our veranda and fell into the scattered cushions on the floor.

Time passed. After a while, I picked myself up from this rosy indulgence to do some necessary bodily maintenance. I heated water to make tea. My movement must have inspired Ior, as he soon got up and headed to the village shop to buy breakfast. When he returned, he cut up some tomatoes and onions and fried the lot with eggs. He cut the bread and brought it all out to the veranda.

It was our daily routine. We ate breakfast and lay there lazily, enjoying the coolness of time as it passed by us in the breeze. Suddenly, Ior announced that he had a story to tell; a story about an alphabet that had been kept within his family.

I looked up at Ior to see if he was joking. I knew reading and writing had never been strengths of his.

"What do you mean by alphabet?"

"My family kept an alphabet where every sound has a meaning"

"What does that mean?"

"A, B, C. Each sound has its own meaning in the Bock Saga that was passed down through my family. 'A' is for 'Aser' – the people who lived in Odenma in the Paradise time and spoke the Root language, the language used in this story. Odenma is the region around Helsinki. Root is Finnish-Swedish. 'B' is for 'Borg', which means castle; but it can also mean 'Brust', which means breast."

While Ior explained these concepts, Aatos, Mikko and I leaned back to listen, but I could see from the corner of my eye Cecile growing restless. She walked in and out of the house a few times first, while the rest of us lay happily absorbing Ior's words. Then suddenly, Cecile lashed out.

"Why have you been listening to these *gammle tanta*, these old aunts! They've filled your head with nonsense, why can't you see that?"

She grabbed the empty frying pan left over from breakfast and threw it at Ior. The plates and kitchen utensils followed.

"But it's a story that's been kept in my family. I've decided to share it today. What's wrong? Why can't I tell my story?"

Cecile just got angrier and threw everything she could lay her hands on at Ior. When there was nothing left to throw, she stormed from the veranda without another word. Could she have foreseen what lay in store for us? The effect this so-called Bock Saga would have on the lives of the people present? I certainly didn't.

Excerpt from the Bock Saga:

The Bock Saga is the story of mankind as passed down through the generations of the Bock family, the Finnish family of Ior Bock whom, according to him, was the keeper of an ancient oral tradition that sheds light on the heathen culture of Finland and its history.

The Bock Saga begins with the first two people dwelling on this Earth and covers a huge time span. It narrates all the events that came to pass during this time in great detail. It's an enormous story...

Ior continued explaining his alphabet.

"'C' is for 'shera', to share; 'D' is for 'dag', day and 'di', drink; 'E' is for 'ek', oak, the family tree..."

Every letter triggered associations with words that we already knew. We lived in a Hindu village in Goa, and we were surrounded by pictures of their deities. Words like 'Krishna', 'Shiva' and 'Ramayana' were explained through Ior's alphabet and suddenly made a lot of sense. Krishna meant crisis. Shiva was a chieftain. Ramayana were Ra and Maija, the king and queen of the world in the Bock Saga. Many words in our different languages suddenly had new meaning. It felt like an inner logic of words.

Ior continued to tell his story throughout the following days. This tale of sounds and ancestors captured our imagination. What fascinated me the most was that each sound had a meaning and could be used as a building block to form a whole, just as atoms form planets and our entire universe. Ior talked about the Paradise time, about the caste system that existed and how its system of selective procreation elevated the human race to a higher plane.

"In the olden days, to enter Hel, one had pass through Helsinki and sing for the key of Hel. Asgard, Valhalla and Hel were located near modern day Helsinki. There lived the untouchable gods. The pantheon

of gods was the pinnacle of procreation of humanity. Ukko and Akka, grandfather and grandmother represented the heavenly gods; their oldest son and daughter, Seppo and Maija, the moon king and moon queen; Lemminkäinen and Svan, the sun gods, and others closely related with a function and title".

Being mythological figures, the gods were immortal. They were represented by mortal humans. When they died, they were merely replaced by someone else carrying the same mythological title. The mythological figure itself does not die − "the king is dead, long live the king!"

Just as a matter of clarity: the gods and goddesses who came from the North Pole where Hel was located were people of flesh and blood. Their only claim to godliness was that they were at the top of a hierarchic procreation system which led to the creation of all new people on the planet. They were god, which in the first language means they were 'good'. If we were to look for the geographical location of the so called Fountain of Youth, the source of eternal life, we would find it in Hel", on an island in front of Helsinki.

Cecile did come back after a while, but she didn't want to listen to the Bock Saga. Ior tried to explain that he was from the Boxström family, which started its legacy in the early days of history. She came from an old family as well. Her family printed the first bibles in Finland in the 16th century and she grew up with family stories about their heritage. Since that time, and probably already a while before that, her family had been wealthy and influential.

Cecile was the eldest daughter and her family had looked to her to guide them through the turbulence of the second half of the 20th century. However, she wasn't really up for that task. She preferred to spend her time on the seven islands teaching 18th century history during her guided tours in Viapuri. That was how she and Ior had met and how they'd fallen in love.

Although Cecile hadn't travelled over land to Goa this particular year as she had done so many other times, she loved to travel with Ior through countries that seemed to reside in another timeframe altogether. Spending time with Ior and his hippie artist friends was much nicer than the heavy responsibility of playing heiress to one of the richest families in Finland.

In the years they had been together, they had spent many

hours on buses and trains, talking. They spoke about where they'd been, what they'd experienced and had shared all their thoughts and dreams. Now, suddenly, out of seemingly nowhere, came a family story, so far reaching that it shattered Cecile's view of life and made her question with whom she really had spent all those years.

Ior spoke of powers of nature: Oden, Ra, Tor, Frei and Freia. He told a rudimentary version of the Bock Saga. He gave an explanation of the Scandinavian mythologies and the difference between the Western mythology of the Vikings and Eastern mythology.

He kept on talking about the alphabet he reached the last letter: 'V' – Vaner. Vaner are the people who were born outside Odenma. Van is their language, which is modern-day Finnish. Aatos and Mikko, who spoke Finnish as their mother tongue, were surprised to hear this.

Because every sound has a meaning, it follows that the alphabet itself is a story. The alphabet tells how in Paradise time the social structure echoed the structure of the complete universe, revolving around the earth axis and galactic axis that connects the North Pole to the Polestar. The Bock Saga shows in a rather mathematical way there is harmony between the lives of humans on earth and the universe they live in.

It was a beautiful afternoon on the veranda of Apolina house. The strong sunlight filtered through the many layers of foliage; each tree scattered with its own vibrant singing birds. The lowest layer of leaves was a bright-coloured bougainvillea. Our small group of friends draped their bodies over the cushions and listened to the last of Ior's introduction to the Root language.

"That is quite the story, Ior," Aatos said, while stirring the leaves in his metal teacup. "I'm trying to grasp it all with my small brain."

"If I understand it right," Mikko cut in. "The backbone of the whole story is the Root language, which is Swedish."

"Who would have thought," Aatos laughed. "The Swedish talk like they've swallowed flip-flops."

"Yes, dipped in soft boiled eggs," Mikko joined in. "Nothing good ever came from a Swede opening his mouth."

"Swedish-Finnish is the first language, and this originated in Hel, located in Finland. It arrived at the Swedes from there; but now, rather than speak it, they sing it," Ior corrected them. "And we Finnish speak Van, which also originated from the sounds in the sound system like all other languages on the planet."

"And so, without us, the Swedes wouldn't have a language at all?" Aatos mused.

"It's our fault they talk so much then!" Mikko concluded, slapping Aatos on the back.

"Thank god they're in their own country now, so we don't have to listen to them anymore."

"Yeah, they've been around forever, but we own our country now. And you're telling us that their language was originally not theirs but ours?"

Ior had told me once that the Swedish language being used in Finland was a sensitive point for many Finns, who were convinced that Finnish was the original language of Finland. For them Swedish was the language of the oppressor.

The message that Swedish originated in Finland would not sit well with some Finnish people, especially since Finland's independence from Sweden was a relatively recent occurrence at that time. There were Finnish political forces that wished to root out the Swedish language altogether to deeper establish Finnish independence. It took a little time, but eventually Aatos and Mikko accepted that the Aser, the Root/ Swedish speaking people, were not of Swedish descent, but the first people who lived in Finland. To our chillum-smoking friends sitting on a sun-soaked veranda, however, all this didn't seem to trouble them much.

According to the history books, no one had lived in Finland until the year 1000 AD. According to the Bock Saga, the first people on the planet were born on one of the seven islands in front of Helsinki and their descendants had continued to live there until today. That's quite a difference. Ior explained that all memory of events that happened in Finland before 1050 AD was rooted out by the Catholics during the third destruction of Odenma in the Third Ragnarök and throughout the hundred years in the crusades that followed.

Ior continued with his tale day after day, week after week. He described how his family had fled to the north of Finland and the head of the Bock clan became the famous figure of Santa Claus. He explained how they had returned in 1250 AD. Ior told that Santa Claus was the same figure as Väinemöinen, the Finnish mythological hero, and Aatos and Mikko could accept this. They could now also accept that the Root-speaking Ior was a descendant of the first inhabitants of Odenma. We realised that we knew something that nobody else on the planet knew about. Ior advised us to think carefully before sharing it with others.

The weight of Ior's story caused stress within the group, particularly between Aatos and Mikko. They wanted to know more, and often argued with each other about what subjects Ior should speak about first. After various misunderstandings, mistrust hung in the air. Both hoped that the other would miss sessions so that they could gain advantage in Ior's teaching. They fell into a frenzy of learning.

I think it became something similar to a gambling frenzy. The feeling you get when you're losing; that urge to gamble more and more. They got into an unhealthy state of mind. You could taste the tension in the atmosphere. And Cecile became more and more convinced that Ior had lost his mind. She regularly smashed kitchenware on his head and would return later with replacement cups and plates.

"What do you think, Casper?"

"About what?"

"About the whole problem." Cecile looked me directly in the eyes, with an intense air about her.

I felt that I was expected to understand something but wasn't quite sure what.

"What problem?"

"This Bock Saga. It's destroying my nerves"

"What's wrong with it?"

"Those two old witches put this whole story into Ior's head. The poor guy took it all seriously."

"It is a wild story, but why's that a problem?"

"What happens when we go back to Helsinki and start working as guides on the seven islands again? What if Ior starts spouting all this pre Ice Age and Valhalla nonsense there as well? Can't you see how worrying this is? People are going to think he's crazy." Cecile closed her eyes and took a deep breath, slowly releasing the air through her mouth. "Does he expect me to join him in this, Casper? Spread this madness to the tourists and school kids?"

"Well, you'll certainly have a captive audience; audiences love to hear what they're not expecting."

"It's a crazy story, and you know it. Ior's lost it."

"I don't know, Cecile. Somehow, it's starting to sound plausible to me. Ior has a logical answer to every objection that's been made so far. With each of his answers, the story seems to gain weight and truth."

"You can't just claim it's true because it follows some twisted logic!"

"But what if it is exactly that logic that makes it true?"

"No, Casper. There's no way that this story is true. Listen, I took a big gamble when I decided to be with Ior. I was supposed to be the heir of a great family and empire. Instead, I chose to spend my life with Mr Bohemian, who's now doing everything he can to make us unwelcome everywhere. How do you think the Helsinkians will react when they hear someone claim that Swedish is the root of all languages, including Finnish? Finnish is the language of Finland. They're not going to care what happened thousands of years ago pre Ice Age, or whatever it is. They're just going to see this as a political attack. Don't you see that?"

"Are you talking about love, Cecile? Shouldn't that be your motivation to be together?"

"I love him, or at least, I love the Ior I knew. I'm not with him for the fame and money, you know that."

"Well, he's not famous, nor rich."

"That's what I mean. And those two dolts on the veranda get on my nerves too."

"You mean Aatos and Mikko?"

"Yes, they're getting worse by the hour. They seem to see themselves as some kind of expert."

"Yeah, they're a bit weird, I'll give you that. But they're not any weirder than your Goa average."

"They think they're somehow special because they know about the Bock Saga. They seem to think that because they now know the story of mankind, they can play a central role in the future of the planet."

"Hmm, yeah. I think you're right there; they believe they're epic. And each wants to be more epic than the other."

"They're just snotty, dim nitwits, getting lost in a story that's far too big for them. I have a bad feeling about this, Casper. It's all slipping through my fingers. It was so good before. We were in love; we were adventuring around the world. We were happy and free. Now it's all just this constant weirdness; our lives are being destroyed and there's nothing I can do about it."

Cecile was crying now. Screams of inner pain shocked through her and tears flowed down her chin. I took her in my arms and tried to comfort her. After a long time, she stopped.

"My gamble didn't pay off, but life goes on," she said, and it seemed as if she'd somehow come to terms with the whole thing.

"Bye Casper," she whispered as she walked past me, a gentle hand on my shoulder. There was a finality in her voice that made me feel like somehow, this time, she had made up her mind to leave our little clan for good. And although Cecile remained in Goa until the end of the season, it was clear that something significant had changed.

The mood in the house became more and more electrically charged. Cecile still regularly lashed out in anger. The two Finnish boys had become strange in the head. They became intertwined with the Bock Saga on a personal and emotional level and felt as if the story had touched upon the very essence of their being. I just took the story as an interesting intellectual exercise. I kept my cool and decided that's the way I wanted to stay.

Cecile had come to India on an airplane that year. Ior and Aatos had made the long trip from Helsinki to Goa over land, as they had done several times before. On long trips of this kind, the relationship between travelling companions changes. It goes beyond friendship, attraction and intellectual bonding. Being so close in strange, changing environments forces you to grow together. When you depend on each other in this way, you start to trust each other blindly. This closeness made Ior and Aatos more tolerant to each other's peculiarities.

Once in Goa, however, where there was no reason for this

level of interdependency, this relationship changed. This was normal. They each went their own separate ways and spent time together when it was convenient. They shared a house and food, and they both loved to smoke hashish from a chillum. This was enough bonding and harmony. This year, however, was different. The Bock Saga changed this dynamic completely. Somehow, Ior's story was both cohesive and disrupting at the same time.

It was evening. The veranda was lit by candles and Ior had just finished giving one of his lectures on the Bock Saga. Mikko and I were trying to sort all the facts we'd just heard into the growing structure in our heads. Mikko's hands gestured wildly as he tried to verbalise a question that he'd just thought of.

It was just at this moment that Aatos, who had stayed on the beach until after sunset, suddenly raced up the veranda steps. His enormous build filled the space around him. Aatos often referred to himself as a gentle giant, and this was mostly the case, but it didn't change the fact that any emotion he had was multiplied by his sheer mass. Emotions were radiating from him now and it wasn't quite clear what was going through his head.

"You Ok?" I asked.

"I don't like this!" he answered, his voice slightly raised and his finger pointing erratically around him.

"Don't like what?"

"All of you talking about the Bock Saga without me."

"Well, you weren't here. Are we no longer allowed to talk when you're not here?" Ior asked, smiling.

"Not about the Bock Saga. I want to know it all," replied Aatos, looking slightly erratic. "And I don't want him to know more than me," he added, pointing a finger a little too close to his friend Mikko. Mikko snapped his teeth in its direction. We sat for a few moments in tense silence.

Finally, Aatos turned away and let out a forced laugh.

"I'm only joking. You guys should lighten up." Nobody else laughed.

After this, Mikko decided that Aatos needed to learn some humility, and he knew just the way to teach him. He silently slipped some LSD into Aatos's tea. The perfect plan, except for the fact that it failed spectacularly. Aatos flipped out completely and ran naked through the village.

An LSD trip lasts a long time, about six to eight hours, during which a kaleidoscope of psychedelic visions and events deeply penetrate the consciousness of the person. It's an impressive experience, even more so when you're not expecting it; say, for instance, when it suddenly descends upon you while you're having a relaxing cup of tea on a lazy afternoon on the veranda of your house. For some people, an LSD trip can feel as if the whole world is falling apart, while simultaneously morphing into a multitude of fantastic dreamscapes. After six to eight hours, the effects of the little pill begin to wear off and all these dream states melt together again into the world you knew before you took the LSD. At least, that's what usually happens.

For Aatos, the effects didn't wear off. He stayed in this psychedelic state for much longer. What was worse, when his body and mind became tired, the experience just continued and extended. In psychology, this is called psychosis.

The Goanese people are some of the most tolerant in the world, but even their legendary tolerance has its limits, and these limits were severely tested by Aatos. His constant screaming through the village of Chapora kept families with small children awake at night. He took food from restaurants and shops without paying. He jumped into a drinking well. Finally, when he started to proclaim himself as the Anti-Christ who had survived the Third Ragnarök almost a thousand years in the past, and who would now bring down the Catholic Church, things became dangerous for him.

There were many locals who believed that the so-called 'bamboo massage' was an effective remedy against all kinds of psychological conditions. The brutal bamboo beating he received didn't help him much, but it did make Cecile and Ior realise that something had to be done to save him.

Meanwhile, Mikko was not much better off. He had been taking too much LSD himself and had come to the conclusion that he was the last member of the Russian Romanov Czar dynasty. It was a combination of too many chillums and LSD that led to this unrealistic identification with some of characters from the Bock Saga.

Ior's story was a catalyst that created a network of connections in Aatos and Mikko's minds. Amongst these countless connections lay many meaningless facts about the world that had already existed in their consciousness before the Bock Saga. Once placed within the overarching perspective of the Bock Saga, these facts and beliefs took on a new life and meaning. Suddenly, the world made sense, and not only the world, but their place in it. They both identified profoundly with some of the characters in the Bock Saga. They went from having an arbitrary existence, to playing a major role in the story, in the ongoing history of mankind.

When you think of the Bock Saga as a story with a purpose and a goal, and make these your ambitions, it's easy to lose touch with the reality that the rest of mankind lives in. It's easy to go crazy. This is what happened to my Finnish friends. In the years to come, I saw this over-identification in other people as well, and it always had a devastating effect on their mental wellbeing.

Close by was the Swedish library, a charitable institute that took it upon themselves to help Scandinavians in trouble. This is where Cecile and Ior brought Aatos. The librarians would take care of him and help him recover from the LSD psychosis that had taken control of his brain. Once this had been accomplished and he was deemed fit to travel, Ior and Cecile would ask the Swedish/Finnish embassy to help provide a strict escort that would fly him back to Helsinki.

By this stage, it was springtime, and all the foreigners were leaving Goa. Visas had expired, money had finished, and the summer was approaching in Europe. Many people would head back there in the quest to make enough money to return for another six-month season the following year.

As usual, Ior and I travelled by boat, bus and train back to Helsinki, while Cecile flew back. As the librarians were taking care of the slowly recovering Aatos, they had given Cecile a letter addressed to Aatos' mother that included information relating to her son's consumption of LSD, his subsequent psychosis and their plan to ensure his safe return to Finland. On receiving this letter, Aatos' mother panicked and thought it best to pass it on to the police, who, in turn, passed it on to the press.

Nothing much ever happened in Finland in the early 80s. Most people lived in the forest, and those who didn't, rarely caused scandals. Cecile and Ior were a well-known jet-set couple. Neither of them had followed the usual career path expected from someone in their position. Ior was well known in Finland through his work in several theatre productions. They both associated themselves with artists and travelled around the world expanding their world views. This jet-set lifestyle was not common in Finland at that time. The newspapers occasionally brought their lives into the news when they departed or returned from exotic locations. Ior and Cecile were called 'The flying birds'.

When Aatos finally arrived at Helsinki airport two month later, there were a lot of people waiting for him there. Apart from his mother and Cecile, there was also a significant police presence. A swarm of photographers and journalists, who had been alerted by the letter the librarians had written to Aatos' mother, buzzed around, attracted by the prospect of a juicy story. They asked Cecile and Aatos many questions about what had happened in Goa. They honestly told their stories, filled with drugs and Bock Saga.

The next day, the headlines were filled with all kinds of variations all pointing to one thing only: scandal! The flying birds, Ior and Cecile, drug-crazed hippies... LSD! Nobody in Finland had ever even heard of LSD, never mind the Bock Saga. But now they were introduced to both concepts, and it seemed clear that the two must be closely connected.

Ior had only just started sharing the Bock Saga with people and hadn't even begun introducing it to the Finnish, but already it had been connected to LSD. Needless to say, it was not a good first impression. This was all happening in 1984, and until his death, Ior was never truly free from the scandals that kept hounding him, many of which involved LSD. It didn't matter that Ior had never taken LSD in his life, or that the Bock Saga rejected all synthetic drugs.

Thus, soon after Ior started sharing his family story, his girlfriend Cecile fell into a constant state of anger and anxiety; his two Finnish friends became raving lunatics; the media connected him and his story to LSD; and everyone else in Goa and Helsinki who had known him as a quiet friendly historian now believed that he'd gone mad.

I knew that he hadn't. Ior was still the same quiet and friendly historian that I'd met all those years before at that dusty bus stop. Only now, instead of speaking about the 18th century, he focussed his attention on the pre-Ice-Age society he knew so much about.

Excerpt from the Bock Saga:

The Yggdrasil, in Odenma's Snappertuna, was the ash tree where the ashes of all the members of the Bock family who held a title, were brought. The tree was first planted by Frei and Freia, the first humans to be born. When the tree grew old, a sapling was taken from it and planted between the roots of the old tree. In this manner, it continued to live through the aeons. During the adventurous escapes that took place throughout the three Ragnaröks, the Bock family managed to keep the tree alive and within their care. It is still alive today.

Yggdrasil is the Tree of Life in the middle of paradise. In the Bock Saga, it symbolises all that lives and recreates.

Ior's mother, Rhea, died on the 6th of April 1984. When Ior arrived in Helsinki that spring, he had to arrange her funeral ceremony. Rhea had left specific instructions and had already organised everything to the minutest detail. All Ior had to do was execute her instructions.

First on the list was to transport the remains of Rhea's sister Rachel and her brother Rafael from a cemetery in Helsinki to the Boxström burial place in Snappertuna. There, all three would be buried in the ground under the Yggdrasil, joining all the previous members of the Boxström family who had been buried there since 1250 AD.

Rhea had specified that the funeral ceremony was to be held on the 24th of June 1984. After a traditional church ceremony in Snappertuna, Ior was instructed to take her friends, who were all octogenarian ladies united in the Freemason society Veronica, to the ruins of the majestic Castle Raseborg and hold a traditional Snappertuna festival there. Rhea had asked her friends and other attendees to come dressed in white or colourful clothes.

"I don't want you to wear black or dark colours. Even the priest should dress in white," she had written in her instructions.

After this ceremony, the plan was to go to the Offerlund, a nearby prehistoric site that played an important role in the Bock

Saga. There in the Offerlund, five fires needed to be lit, each representing one of the five powers that Ior had outlined in the Bock Saga thus far: Oden, Ra, Tor, Frei and Freia. According to Rhea's instructions, Ior was to introduce the remaining three powers of nature in the Bock Saga at a later stage.

The old ladies who were members of the Veronica society would be seated on benches within the circle of fires and would wait there silently until the fires died out. Then, Ior would speak about the Bock Saga. He would explain that, according to Rhea, two symbols of the Bock family were buried under the two oak trees that grew on the Offerlund. These symbols consisted of solid gold statues of a bock[2]. The plan was to dig up the statues soon after.

"It's all wrong!" Cecile insisted. "Rhea's ashes should be placed in the Svedlin graveyard."

"But her wish is that they should be buried in the Boxström graveyard, under the Yggdrasil," Ior countered.

"She lost her claim to the name Boxström when she married a Svedlin. Why must you always insist on doing everything differently?"

"It's her last wish, we should respect that. And it's not different. All Boxströms have always been buried under the Yggdrasil."

"Not this again, please. You can't possibly believe that fairy tale. The Yggdrasil tree wasn't planted by the first humans. You're crazy if you think that. It's already bad enough that your mother was cremated instead of being buried. Cremation is for the heathen. You know that burial has always been the Christian custom in Finland. And now you want to bring her where she doesn't belong? Oh god, why is this happening?"

"It's our custom, and it's my responsibility to make it happen. Enough!"

Cecile got up and strode out of the room slamming the door so hard it shook the house. At the end of the day, it was Ior's mother and not hers, so there was only so much she could argue. It turned out that it was the last time she slammed a door in Ior's face.

Cecile decided to take her hands of this new Ior Bock. She

---

[2] *For those who aren't familiar with the word, a 'bock' is a billy goat.*

had met him as Ior Svetlin. They were both tour guides. They were both from the old aristocracy of Finland. They travelled the world together in a most adventurous way. They were popular socialites. Their lives were like one long honeymoon.

Without any warning, the love of her life had changed his name into Ior Bock. He claimed all kind of dangerous things like that his family had produced the All-fathers of the planet. And Helsinki was somehow connected to hell. That certainly would freak out the Bishop of Finland if he'd ever hear that story. And on top of that, suddenly they were surrounded by madness and drugs.

Cecile lost grip of the situation. She lost touch with Ior. She decided to leave him and mourn for the loss of their beautiful relationship alone.

Word of these peculiar funeral arrangements reached the Bishop of Finland on the eve of the funeral. He immediately jumped into action and forbade the entire ceremony. He proclaimed that Finland was not a heathen country, but a Christian one. He even spoke on a radio interview claiming that Rhea's funeral wishes were a heathen aberration. The bishop was a regular guest at the Bock family estate in Akanpesa, Gumbostrand, so it wasn't a personal grudge but a professional point of view that forced him to take this stance.

Ior feared blowing up the confrontation out of his control. He knew from history and from the Bock Saga the sort of damage religious and political forces could do. Every life- and society-changing event his family had endured was always brought about by such forces. After all, his family was one of the most conservative in the world, wanting only ever to preserve the cultural heritage they had worked so hard to protect.

The Bock family never took an aggressive or reactionary position when such forces were exerted upon them. They always took their time, often a long time, to think carefully about each situation before doing anything about it. Their preferred reaction to any change or event was to do nothing at all. Since the beginning of mankind, the Bock family had simply tried to sail the prevailing winds of time as well as was possible. They never took sides in conflicts. This was their experience for countless generations. If an action was deemed necessary, they would choose a defensive or retracting strategy.

It was exactly in this same fashion that Ior handled the case of the golden bocks and the Catholic bishop. He avoided clashing with the religious forces by not fulfilling his mother's funeral wishes. No five fires burned at the Offerlund, the golden bock statues remained buried under the oak trees and the general public attending the funeral never heard the revelations of the Bock Saga.

Excerpt from the Bock Saga:

When the Helvetian army raided Odenma in 1050 AD during the crusade called the Third Ragnarök, the Bock family were able to escape miraculously. Two golden statues that were used in rituals since the Paradise times were hidden under a hill called Offerlund. To mark the site, three oak trees were planted on top of the treasures.

In the Snappertuna region, legends of these golden bocks are still told amongst the locals and appear in the church books found in the church of nearby Tunakullen.

The Finnish media made a big deal out of the story. Why would the bishop forbid the funeral wishes of a harmless old lady? Ior was interviewed and stated that, since the bishop seemed to feel so strongly about the matter, he would not fight to oppose him.

Ior's decision not to tell the Freemason society Veronica about the buried bocks on that midsummer day in 1984 meant that Rhea's plan would unavoidably be delayed. Rhea had hoped that when these elderly and influential ladies heard there were ancient gold statues buried in Offerlund, they would initiate an excavation. The success of having predicted the location of the golden statues would have given him and the Bock Saga credibility. He would have gotten support to excavate the Lemminkäinen Temple mentioned in the Bock Saga, which was planned for three years later, on the 24th of July 1987. At this point, the Bock Saga would be public knowledge and proven true by the discovery of the artefacts in the Lemminkäinen Temple. This excavation would change the world, and the study of these ancient insights into our common history would be allowed to flow freely, without the drama that was to follow.

If things could have happened in this 'normal' and 'civilised' way, by this stage, all would be said and done, and you'd be hearing to a much shorter story today. To Ior and my surprise, this didn't happen. Instead, so as not to infuriate the bishop, the ladies from the Veronica Freemason society, Ior and some of our friends from Goa attended a simple ceremony in Snappertuna church under the Yggdrasil growing in its garden.

In accordance with Rhea's wish, everybody was dressed in white; even the priest had found some white robes to wear that day. Ior put two bouquets of flowers on Rhea's urn, freesias and lilies. Then the ashes of Raphael, Rachel and Rhea were placed together between the roots of the ash tree Yggdrasil, in this little churchyard. Ior knew that this would be his last resting place too.

After the funeral ceremonies were completed, Ior contacted Museovirasto, the Finnish Heritage Agency. He told them that he wanted to share his family story along with information on prehistoric Finland. He knew the institution well, through his tour guiding job, and was in regular contact with them. The institute director, Gardberg, was a friend of Ior's. Responding to Ior's message, Museovirasto sent two interns to his apartment to hear what he had to say. Ior gave them a rough outline of the Bock Saga and told them it took him twenty years to hear the full story in all its complexity. He then told them that it would take him a further twenty years to share it with the world in its entirety. It's such an expansive story that a human mind can't possibly grasp it fully, along with its connotations, associations, and consequences, in a shorter time span. The two interns never came back, and it was the last time the Museovirasto ever took interest in the Bock Saga.

Ior Bock had only just started to tell his story to the people that happened to be sitting on his veranda in Goa on the 24th of February in 1984, but the chaos it had unleashed was already enormous. He realised this was only the beginning and that the octogenarians were not going to help him out.

If he ever doubted whether his mother and aunt were in their right minds when they told him such an alternative history to mankind, seeing the effect the story had already had on the people around him, not to mention the Bishop of Finland, convinced him of the power held within the Bock Saga.

Witnessing his friends and girlfriend flipping out after hearing his story, seeing how angry the funeral had made the Bishop of Finland, Ior thought the world had gone mad. The world, on the other hand, thought that Ior was the one who'd gone mad. It's difficult to say who was right, even to this day.

Right after the funeral, I'd left for Crete with my girl-friend Susanne and stayed there all summer. She worked as a hotel hostess, and I was working as a carpenter for various hotels and restaurants. I travelled all over the ancient island with its quirky people. When I met Ior again in Goa the autumn of 1984 to make the long overland trip to India again, he filled me in on what had happened in Finland. I was surprised at the level of resistance he'd faced and especially that he'd failed to dig up the golden bocks. When I'd first heard of the existence of the golden statues the previous year, I'd been convinced that this crucial first step would be simple. And then, once we had this physical proof, being the golden statues, to support Ior's story, everything else would become easier. I really couldn't have imagined that this 'little' hurdle would occupy us for the rest of our lives.

Ior had changed somewhat, and it wasn't just the beard he'd grown. The monumental Bock Saga had started to cast its shadow over him. It had dawned on him that his role in its telling came with costs and losses. He had lost Cecile both as girlfriend and colleague. He had lost the tour guide job he had held at the Ehrensvärd Sveaborg, which was the setting of Hel and Valhalla in the Bock Saga, although he was still allowed to guide visitors on his own accord. The Finnish nobility kept their distance, eager to avoid being contaminated by the strangeness of the Bock Saga and the drug scandals that shrouded Ior.

He was no longer the worriless, open and spontaneous person I'd met years ago. He'd realised that his knowledge of the Bock Saga, however magnificent, was also a burden. He started to distance himself from other people. He still kept close relationships with his friends, but he was more careful with what he said and to whom he said it. He knew, of course, that he had only just started to share the Bock Saga with the world and that there would be plenty other occasions for people to become irritated or offended. He knew the scandals weren't over.

We spent the winter of 1984/1985 together in Goa. Ior would sit on the veranda of Apolina house every day and tell his story. A group of about ten to fifteen regulars visited the veranda, shared and discussed the latest parts of the Bock Saga. They brought their newfound interest and knowledge to various other verandas and tea houses in the area.

In other words, the Bock Saga started to grow its roots within a slightly larger group of people than the previous year. When we weren't in an intellectual mood, we'd be on the beach or dancing at one of the famous Goa parties instead. It was a harmonious and intellectually inspiring time.

On one of these sun-soaked days, a young local boy I'd seen occasionally in the village walked up the steps to Ior's veranda.

"I'm just going to hang my hammock here in the corner," he told the curious eyes that were demanding what he was doing in our territory.

"No problem. It's out of the way."

When he'd finished fiddling with the ropes and knots, he tested it, sinking down into the soft netted threads.

"That's just fine," he smiled.

He wriggled around for a bit until he found the perfect position and then immediately fell asleep. When he woke, he went to the kitchen, not disturbed by our wondering eyes. When he came out with a pot of steaming tea, he asked us if we cared for a cup.

"Oh, by the way, my name is Soma."

From that point onwards, he was a regular. He always seemed to peacefully sleep in his hammock, but later we discovered that he'd always kept one ear open to absorb Ior's story. Soma became Ior's helper and travelled with him to Helsinki in the spring. For many years to come he would remain a faithful companion to Ior.

Cliff Barber arrived on our veranda in the spring of 1985, when Ior had already left for Europe. Cliff was a yoga teacher from the United States, and after his morning lessons on the nearby beach of Vagator, he would sit with us and listen to our discussions. I told him parts of the Bock Saga and the story captured him immediately and with force.

What he was most interested in was the underlying sound system of the alphabet and how it formed the Root language. Using his great mathematical and philosophical skills, he designed a geometrical construct of the alphabet using circles and lines. He connected language with a procreation system and with the structure of the universe just as Einstein had connected energy, mass and the speed of light into one equation.

Suddenly the Bock Saga was not only just another creation story, it turned into inevitable logic that expressed the beauty and harmony of the nature around us. The Bock Saga was growing ever larger, and we were excited.

At the end of the season, I went to Japan. One of my life-long wishes was to experience the Trans-Siberian Railway. I took a boat from Japan to Vladivostok and from there the train to Helsinki. There, we spent the summer of 1985 with a small group of Europeans who were interested in listening to Ior telling the Bock Saga.

Fresh scandals that had hatched during the winter were lying in wait for us in Helsinki. While in Goa, Ior had rented his Helsinki apartment to a violin player from the Helsinki Philharmonic Orchestra. The only thing this guy knew about the Bock Saga was that it was some sort of pagan story, he really wasn't involved with it at all.

Anyway, he'd just came back from a holiday in Sri Lanka when he started renting Ior's apartment in the autumn of 1984. In Sri Lanka, he'd fallen in love with the sweetest baby monkey. He'd somehow managed to smuggle this little darling to Finland and brought it with him to live in the apartment. During the winter, the little monkey grew quickly and loved to jump around and climb the curtains.

Because the apartment wasn't very big, the violin player would occasionally let the monkey play out on the balcony. From here, it happily jumped from balcony to balcony, and soon everyone in the apartment block knew and loved him for his courageous moves and happy character.

One cold winter's day, the violin player left the apartment for a rehearsal at the Helsinki concert hall. The monkey had been playing out in the balcony and for whatever reason wasn't able to get back into the apartment. When the violin player returned, he found his sweet little friend frozen outside.

Greatly upset by this death, the violin player decided to give the monkey a traditional Buddhist funeral, as was custom in the country where it had come from. To do this, he had to find a way to cremate the body. A funeral pyre was out of the question, especially since it was −30°C outside in a city with a population of more than one million people. No, a funeral pyre in the middle of Helsinki central park would have been impossible.

So, our violin player decided that the best alternative was to burn the little monkey to ashes in the oven of Ior's kitchen. Although it was indeed little, it was not small enough to fit easily into the oven, so he cut the monkey into pieces and set the oven to its maximum temperature. Then he waited.

An intense smell of burning fur spread through the kitchen, then the apartment, until it engulfed the whole building. After many hours, the body still hadn't turned to ashes, but had turned black and crusty instead. By this stage, the violin player had realised that the oven would never turn the body to ashes, it simply wasn't hot enough.

He decided that he'd done the best he could for his monkey friend's soul and karma. He put the various body parts in a few plastic bags and grabbed a box of incense. Setting out into the long, dark winter's night, he headed to a nearby park and tried to dig a hole in the frozen ground with a pickaxe he had bought.

It was a difficult and laborious task for our delicate musician. As he hit the frozen Earth over and over again, an elderly lady caught sight of him from a second-floor window of the apartment block. She was convinced that the dark shadow wielding a pickaxe was clearly burying the body of a small child, so she called the police who came in force and arrested him.

The police informed the media and before long, the TV and newspapers were covered in headlines that screamed garbled fantasies about burnt, dead monkeys in apartments and pagan rituals. And at the centre of it all? Ior Bock and the Bock Saga, of course.

At more or less the same time, in Chapora, Goa, a Finnish guy had overstayed his visa and finished all his money. You see, it's easy to lose yourself in the paradise of endless parties, drugs and sunshine and forget the inevitable reality of life lying in wait on the other side. This reality often involved flight tickets home or a new six-month visa, both things that could best be solved with money, something our Finnish friend didn't have anymore.

He had postponed these inevitabilities as long as he could and had finally come up with a solution that didn't require money. He would jump off Chapora fort, which stood above Ior's residence: Apolina house. His plan was to break a leg or cause some minor injury so that his insurance company would repatriate him, thus solving his two problems with a complimentary ticket home and a hassle-free trip through customs irrespective of his expired visa. His gravitational estimations were wrong, and he died at the bottom of the walls of the great fort.

Ior helped his family repatriate his body by mediating between them and the local authorities. I'm sure you know what came next. The Finnish media heard of the story and didn't waste any time incorrectly connecting the dots. The Finnish Goa freak had jumped to his death right next to Ior's house and Ior seemed to be somehow involved.

LSD was mentioned and a recognisable pattern emerged. Surely, Ior was responsible. Not much happened in Finland those days and it wasn't always easy to fill a newspaper. I'm sure the journalists loved Ior. The man seemed to spawn one scandal after another, and it didn't matter that he never directly had anything to do with them, nor that he'd never taken LSD. These two stories, the burnt monkey and the guy who jumped, would in later years come back to haunt us in the most unexpected way. By then, we knew that 'unexpected' was the connecting thread in our lives... But back in 1985, we tried to ignore this kind of attention and just continued listening to Ior's ever-expanding story.

As we've established, Ior's social life had changed quite drastically once he'd started his telling of the Bock Saga. Most of his old friends in Finland didn't know what to make of it. It used to be *en vogue* to know Ior Bock and hang out with him. The Bock Saga had isolated him from many of his good friends, and in general, nobody wanted to be associated with him and his crazy Bock Saga. In a way, it made Ior quite lonely.

The empty space left behind by his Finnish friends was filled by what we came to call the 'via-via group'. This group was made up of all sorts of people who would come into contact with us via some acquaintance and who had some interest in the Bock Saga. Throughout the years, many people found us in this way. It was a colourful bunch; some were extravagant, some crazy and some, had a similar mission to ours. They all came and went. When we started digging for the Lemminkäinen Temple in 1987, however, Ior lost the sympathy of the major-ity of even this free-minded group of people. The opposition to Ior's story was growing in intensity and many thought that Ior had overplayed his hand by telling increasingly unbelievable stories. Many also thought that he'd lost it completely.

I had known him well both before and after he started telling the Bock Saga, so I knew that his personality hadn't changed; nor was he crazy or mentally ill. During the temple excavation, it was mostly only the Goa freaks that persevered. But let's not get ahead of ourselves here. That comes later.

I had just finished an enthusiastic, two-hour-long mono-logue about the Bock Saga.

"Well, what do you think?" I asked my sole listener, Seppo, expectantly.

A round, worried face looked back at me.

"I mean...Isn't it a bit too big a story to actually get into?" he asked, leaning back.

"I love this planet and I love people. I'm all in, Seppo it's part of me now and I can't change that."

"Casper, have you somehow got yourself stuck in some weird cult?"

"It's not a cult and it's not a religion."

"Well, it sounds like a belief system to me. One with all kinds of consequences to daily life."

"But it's all true and I like the consequences."

"Not my piece of cheese, bro."

"Just a perfect day, feeding animals in the park. Just a perfect day, problems are left behind. Just a perfect day and I'm glad I'm spending it with you. And later a movie too," I freestyled my own interpretation of a popular song I'd heard on the radio. It was a perfect day with Susanne.

"Look how cute those kids are over there," she pointed, turning to me with that smile I loved.

I couldn't deny that the whole scene was incredibly cute. The kids had made sailing boats out of folded leaves and were sailing these across a pond in great excitement.

"If you had a son, do you think he'd play with little sailing boats like that?" she asked with an innocent look on her face.

I was silent.

"Or a daughter?" she pressed on.

"I'll never have children, Susanne," I whispered.

"Why not?" asked Susanne, shocked that I had such a definitive answer.

"Well, Ior says that in Paradise time men had to be at least six foot tall to become fathers."

"That's the dumbest thing I've ever heard."

"It's all about selection. It's needed to make a better race of people."

I could see what was coming from the look on her face.

"Hasn't anyone told Mr Bock that Paradise time is over? Oh, and please do tell, how would these half-apes even know what centimetres were? Are you sure it wasn't inches they used instead?" She scoffed. "And don't get me started on 'selection'. Can you hear yourself, Casper? Are you Saga-heads Nazis now?"

"Nazis selected people after they were born. In the Bock Saga this is done before. We select animals and plants through breeding, is it that far-fetched to imagine doing this with people too?"

"Oh, I see. Now we're just some kind of farm product. And who's Ior? The great farmer in the sky?"

Although the main reaction the Bock Saga caused in the Finns was disbelief, its stories nevertheless seemed to stick in their minds. I've noticed that they always react in an emotional way when they hear the Bock Saga, and this is quite remarkable, as Finnish culture doesn't generally promote emotional expression, or any expression whatsoever really.

For us foreigners, the Bock Saga was, and is still, mostly an intellectual story. Sure, the way our world went from being a paradise to what it is now is interesting, but for the Finns, the whole thing seemed to strike a chord in their soul like music. I reckon that the reason for this is that the sound system and all its associations rings so much clearer in their language. And in this way, their language speaks to them, so to say.

In September of 1985, Cliff the yoga teacher that frequented Ior's porch in Goa knocked at the door of Ior's apartment in Helsinki. He had arrived already three months earlier and had spent that time finding Ior's address. These were the times before the internet. He was welcomed and a lot of Saga discussions and listening ensued.

Cliff wanted to share a geometrical concept that we could never have imagined before he'd shown us. He drew various shapes and lines that expressed the relationship between the letters of our alphabet in a mathematical way. He could do the same thing with the Hebrew and Roman alphabets, amongst others.

He even discovered a similar system within numbers where each number had its own meaning. Cliff was able to show the relationships between these numbers and meanings. Thus, not only the alphabet, or the Alfarnas-Bete, the rhyme of the All-Father, but also the numbers 0, 1, 2, 3, 4, 5, 6, 7, 8 and 9 told a story: 0 = Oden, 1 = Lemminkäinen, 2 = Svan and so on.

Cliff is an absolute mental giant, who could understand much more than anyone else, including all geniuses I ever met. I believe it a great loss to the Bock Saga that Cliff retreated from it some years later and thus never finished this line of research. He wasn't a fan of all the scandals and decided to dedicate the rest of his life to researching a 'universal truth' and its expression through 'Pure Mathematics' as proposed by Plato. He abandoned the 'cultural truth' that the Bock Saga described.

The thing that really gets me is that I believe he left the Bock Saga too early. Ior still hadn't completed his narrative of the 'Wheel of Life'. He was only halfway through by that point, so Cliff never discovered the full cycle.

I reckon that if he'd stayed long enough to witness this beautiful principle, he would've stayed with us a while longer. But then again, maybe he wouldn't have. The drawings he made while he worked on the Bock Saga are mostly lost forever. What's left of them, and the rest of his exceptionally beautiful and interesting life work was recently published in the book: *Cliff Barber and the Flower of Life*.

Cliff had made some audio recordings from the early veranda sessions in Chapora, which he took with him to Hawaii. This is where Mr Yeah arrived into the Saga scene. Mr Yeah listened to the recordings several hundred times and then decided he would produce a video recording of the Bock Saga in Chapora. It took a considerable effort to get all the necessary equipment together, which was fully funded by Mr Yeah.

Finally, in the spring of 1986, the famous Bock Saga video was made. The video consisted of Ior speaking about the Bock Saga for three hours in front of an audience consisting mainly of Dutch artists visiting Goa. This was the very video that Ronan and Lola watched in a restaurant later that year. The video was like a stone thrown into still water; its ripples ever growing, even until today.

The sound quality of the videotape was terrible. You can hear wind blowing into the microphone continuously. A goat was bleating in the background, making it even harder to hear Ior's story. The tape contains the chronological historical sequence of the Bock Saga in its entirety. However, Ior had not yet introduced the Offer-Ring system by that stage, which forms the second half of the Wheel of Life. So, from today's perspective the tape isn't complete. Still, this video turned out to be essential in all that was to come.

The three-hour tape of Ior telling the Bock Saga was brought to the United States by Mr Yeah, who had a hundred copies made by a high-tech company. This was all before the digital revolution, so it wasn't easy to produce the tapes. The whole project had been a financial marathon for Mr Yeah, who shouldered all the cost. Mr Yeah sent fifty tapes to Ior so that he could bring them to Goa and spread them amongst interested people.

Throughout all those summers in Finland and the ones to come, Ior continued to work in Sveaborg as an independent tour guide. Then every year in Goa, he worked his way through old thick and dusty 18th century books that he always brought with him to prepare himself for the next summer.

He would sit hour after hour in his Apolina house with a candle on his desk and a magnifying glass between his eye and a book, reading word by word. According to Ior, the boreal world had its greatest changes in the 18th century. The Bock Saga was his life, but the history of the 18th century was his job and his hobby.

Apart from the large collection of books that his family owned, he also had access to the enormous treasure trove of information contained in letters written in that period. Over many years, Rhea and Rachel had asked the Finnish nobility access to letters written by their ancestors. The ladies, possibly with the help of some scribers, then copied these letters. These gave great insight into the communication that had taken place between the royals of Europe and between diplomatic officials. Of course, the best part of the collection was formed of gossip between the wives, court ladies and servants of all the important aristocrats of the time.

This wealth of information was only available to Ior now, and it often gave him a surprising view of how history had played out. It also more than once brought him into conflict with the envious colleagues of the Museovirasto.

Ior was a highly respected tour guide who produced his own programme every year. When foreign officials visited Finland, Ior was often recruited to give them a tour through Sveaborg and, if required, through the rest of Finland. He spoke English very well, and this was uncommon in Finland those days. He also spoke Swedish fluently. It was after all very similar to the Root language that the Bock Saga describes as the first language of mankind.

Public knowledge: Nukke Mestari

Till his death in May 2012, media tycoon Nukke Mestari was one of the richest men in Finland. Nukke Mestari was the most significant publisher in his country and the owner of the Helsinki Raportti, the largest newspaper in Finland. He was also a key player in the Raportti Group, which rose to become Scandinavian's leading media corporation from the 1960s onwards to the present day. During Nukke Mestari's time with the Raportti Corporation, the company's net sales grew from FIM 3.5 million to FIM 2.75 billion. As the largest individual shareholder in the Raportti Group, Nukke Mestari was definitely one of the top richest individuals in Finland. He married Jane Mestari in 1959, but the couple had no children.

His father was the foreign minister of Finland and negotiated with the Soviet Union before the Winter War started in 1939.

"Nukke Mestari was at heart a newspaper man. *The liberal ideology of the Mestari family towards the publishing of newspapers was to give the editorial staff of the paper the journalistic freedom to write, and then to analyse the results afterwards", writes a former Helsinki Raportti editor-in-chief.*

Nukke Mestari was an international Finn. He maintained his family's traditionally strong and high-level links with the United States and was also familiar with the Royal Court in Sweden.

It may have been that the role of a publisher, though carried off with aplomb and no little success, was not his first choice.

Mestari himself recalled later in life that what he would really have preferred was a life at sea enjoying the freedom to move. Nevertheless, the traditions of the family set certain obligations, and limited his marine ambitions to a love of steamships and support for maritime museums amongst his many charitable commitments.

One day, Ior was hired by Mestari to give a tour to *the crème de la crème* of the Scandinavian media. Everyone who attended the tour with Ior that day was a newspaper, television or radio director. It was a pleasant afternoon and when the tour ended, Mestari jokingly asked Ior if he had anything to explain about Valhalla.

Ior had never incorporated the Bock Saga into his tours, and he wasn't ready to do so yet; even if it just so happened that the spot where they were standing was the exact location of Valhalla according to the Bock Saga!

Ior suddenly remembered that he'd picked up the fifty videotapes from the post office just before starting the tour. He took one videotape out of his bag and handed it over to Mestari, telling him that if he really was interested in Valhalla, he would find all the information he wanted here.

Mestari and his media friends just thought that the videotapes contained Ior's tour and more information about Sveaborg, so they all gathered round him each asking for a tape of their own. Finding it hard to refuse them, Ior gave away all of his copies. I guess he could have seen it as a good opportunity for the Bock Saga to get some airtime.

All those big media bosses returned home with a video tape. What happened afterwards you ask? Well... nothing. Or at least, it seemed like nothing to us at the time. Much later, one of the directors present that day brought us a story. He asked to remain anonymous until after his death, for reasons that became obvious as he gave us his information.

Apparently, as soon as Mestari had seen the videotape, he gathered everyone who'd taken part in the tour together and ordered them to never speak of or refer to the contents of the videotape to anyone. Each person was ordered to destroy his personal copy, and Mestari promised them that if he ever heard any mention of this Bock Saga on any of the Raportti Media, there would be serious life-changing repercussions.

Having finished dinner, Nukke and Jane Mestari sat by the wood fire, watching the flames rise and dip.

"How was your day, dear?" asked Jane.

"Quite a lot of fun actually. I spent the day with a group of Raportti directors at Sveaborg. We went on a tour that was taken by this guy, Ior Bock. He had an interesting story to tell about the place and how, in a way, the foundation of the modern times we live in now was laid out in that very location in the 18th century. He went on to explain the important role Finland played in the Crimean war in the 19th century. The seeds of our independence from both Russia and Sweden were laid in that war and Sveaborg was essential in it. It was really fascinating, Jane. He has a very distinct view of history and our present time; I've never really heard anyone else tell it the way he does."

"It's strange, seeing the past in a different light, suddenly makes you see the present differently too. Ior is a great storyteller and knows how to captivate an audience. I was thinking that it might actually be quite interesting having him on our TV shows now and then. I think the public would enjoy being educated on our nation's great past, even if he does deviate from actual history from time to time. It's important for us to have pride in our past and in ourselves.

We've always been part of some other country's scheme, but now we're on the same eye level as the Swedes, Russians, Germans, and Americans. Ior might provide the pride we need to lift our status as a nation. Through his stories, the Finnish people can build their self-esteem. That's what we need if we want to continue being a world player. You know, at the end of the

tour I asked Ior about Valhalla and he gave me this videotape."
Nukke got up from his armchair and brought the tape to his wife.

"Shall we watch it?"

Nukke and Jane sat together and watched the Bock Saga video. As the story unfolded, Nukke grew more and more restless and aggravated.

"What is it, don't you like it?"

"It's not that I don't like it, I do like it. But this is the opposite of what we need. The Finnish people want to be independent and Finnish, but in a quiet way. This guy claims that Finland was the centre of the world, that Paradise was here, that the great 'All-Father' was a Finn. What do you think the bishop would say to that? This hippie is claiming that all that's ever happened in the history of mankind was somehow caused by and related to our Finnish ancestors. We want to live in peace. We're not great and powerful like the Swedes, Germans, or Russians. Our independence was only granted because they grew tired of fighting each other over Finland, not due to any sort of real strength or victory on our part. We don't want to disrupt anything, and we certainly don't want to unleash some heathen lifestyle upon the whole world. We just want to be left alone. Do you understand what I mean?"

"Yes, I do understand, but I think you're being overly emotional and blowing this out of proportion. It's just a nice fairy tale set in our past. It doesn't really matter. We've got plenty of other stories like this in Finland, you know that."

"Sure, we've got the Kalevala and all those other folk stories that have never been written down. But they don't have the same implications that this Bock Saga has. They have no implications at all except that people liked to listen to them in the past. This Saga's different. It says that under the perfect circumstance of Paradise time, the Finns were the rulers of the world. And they did this by having babies with women of lower castes, of all things!"

"Oh, you're such an idiot!" Jane burst out angrily. He'd touched her sore point. She withdrew in her own safe house of thoughts, like a snail that's been touched by salt water.

They had no children of their own. It was her greatest wish in life, and she felt somehow guilty for it and had no way to compensate but to spend time with the children of others. Poor children that were in need of help. Her help. She engaged in all kinds of community help for poor and depraved children, who did not have the advantage in life to be born in a billionaire family. She regularly spend more money than her husband was aware of to all kinds of projects to help and protect vulnerable children in the first years of their lives. Of course, what she really wanted most was to hold her own baby in her arms. For some reason beyond her, god, or whoever decides over such matters, had not granted her that luck. Not only did she not have children, she would not have grand children as well. Her life when growing old would be empty.

Having watched Ior's tape, she wished that she could be the Svan in the Bock Saga with her many children. Oh, to be the king and queen of the world and the creators of a new generation of people. Nukke had been successful in his life. He was probably the richest man in Scandinavia now and the most powerful. He decided what people in the large, spread-out region would see on television and read in the newspapers. Whatever TV or news they encountered: it would carry Nukke's fingerprint. Scandinavia was proud to have a free press; free of state censorship, yes, but not free of Nukke Mestari, who owned it all.

Thank God he was a wise and good-hearted man that had our world's best interests in mind. He was the perfect gatekeeper to decide what news was presented and how. And the difference between Nukke and a president of a country was that he would stay in this position not only for four years, but for life. But what was it good for? All the riches and power in the world would still not bring them eternal life. Not even Jesus Christ, Mohammed, Buddha and Mahatma Gandhi had lived forever. Nukke and Jane would grow old and then they'd die, and everything they'd achieved would fit in a dusty cabinet in the basement of a concrete newspaper building. It was all so empty.

The only real fulfilment in life would have been to have children and grand children. That would be the closest thing to eternal life. Or at least it would be a good feeling to pass over our world to the next generation, our kids.

Nukke could give his energy to the company that made him rich and powerful. Jane knew he could live like the Lemminkäinen in the Bock Saga, with all those beautiful girls. Helsinki had plenty of beautiful girls and what Nukke did on his foreign travels, nobody knew and would surely never be published in any newspaper, since he owned them all. Jane didn't want to know either.

Nukke knew what the sudden silence from his wife meant and where her thoughts would inevitably go.

"I am not Lemminkäinen," he said slowly, as quietly as he could, his heart thumping.

"Lemminkäinen does not exist. It's less than a fairy tale. I will make sure that no one ever hears this story. It disrupts our country, and it disrupts you. I've had enough. Ior Bock will never tell his story on my media and if he tells it anywhere else, I'll make sure that it is ridiculed. And that's the law of Mestari from now on. And this law will stay in place for the next thousand years! Am I clear? I never want to hear anything about this Bock Saga again!"

Nukke took the video from the player and threw it into the fire. He then retreated to his home office. He was on the phone all evening with the people that had accompanied him that afternoon. They were surprised to receive a call so late in the evening, but they knew their ever-calculating boss never did anything without good reason. Besides, Nukke Mestari's tone made it clear that there would be no discussions nor questions asked.

In the winter of 1986, I once more spent a lot of time with Ior and our group of friends on the veranda in Chapora. We learned more and more about his family history and thereby the history of mankind. It's also a story that needs to be understood properly and for this, the workings of the Root language are crucial. By testing this language and the underlying sound system with visitors who came from all over the world to our veranda, we gained great insight. We did all kinds of so-called parlour games.

We took a word from one of the many languages known by the people present and tried to dissect it, dividing it up in sounds and meanings. The others present from other countries would try to find the equivalent word in their own language. Then, we would take each apart in sounds and try to figure out how the meanings of the sounds could be applied, and how that particular word would correlate to the meaning and sounds in the Root language.

Another variation of this game was to take a word from any language and each person present would try to find a similar sounding word in their own language. Together, we tried to find similar meanings in the similar sounds. We were often surprised by the results. A lot of them sounded far-fetched at the time, but it was clear to everyone who participated in the games that there was much more meaning hidden in our languages than we could ever have suspected. We all learn to associate sounds with letters and meanings from a very young age, so it's easy not to recognise the most obvious connections.

On the porch, we heard all kinds of European languages. As well as this, there were several Indians most of whom spoke at least four languages. There were Japanese, Chinese, Afghanis, Turks and many other nationalities. It was actually the hardest for those of us who had English as their mother tongue, because they could not pronounce the Root sounds easily and they usually had only one language in their brain. The people that already knew two or more languages could play these games by themselves. We noticed that the Indians had a great talent at learning the Finnish language; a language that the Europeans found so difficult to learn. Later, when some of the Indians went with Ior to Helsinki for extended periods of time, they could speak and understand Finnish within a few months, even those who were illiterate!

The veranda was filled with people, smoking chillums, laughing, and chatting. Ior stood in the doorway, dressed only in a loin cloth.

'Rettekettette, Retteketaaah!' he declared through his cupped hands. "I have an announcement to make of great importance!" He marched up and down the veranda with great aplomb, like an emperor addressing his subjects.

"I hereby announce the birthday party of my aunt Kristina Victoria, which will take place on the 24th of July 1987. The party will be held at the family estate: Akanpesa in Gumbostrand in Finland. Everybody's welcome."

There were loud cheers from everyone present. Although the party was far away in space and time, it was a happy announcement and taken as such.

In the ensuing chaos, somebody yelled: "How old will your aunt be?"

"130 years old!" Ior exclaimed proudly.

"Won't a party be a bit too wild for her?"

"She died before I was born. The party is to commemorate her birth. She was an important lady for our family."

"Important in what way?" I asked.

"I will tell you one day," Ior smiled mysteriously. "Oh, yeah, I almost forgot! We're also going to dig up a piece of wood that my ancestors buried behind the estate exactly one thousand years ago."

There were more cheers and pledges to travel to Finland in the coming summer.

After a few months in Goa, I travelled on to Thailand, Japan, and the Philippines. My head was full of the Bock Saga and on the way, I spewed out all I had learned from Ior to anyone who was polite enough to listen or too shy not to chase me away. I blasted them with pre-Ice-Age society structures, the origins of languages and explained the meaning of just about every symbol that could be found on the planet. The subject was too large to be covered in a few hours, but I did it anyway, just as it had been done on the 1986 tape.

Talking about the Bock Saga became a natural state of being for me at that time. My mouth overflowed with what my head was full of.

The only effect my lectures had was to make people tired of me. I think that for most people, it was a bit too much information. It started the trend in which everything I wanted to accomplish would have the exact opposite effect.

I arrived in Akanpesa, the Bock family estate in Finland in the spring of 1987. Ior had already arrived from Goa with Soma, the guy in the hammock. Ior asked if I could restore the estate to the condition it had been in when the family bought it in the 1930s. It was a lot of work. I repaired the roof, I painted the walls in the traditional colours, and I restored a lot of woodwork and carvings both within and outside of the building. The garden needed a lot of love.

As my work progressed throughout the spring, more and more people arrived from Goa. Lola, Mr Yeah and Cliff were there and did their share of the work clearing up the big mud pool in front of the Etta Stupa. One day, Ronan arrived with Swedish Mats, another regular on the porch of the Apolina house. Ronan had a buckets full of questions related to the Bock Saga.

Lola

One of my earliest memories is of wallpaper. Large baroque motifs in plastic pink and heavenly blue. Our whole apartment was covered in it, including my bedroom; although, it was my bedroom only in the beginning. In later years, I was forced to share it with an ever-increasing number of brothers and sisters. In the end, there were seven of us sleeping in it. Another seven were sleeping in the second bedroom and the last two slept with mother in the living room.

Our world consisted of large institutions. The largest of them was the enormous concrete building we shared with hundreds of other families. It was a city of its own. The other institutions were the Catholic Church, school, and Franco. They all blurred into each other. It was all about truth and lies, rules and exceptions, power and weakness. The truth was poured over us by the priest, Franco, and my father, all in the name of the universal supreme male: God. It was all about good and bad, both in extreme forms. They talked about the good and then lived the bad. There was no love, only repression and it was clear that everything they told us was lies.

My father wasn't home often. When he was, I always remember him either drunk or asleep. He beat and raped my mother regularly. My brothers, sisters and I were all a product of rape. Our church and school were covered with little statues of Mother Mary and her Child. They were worshipped. That was one of the lies. Many years later, I talked with my mother about it all. She had no real understanding of contraception except that the priest said it was wrong. She had never enjoyed sex in her life. Neither had my father. Franco and the priest had taken care of that. Love existed only in the movies, foreign movies from Hollywood.

My mother had a full-time job in between giving birth. The children had to mostly take care of each other, the older ones taking care of the younger ones. I was the oldest, and ever since I remember, I was the defacto caretaker of the household and the children. With so many kids around, there were always at least a few of them crying, sick or fighting. As soon as they could walk, I kicked them out onto the street where they could play. In the Franco era there were no cars, so the streets were safe. That has changed. I was out on the street too, mostly making sure no one got lost. I didn't play much myself.

I listened a lot and talked a lot, though. That was and is my main occupation in life. I can talk forever. When no one else is around to listen, I talk to myself. The only thing that really set me apart from the other people in our concrete behemoth, I think, is that I liked to learn words from other languages. Through a small transistor radio, we received French and English music. I could soon speak those languages. Well, strictly speaking, I couldn't speak them but sing them. I had no idea what the words from the songs meant. I guessed it was mostly about love, falling in love and breaking up. New concepts to me. It was the opposite of getting married due to your parents' decision, being beaten up and raped, giving birth and having a statue dedicated to you in the church.

When I was thirteen, I got a job in the markets. There, I was able to learn the languages of the tourists who visited our city. I learned to understand and speak the main European languages. Finally, I learned something I could use in life.

In 1975, when I was seventeen years old, the three most important people in my life died: the priest, who's probably burning in hell now, Franco and my mother. My father signed a piece of paper that assigned all the kids to a monastery. I escaped to France. I was free for the first time in my life. I ate an ice cream every day, although that was mainly because I sold them on the beach.

Somehow, the ice cream set free from their colourful wrappers, melting in the shining sun, made me feel worthy and happy. I lived day by day. Sometimes in the evenings, sitting at a campfire with other immigrants from Spain and Africa, I listened to their stories and thoughts. Some had great dreams of what they would do and be in life. I'd never thought about these things, at least not more than wanting to be a famous and beautiful film star. But I realised early on that this was just a dream and not something that would ever materialise.

The only practical thoughts I could formulate focussed on what not to do or be. I knew I would never trust a priest; I would never listen to such a person again. Nor would I listen to Franco-like people in uniforms. I would never marry or be abused. I would never have children. I'd already raised enough of them by this stage.

I also made the decision to never be dependent on anyone and, most importantly, to enjoy my life. I had no ties and obligations. Apart from staying alive, I had no ambitions nor obligations, so I decided to explore the world. I worked in markets in France, travelled with market merchants to other places and, in this way, ended up in Berlin.

There I met Ronan, a cute boy who'd had his roots cut off like me. He took me with him on adventurous nights, spray painting graffiti on bridges and trains in the dark. In the beginning it was scary, then exhilarating and then great fun. There was always a chance we'd get caught, but we outran every night guard and cop. We were a great team. One day, he asked me to come with him on a great trip to distant lands I'd never even heard of. Sure, I'll jump on your white horse, Ronan.

Ronan

I was born in 1958 in East Berlin. The fumes of the Second World War had never left the city. Many buildings wore the pockmarks of fighting; others had never been repaired. These made great playgrounds. My mother worked long hours, so when I wasn't in school, I was in these ruins with the neighbourhood kids. I was a shy boy by nature, but in the rubble of East Berlin I became streetwise.

My father died when I was young. I have no memories of him. My mother told me he died years later from the wounds that he sustained in the Russian prison where he ended up after the war. I felt sad for him and for me, but I didn't know much better and took life as it came. I felt the sadness most of all at Christmas time. The apartment was dark and cold, and I was always alone with my mother. She was tough and hard. I felt safe with her, but not warm. And I knew that you were supposed to feel light and warm on such an evening. I saw in my mother's eyes that she'd seen many things that shouldn't have happened. These Christmas nights, I would sit and watch over the Berlin wall. On the other side it was warm and light.

We used to listen to a radio station from West Berlin. Not too loud though, because it wasn't allowed. But we loved to hear the Beatles.

"Hey, Love me do, You know I love you, So pleaeaease love me too!"

I'd wish so hard to be in West Berlin. There, you could play the radio as loud as you wanted. I wondered if the people in West Berlin listened to the same radio stations as we did at Christmas time. I didn't know what was true and what wasn't. Our apartment only had one small window. I spent many hours looking out of that window over the city. Out of boredom I drew the cityscapes. I must have sketched hundreds of them; all of them the same. The only variation was the season and the tiny people and animals I drew into them. I imagined the adventures they had in that endless city. My little creatures climbed the buildings and when they reached the top, they continued climbing into the sky. There, they were happy.

After high school, I was selected to go to art college. They told me I was a talented painter and drawer. Art college was strict and technical. All art should express the glory of the fight between the different social classes. I didn't see many social classes. Sure, some were part of the communist party, while others weren't. Some had Nazi backgrounds and were demonised. But all were poor. This wasn't what you were supposed to draw, though.

All decisions at home were made out of poverty. It was hard to do anything about it because earning money outside of the socialist factories was considered stealing. We were stealing anyway, whenever we could. We went into old houses and took metal parts from the hinges and waterpipes and sold them. It was tricky. If you were caught, you'd be in big trouble.

In my third year in art college, I was chosen to partake in a student exchange and was sent to Kazakhstan for six months. It took me a whole week to get there by train. That opened my eyes. I'd never realised that the world was so large and that there were so many different types of people populating it. Kazakhstan was very colourful compared to the city I came from. It was from another century. It still existed in the times of camel caravans. Berlin was grey in summer and winter; the people were grey. They were all working in grey factories, making grey stuff. There was no joy and hope, or so it seemed to me. The socialist propaganda was constantly blaring how fantastic it all would be if...

In Kazakhstan there were tribal men and women dressed in colourful wild dresses. It scared me in the beginning. They looked proud. What a difference from the bent, broken backs in Berlin. The Kazakhs looked serious, and their dark eyebrows gave them an angry look, but you could tell they were happy. Happy with who they were, happy with the world around them and happy with their position in it.

And somehow, it felt like they knew a secret that you could

only know if you were one of them. Even the kids had this knowing look. I wished I were one of them. I made some drawings of them, but they weren't appreciated in school. People weren't supposed to be divided into tribes. We all had to be glorious socialists, all of us the same; and the same meant being something like us, grey.

At some point I got a message that my mother was ill. Shortly afterwards I got a message that she was very ill. I made the long train ride back to East Berlin. When I arrived, I learned that she had died of pneumonia. Our apartment had already been rented out to another family and I was assigned a small student room. I was alone in the world with only my drawings now. I had no concept of how to live my life from here on. Should I find a job at some newspaper and draw glorious socialists until my death? I had no idea or vision of how to have a real life. In my mind, I couldn't make the compromise of staying on the beaten track forever merely for the sake of being a good citizen.

The defeated evil empire, the socialist paradise, the capitalist hell. These were the three possibilities of the state of the world presented to us. "Is that all there is?", I thought to myself. "Surely, there's more, like Kazakhstan. I'll search for a place like that, where I can be part of a tribe and be happy and proud to be myself." I had no idea where to look for this tribe. I saw from the window of my room the bright lights of that mysterious place called West Berlin. There were no tribes there. I was told it was the centre of slavery and injustice. It might be, but it was at least different from where I was now.

On this beaten track, I couldn't see a life I could live. And outside of this beaten track, all I could see was myself joining the fight against, and attack on, the mighty Russian Empire. I didn't have even a slight chance of success with this alternative. To be honest, I didn't even know what success looked like. The only sense of success I'd ever seen was in the eyes of the Kazakhs.

We weren't free to travel at will. There was no way I would be allowed to go to Kazakhstan and even if I were, I couldn't just become one of them. It was a matter of birth. I felt so suffocated. I needed freedom. I searched for options across the cityscape below me, but my cage was closed. Darkness was approaching, and in the distance, I saw the lights of West Berlin. Could they be the lights of freedom? It was worth a try...

Being smuggled to the other side of the Berlin wall comprised of some terrifying and hairy moments. I made it, and soon after I was able to acquire a legal West German passport. I was free to go where I wanted in the world, or at least this half of the world. I learned that a lot of what we'd been told about the capitalist West Berlin was true. It was all about money. A great deal was possible if you had money. To get this, you needed a job or to be exceptionally lucky; to get paid well, you needed skills.

Drawing was considered a hobby and was poorly paid. I hardly managed to stay alive. West Berlin was like a beautiful palace I could enjoy, but I was the palace butler, not the king. That's not to say that there was no art scene in West Berlin, there was, but I had trouble connecting to it. I liked to draw and paint, but I wasn't a passionate artist. I had no intention of cutting off my ear like Vincent van Gogh, and I was no master of publicity like Salvador Dalí. I was just Ronan from East Berlin, drawing advertisements for stuff found in supermarkets.

I realised that even with great talent and hard work, I wasn't set for success. That required skills that I didn't have, like a burning and unrelenting drive, for instance. Success was not my main goal. I just wanted to have a life, to explore and enjoy the world, to have adventures and so on. I mean, to become a successful designer you had to sit all day with a pencil in your hand, watching the paper in front of you turn dark. I wanted to really live. I wanted to be in the drawing, my drawing. And yes, I needed money to do that.

For the moment, the closest I came to living in a drawing was by participating in the habit of West German freaks to paint everything around them. We went out in the night with spray cans and went wild painting underground trains, walls, bridges, every urban canvas we could find. In the daytime, we painted our friends' cars and even our own clothes.

The mood portrayed in the graffiti of my friends was getting darker by the day. It was the punk era, and their artwork was heavy with political meaning. My artform, on the other hand, was meaninglessnessism. I had seen enough dread darkness. I came from an apartment with one little room in East Berlin. I loved the colours. I liked to brighten things up. I wanted to contribute to a colourful and happy world. West Berlin might not be paradise on Earth, but it was a huge deal better than the institutionalised boredom of the East.

Then I met Lola and fell in love immediately. She was mysterious. She had platina white hair and a light shone behind her dark eyes. She was wild, independent; she was alive and happy and adventurous. We started an intense relationship. I tried to draw her, but she couldn't sit still. So, I drew her while she slept.

Lola came with us on our nightly adventures. She'd never drawn anything in her life and had never used a spray can. But her savage animal instinct was expressed in her artwork. She loved bright contrasting colours. She was much more talented than I was. We were a great team together. I sprayed compositions and she went wild on them. In each hand she swung a different colour of spray paint can and gesticulated like a passionate orchestra conductor, directing the drops onto the wall.

Within the art scene there were some free-minded people, and they told us stories about the big world outside our walled-in city. Some had travelled to distant lands that existed, not only in fairy tales, but in our reality. They were far away and would require long journeys, but Lola and I shared the same ambition. We wanted to be like Sindbad the sailor or Marco Polo and travel to distant lands, just for the fun of it. Let's escape this golden-caged city and discover the world. Although my decisions were mostly of the romantic and dreamy kind, I realised now was the time to get rational and find some money for our trip. I'd escaped once before, this time it would be easier. To earn money for our trip, we worked relentlessly in a silkscreen print workshop. It was an unhealthy job. We were in continuous contact with bad solvent fumes that seeped out of the ink. The long hours made me weak, and I developed a bad cough. After what seemed like an endless period of time, we decided we had enough money to make the jump into the great big world. We managed to hook up with a caravan of three hippie vans that was leaving West Berlin in a south-east general direction.

And so, one cold and drab morning, we waited for the vans from a petrol station on the outskirts of Berlin. I kept a look out for the hippie vans, eager to see them come round the corner. Around us were concrete buildings and highway roads, some covered in our graffiti. Huge women looked at us seductively from large billboards. Bright colours and bright lights tried to sell us all kinds of crap, none of which were real or important. We ached for real things like fresh air and mountains, and we imagined these things through the eyes of the tribalistic men and women of the mysterious East.

Then three colourful Mercedes 508 vans came into sight. We got onboard and everybody was excited and ready to get going. We were full of anticipation of where our adventure would lead us. As long as the rest of the world wasn't the same as Berlin, we'd be happy. The engines roared and spewed out big dark clouds, like an old steamship setting out for a transatlantic voyage.

During the next few months, we drove and drove through beautiful landscapes towards ever more exotic places. We entered the land of a thousand and one nights. It seemed that for every kilometre we drove eastwards, we travelled back one year in time. Not much had changed since the days of the silk caravans. In many places along the trip that led us through Turkey, Iran, Afghanistan, Pakistan and eventually India, the locals had never seen Europeans before. We were welcomed as important guests at times. We got invited to the courts and palaces of princes, Khalifas and other high functionaries. Who would've expected that a bunch of escapees like us would get such treatment?

The further east we travelled, the harder it became to protect my fair princess from the possessiveness of the local aristocracy. On a few occasions, our hosts demanded that Lola should become part of their harem in return for the hospitality they'd given us. Presents were offered as well: camels, racing horses, jewellery. She needed a permanent escort; her shiny white hair meant that even a girl of Lola's calibre could vanish in a moment. This stressed Lola out quite a bit as she had no intention of living her life in a harem, which resembled a lot to slavery.

"Nonsense," she pointed out irritated, when I suggested that she was too jealous to share her Prince with other beauties. But in a way, she also liked the attention, and she liked the idea of me chaperoning her through the dangerous lands of the dark-eyed sultans, sheikhs, and maharajas. It gave her a sexual thrill. It gave me the shivers.

Lola

Yes, it was a beautiful trip with many breath-taking wonders. We met so many beautiful people. But behind the beauty and veils, I saw many women in the same situation my mother had been in. Ronan thought I was jealous.

No, I just knew what it meant living under such dominant male authority. It might seem like a romantic idea, falling in love with a Persian or Afghan prince, but after you marry, the rules change. I had no illusions about that. A woman's voice could only go so far in a place like this. Ronan told me that at the end of our trip there was a beach and an easy life together. I wanted to get there unharmed and keep the independence I'd fought so hard for. Beautiful and mysterious as those lands were, they were dangerous too.

At the end of our journey was Goa. We moved into a house overgrown with bougainvillea on a beach in south Goa. From the porch, we saw the sun setting over the Indian Ocean flanked by swaying palm trees. It was so romantic. We felt at home. The locals were friendly, and we made many new friends from all over the world who'd also found this haven of goodness. The climate was perfect for human bodies, the nature was beautiful and generous. Everything we needed was at or fingertips. If I was ever to be homesick again, it would be homesickness for Goa.

The feeling of time and alternating seasons was gone. Many months had already passed since we left West Berlin and the presence of Europe was fading from our minds. The idea of ever going back to the grey concrete of Berlin was like a nightmare lurking on the edge of my thoughts. We belonged here. Time was never a problem, but our money was getting low, and our dwindling purse demanded attention.

The guy we were renting the house from offered us the job of selling charas, a popular local marijuana product. He had brought a few kilos from Manali in the north of India to Goa and needed someone to distribute them. I was scared. I thought it was a dangerous proposal. Why did he not just sell it himself if it was such a walk in the park, as he put it? Even if it ended up working out, our paradise, our dream life would be over, as I'd just be worrying myself to death.

Ronan and I had many arguments about it. He thought it was a good idea, as it was a clear solution to our problem. I told him it was a very different thing to spray paint on some anonymous piece of concrete in Berlin than to sell drugs here. Fuck the money, we would survive somehow. I'd always survived without money with all my brothers and sisters under my wings.

Ronan

It sounded like a good opportunity to me. and it turned out to lead to quite a nice lifestyle too. It was my first truly capitalist experience. Every morning, I walked along the beach trying to sell my merchandise to the few sunbathing Westerners.

Then, when the sun climbed higher towards its zenith, I walked on the back side of the dunes, where the Westerners' houses lay scattered between the palm trees. I visited the houses where people were having lunch. In the evenings, I headed to a few restaurants to catch the people I'd missed during the day. There weren't many Westerners, but those I found were mostly stoned all day, so I sold so much that I had more money than when we left Berlin.

On one of these working days, I met William a guy from Amsterdam, who had his own story to carry around on his shoulders and was happy to be relieved of it here in Goa. Most of the Westerners had some history and reason to leave their home for so long. He sometimes visited us on our porch for a smoke at sunset. He never bought anything, he had his own, but we did sometimes swap some.

My little business went well, but it didn't make us millionaires. In the end, our visas expired, our money ran out and we headed back on the long journey to western Europe. My relationship with Lola didn't last. After having been together day and night for over a year, there was not much left of the mystery that had attracted me in the beginning. I think she was fed up with me as well, to be honest. I still liked her and loved her for who she was. After we got back to Europe, we went on our own ways, but we remained in contact over the years.

I'd tasted adventure and the good life and wanted nothing else from now on. Berlin had nothing to offer me, and I wanted to leave again as soon as possible. I'd heard that in Alaska there was good money to be made on the fishing boats. And I'd heard in Goa, where such matters are discussed all the time, that hashish in Alaska was in high demand, rare and easy to sell. I decided to go for both options.

Amsterdam was the hashish centre of the world in those years, and you could buy it cheap and almost legally. That would be my first logical stop. I met William in Amsterdam, and he brought me half a kilo of dope to sell in Alaska. I found out how to smuggle dope onto airplanes. I cut it up into small lumps, carefully packed each up and swallowed them all before boarding the plane to Anchorage. I hoped to God that this pseudo-science worked and that the packets didn't open in my stomach. Shitting it all out from fear seemed too real a possibility.

The trip from beginning to end was more than twenty-four hours long, and I spent all of it hoping to God that I could keep the merchandise in my stomach. If I had to crap while still on the plane and the little packets of dope came out, I'd have to swallow all the stinky brown bullets again in that little claustrophobic toilet at 30,000 feet of altitude. What a nightmare scenario! I'd taken pills to induce constipation and just prayed for the best. I ate none of the food served on the plane and drank no tea or coffee.

My stomach felt hard and full the whole way. The tension of smuggling added to this discomfort. In the meantime, I tried to look as relaxed and normal as possible. Later, I thought: "In what world does a long-haired hippie, dressed in colourful hippie clothes look like he's not smuggling?"

After landing in Anchorage, I encountered the customs. The only thing they were interested in was if I was going to work in Alaska, which was not allowed on a tourist visa.

"No way!", I declared, pretending to be disgusted by the idea. They stamped my passport and waved me through. All went according to plan.

From Anchorage I flew on a small plane to Dutch Harbor. When I arrived in a little guest house, I could finally release myself. I fished all the packets out of the toilet bowl. The smell was terrible. I hoped that the dope didn't smell like shit too. I washed it again and again with water until I couldn't smell it anymore.

Life was rough in the fishing world, especially for a colourful artist who found himself amongst ruffians whose hobbies included drinking beer, fighting, and shooting guns. Luckily, selling dope gave me a protected status. It was in high demand and supply was incidental. I sold half of my supply in bars until I found a boat to go fishing in.

On the boat, I sold the second half to the captain and the crew. I made more money than I'd made in my whole life. I finally knew the taste of success. I was travelling the world, living an adventurous life. Everything seemed to be working out for me. I grew more and more excited every moment that passed. I'd come from such a depressed place, filled with depressed people who were all resigned to a depressing future. I'd escaped and constantly remembered this fact. I felt happy and satisfied.

When all my merchandise was sold and the work was done, I flew back to Amsterdam and headed to Goa. This time, I skipped the long overland route. From my financial fortune, I bought a plane ticket to India. I was looking forward to a six-month holiday in Goa, more travelling and adventures and my next step towards even greater success.

The next months were great. The days were filled with beach racket, smoking chillums and enjoying psychedelic parties that lasted all night and seemed to last longer each time. The first few parties lasted through the night, the next few until noon, and later, some even lasted until the next sunset. After the parties, we slept in hammocks and drank fruit juices.

Somehow, these long parties never wore us out, but gave us loads of energy. We felt that we were doing stuff that was good for our bodies and minds. We even talked about bringing these parties to Europe and other places in the modern world that needed brightening up, although it was hard to imagine how we could manage all the practicalities and logistics involved. If that were possible and successful, it could pay for our lives, and we'd be giving the world something that was good for body and spirit.

Our lives in Goa consisted only of these things, and we spent all our time with freaks and the local Goanese people. We had no idea what was happening in the rest of the world. There were no newspapers or televisions available, and intercontinental telephone lines were something that existed only in science fiction. The internet, on the other hand, still didn't even exist in science fiction. News from the outside was scarce and didn't affect our lives. Truth be told, we didn't miss it, we were happy in our world as it was.

Lola

When we returned to Europe, I realised I'd added a few things to my list of 'never again in this lifetime'. I would at all costs avoid countries and places that had an institutionalised system that repressed women, like what I'd experienced in Spain and like I saw in some of the countries we passed through on our journey back to western Europe. Later, I revised this statement, realising that the world would become too small a place if I strictly adhered to it. I would just avoid places where I couldn't be free.

The second new item added to my list: I would never again involve myself in suffocating relationships. I loved the sex and friendship, but somehow, my relationship with Ronan had come with an invisible contract. There were all kinds of behaviours that were allowed or weren't allowed, and there was jealousy that stemmed from the fear of losing each other. Being afraid had not helped us and I'd been no better than Ronan. The traditional monogamous relationship had not brought out the best in either of us.

What I did love was travelling and Goa life. To continue this, I needed to find extra money on top of the money I needed just to stay alive. Many of the Goa freaks were smuggling hashish all over the planet, but in my opinion, this was a road to ruin. They were smuggling small amounts, just enough to pay the next airplane tickets and for the next few months of living. They weren't big time gangsters, gangsters made a lot more money, but both could end up in jail.

On my way back to Europe, I'd bought lots of little souvenirs in the bazaars that we passed through. It was cheap jewellery, rough but beautiful printed cotton cloths with Eastern motifs, along with some girls and women's clothing. Ronan had thought it a waste of precious money. I tried to explain to him that it would pay for our next trip to Goa. I had plenty of market experience and knew it would sell for profit. The profit margins were even higher than with the hashish.

I sold it easily on the markets in the south of France. I found people who'd imported more than they could sell themselves and sold their merchandise too. I was doing great. I was well on my way to having the money to buy myself an airplane ticket to Bombay in autumn and spend another season on a Goan beach. On one of these markets, I met Xevi. He was of the Catalan brand, like I was, but from the French side. A part of Catalonia is in France. He spoke my language, but more than a Catalan he was a Buddhist. He always carried with him a little Buddhist book called the One Hundred and Fifty Verses of Mātṛceṭa. It was a collection of poems. Sometimes, when we lay lazily in bed, he would read it to me. I didn't understand much of it, but the sounds he formed with his lips were intensely beautiful. "To feel it is enough," he'd tell me. "To study it takes a whole lifetime and probably even that wouldn't be enough" He was a charming guy, not as tight as Ronan. He loved enjoying the pleasures of life and I was one of those pleasures. I loved being this for him and I loved being loved and treated like someone special. He often told me I was more beautiful than Gina Lollobrigida, the film star. I was more beautiful than Sofia Loren. I was the most beautiful woman in the world, and the most interesting and talented as well. We had something in common too: he'd been in Goa that winter. This meant we didn't need to waste time explaining what paradise was to each other.

After the summer, we returned to India together. Before heading to Goa, we travelled through romantic Rajasthan. Once more, I found many items in the markets that would sell well in Europe. I bought a lot of colourful sheets and saris and sent them directly to France. When we arrived in Goa, I bumped into Ronan at the flea market. He frowned darkly when I first told him about Xevi, but it never turned into a problem. The two guys hit it off.

Ronan

After a few months in Goa, I left for its neighbouring state, Kerala, with my new friend Xevi. He knew where the legendary marijuana grew. We spent a few weeks in the mountains and came back with our bags full. From then on, I went back to selling dope on the beaches and making my rounds along the houses rented by Western freaks like me. It was nice; I was welcome everywhere. I replenished the coffers and made a lot of friends. One afternoon we were on Lola and Xevi's veranda with some friends, looking out over the Indian Ocean. We were smoking chillums as usual, and a guy called Mr Yeah passed by. We'd already seen him dancing at the parties. He was a good-looking guy and full of energy, the type that all the girls fall in love with. He used to say that we all originated from the energy of the sun.

"The roots of all people are in the North Pole that used to be in Hel, near Helsinki. Sing for the key of Hel. We lived in a Ringland around the pole. The ring is Pi or π, the Greek letter that represents the ratio of a circle's circumference to its diameter. We are Pi-Pole so to say. The Catholics hated Hel and burned it down and made it into the hell they describe in their holy Bible. 'Holy, Whole-i' means all of the 'i'. 'i' is the prick of the Bock who is the All-Father and the dot on the 'i' is his sperm." He told us a story that was going around called the Bock Saga. It was the history of mankind.

"Oh, really?"

This was by no means the first strange story we'd come across in Goa, but this one sounded particularly weird. I didn't pay much attention to it at the time. There were beautiful girls on the veranda, and we were all stoned, that was enough. Mr Yeah invited us to come to the Marina Restaurant that evening, where a movie would be shown.

"A movie?"

That sounded nice. I'd been without any movies or other Western cultural expressions for many months now. A movie sounded just fine.

That night we went to the restaurant with some friends to watch the movie. I expected an American action flick or something of the kind. But that turned out not to be the case. It was a movie, that much was true. It had been shot earlier that year in the Chapora fort and consisted of a man called Ior Bock telling the Bock Saga. The audience in the videotape was largely made up of the Dutch Balloon Company. I knew the 'Balloonies' as a colourful group that travelled all over the world to the most exotic places, putting on theatre shows along the way. Usually they were loud scatter brains, but on the day the video had been shot, they all listened in awe.

I must admit, I didn't get much from that movie screening. The television was small, had a blurry screen and was screwed to a far wall. The sound quality was terrible; the restaurant was noisy, and we were sat next to a busy road. It also didn't help that we were smoking chillums and joking around.

But one thing in the story did catch my attention. It made a big impression on me and was the reason I later listened to the Bock Saga again. In the procreation rituals of the prehistoric people, Boxing Day played an important role. 'Sing for the Bock day'.

I had always wondered why the day after Christmas was called Boxing Day. It seemed to make no sense at all. In the Bock Saga, it was a festival day during which men were tested for their manly skills. Games were played like 'hop the bock' and 'sparring'. In the Bock Saga, this day made logical and harmonious sense and once I'd heard this explanation, it was hard to imagine a time where I hadn't known its meaning.

"Aha!" How could I not have seen that before? Many more of these moments were to follow.

In the week after this pretty unmemorable event, on one of my dope-selling wanderings, I came near the Chapora fort into a dead-end footpath. Huge bougainvillea covered the path and created a soft light. An amalgam of conflicting smells filled the atmosphere. Light fragrance of flowers danced on top of the heavy tar and fish fumes of the nearby harbour. Little birds were singing and talking to each other. Hummingbirds were collecting honey.

Under a large tree that seemed strangled in a century long dance with the bougainvillea stood a little house. Above the entrance of the porch was a sign with the name of the house: Apolina house.

Some people on it were just lighting a chillum. Big clouds of smoke entered the mix of smells. I walked up and asked if they were interested in some grass from Kerala. As I was invited in to join them for a smoke and tea, I didn't realise that it was Ior Bock and his friends I was about to meet.

But this didn't last long because there was only one topic of conversation on that veranda. Ior was in the middle of explaining details of the Bock Saga. I stayed until it got dark, listening with ever-growing fascination. I went home with a head full of new information on our ancient past. I was hungry for more and the next morning I headed once again towards the veranda. From then on, I listened all day, every day to Ior, who never seemed to get tired of talking. He had so much in his head. He never spoke of the same thing twice, or at least never in the same context.

I learned that the house next door was available for rent. I moved out of William's house, where I'd stayed until now and moved in next to Ior. Over the next weeks, I gained a much deeper understanding of the Bock Saga, spending every day on the veranda.

I was not alone. Sitting next to me were other people that would play a role in the events of the coming years. There was Mats, a Swedish punk and Cliff the yogi, who had brought some cassette tapes to Hawaii and introduced the Bock Saga to the yoga/alternative scene over there. Mr Yeah, who had heard those tapes a hundred times in Hawaii and had financed the making of the Bock Saga video. Soma, a local guy, who quietly hung in his hammock all day and slept with his ears open. Many other interesting characters that had been attracted to Goa passed by occasionally and stopped on the veranda for tea, stories, and a smoke. Now and then, I asked Ior a question about some detail in the Bock Saga or some correlation between the trillions of facts. He would then pretend to give me an answer, but what he was doing was continuing with what he'd already been talking about, without deviation.

He seemed to follow a plan and knew exactly what to tell us and what not. I sometimes asked him about Greek mythology, which seemed to have a similar pantheon of actors. He replied that he didn't really know and didn't want to spend time on any other myths apart from the Bock Saga.

"This is already enough; all the answers are in here."

But he did make some exceptions. We lived in a Hindu village and there were plenty of Hindu rituals and festivals in the temples around our house. Ior would sometimes explain these rituals as we watched them unfold, explaining the name of the ritual, like Holi, Diwali, or Shivaratri, with the help of the sound system of the Bock Saga.

It was so intriguing to see the symbolism of the rituals match the meanings of these Hindu words when the sound system of the Root language was applied. All these rituals were suddenly not religious and philosophical, but practical and logical. The Bock Saga is the most logical story I've ever heard.

Ior told us: "The difference between Root and our conception of modern language is that, in modern language, the sounds themselves do not have a specific meaning whereas in Root, the meanings are already locked into the sounds. That limits the amount of true statements one can make.

A useful analogy is that of music, whose sounds form different chords and harmonies. In the Root language, as in music, it is by listening that one knows whether sounds are out of tune, or untrue, or whether they are in harmony with one another and therefore true.

The Bock Saga contains an inner harmony like music. When in symphonic music a discordant note is played, you can immediately hear it is not in harmony. The same is true for spoken words that do not fit into the Bock Saga. When names or facts are given that are not in harmony with the sound system, we know they do not fit into the story and are therefore fictitious.

It is the rigidity of the sound system principle of the Root language that secured the oral tradition of the Bock Saga. This principle made it possible for the Saga to be passed on by countless generations without any changes.

The Bock Saga states that the plan for our planet (Root: Planet, which means 'planet' as well as 'family plan') is encoded in the Root language. This turns Root into a prophecy. And since we are already far into this prophecy timewise, one can safely deduct that our history is also encoded in Root.

As we know by now, the meanings of the sounds in the Root language are the building blocks of the Bock Saga. These meanings have been with us since the first two humans and form part of what makes us human. Just as a duck says 'quack' and a donkey says 'hee-haa', humans say 'ABC'.

The first humans were born in the great outdoors surrounded by trees, rocks and the seas, as well as by this language. The Root language is not a human fantasy but existed in nature of which these humans formed an integral part. This is a fundamentally different concept of language than what most of us have today. It has many consequences for our beliefs and thought processes which will become clearer as one learns more about the Bock Saga.

The Bock Saga states all languages are derived from the sounds and meanings within Root. That means that in every language spoken today these meanings can still be found. And therefore, it should be possible for everyone to understand the Bock Saga with the help of both emotion and intellect."

But I could never explore any subject in more depth than what Ior would allow. Sometimes new people appeared on the veranda with questions to which Ior would respond with a lengthy recitation about something else entirely, totally baffling the newcomer. He'd probably already planned to speak about that specific subject and did so, no matter who was in front of him. At least the seniors, to which I already belonged to by now, knew what he was talking about.

His lectures revealed how much knowledge I already possessed and how far my way of thinking within the Bock Saga had evolved. Some people, like William, thought we were being brainwashed. He said that even if it was all true, it was still brainwashing. I didn't agree. Surely, if it was all true, then it was the religious and cultural crap we'd filled our brains with prior to hearing the Bock Saga that had brainwashed us.

Things got even more interesting when Ior told us that there existed physical proof of the story. Ior explained that his family built a magnificent castle called Raseborg about 9,000 years ago. In this castle was a life-size statue of a golden bock on display. In the year 1050 AD, during the Catholic crusade that destroyed Odenma, this and a second statue were hidden in a place called Offerlund under oak trees near Helsinki. A third statue was hidden in the well of a castle ruin in Kajaani in the north of Finland.

Ior knew exactly where these had been hidden and told us that the statues should still be there, waiting patiently to be dug up by our generation. He even invited us to help with the excavation and join him at his ancestral estate in Finland that summer to celebrate the 130th birthday of his auntie Kristina Victoria.

Of course, she'd already died before Ior was born, but he always talked about her in a loving way and told us she was important for the later events within the Bock Saga. He remained vague about what these events actually were, he just told us that he would explain in due time.

Digging up golden statues sounded like a good idea to us. A party was even better. It was what we spent most of our time doing anyway, when we weren't listening to Ior on the veranda.

Lola

I kind of liked the Bock Saga. I especially liked the language side of it. I grew up with Spanish and Catalan, and through Ronan, I became fluent in German. Through Xevi I was learning French. I didn't read books in those languages. I just listened and talked. Both Ronan and Xevi agreed that I talked too much. Talking is a good way to practice, though. Of course, there must've been one original language.

I mean, someone in the past must've started talking at some point and that became the first language. Probably a great-great-grandmother of mine. The notion that the first language had sounds that had specific meanings seemed logical to me as well. Why utter a sound that has no meaning? It's logical too that from these sounds all words and, later, all other languages were formed.

Yes, sure, Ronan was taking it all a bit too seriously. He believed that somehow this story would change the world. I didn't believe that. Xevi liked the Bock Saga too, but he wasn't that fanatic about it. He was more into his Buddhist trip. They got along very well, though. It got to a point where Xevi was spending more time with Ronan than with me. But that was ok.

What was strange though, was that all my boyfriends turned into dope dealers after a while in our relationship. It was never to pay for my exclusive and luxurious lifestyle. I paid for myself. Everything I ate, everywhere I slept and everywhere I travelled, I'd pay for myself from money that I'd earned. I hoped that this boyfriend-turning-into-dope-dealer trend didn't become a pattern.

William

I grew up in a small village in the middle of the Netherlands
in the 1960s. The village was divided in two by a railway track.
There was a small railway station with huge trees around it.
A few times a day, a commuter train stopped, but most trains
passed by without stopping. Not many people needed to get on
or off the trains in our little village. It was clear to me from a
young age what the true purpose of the railway tracks was, they
served as a social divide.

On one side of the tracks the houses and the trees were bigger. That was the Catholic side. This was where the mayor, the
notary, the priest, the doctor, and other notables that had attended good schools in big cities lived. All these notables had
good connections, albeit mostly to each other. In the centre was
a huge Catholic church that could easily hold the whole Catholic
population of the village, including the Catholic farmers of the
surrounding region.

The other side of the tracks was for the Protestant Christians.
They were mostly labourers. I can't say the people were poor,
but they certainly weren't rich. Most didn't have modernities
such as televisions and washing machines. The people on the
protestant side had a thin socialist lining to them, as sharing
wealth is more convenient for the non-rich than for the rich of
this world. I think their religion told them that material pleasure was not for them, and suffering made them good Christians.

What the people on both sides of the track had in common,
was that they weren't much in contact with the big world outside the village. Not much good came from there, like world
wars and social disruption. Both sides were strictly religious

and strictly divided from each other. And everyone wanted to keep things that way.

The Protestant labourers worked in Protestant factories, did their groceries in a Protestant shop, and bought Protestant bread from the Protestant bakery. On the far side of the village, beyond the Catholic part, was a Protestant school, where the Protestant children learned to read and write and were taught the Bible and what was right and wrong.

Sundays were spent in a Protestant church, which was next to the school. Any other activity on Sundays was strictly prohibited. For the children that meant no playing, just waiting until the day was over while attempting not to spoil their good Sunday clothes.

Since televisions were still extremely rare at that time, most people that lived in our village had no idea that life could be different. The feeling people had was that everything had always been like this (it hadn't) and that everything would stay like this forever (it wouldn't).

Our family lived on the Protestant side, and we were atheists. Fundamentally so. Our family, I learned at a later age, had never been Christian as far as our generational memory could recount. My father was a geologist who believed that the Earth was billions of years old, that life on it was a billion years younger and that he could prove it. He knew the world was a ball, and people repeating for millennia that it was flat had not made it anymore flatter than it ever had been.

I remember asking my father once: "Daddy, what are socialists?"

He replied: "Socialists are people who steal your money in the name of charity and divide it up amongst each other."

"Daddy, what are Catholics?"

"Catholics steal your money and promise to give it back after you die."

Therefore, my brother and I were allowed to play on Sundays. And we did. We played football, drove our little bicycles and climbed trees, while the other kids watched us from inside their houses that must have felt like prisons. The parents also watched us and thought we were possessed by the devil. Our family was not only atheist, but we were worldly too.

Although we were citizens of the Netherlands, my father and

many generations before him, were born in Indonesia, which was a Dutch colony. After the Second World War and subsequently the independence of Indonesia, he ended up in Canada, where my brother and I were born. I was almost four years old when I arrived in the Netherlands.

I remember the first years in the Netherlands as being playful. All my memories revolve around playing. My father liked playing too. Not just with me, but by setting a playful example, always inventing things with electricity and physics at their base.

In addition, he made beautiful paintings in oil and could play any musical instrument without needing to read the music notes. This period came abruptly to an end for me when I had to go to the big school at the age of six. Suddenly, everything became serious, and the playfulness of my father was gone. Good marks were all that mattered and even when they were fantastic, it was never enough. Darkness ruled my life.

My father's family has a long and great history, with some legendary people in it. And on many occasions tales of adventures were told about them. Until the Second World War, the family had been lavishly rich, owning huge territories around the world, mainly in the Dutch colonies. They owned plantations, factories, were governors of countries and had positions in the Dutch overseas army.

In the old days, not everything had a monetary value and much of the mysterious power the family seemed to have was neither bought nor bribed. Within the family it was conceived that the nature of our position was a logical consequence of us being superior. What that meant exactly, was never much discussed. The family were not exactly racist, because our position was the same compared to any race. It was somehow a natural state of the universe that we were elevated somehow.

Old and rich aristocratic families often spread their wealth over the planet to make sure that whatever disaster might strike, they could always maintain the lifestyle that belonged to their standing. That's a good strategy in most cases, but the great depression of the 1930s and World War I and II were disasters of a global scale and had erased all our assets.

My grandparents, uncles and extended family suffered in Japanese concentration camps; while in Europe, my father and his sister were on the run from the Germans. All survived miraculously and came out of the war with many stories that were often repeated at the family gatherings.

Other stories, however, were not shared and that added to the mystery. But the beautiful estates, castles and art collections were all gone, and with it our aristocratic standing. The family came to realise that the post-war world was a monetary and economic one.

Just after the independence of Indonesia, my grandfather and grandmother found themselves with their kids living in a one-room apartment in a soon-to-collapse house on one of the famous canals of Amsterdam. The past was a dream now and they had no experience of how to survive as part of the common people, which probably meant having a job.

The reason I tell you all this is that it was perceived in the family that the eldest son of the eldest son (and so on, and so on) would become the clan leader. When the clan leader's son was stronger than his father, he would become the next clan leader.

Of course, the old clan leader would hold on to his position as long as possible, or at least pretend to. He would require proof from his son that he was indeed stronger and fit for the task. If challenged by his son, there would be some kind of match or struggle, the rules of which would be set by the older clan leader.

Sooner or later, the new generation would take over and remain clan leader until he too was challenged by his own eldest son. Each time the process would be different, depending on the situation and the characters of the people involved, but the outcome would be the same: the father would give the ancient seal ring with the family crest to his son. This meant that the son could now stamp official letters in the family name. It was a natural process, I guess.

The task for the next clan leader after the Second World War, was to bring the family back to its original status. He was to recreate an empire similar to that which the family had held before, with all the responsibility that went with this.

That person was to be me. How I would accomplish this formidable task, living in a small village and going to a common public school and without any access to important people and resources, was never explained. Although I was supposedly superior by birth, I did everything wrong in my father's eyes. He believed I was as immoral as one could get.

I, on my side, did not see how I could ever acquire an empire by getting good marks at school and living in this small village where trains didn't even bother to stop. I knew for sure that I would never get the ring from my father as he held me in such low esteem. But to be honest, I never wished to have it either.

Thus, my world consisted of Catholics, Protestants, the heroic past and a bleak future. Then something happened. My father made the grave mistake of giving me a radio at the age of nine.   On that radio I discovered Veronica, a pirate radio station that broadcast from a ship moored in international waters in the North Sea.

Through radio Veronica, I entered the world of the Rolling Stones, David Bowie and Alice Cooper. I learned about hippies in San Francisco with flowers in their hair and the existence of freedom and choice. I learned about Andy Warhol and his indifference towards all the so-called important stuff of our culture. I was injected with the dreams of Salvador Dalí and realised that dreams could be as real as anything else.

In other words, I completely rejected the cause and culture of the setting I was brought up in. I was not a Protestant, Catholic, atheist, communist, capitalist and certainly not a builder of empires. The contours of all that I was not, or didn't want to be, started to appear. And with that, all the things that I wouldn't want to do in life started to become clear.

I still hadn't any idea of what I *did* want to be or do, except maybe to be an astronaut and fly away as far as possible from it all and never return. I saw the men land on the moon and defy gravity. I had great admiration for these astronauts, but I wouldn't have come back to Earth; that was their only mistake. Already at that age, I felt no real connection to anyone in my real life anymore. I had a deep distrust of all grown-ups, who gave me impossible tasks or propagated a moral expressed in words but denied by example, like the Christians. Nobody around me could follow what was going on in my mind and nobody had a grip on my behaviour.

At the age of sixteen, I decided not to finish school, to ensure that I would never end up in an office building like my father. When I was seventeen years old, my father miraculously survived a suicide attempt. In his farewell letter, he'd written that he'd taken all those pills because he couldn't live with an amoral son like me, who refused to live up to his family heritage. A few months later, I left for the big world: Berlin.

It was the darkest days of the Cold War and Berlin was at its centre. Between the capitalists and the communists were the outsiders who couldn't care less about it all. Punks, drug addicts and artists. No ambition, no future. There are many anecdotes from this strange and detached period, all playing against this dark backdrop.

And it got darker and darker. My friends and I were using more and stronger drugs. Accidents happened. It's all the usual stuff. We were low-life city rats. I realised that I didn't want to spend all my life in this way and decided to prepare an escape. I wanted to get as far away as possible. I wanted to travel the world and never come back.

To accomplish this, I had to make money to pay for my tickets and life in another place. The most obvious way to do this was to sell drugs. And while I did this, I discovered I had a talent for it. I even liked it quite a bit, it was like a game. I was rich for the first time in my life. Then I got arrested and spent the next eight months in jail. There I met the real low life, most of whom couldn't read or write. I had the highest education there, without any diplomas!

I realised that an even greater radical change in life was needed, and I decided I would definitely leave Europe once I was released from prison. I had lived long enough in the decaying cities of the 1980s with decaying friends. We had revelled in a post-everything punk, fuck-it-all trip long enough. I realised that I would only live once and that spending time in dark dead-end streets was not the only thing I wanted to experience.

This time I settled for a longer, less luxurious trip. I worked my ass off just to have enough money for a ticket to anywhere far away. In the end, I decided that India would be my destination. I bought a flight ticket with PIA (Pakistan International Airlines, or as it is better known, Please Inform Allah), with a three-day stopover in Karachi, Pakistan, before continuing on to Delhi in India.

Before I left for Asia, I visited my father in his house in London. We had dinner together in the usual tense atmosphere that was the main characteristic of our relationship. He didn't like how I lived. I liked him and admired him for his charms and genius but hated the fact that he wanted to recreate me into someone I wasn't. We sat in silence for most of the dinner, with occasional tense small talk. We both felt awkward. After dinner we continued to sit in silence, the room heavy with the discontent we felt for each other.

To break the icy atmosphere, his wife suggested: "Why don't you two play a game of chess?"

My father and I looked at each other, knowing the significance such a game would have. But we also both realised that it was a good way to break free from the charged electricity of the room and a good way to pass the time. We both knew that he'd probably win and see this as confirmation that he'd been right about me all along.

He was a good amateur player, just one degree below fanatic. He even had a couple of chess computers, a novelty at that time. He played a lot on these things on a high level. He even replayed the final world-championship game between Fischer and Spassky, trying to find the moment where Spassky could have won if he'd played something different. Then he'd let the computers run for days to see if his play really could have worked. And yes, he found a way for Spassky to become world champion. If only Spassky had played my father's move!

That was what I was up against. We started playing in the early evening.

After a few moves, he wanted to advise me on my position. I told him I wasn't going to take advice from the enemy and would appreciate it if he'd let me think in silence. Every move he made, he tried to force me in some direction. I excluded these obvious responses in my deliberations. I just kept on thinking of possibilities that were outside the box, hoping to find a way to win. I knew that was my only chance: to make moves that weren't in any textbook, that were unpredictable and opportunistic.

The game went on and became a battle. At three o'clock in the morning he realised that he was in trouble, deep trouble. One hour later, he was sweating, and I was smiling. I knew I had him by the balls. He was struggling, squirming, trying to escape, and I just kept smiling.

I knew that it would only take a dumb mistake on my part for him to still win, but I didn't make that mistake and I won. It was early morning. He shook my hand and congratulated me in all honesty. We fought hard and he lost, but he awarded me the victory with respect.

We went to bed and had a late breakfast. I'd already packed my stuff, ready to go to the airport. To my big surprise, he stopped me before I left and told me he had a present for me. "Actually, it's not a present. I think you've earned it."

I had no idea what was happening. He took the family seal ring from his finger and handed it over to me. I was in complete shock. As I put it on my ring finger, I realised I was now head of the clan, whatever that meant. I took this as a good omen for my trip into the unknown.

The plane arrived in the night at Karachi airport. When the doors opened, the Karachi air streamed in. It smelled spicy and rosy, mystically Eastern. I'd been warned by friends who'd made this trip before that, upon arrival in a Pakistan airport, there would be a wild crowd of pushy taxi drivers all of which had the same holy mission: to rip off the foreigner.

I arrived in the late evening, and in the half-lit exit of the airport, there were the taxi drivers waiting in assault formation. I walked through the doors and a crowd of heavily moustached, turbaned, and wild-eyed taxi drivers jumped on me. My friends had been right. They all wanted to push me into their taxi cars.

There was fierce competition between them, which at least meant that they weren't teaming up against me. I was somewhat scared and realised I didn't have the situation under control. The energy they produced was volcano hot. Something had to happen, something that would direct this scary energy in another direction, any direction except mine.

I looked around and realised that there was no one else coming out of the airport. All the other travellers had disappeared, and I couldn't see any security uniforms around. It was just me and the taxi drivers. I felt I had to do something.

So, I chose the guy with the biggest moustache and hoped he'd take me away from the crowd to the safety of his car. My decision had a rippling effect of anger, followed by excited screams and even wilder eyes. But I stuck to my decision, scared of creating further chaos.

My new friend guided me away from the sticky crowd towards his car, which was parked about one kilometre away on a dark parking spot. I saw it in the distance, shining in the moonlight. It wasn't a model I'd ever seen before; it didn't even look like a car. It looked like an intense bouquet of baroque flowers on wheels with stainless steel fringes and colours and shapes of repeating fractals. It looked like twenty Hindi paintings overlaid one on top of the other. The interior was in the same style. The car manufacturers had not restrained their passion for frills. Mr Big Moustache looked at me and asked where I wanted to go. A hotel please, a cheap one.

"$20," he replied.

"Hmm, that could be worse," I thought.

I tried to negotiate a better price just for the sake of it, but did so softly, realising my weak negotiating position, and we finally agreed on $17.50.

"I don't have any money, by the way. I tried to change an American Traveller check in the airport, but the bank was already closed. Do you know somewhere where I can change a check for Rupees?"

He said it was no problem, and we'd go to a nearby big international hotel and do that, for $2.50 extra. Afterwards, he'd drive me into town and bring me to a more affordable hotel that belonged to a friend of his.

"OK, that sounds reasonable."

We drove in his museum on wheels to the Hilton. There, they told me that I could only change a check if I booked a room. The room rate was super expensive; I only had seven days of Hilton money with me that needed to last me a whole winter in Asia.

"No problem," said my taxi driver. "We go to another hotel. $5 extra."

We went from hotel to hotel. It was already late into the night. All the hotels gave the same response: book a room and we change your check. My bill with the driver rose higher and higher. For the last few hotels, it went up to $10 to drive between them, and later this increased to $15. I protested in the beginning and argued that he'd told me I could change checks at these hotels, which had turned out not to be true.

He should know, being a local. He was wasting my time. Instead of driving around on a wild goose chase, he should bring me to a place where I could change money and then to a place where I could sleep. But as my taxi bill surpassed the $100 limit, I started to think that it would've been easier to just take the room in the Hilton and have a proper sleep after my long flight from Amsterdam.

"Please bring me to a hotel where the bill can be paid the next day. Tomorrow, I will go to the bank and pay you as well as the hotel."

He realised that this was the only practical solution. We drove into the huge city of Karachi, but it wasn't easy to find a cheap hotel that would provide a room with only the promise of money. At every hotel that refused me, the taxi price went up exponentially. It had started at $17.50 and now it went crashing through the $250 barrier. I was so tired and still didn't have a place to rest my head. Oh, how right my friends had been about the airport taxi drivers. I was exhausted.

The Karachi architecture silhouetted against the morning sky when I got out of the car for the hundredth time at the entrance of some bland hotel. I finally managed to get a room with my promise of cash. I had to give my passport as warranty. I told the taxi driver to come back in the afternoon to bring me to a bank. I took my bag to my room, threw myself on the bed and fell asleep.

I woke up shortly after from a loud *bonk bonk bonk* on my door. It was nine o'clock in the morning and the taxi driver was ready to take me to the bank. He had raised the price again. For the money he was asking, I could have stayed in the presidential suite of the Hilton. I asked to borrow some Rupees from the hotel to pay for food and get around. My request was granted. We went to the American bank, but it was closed as it was Sunday. I agreed with the driver to meet the next day and then walked around Karachi, made some friends, was offered drugs by people who turned out to be the secret police and made some real friends who showed me around. It was a strange place for a suburban European guy like me. The food was fantastic, though.

The next morning at nine o'clock sharp, the driver was at my door again. He'd raised the price once more and so had the owner of the hotel. I told them both that I would negotiate with them when I had money in my pocket. I would give each of them a fair amount for their services, not to worry. But I certainly wouldn't give them the ridiculous, far-fetched prices they were dreaming of now.

We drove to the big American international bank that was not far from the hotel. It was closed again because of some bank holiday in the US. The situation was dragging on now, but what could I do? There was nowhere else I could change my American traveller checks and I had no cash or credit card. I spent another day exploring the huge city of Karachi and visited the harbour and a bazaar. Again, I had mixed feelings of excitement at being in a faraway place and fear of being ripped off, cheated, tricked, or robbed. I had a general feeling of uneasiness in this place and with reason. Karachi is a place where one can disappear in broad daylight without a trace.

The next day, I had to leave Karachi in the evening to fly to Delhi, India. I woke up early. This time, it wasn't the taxi driver with his enormous $500 bill to wake me, but my jet lag. I thought I could head to the bank alone this morning. I knew where it was located by now, having been there every day of my stay in Karachi.

It was about a one to two-hour walk, but this was doable, even in the humid tropical climate heavy with the smog of a zillion diesel trucks and rickshaws. The hotel owner was becoming impatient with me. He wanted his money too. He had increased the room rate every day and the bill was now more than $700, having started at $12 on the first night. I asked him for my passport, which I needed to identify myself when cashing the checks at the bank.

On an intuitive hunch, I brought my travelling bag with me. I walked through the madness of the Karachi traffic to the bank and cashed a check for $50. In the quiet and airy marble bank, surrounded by leather chairs, I suddenly realised that there was no point going back to the hotel. There, I would be forced to fight with the hotel owner and taxi driver over their enormous expectations.

Instead, I could simply disappear and fly off to Delhi later in the day. I sneaked out of a side entrance and stopped a rickshaw with curtains. Do you want to bring me to the airport? Yes, sir. And so we went. During the entire trip, I was terrified that the taxi driver would somehow find out where I was heading. The journey to the airport was a bit too long for the little rickshaw, the airport being quite far away from the city. It seemed to take forever. As soon as I arrived, I rushed inside and went through the customs as fast as possible.

As I sat on a sofa in the Western world of the tax-free area, surrounded by perfume and whisky, I realised that all the warnings I'd received about Pakistan had been justified. The taxi driver and hotel had really tried to rip me off, and the secret police had tried to sell me drugs so they could arrest me and receive a bribe for my release. But the end score was: William 1 – Pakistan 0.

I felt proud of myself. I didn't like stealing from people, but it was easy to see the situation as a game. I'd enjoyed playing it and I was happy I'd won. It gave me the confidence to embark on the next part of my journey into the unknown.

Like many poor or stingy hippie travellers, I ended up in Paharganj after landing in Delhi airport. This was an old marketplace flanked by drab and sleazy hotels, which had a buzzing street life with an intensity unknown to suburban city dwellers from the West. Each square centimetre of Paharganj was filled with many different creatures, human and non-human, all in constant movement and making a ruckus. On top of this, a multitude of contrasting smells attacked my nose.

Rose water, exotic flowers, amber, beedis, unknown masala spices and curries, strong acids and chemicals used to turn hides into leather, rotten sewers, camel, cow, dog and human shit and many other evaporating molecular combinations with no fixed definition. There was a cacophony of competing sounds from black smiths blowing into the fire and beating fiery steel, to wood workers sawing planks and cutting wood into woodprint blocks used to decorate ladies' saris.

There were all kinds of transport machinery like big trucks, rattling bicycle rickshaws and carts with big wooden wheels pulled by oxen. People were shouting and screaming at each other for unknown reasons. There were at least five different types of music competing with each other.

There was live music performed by half-naked street musicians with painted faces, blowing into shrill flutes that split brain cells into protons. My body felt hot, but my sweat was cold. I hadn't yet adjusted to the moisture and tropical heat. I sat on a stone at the side of the road watching the whole theatre of Indian street life. I nibbled on a snack: pakora with chutney. Each spice danced on my tongue, fighting for attention.

Somehow, amongst this plethora of sensual attacks of all that is 'Indian', I discerned a soft and repeating *sweesh* sound. I looked around for what it could be. At first, I couldn't find its source and was about to ignore it along with all the other unknown sounds that bounced between my ears, when I suddenly looked down and saw what was inching by.

It was a small man lying on his back. He had no legs or arms. He was consecutively arching and stretching his malformed body, and in this way, was moving forward about fifteen centimetres with each leap. It really looked like he was imitating an inchworm.

As he arched his back, he also arched his neck and grabbed a metal bowl with his teeth. The metal bowl was filled with paisa coins. Every time he stretched his body, he managed to jettison the bowl a few centimetres in the direction he was going. This is what was making the sweesh sound. The sound was meant to attract attention to his miserable fate, and it was with this that he begged for money.

I was in shock, cultural shock. I came from a country where unemployed people, like I'd been myself, were given money from the government to pay for rent and food and clothes. We even received money for holidays. It was possible that the poor guy in front of me had had his arms and legs cut off by his own family so as to make him look more miserable and increase his success as a beggar. He probably couldn't even spend the money he collected himself, as some beggar prince would take it from him every night, as he did with many others. His fate had been sealed the moment he'd been born in the beggar caste. It shocked me that a culture where this kind of scene was deemed normal still existed.

But I was the only one looking surprised at the beggar. Would I have to stretch my tolerance and acceptance for cultures not my own so far as to think it normal to have a caste of beggars who, generation after generation, inflicted the most horrendous mutilations on each other?

I was in total paralysed shock at the scene in front of me and was trying to decide if there was anything I could do to help the beggar, when a rickshaw driver approached me.

"You look distressed. I think you'd like to go to a nice place. Is that true?"

"Yes, that's right," I replied, surprised at the sudden change of events.

"I know a nice place, but it's too far for my rickshaw. I can bring you to the bus station from where a bus drives to this beautiful place outside the city. And I can help you buy the bus ticket. It's 75 Rupees and my fee to bring you to the bus station is 15 Rupees."

I asked a few questions to try and understand where and how far away the place was, as well as its name, but I didn't get very far. I didn't recognise the names he mentioned, and his accent was too strong to really understand any of his answers.

"Is it surrounded by nature?" I asked him.

"Oh, yes, lots of nature, with very many trees and mountains."

I imagined some kind of park. As it didn't really matter where I went, I decided to leave it up to destiny, in this case the rickshaw driver, to decide my destination.

The rickshaw driver guided me through the chaos of Delhi traffic and brought me to the bus station. He showed me the ritual of pushing through the crowd to a little mouse hole in the wall from where bus tickets were sold. I now had a seat reserved on a bus that was leaving soon. With the help of my guiding angel rickshaw driver, I found the bus and sat down on my designated seat.

Aah, a moment of rest was exactly what I needed. Although, the wooden bench was hard, and I hoped the bus ride wouldn't take too long. Neither the signs on the bus nor the bus ticket told me where we were headed. Everything was written in Hindi. I decided to just appreciate the moment and look around me. From suburban Europe, where I'd been just a couple of days before, I'd landed in a world so different that nothing could have prepared me for it. The ladies dressed in saris, the men in lungis, with everyone wearing all sorts of strange and exotic headwear, footwear, and accessories.

I was not only on another planet; I had landed in a different age. Nothing was electronic and only a few things were mechanical. The main source of energy seemed to be the muscles of humans and oxen.

I watched the fairy tale scenery for a while and accepted a cup of chai from a tea wallah through the open window of the bus. There was a great variety of clothing. There were businessmen dressed in white shirts and suits, there were traditional Hindu dresses and ancient looking tribal clothing. There were people from all kinds of different national backgrounds: Tibetans, Sikhs with beards and tight turbans, Rajasthani with impressive moustaches, and beautiful women in colourful saris.

Regardless of how wildly dressed, every person there had a role to play and knew exactly what that was and where they were going. There was only one lost-looking, long-haired Westerner with no idea who he was or where he was going, and that was me.

My thoughts meandered as I looked at the beehive of the bustling bus station through the window of the waiting bus. I was a little above street level, so it was like watching television and the distance comforted me.

Suddenly, I was brought back to the raw here and now when a screaming row erupted just a few seats away from me. At first, I had no idea what it was about, or even if the people involved knew each other. One lady in particular seemed to be the instigator. She screamed ferociously at two other men. She was an older lady and would have been beautiful if it wasn't for the anger she was spreading. Her upper lip was raised showing her red teeth as if she intended to leap out and bite someone like a cobra. She looked dangerous and angry.

She then abruptly turned towards me. A wave of angry words rolled over me. She held a bus ticket in her hand and was swinging her arm around like a sword. I figured her anger had something to do with the seats. I tried to stare as blankly as possible, hoping it would communicate my total bewilderment, lack of understanding and overall inability to helping her solve her problem.

The ticket inspector then arrived on the scene. Further screaming from more people ensued. The ticket inspector asked to see everyone's tickets in an attempt to resolve the situation. As it turned out, everyone was in their right seat, with enough space for us all. This seemed to settle the situation and the atmosphere turned friendly again.

Yet another culture shock! In our northern European countries, the whole situation would've been seen as a logistical problem with an easy solution based on rules and facts. Strong emotions would've been seen as counterproductive and extremely rude. I was shocked that such a small matter could provoke such strong emotions and was surprised that as soon as the initial problem had been resolved, all that anger had simply dissolved. It sounded like many harsh words had been said, but this was all forgotten now, and people were even sharing food with each other. I got offered a snack from the lady who'd now turned beautiful again.

The bus started its engines, big clouds of diesel smoke signalled our departure. We drove for an hour or so through the city. As we travelled along, the buildings became smaller and smaller until they weren't really buildings anymore. We drove through slums made of blankets and cardboard. These places were dark and crowded, the people living there were dark and skinny, and naked kids played. I realised that this was real poverty that you couldn't understand on an intellectual level. This was an experience.

Then we turned onto a bigger and straighter road, a highway. I hoped we'd reach our destination soon. I'd already spent more than two hours on the bus and the wooden bench was hurting my skinny ass. A few more hours went by, and dusk was setting in. The bus stopped at a parking lot beside the road. I first thought we'd reached our destination but was told it was just a stop.

I couldn't see much except the silhouettes of trucks, tents, turbans, and saris. Under large sheets of tent canvas was a kitchen where large pots were brewing and boiling on fires. Spicy scents filled the air. The food was hot, sharp, and tasty. Everything was so different from what I'd known. No meat, no alcohol, no uncomfortable plastic seats in a Burger King, but beds to relax on and stretch the body. Real ingredients instead of fried frozen prefab food.

I started to appreciate the fairy tale land that I'd fallen into. After the break, we piled back into the bus and continued our journey. It was dark now; pitch dark except for the lights of trucks and buses that were coming from the opposite direction, their lights flashing by. I still had no idea where we were going. Sleepiness and dreams crept up behind me. We are nowhere. No-where? Now-here...

I was in between sleep and waking and dreaming, as the bus ploughed on. The other three men on my bench were hanging over each other and over me, sleeping too. We moved simultaneously with the movements of the bus. When the bus stopped, it was dawn. We got out and looked around. Again, a parking lot, this time surrounded by the biggest mountains I'd ever seen! We were in a deep valley with enormous masses of rock stretching into the air on either side. The mountains reached above the clouds and were topped with glittering white snow. It was cold; we weren't in the tropics anymore.

After breakfast, we moved on. The engine of the bus worked hard as the road rose higher and higher. It was a narrow road and busy in both directions. It was cut into the steep sides of the mountains. In both directions were long convoys of buses and trucks. They were beautifully decorated with wood carvings and shiny metal sheets. The mythological Hindi gods were painted on them in flashy colours. The driver cabins were filled with turbaned people with big black beards covering their faces. On the outside of the trucks, on top of these cabins, were more people sitting.

The trucks were top heavy, overloaded with bales of cargo, swaying dangerously on the bends of the serpentine road. Every driver seemed to be in a deadly hurry, as each continuously overtook the other, even when there was traffic coming from the opposite direction. They often raced beside each other, only at the last second somehow swerving back into the safety of their lane.

On one side of the road, the mountain climbed steeply up as far as I could see. On the other side, the rock stretched steeply down into nothingness. This precipice had no rails and the only things that stood in between the road and this realm of unchecked gravity were white painted stones marking the border. It all looked very dangerous. I'm not going to lie, I was scared. But then I realised that this road and its traffic had been here long before I'd come to this place. Surely, they knew what they were doing. If so much traffic, with this many people involved, used this road every day, every year, then it should be considered a functioning infrastructure.

I decided that I couldn't trust my eyes and ears to interpret the traffic situation correctly. It was clear that culture shock was blinding me from seeing how things were for the people around me. Thinking this helped somewhat, at least until I noticed that some of the white stones on the side of the road were missing.

Then I saw that, corresponding to these missing stones, deep down below on the bottom of the ravine, were wrecks of truck and buses that had crashed, now in different stages of decomposition. When I looked closer still, I realised that the bottom of the ravine was littered with these wrecks.

What could I do? Should I get out and walk? With all the heavy traffic this was certainly not a place for walking. Taking a shortcut by foot through or over the mountains was obviously also not an option. The mountains were too high and huge and uninhabited. There was nothing I could do but accept the situation, hope all would be well and curse the rickshaw driver in Delhi who was the reason I was here. I'd assumed he'd sent me to a natural park outside Delhi, not on a never-ending voyage into the Himalayas!

I realised for the first time that the value of a life, or even many lives, was not high in India. How could it be if even a simple bus trip to another part of the country was a potential deadly event. This unsettled me greatly, as I didn't believe in reincarnation or second chances. The life I have now is the only one I've got!

We arrived at our final destination as dusk approached once more. I stepped out of the bus, cold and stiff, and walked to a kitchen to sit by the fire and have some tea and food. A young boy tugged on my elbow and asked if I was looking for a room for the night. Yes, I was.

"I have a room on a houseboat," he informed me happily.

I looked around at the majestic Himalayan mountains glowing white in the moonlight.

"A houseboat? Is this a joke?" This was the last thing I'd expected to hear, even if it was indeed a joke.

In the dark, we walked from the bus station through a medieval city where all the houses were built on top of each other. There were countless little alleyways, passages, corridors, and bridges, and it was obvious this city had grown organically over time rather than by architectural design.

I made sure not to lose my new friend in this partially lit and unknown maze, and he made sure not to lose me, his potential client. We came to a quay and – behold! There floated the houseboat. It was made from beautifully hand-carved wooden panels.

We went inside. A fire was burning in a steel stove and the rooms were separated by additional wooden panels. In the corner stood a bed covered in thick woollen blankets inviting me into its folds. After a chai, I accepted the invitation, crawled under the pile of blankets, and enjoyed a dreamless sleep.

When I woke up, sunlight was filtering through the thin splits in the wooden panelling. I slid one of the panels to the side and peered out to see where I was. I saw that my houseboat was moored to a quay and that behind it stood the contours of an ancient city. The slim towers of a mosque pricked the hazy morning sky. I opened a panel on the other side of the boat. From here I could see that the boat was floating on a large lake rimmed by ice-capped mountains. The air was clear and fresh on this side. What a difference from the crammed space of bustling beehive business that had been Delhi! The houseboats reminded me of Holland, and I felt at home.

A man dressed from head to toe in many layers of wool stepped onto the boat.

"Tea?" he asked.

"Oh, yes please," I replied.

He lit the stove with wood, boiled the water and added leaves. As we sat and drank our tea, we negotiated the price of the houseboat in a pleasant atmosphere, after which he offered to show me around the lake by boat for a reasonable fee. Then, he became suddenly annoyed at me because I hadn't brought any European razor blades.

"Why not? You could have easily brought a bag, or at least ten packets of them with you!"

"Yes, I could have, but how could I have known that you needed them? I'd never even heard of you, or this city, or the name of the whole state. I thought Kashmir was the name of a Led Zeppelin song!"

"Of what song?!"

My new landlord explained to me that sharp razor blades were in high demand and that he thought that this fact was common knowledge throughout the world. I realised how incorrect – or at least incomplete – his world view was. He believed that the whole world resembled what he experienced around him, and that, therefore, everyone in the world must also be aware of the blunt-razor-blade problem in Kashmir. His world view was never challenged because everybody he ever met confirmed this point of view. And yes, the men in Kashmir really did have heavy beard growth!

My culture shock deepened, especially since I'd now been jettisoned from 20th century suburbia to medieval India. I started to realise that everything I understood as true or real was just a point of view. If you never leave the place you're born in, you can easily take your world view for granted, like my landlord had. I'd grown up with some experience of different world views.

The Christian view on things differed greatly from the atheistic view my father held, for instance. But even so, I now realised that my world view, whatever that was, was potentially distorted from true reality. How else could I believe that this medieval houseboat on a lake surrounded by the highest mountains of the Earth was somehow similar to Holland?

I wasn't sure how to communicate these philosophical thoughts to my now slightly aggravated companion and even if I could, whether it would clear the atmosphere between us. He frightened me a little with his enormous curly moustache and large, wild, wide eyes, dressed in tribal wool with shoes that ended in long curling points.

If a trivial subject like razor blades could cloud the relationship between strangers to this degree, then how could stuff that really mattered ever possibly be resolved? What about the subjects that newspapers write about: territorial claims of states, religious tensions and so on?

To clear the air between us, I tried a tactic I'd learned from Monty Python:

"And now for something completely different. Are there any

particular birds of interest in this area?" I asked him.

"Oh, yes."

He started to speak passionately about his beautiful lake and mountains and everything that lived and grew there. Soon, we were in a little rowing boat, gliding through the dark waters, the only sound, the soft splashing of the oars. He insisted on rowing. I liked rowing, though, and thought it inappropriate that a young nitwit like me should be rowed along by such a proud warrior-looking man like him. In the end, we took it in turns.

He showed me floating peat on which vegetables grew. It was so wet that it couldn't be walked on. The vegetables had to be cultivated from the boats. We passed a large houseboat where several people were carving wood. They were making all kinds of intricate boxes with hidden chambers in them.

"For whom are those?"

"For the tourists."

"Are there tourists here?"

"Yes, some."

We drank tea and he rolled a joint and lit it. Twirling filaments of smoke that smelled of fresh and fruity hashish floated by and disappeared over the lake.

"We make this here," he proclaimed with a vague gesture of his hand. "Do you want to see?"

"Oh, yes please!"

I'd decided before getting on the plane in Holland that during this trip I would try to always be positive and generally say yes to everything. That said, I really didn't need much persuasion to say yes when it came to visiting the place where the world-famous Kashmiri hash was grown and produced.

It was another hour of rowing across the lake and then a two-hour walk to get there. The spicy scent of the marijuana plants guided our way. We finally arrived at a shack, the farm. Here were more tribal men and tribal women and tribal children. They looked surprised to see me. I guess they didn't expect a Westerner here. The kids were shy and stared at me from a distance. Lunch was served, then tea, and a water pipe was filled with tobacco and hashish. It wasn't long before I was stoned.

"Is this real?" I asked myself. Only last week I'd been in suburbia-normalia and now I was here smoking water pipes with tribal Kashmiris. I hadn't planned this in any way. I'd never even imagined a scene like this before. I felt like the reigns had been yanked from my hands and I was galloping into a new world of adventure. So far, the gods had been on my side.

"Do you want to buy some hashish?"

"Sure, that's a great idea."

To be honest, I was so stoned that I had no idea whether it was a good idea or not. I was doing all I could not to pass out. My eyes saw everything in shades of brown: the faces of the kids, the wool of the tribal wear, the Earth on which we sat, the dried leaves of the hashish, the hashish itself. All was melting together, and I tried to stay cool and strong and to focus on keeping my head and upper body upright until I couldn't anymore.

"Can I rest for a while?" were my last words before I slumped down.

When we arrived back at the houseboat at the end of the day, I was the proud owner of a kilo of hashish. The next day, when the clouds in my head had dispersed, I still thought that buying the kilo had been a good idea. I didn't spare a second thought to the potential danger of travelling with it in my possession. I was in the huge country of India where there were no borders to be crossed, I thought. And no borders meant that I wouldn't be smuggling anything.

If I didn't do anything seriously stupid, the police would never search me. Owning so much hashish meant that I would never have to buy it again during my stay. On top of this, I could always sell some if I needed the money.

I had no idea where I'd end up, but wherever it was, prices wouldn't be lower than at the source here in Kashmir. These thoughts gave a feeling of rationality to my decision, even though it had probably never even been my own. The decision had more likely been made for me by the tribal men who saw in me not much more than a young and green Western wallet.

Now, many years later, with all my experience, would I have made that same decision? No way! I had no idea what I was getting myself into. If anything went wrong, the consequences would be horrendous. I didn't know it at the time, but the minimum punishment for drug-related offences was ten years in prison. An Indian prison that is.

I stayed another week or two on the houseboat and made many little trips across the lake and in the city. Then life got boring. It was a strictly Muslim place, without any nightlife or partying. Sitting with the tribal men was pleasant and interesting, but the beautiful tribal ladies were forbidden territory.

I soon bought a bus ticket to the nearest railway station. At six o'clock the next morning, I was at the bus station looking for my bus. It was the beginning of November and freezing cold; you could feel the winter approaching. Snow was swirling down from the white sky. I wasn't looking forward to the scary road, it was now probably even more dangerous than before thanks to the ice that had formed over it. Nor was I looking forward to being driven around by some maniac who believed in reincarnation and heaven. Waiting at the bus station was already scary enough.

The drivers seemed to be pouring petrol over their diesel tanks and setting them on fire to warm up the thick oily fuel. All around me stood buses and trucks with burning open fires on their fuel tanks. I really hoped they knew what they were doing and that I could get out of there soon.

European trains always remind me of modern hospitals, all bright lights, and sterile surfaces. On a European commuter train, everyone's expected to sit quietly out of respect for their fellow passengers, just like you'd be expected to sit while in the waiting room of a European dentist. Indian trains are the opposite of this; they're a concentrated snapshot of the contrasting elements of Indian life.

All kinds of different people from all kinds of different Indian cultures and tribes travel alone or in groups. India is a large country, and the trains aren't very fast. Being on a train for a full day is normal, and so, normal life continues while you're on one, with all that comes with that. Food, drink, sleep and countless interactions. In those days, instead of windows, the trains had steel bars. These made the outside world seem closer still.

India's a fascinating place, and just watching it from the window of a train is a thrilling activity. Cities, villages and natural landscapes all passed us by. Weddings where rice that was thrown landed inside our carriage. Ten-year-old kids riding colourful painted elephants. Ladies beating their clothes on the side of the river to wash them. All accompanied by exotic smells and the sound of laughter from playing children.

Night had fallen. The train was slowing down as we drove into urban territory. We were approaching Bombay Central Station; the name was written on my ticket as the final destination. I'd heard the name 'Bombay' before but had never really known that it was in India or that I'd ever visit it.

Baghdad, Beijing, Bombay, I had no real concept of these places. From the window of my train, I could see candles and oil lamps burning everywhere. Bombay looked like a snug place at night. We arrived at an enormous train station that had been built by the British in the 19th century. To my surprise, the platforms and the big hall were also lit by candles. These Bombay people must be such romantics!

I took a rickshaw to the centre in search of a cheap hotel. This led me to the bay of Bombay. I checked into a hotel that was anything but romantic and went out for a stroll along the waterside.

The Indian night sky was filled with stars. The bay was scattered with hundreds of little floating candles. It all looked so beautiful. Someone asked me if I wanted to take a boat out into the bay and my now-habitual answer was, yes.

In a small rowing boat, we drifted amongst the lights. The captain explained that tonight was the festival of light, called Diwali. I only really understood what that meant much later.

The next day, I walked through the city and decided that it was busy and business-like. The magical atmosphere of the previous night was now replaced by exhaust fumes spewed out by hurrying cars, buses, and trucks. It didn't have that special Indian feeling I'd grown to expect, and I decided I wouldn't stay long.

On my wanderings, I met some Westerners, freaks, who advised me to take a boat to Goa. By 'freaks' I mean that they didn't belong to any specific group. They weren't hippies, or rockers, or punks, or straight (conservative and materialistic). They were people without any real ideology that just wanted to be off the beaten path. They were like me. I'm sure there are other better definitions for this band of people, but I identified with this one most of all.

I found my way to the harbour and some hours later, I was on the ferry to Goa. It was a twenty-four-hour boat ride and it turned out that life on a boat wasn't much different to that on a train. The main difference was that the boat was full of Western freaks. Most were in their early twenties like me, many were travelling alone, and it was easy to start a conversation.

I met some people on that boat that I still know today. From the deck of the ship, we could see India's shoreline made up of beaches and palm trees. The climate was perfect: twenty-five degrees, blue sky and a soft wind that made the hairs on my arms tremble slightly. Everything was going well; the gods must love me.

The next day, we arrived in Panaji in Goa. High from the upper deck of the boat I could see a friendly-looking Portuguese-style city. Big bougainvillea plants painted the streets pink, and the buildings were decorated with colourful tiles.

The mood on board was good all round. The Goanese who worked in the big cities were happy to be arriving home. The Westerners were anxious to arrive in what they knew was a hippie paradise. The gangplank was lowered, and people flocked out of the side of the ship.

I looked down at the quay and saw to my alarm that police officers were checking Western freaks and their luggage. The police too seemed to be enjoying the arrival of the freaks.

I asked Mark, a friend I'd made on the boat, what they were looking for. Drugs. Shit. What was I supposed to do with my kilo of hashish? I could either leave it behind on the boat and be safe, or I could risk it all and hope for the best. It hadn't been long since I'd spent eight months in jail, and I really didn't want to repeat that experience.

I couldn't picture myself as a hardened criminal and didn't want to be a loser in life but leaving the hashish on the boat was also maybe not a great idea. I decided to take the risk. I had a feeling that everything would be fine; the gods loved me after all, Inshallah, Hallelujah.

I walked down the stairs of the boat, onto the gangway; my heartbeat hard in my chest, *bim bam bom*. I was sure they could hear it. There were three officers stopping and checking Westerners, and a few more in the distance, just watching.

I saw one of the police officers take a step towards me. I tried to disappear from his line of sight by stepping behind another Westerner. I pretended to tell her a joke and laughed light heartedly. The officer took another step in my direction and at the last moment decided to grab the person next to me. I swayed along, past the second row of policemen, feeling happier with every step.

I'd made it. Oh, how differently my life would have turned out if I'd been captured with a kilo of drugs. Yes, I realise now that all the wise and smart views I had on life could have been radically changed if the gods, or fate, had decided differently on that sunny day on the quay of Panaji.

Mark seemed to know where he was going, so I took the bus with him to Colva. It was already dark when we arrived in the tiny village. A few small houses poked out amongst the dunes. They looked exactly like the houses a child would draw, with roofs made of palm leaves. After a short negotiation with the beautiful Juanita, we rented a room in her house.

The floor was made of a mix of dried mud and cow shit. The bed frame was made from wooden sticks with ropes stretched over them. Every now and then, huge beetles fell from the palm-leaf roof. Of course, there was no running water or electricity, but I felt immediately at home. After smoking a couple of joints and discussing our boat trip we fell asleep.

I woke up early the next morning. I realised from the sound of the waves that our little hut was close to the beach, so I went to look for the sea. I made my way through a forest of palm trees, over a dune, and was suddenly confronted by the majestic Indian Ocean. To my left and right was a pristine empty beach lined with palm trees as far as the eye could see. It was stunning.

"Yes, yes, yes, yes! This is what I want. I've found paradise."

Until that moment, I'd only ever been sure about what I disliked in life. I didn't like having a job, a career, studying; I didn't like anything that had, until that point, been presented to me as a potential life-fulfilling activity. I realised that I'd been drowning in a deep depression since the day I'd started school and that this depression had finally lifted when I saw that beach in Goa. One day long ago, when the world was still on a black-and-white screen and I was a four-year-old riding a three-wheeled bicycle, my mother told me that I had to start school the following day. I somehow realised that the holidays were over; my youth was over.

I'd lived in a world where every adult was a dictator. My parents, my teachers, anyone who was larger and older than I was had authority over me. I was told that we lived in a part of the world that was free and had a democracy, that we were under the permanent attack of communists and fascists and had to be defended by big armies. There was a clear wrong and right side to the world, and we lived on the right side.

And yet, the generation before mine, moral crusaders that they were, had destroyed the world and each other on a scale that had never been seen before in the history of mankind, all the while insisting that they'd made a giant leap towards a more civilised and scientifically conscious society. They'd already divided the world up amongst themselves and there was nothing left of it for us. Everything belonged to them, and nothing belonged to us. Unless you wanted to join their lifestyle of school-office-death, that is, and live in a concrete box and watch TV every night.

Far away in space and time from that early darkness in my life it seemed I'd finally found some space and time that I could call my own. I'd escaped into the unknown and it turned out to be paradise. I took off all my clothes and ran naked into the sea. It was salty and warm. The foaming sea washed all those memories away, like a miraculous cleaning agent on a television commercial.

Thick layers of worry, assumed responsibilities, feelings of guilt and many other negative emotions that had accumulated during my youth and even during the generations before me, dissolved in the Indian Ocean. From under it appeared for the first time something that I had not known it existed. It was the original real and clean me.

I found out that more people like me had found that paradise. One of them was Ronan. He'd travelled over land all the way from Berlin with his jealous, blond girlfriend. They lived in a friend's house on the beach. He was making a living by selling the hashish that someone had smuggled into Goa.

Yep, turns out I wasn't the only one who'd taken that risk and been lucky. I was not his competition, however, as I wasn't selling any of my own kilo of hashish. I had it hidden in my rented room and was too scared to share this secret with anyone. For now, I just nibbled little pieces off and used them to roll joints for Mark and myself.

The next few months went by as if in a dream. There was harmony between the four elements of old: Earth in the form of beach sand being washed away by the Water of the Indian Ocean; Air from the smoke rising from the chillums; and Fire in the form of the sun shining and warming my tanned skin. As a fifth element there was the Greek Aether, which was lots of nothingness with time passing through it.

Of course, I didn't really believe in any of this four-element stuff, but it was a nice way of looking at it. I became more relaxed than I'd ever been in my life. I loved Goa and everyone in it. The nature around us was friendly and it felt safe living in this huge garden called India.

When my money dwindled, I decided to sell what was left of my kilo of hashish. This turned out to be easy. Only one hour after making the decision, I found myself with a considerable amount of money in my pocket. No longer feeling worried about monetary matters, I decided to embark on a trip through the garden of India. By bicycle.

I bought an old-fashioned Indian bicycle, the brand of which was called Hero. I felt like a proud hero myself, entering a mythological land. I had no urge to visit any cultural or architectural places in particular, or to see any specific famous monuments, but just desired to immerse myself in the strangeness of the country I now felt a part of.

I thought that by travelling I could give fate a chance to sprinkle coincidences across my path and continue to make my life interesting. The fact was that even without coincidences, life on the road was intensely fascinating in India. Daily life for a foreigner here consisted of a permanent stream of unforeseen events and insights. I think every traveller who's been to India will agree with me on that.

I ploughed along on my Indian bicycle that weighed a tonne and had no gears. This made it a perfect vehicle for travelling slowly and experiencing more than just racing between bus and train stations in mechanical monsters. I witnessed a range of beautiful, ugly and strange events, and I believe that India is the strangest country in the known universe.

The description of my bicycle trip would be more appropriate in a National Geographic magazine. I experienced beautiful, exotic people and their culture, breath-taking landscapes and a multitude of sunrises and sunsets over rivers, rain forests, mountains, and deserts.

After three months of this deep immersion, I arrived back in Goa feeling wiser and more experienced. I was looking forward to another few months of lazy beach life, interrupted only by beach parties that lasted all night and all day.

Throughout my trip, I'd met many people, most were local Indians, of course, but some were Westerners, many of whom I'd meet again in Goa or in Europe. I was becoming a part of a big global network of travelling freaks. I no longer felt like I originated from a specific city; I was a globe-trotter now.

This time, I searched for a house in the northern part of Goa, where there were more hippie happenings. I found a nice room behind the legendary Shore Bar in Anjuna. It was by the sea, near the famous weekly flea market, and a gossip hotspot. Again, I enjoyed the simple pleasure of lying under a palm tree, watching the sun rise in the morning, following its course across the sky and watching it land in the Indian Ocean at the end of each day. In between, I swam, smoked chillums, talked with other freaks and locals, drank fruit juices and was just content with everything as it was.

On one of these sun-filled days, I was invited to attend a gathering during which I was told a special story would be shared. "It's a family story that starts with the first people on Earth and explains in encyclopaedic detail our so-called dark past, our prehistory, what the Bible calls paradise time. It talks about the first language and what the sounds of our current languages mean. We all come from the North Pole. We are the people, 'Pi-Pole'. 'Pi' is the circle around the North Pole, which in pre-Ice-Age time used to be in Helsinki."

"Uhm...Nah. Thanks but no thanks, I'd rather stay on the beach".

I was reading a Dostoevsky book at the time called *The Brothers Karamazov*, which is a heavy Russian family story, full of melancholy and depression. I'd thought that a tropical beach was probably the only place on Earth to read something like this without falling into depression myself. But one such story was enough. This gibberish about 'Pi-Pole' and 'Hel' sounded weird and possibly religious. Some Westerners in India were open to Eastern philosophies and others even spent time looking for a guru to follow. I wasn't one of them. I imagined that this Pi-Pole stuff was probably just another guru looking for disciples. I wasn't about to make an exception. Njet.

Later, I heard from others who'd attended the event that it had been quite interesting; apparently, no philosophy or religion accompanied this so-called Bock Saga. It was simply the history of our ancestors told in a 'matter-of-fact' way. There were voices that a video had been made of the storytelling session, which would be played later in one of the restaurants.

"Oh, really?"

After processing this information, I went for a swim, played some beach racket, had a fruit juice and forgot all about the Bock Saga. Not attending the Bock Saga event had no consequences whatsoever on the events that would happen over the next years. It was all inevitable, it seems. The force of the information in the Bock Saga is stronger than the specific actions of any one individual.

Life went on in this same style until my visa and money ran out. I took the boat back to Bombay.

In the years after my first encounter with Asia, I travelled each winter to India, making additional trips to the Philippines, Sri Lanka and other countries along the way. During the summers, I worked in France as a DJ in a tourist destination on the Mediterranean Sea. A guy called Xevi was my boss, and this work provided me with the money for the next winter season in Asia. I tried to escape my home country as much as possible.

This particular year, I found myself again on the twenty-four-hour boat trip from Bombay to Goa. From the harbour of Panaji, I then took the bus to the north. It was October, just after the rainy season, which meant Goa was a fertile green and the sun spread a perfect temperature from a blue sky dotted with fluffy clouds. The rural land was napping lazily in the sunshine.

Our bus caterpillared along the rows of coconut trees that lined the dams and levees dividing the rice fields into a chequered pattern. Occasionally, we crossed rivers and streams, passed muddy ponds in which buffalos bathed with big white birds standing on their heads. The water buffalos didn't seem to react to our bus, except for a gentle waving of their ears by which they communicated our sighting to other water buffalos nearby.

Even the coconut trees seemed to understand this language and relayed the message by waving their leafy fingers, signalling to the rest of nature the arrival of the bus filled with local men dressed in white office shirts and lungis. In amongst these men were local ladies dressed in Indian saris or in traditional Portuguese dresses with cute balloon sleeves, as well as a few of 'us', the Western self-declared outcasts.

We were labelled as 'hippies' by the locals. This was mainly because the first foreigners who arrived in Goa in the early 70s were indeed hippies. In the West, culture had evolved since then, and the idealistic long-haired hippies who wanted to change the world for the better were being replaced by the so-called Generation X. That was us. We didn't want to change the world; we didn't think it was ours to change. What we wanted was to have nothing to do with anything; we just wanted to have a life. Our life, not what somebody else figured was best for us or for some grand idea. Maybe not everybody in Generation X felt like this, but I certainly did.

These nuances were of course lost on the locals who just saw us all as alike and equally alien. For them, all foreigners were hippies. In fact, in 1983, when the commonwealth organised a big conference in Goa, which was attended by the prime ministers of the UK, Canada, Australia and other former colonies of the British Empire, the locals declared to each other: "Here come the big Hippies!".

It's probably the only time Margaret Thatcher has ever been called a hippie! This conference had quite a big impact on our everyday life in Goa. Special telephone lines that connected to the international telephone grid were installed for all the attending world leaders. After they left, these connections remained in working order, which meant that we could now phone to Europe.

My local phone was found in the restaurant Cocquiero. Since there was only a limited number of telephone lines, there was always a long waiting period involved, during which one could have food from the dangerously dirty kitchen. Having a drink from a bottle was a better idea and having this cooled by big lumps of ice from a nearby fish-processing plant added to the luxurious colonial feel of the place.

Telephone calls could only last three minutes, and you had to scream to be heard by the people on the other side. Because of this, you couldn't really share much information via these conversations, but at least you could every now and then let your parents know you were still alive.

Before this important lifeline existed, I would have no communication whatsoever with my family at home from the moment I left Europe in autumn, until my return in spring seven or eight months later. Sending letters was an option, but not many arrived. Later, I heard that the postal workers sometimes took the postal stamps off the letters instead of stamping them, just so they could sell them again.

We did look like hippies, to be fair. We had long hair. But this was because we didn't go to a hairdresser, rather than due to some underlying fundamental philosophy. We thought going to a hairdresser was a waste of money, and money was the ticket to staying longer in Goa, our main goal in life. We dressed in colourful clothes, as these were cheap too. We looked like Christmas trees with colourful paraphernalia hung from our clothes and body parts.

We decorated the old Portuguese-style houses that we rented from the locals with colourful pictures of Hindu gods like Shiva and Ganesh. Outsiders often interpreted these habits as openness for the Hindu culture on our part. People like sociologists or our parents, anyone with a suit and tie, thought that we had some ideological connection with Hinduism and spiritualism and that we were looking for a guru to guide us.

But this wasn't the case. We liked the Hindu paintings because they were cheap and colourful. That's all. We didn't have that intellectual or spiritual hunger. We were Generation X. We were looking for nothing (apart from maybe parties and drugs). This 'nothing' could only be found far away from our homes in urban Europe, USA or Australia. We were glad we'd found it here in Goa.

In the last two years, some slight changes had occurred among the so-called hippies in Goa. Colourful clothes were still the craze, but now they'd become fluorescent too. The hippies used to travel from beach to beach in Goa mostly by foot, but now motorbikes had become available. The parties on the beach were no longer accompanied by acoustic guitar and sitar music, but by electric amplification. And the music itself was no longer rock and folk, but a new invention called 'Goa trance'.

This style of music used ingredients like the rough and spacey psychedelic acid-rock of artists like Hawkwind, along with the kitsch and up-beat Italo-summer-disco, melted and brewed into something unrecognisable by the newly invented German computers. It was served with the slightest whiff of melancholy, as all summer music is, to emphasise the transient quality of holiday happiness.

During the first few years of Goa trance, musicians and DJs were still searching for the sound that would best epitomise the party scene in Goa; one that would capture the dusty fields of coconut trees and the sandy crash of the waves.

It took some time to bid farewell to lyrics, but words were too specific to successfully catch the imagination of the drug-crazed freaks. The beat got faster and faster and created a happy psychedelic sound with a continuous stomping bass kick at its centre. Other improvements were made to the music, and as a side effect, a whole bunch of DJs popped into existence, each claiming to be the inventor of Goa trance.

This new style of music was fast and loud, making it perfect to dance to through the night. We were lucky the Goans had a high tolerance for noise. The parties lasted all night, with some lasting both night *and* day. They also started occurring more and more frequently. In the early days, parties happened for a specific reason, like the celebration of the New Year, a birthday or to mark certain astrological events.

But these reasons became less specific and much more frequent until, in the end, there were only seven reasons left: Monday, Tuesday, Wednesday, Thursday, Friday, Saturday and Sunday. The parties were so loud that it was common to have three villages lying awake at night listening to the bass beats in the distance.

The only time quiet was enforced was during the school exam period at the end of March. Since by this stage the temperatures had started to rise dramatically in the lead up to the scorching Indian summer, and since most six-month visas expired around this time, March was considered to be the logical end of the Goan season.

My mind was drifting away, still sitting on the bus on that warm afternoon, all these changing trends were not yet that obvious to me. The bus was inching from stop to stop. Beautiful Goanese girls walked to and from water wells with pots on their heads and at their hips. Sunlight filtered through the leaves of big banyan trees, their hanging roots reaching down to touch the ground. Kids played in little streams building model boats. Strong men ran up palm trees to cut the coconuts down and milk the trees for palm wine and hearts of palm. It all looked so peaceful and so much like what paradise had been described to us in school.

The bus finally arrived at its destination: Central Anjuna. I think that this area was established as the 'centre' because of the big red football field found here. This was where all the boys would assemble before dusk for the main social event of the day. The field was red because all the earth in Goa is red. The colour is the same as rusted iron and that's exactly what it is. A long time ago, before men roamed the planet, volcanos had existed in Goa and had spewed lava mixed with iron from deep within the earth. This had rusted and now every after-noon, football games are played on it.

Fathers who had themselves played when they were young came to watch the games and their wives and daughters came to watch the players. There was a little post office with poste restante, the only address in Anjuna where foreigners could receive mail. After getting off the bus and retrieving my travel bag from its bellows, I sat down in the local chai shop and took in the surrounding scenery.

"One cup of chai, please."

I realised that I needed to rent a room soon if I wanted to find a place to stay before dark. The paradise-like view in front of me would change quickly after dark. Dark is dark. There was hardly any electricity around in those days and it was hard making good decisions blindfolded.

There are quite a few things that can be difficult in India, especially if bureaucracy is involved, but usually it only took wishing for something to make it available. This wasn't magic. It was just that the locals knew what foreigners wanted and were willing to provide this for money.

Although it didn't seem like a lot of money in our opinion, from their point of view, we foreigners were willing to pay a lot for things. India was much cheaper than life in Western countries and its people earned much less.

I n Goa, most locals were fishermen or worked in the rice fields, which meant that they made even less; their wages were often paid in rice, coconuts, and fish. The Indian Rupee was under-priced compared to Western currencies by a factor of fifty. This made Europeans rich in India, even though we were poor in our own countries.

We didn't spend our money on luxury because there wasn't any. India was a completely closed economy; everything sold there was made in the country. We spent all our money on time. We were rich on time. We were time millionaires. Time to relax; time to go to the beach; time to blah; time to be creative; and above all, time to party! Free psychedelic Goa parties with lots of free LSD and loud Goa-trance music.

"Do you want to rent a room?" somebody asked me.

"Yes," I replied.

Two minutes later, I was sitting on the back of a motorbike belonging to Thomas from the Nelson gang who could fix anything in the area and who drove me to what would be my home for the next six months.

It was a short ride down a dirt track through rice fields and coconut trees until we reached a cute Portuguese-style house with a veranda, which was for rent. In between the pillars of the veranda, I could see the sun setting behind a row of coconut trees, which I was told lined the beach.

"How long do you want to stay?" the landlady asked.

"Forever," I replied.

After a short negotiation, we agreed on the price and other conditions that left us both happy. I rented the house for six months and paid the whole amount immediately. This meant that I wouldn't be at risk of losing my house if for some reason I lost all my money. Yes, even in paradise people steal, and houses did get robbed from time to time.

The landlady and her kids helped me get settled in my room.

She let me borrow some kitchenware, a mattress, chairs, and a table. They gave me a clay pot and filled it with drinking water from the well. She brought me candles so I wouldn't be in the dark. They were so sweet and hospitable, and I loved them already.

In Goa, when the foreigners spoke of their family, they weren't referring to their fathers and mothers, but to their Goan landlords. This showed how close we were to each other. Where else in the world would you call your landlord family? That's how we lived when Goa was still in paradise time.

I dedicated the next few mornings to making my little house cosy. I went to the nearby town of Mapusa with the caterpillar bus; there, a busy market offered everything one could ever need. All the stalls were submerged in a thick cloud of fragrant herbs and spices. Sheets of jute were hung above to protect sellers and buyers from the sun. Little birds loved using these sheets as building material for their nests and constantly stole pieces of the fabric. Sunlight glistened through thousands of little holes and danced on the dust that rose from the baskets of rice, flour, spices, and countless other unnamed substances. Huge flowers, bright garlands and incense were sold for Hindu ceremonies and the neighbouring fish market competed with the smell of the herbs and spices.

I quickly found what I needed, had a shave at the barbers, ate a lunch of bean bhaji with a cup of chai and jumped on the bus home to Anjuna.

In the afternoon, I walked to the beach. There were people here and there scattered on the sand, some were playing beach racket, and some were in the sea. It was Wednesday, which was when the weekly flea market was held. The flea market was created years ago when the first hippies realised they could sell Western-made stuff to make enough money to extend their stay in paradise.

As I mentioned earlier, India was a closed economy and anything foreign was in high demand. Electronics, magazines, jeans, shoes, no matter how old or worn, were sold for much higher prices than they'd ever cost in the West. Busloads of prospective buyers came from as far as Bombay and Bangalore for a chance to buy second-hand foreign stuff. And if they couldn't find what they were looking for, they could at least goggle at the foreigners with their strange white skin and blue eyes.

Yes, it was strange, we were such a rarity to most of them and they thought so highly of us in a kind of racial way. They could look at us in bewildered wonder for extended periods of time, simply staring. It made us feel uneasy at times; the girls especially felt like they were being x-rayed by prying eyes.

On flea-market Wednesdays, groups of Indian tourists dressed in office clothes and black shoes walked up and down the beach to see the legendary semi-naked foreigners. They held themselves and their country in such low esteem, it was sad really. Thirty years later, this has changed, thank goodness.

As I approached the flea market from the beach, I saw growing throngs of people. Apart from the tourists in office clothes and the hippies, there were all kinds of tribal people from all over the Indian sub-continent. Tibetans, Gujaratis, Kashmiris, Keralites, Bengalis and many others. They had gradually added their shops to the growing flea market. It was a great improvement to the diversity and colourfulness of the weekly event. Big handmade sheets, block printed and full of embroideries waved in the lazy wind like sails.

Strange ancient tribal art in a huge variety of different shapes and textures and materials was on display. There were beads and wearable mirrors, miniature erotic paintings in ivory, gold figurines from a forgotten time and many other mystical and mysterious objects. There were even human skulls for sale that had spells carved into them in unknown alphabets.

The tribal ladies were all dressed in their respective traditional custom-made clothes. They wore handmade dresses with beautiful intricate embroideries and complicated jewellery laden with symbolic shapes and figures. It was like a museum of people with a large collection of different languages, races, and stories.

At the other side of the buzzing market was a bar where Westerners hung out. I was curious to see who'd made it to Goa that year. It was a long and expensive trip and not everybody was always successful in finding the required time, money, and luck to get there. But many did. The bar and the terraces around it were full of long-haired colourfully dressed freaks. It had always surprised me that people from this many diverse backgrounds could all look so similar. I always felt immediately at ease with these hippies and freaks, my beloved Generation X.

Some Westerners travelled all-year round along the hippie market trails. They sold electronics and jeans in Goa and bought silver in the north of India. At the end of March, they went to Bali to add swimwear and other clothes to their collection, after which they made sure to be in Ibiza in time for the European holiday season to sell these goods. Then they returned to India with bags full of merchandise to sell on the flea market and the whole cycle would be repeated. Many knew each other and met at the different locations around the world.

Some of those travelling traders took holidays in between this cycle and travelled to other countries where they combined the hunt for new beaches and natural, cultural experiences with the hunt for exotic tribal antiquities to sell in rich countries. And thus, they scavenged in Laos, Cambodia, the Philippines, Tibet, Kyrgyzstan, and other places Westerners had never even heard of. Other Westerners returned to their home countries every spring to do seasonal jobs in tourism and agriculture, and some lucky ones lived on trust funds like aristocrats and didn't have any monetary worries.

Many of the regulars I met in the flea-market bar were scammers and drug smugglers. It wouldn't be polite to mention them by name but rest assured that there were many colourful personalities amongst them. These individuals were important to the rest of us as they proved that even if you came from a simple suburban descent, you could become a *someone* and live a hero's life.

You could be rich; you could have adventures. You could add something to a new culture and become part of a new aristocracy of hippie, freaky royalty made up of free people that weren't bound to small-minded conventions dictated by hypocrite religious and political leaders. Thank God we were free of any mass media in India during those years. These celebrities showed us in person how to live as celebrities ourselves.

Many of them are no longer alive, and not all of them died of old age. Apart from being adventurers, many of them had a wide variety of other qualities as well. There were DNA scientists, painters, musicians, and classic English Shakespearian actors.

What they all had in common was that they refused to follow the beaten path or work from nine to five until oblivion. They wanted more from life and accepted the risks involved in freeing up enough time for their talents to thrive in, for their love of life to flourish and for the parties under endless waving palm trees on the Goan shores. Smuggling drugs was the perfect way to achieve this. They liked drugs, especially charas (the Indian variety of cannabis) and LSD.

Charas was easy to buy in different locations, and the general rule of thumb was that the closer you got to the production source, the cheaper it was, the further away, the more expensive it became. Risk equalled money.

Manali in the north of India was one of these production regions and most of the cannabis that was smoked in large cloud-producing chillums came from there. There're lots of exciting, absurd, happy, and tragic anecdotes about the smuggling that happened during those years. Some of these stories are told by the light of wood fires around the world where hippies and their offspring gather. Some are whispered informally on a need-to-know base. You'll hear some of these stories in this book. There are stories of legendary proportions that never really happened. And certain anecdotes are best forgotten.

LSD was a different game altogether. There weren't many people in the world that knew how to make it or had access to the facilities and materials required to do so. It's possible that at that time there was only one source of real LSD in the world. But smuggling it was easy. It didn't smell or look like a drug. One gram was enough for ten thousand LSD trips. One kilo or litre was enough for ten million trips.

That was a lot of trips and a lot of money. But it was a risky game because the governments around the world considered LSD as more dangerous to society than plutonium. If you were caught smuggling or selling large amounts of LSD, you would spend most of the rest of your life in jail.

Surprisingly, most of these smugglers fared well. There were casualties and people were caught and did spend time in jail, but I think that if you compare how much time and effort the governments spent on the so-called 'war on drugs', relatively few drugs were confiscated and the main effect of this 'war' was to raise the market prices.

The heroin traders formed another group. Heroin came from Afghanistan and found its way through Goa to the rest of the world. For the Afghanis, Goa was the last stop of their opium and heroin delivery before handing it over to the Westerners, who would then bring it by boat, plane, or whatever other means of transport, to the West and to Australia. The faith of these smugglers and traders wasn't great. They endured many adventures that mostly ended in hospital, jail or death.

Cocaine wasn't around in those days and only appeared a few years later. The cocaine traders suffered the same faith as the heroin traders. May they rest in a peace they never knew during their lives.

All these groups of people I just described, evenly divided between male and female, young and old, were represented at that bar on that Wednesday afternoon, drinking tea and beer and producing huge clouds of tobacco and charas from their chillums. Every time a pipe was lit, a loud 'Boom Shankar', or similar prayer to Shiva the god of dope smoking, was proclaimed by the freaks who sat in a circle in anticipation of the chillum, which was being passed round counterclockwise from mouth to mouth. As I approached, I was welcomed by Ronan and other friends.

"Hey, light this chillum!"

I sat down in the circle of friends, covered the bottom of the chillum with a wet cloth and put it to my mouth. It took two matches to light it.

"Bombule bulenat bom Shankar bombule Shiva Shankar i alek Shiva Bom!" resounded through the bar and into the flea market.

I inhaled deeply and exhaled billowing clouds of smoke. I tried not to cough. This was difficult due to the quality of the tobacco but would have been considered very uncool. I just about passed this test and handed the chillum the person next to me. A feeling of happiness overwhelmed me. Here I was, stoned with my stoned friends, smoking huge chillums under the palm trees in Goa, a billion light years away from the seriousness of our home countries. We were lucky that the gods loved us, each and every one of them.

After the initial kick of the chillum had passed, we talked.

There was so much to talk about. Where had we been during the European summer? Where had we travelled to? Had new places been discovered and were they more beautiful or cheaper than Goa? Where was the best fruit juice in Goa? Had everyone already rented a house for the season?

"Yes, in Anjuna."

"Can I live with you?" Ronan asked.

"Sure, you're always welcome."

And most importantly: was there a party tonight and if so, where? Yes, there was, but its location had not yet been revealed. That was normal, of course.

After we'd watched the sun disappear into the Indian Ocean, we headed to the little fishing village of Chapora, in the centre of which grew an impressive banyan tree that was already several hundreds of years old. Under its long hanging branches and roots, people gathered for a fruit juice accompanied by more chillums.

This was the place to go if you wanted to find out where a party was because the wallah, who ran the fruit juice bar was also involved in renting out the sound system. And yes, we got some hints and gossip, but its location still wasn't 100% clear. After having dinner in one of the local restaurants that served rice and fish curry with chapatis, we freshened up, jumped on our motorbikes, and drove off in the general direction of where we suspected the party might be.

This was always an amusing ritual. People on motorbikes criss-crossed the Goan roads, stopping here and there to switch off their engines so it was silent enough to hear the distant bom-bom-bom of the party. Remember, there were no mobile phones, so we had to find the party in other ways. There were a few standard locations, such as Chapora fort, Bamboo Forest, Hill Top and some beaches and river sides; all of them places of dreams, psychedelic dreams.

Most of the parties followed a set of norms. Music started at about midnight. The sound system that was used had originally been brought to Goa by a famous rock band who had donated it to the residing hippies; they in turn had sold it to a few entrepreneurial locals who rented it back out to the hippies. The money made from this sound system was used to partially pay the police who would then allow the party. The other part of the police bribe was paid by whichever bar had control over the drinks sold the night of the party. Good business, everybody happy. Entrance to the party was always unrestricted and free. There were no fences or borders and no security personnel. That would have been really unthinkable.

The party grounds were mostly decorated with Christmas lights, which were easy to find in Christian Goa, or Hindi festival lights, which were equally easy to find. Palm trees, bamboos and banyan trees were coloured with fluorescent pigments used in the Holi festival. Hanging between the trees were colourful sheets decorated with Hindi gods, psychedelic motives, and mandalas.

Each party usually had no more than two DJs: one for the night and one for the morning. Few people wanted to be a DJ, as it meant you couldn't dance and party yourself. Most DJs were too stoned to dance anyway. At that time, DJs weren't seen as celebrities and not many would sacrifice themselves to stand all night and play music. The music was pre-recorded and played from now-obsolete cassettes. The sound was far from crisp, especially if you compare it to what we're used to now, but for us it was heaven.

Around the dance floor were chai shops, run by chai ladies. They sat on mats and made chai, coffee and served snacks by the light of kerosene lamps. They were an important point of stability for many of us. At the start of the party, we gave them all our belongings, including our money, and they would take care of them for us all night. Each of us had our favourite chai lady, usually someone from the village where we lived. At many of these parties, certainly in the early years, the LSD was free. Somewhere in the party ground was a bucket of fruit juice spiked with first-class pure LSD that one of the hippie legends had provided.

After a confused criss-cross drive through the Goan rice paddies, we finally heard the party in the distance. It took another thirty minutes of trial and error before we saw the Christmas lights shining in the trees. Many motorbikes were already parked nearby. Some locals taxi wallahs buzzed around the entrance of the party ground offering their services, selling anything from cigarettes to drugs, while others were beggars from neighbouring states.

Our little group of boys and girls didn't stand out much from the rest of the crowd. In any other place in the world, we would have. We were dressed in fully fluorescent pants, strange-shaped shirts and jackets, wild hairy-hairdos and lots of paraphernalia. I made a tour around the dance floor to determine where the best sound was. I was still relatively sober, considering the chillums I'd smoked, but later in the night, I would be tripping on LSD. I made sure to check that there were no unexpected water wells or ditches to fall in; then I went to look for my favourite chai lady.

I met some other old friends on the dance floor, and we celebrated by smoking a few more chillums. The music grew louder and louder. These sounds were all new to me. It was the first year I'd heard Goa trance. Someone pointed towards a little ruin in the corner of the party ground. A mysterious light shone from inside it and I could see the silhouette of an Indian lady at its entrance. People were coming and going.

"Go there..." my friend pointed.

I approached the Indian lady dressed in a psychedelic sari.

She smiled and whispered: "Do you want?"

I didn't know what she meant by this, but I nodded anyway. She used a long spoon to stir the shiny orange liquid that filled a large clay pot. She stared at me intensely. Then she brought the spoon to my lips. She smiled.

"Go now and fly."

I left wondering what lay in store for me and continued to explore the party, in search of nice girls. I'd always been shy with the ladies but hanging around them as friends was easy. I stepped onto the dance floor. It was dusty and dark, and the little party lights spread a romantic patina over the place and people. The music was strong. I danced, loosening up my muscles. The beat carried me along for a while until in the distance I heard the crashing sound of marching elephants. The tremors increased as the elephants energised the air with blasting waves that erupted from their trunks. They were accompanied by the screeching of huge feathery birds who flew above us, brushing the tops of our heads. I saw a troop of monkeys beating sticks in a coordinated rhythm as they jumped up and down and threw their arms and legs into the air. The palm-tree leaves click-clacked their fingers in tune with the jungle animals around them.

Then all these sounds and lights liquified. The whole thing was driven by an enormous force that we were all part of. This force shredded the matrix of our universe, and everything fell apart into sub-atomic particles. I could see everything in the minutest detail, in the smallest of scales; I could see all the way to the other side of the party. I worried for a moment that maybe the world had fallen apart to such a degree that it could never be put together again.

This worry morphed and manifested into a guy dancing beside me with a pineapple head. I laughed and laughed as I watched him shake his pineapple leaves to the music. Beside him danced a flamingo flamenco ballerina with glittering bird wings. I laughed at how serious she looked as she stomped around the dance floor. Her fingers snapped stroboscopic light that flashed and vibrated around us.

Behind me, an Indian goddess with hundreds of snake arms blurred the air around her. The snakes in her hair also danced in harmony with the tall arms that had started to grow from the ground. A juggler juggled countless invisible balls high into the sky, defying gravity, while a long black waterfall of hair flowed from a smiling head and spread love. The hair was so black that it absorbed all light and energy before radiating it out in a loving frequency so that everybody could be enlightened. I was caught in its mysterious tangles.

I felt so smart. I knew everything there was to know and re-alised that no words existed to explain it all. I knew more than language could express. I heard the echo of sounds before they happened. I could hear with my eyes and see with my ears. And there were other senses too. I was connected to the soup of a universal everything. I was the opposite of lonely and it lasted forever.

Behind the palm trees the sky had turned orange. Morning had come. What a perfect reason to make the music louder and faster! And happier too. All the strange creatures on the dance floor turned into people, freaky people. In between the sweaty, dusty, and hardworking bodies, arrived fresher bodies of young mothers who'd just showered with scented oils. Everything and everyone danced.

A little later, the sun spilled over the horizon. Its rays filtered through the dust and palm leaves. For the first time, I noticed that the beach was only fifty metres away. The sun caressed my skin. Semi-naked people danced on the sand to the never-relenting beats. Local kids walked around selling watermelons. I sat down under a palm tree and asked for one of the juicy green balls. I pointed towards the chai lady who had my money. I saw that the beach consisted of zillions of grains of sand.

The universe, which had fallen apart into sub-atomic particles not long before, had come together again; all except for the beach that still remained a heap of loose sand. No problem. I kissed the watermelon and the salty sweat and dust on my face mixed with its sweet juice.

I decided to swim in the ocean. I took off all my clothes and the saltiness greeted me as I plunged into its depths. Pffiishaaahhhh. Oi. Oof. Ahh. That's nice. Gentle waves rolled a new layer of reality over me. This new reality warned me.

"Watch out. You're tripping and you're in an ocean. There might be currents and unknown dangers."

I accepted reason's cue and swam towards the beach. The music was still going strong, and I saw from the dust clouds that the energy on the dance floor was exploding. I walked back and sat under a palm tree beside the dance floor. I watched my friends, now human again, dancing and enjoying the party, the music and each other.

When the sun reached its highest point in the sky, the music finally stopped. We could have gone on forever. My body felt strong and lean after this marathon of dancing, but my mind was spaced out. I walked for a few kilometres with my friends and crashed on the veranda of a house. There were pillows, hammocks, flowers, tea and fruit. Everything felt friendly. We were all good friends sharing paradise with each other.

As I repositioned myself on one of the pillows, I tuned in to the conversation around me. Mr Yeah, Mats, Xevi, Lola and some others were talking about prehistoric times, about how the North Pole had been in Helsinki and how we'd all originated from there. They talked about Paradise time in great detail. They described how people used to live during that period and insisted that everybody could return to this way of living once more if they gained an in-depth understanding of the Bock Saga. If this could be accomplished, the world could once more return to Paradise time.

Mr Yeah proclaimed: "I don't just believe the Bock Saga; I know that it's true, because I understand it, because it's logic. But the rest of the planet requires proof, and this is something we can give them. There are golden bock statues from the pre-Ice-Age period buried in Finland. If we dig them up, we prove the Bock Saga is true, and we never have to live in a money rat race again. On the 24th of July is the 130th birthday party of Kristina Victoria at Ior Bock's mansion in Finland. That's when we're going to dig up the golden bocks. Let's all go there together!"

"Oh, no. Not this Bock Saga again," I thought. "What a waste of time. Even if Paradise time did exist, it'll never come back, no matter what you find in the ground. Paradise is here and now and at the next party."

But I saw a burning light radiate from my friends' eyes, and it was clear that they'd somehow been captivated by the idea.

Ronan

My hunger for knowledge was like a vampire's hunger for blood. I decided I needed more, and I got frustrated that I lacked a better overview of the story. All the facts I'd already gained rang like bells inside my head, echoing and contending with each other. It was like the music of knowledge. I could hear the different instruments, but I lacked the educated ear and elevated position of a conductor to combine it into a symphony.

I decided that I needed to find Casper. He was the man sitting next to Ior in the video. He would be able to answer all my detailed questions. He was a guy like me, a normal twentieth-century urban kid that I probably could relate to easier than Ior and his prehistoric mind. Casper was not in Goa at the time, but I'd heard rumours that he was in Boracay.

This was a small island somewhere in the Philippines and supposedly one of the most beautiful spots on Earth. White beaches, palm trees, no roads, no cars, no electricity, or any other landscape-destroying inventions of our times. It was far away and an expensive trip, but I was still rich enough to afford it. The nearest international airport that had flights in the direction of Manila, the Philippines, was in Sri Lanka, in the south of India. Xevi decided to come along for the ride, at least until Sri Lanka.

Flying was expensive at the time. Going from place to place by plane and partying along the way was referred to as the jet-set lifestyle, which usually meant you were exorbitantly rich without needing to work. I was not rich, but as long as I brought a kilo of hashish with me on each flight and sold it in the next place of arrival, I could pay the fares and stay for free in that country for a while. As long as I wouldn't be caught with it, everything would be alright. Or at least, that's what I thought.

Being a stoned and psychedelic freak with a head full of Saga, trouble was bound to find me sooner or later. But I wasn't worried about this at the time. No, I was sure that Öde was on my side, that it was directing me to find the golden bocks, proof of the Bock Saga, and giving me the tools needed to change the hopeless path that humanity was on into one of hope and happiness. I still believe this now, thirty-five years later, except that I now think that Öde doesn't really care about the fate of any one individual, not even that of those who, like me, dedicated their lives to the Bock Saga.

Excerpt from the Bock Saga:

Öde = Fate, determinative event of natural law given by Oden, the universe.

Through the so-called coconut-connection system, which was an informal, oral information system between the hippies and freaks in Asia of what to buy where and from who, I got the address of Kemal, who was supposed to be a marijuana farmer in the legendary Kerala mountains. Xevi and I took a twenty-four-hour train ride southbound to Cochin. From there, we had another eight-hour bus ride, followed by a further two hours on a different bus and a few hours walk, until we arrived tired and dusty at Kemal's farm.

After the initial introduction rituals, mainly consisting of gossiping about common acquaintances, to confirm our identities, and drinking tea and smoking joints, he took us on a walk through the jungle for a couple of hours. After a few steep inclines, we stood on the edge of a sea of green. A wide valley overgrown with marijuana plants stung the green retina receptors of our eyes.

"My friends, here are the secret marijuana plantations of Kerala."

"I'm... I'm just overwhelmed. There're more plants here than I've ever seen, touched, or even dreamed of," I said in pure awe.

"This is marijuana heaven," Xevi agreed.

"The whole field is ripe and ready to be picked. However much you want, it's yours," smiled Kemal, our cannabis angel.

"Bingo! Deal!"

"There's just one catch: you have to cut and procure it all yourself."

"Are there no hands available to help?" I asked lazily.

"No, we used to sell it only to the locals, and the police never cared as long as we gave them something to smoke. Since you foreigners arrived, the game has changed. Inevitably, stories of smuggling, seizures and other foreign intrigue have bubbled to the surface. This makes us an easy target. There are no secrets here. Whatever we do or are involved in is known and known forever. For you guys it's different. Whatever you do, leaves with you and is forgotten as soon as you take the bus. So, what are you waiting for? Get to work!"

"Fine. Just make sure your policemen have plenty to smoke so we can leave in peace when we are ready to go," Xevi instructed.

We were in a green world with a blue sky above us with hot red faces dripping in sweat. For a few days, Xevi and I harvested the plants. We dried them and processed the hashish. It turned into beautiful, black, fragrant and potent Kerala cream. On our last day, we walked back to the road from the marijuana fields and waited for a bus to bring us to the market in the next town. We bought two pairs of luxurious leather sandals in a Muslim shoemakers' shop. (Hindus don't use leather and in reality, these sandals weren't exactly Halal either, since the leather came from pigs. Turns out, walking on a pig is different from eating it.)

Then we bought glue that was strong enough to bind leather. When we arrived back in our shack that evening, we got to work. Carefully, I cut open the new sandals. I removed some of the sole and added extra leather to the sides. It took me the whole night to prepare the sandals and when I was finished, I had four sandals with 450 grams of hashish in each. They looked sort of convincing, but some luck would still be needed if we wanted to board a plane and pass customs twice without being stopped. It was imperative that we didn't sweat too much and concentrated on moving lightly and naturally. We were long-haired freaks; we would be suspicious at any customs.

We set off. There were more trains and buses before we got to the tiny airport in Trivandrum, where we donned our new sandals and walked in. This was south India and the hot season had already started. In the streets it got so hot that we saw slippers stuck to the molten tarmac. We tried to walk in the shade as much as possible.

Air conditioning still hadn't graced Indian airports and all you could hope for were big fans that moved the hot air around. I felt the hashish in my sandals liquify. It made it harder to walk naturally and maintain the forced cheerfulness I was trying to emanate. I looked sideways at Xevi. I saw he was sweating too. You might think that sweating is normal in the tropics, but there're different kinds of sweat.

Our sweat at that moment was as suspicious as the hashish that was sweating out of our sandals. The combination of the hot street and the pressure of each step we took was causing the drug to expand. It tried to escape the narrow prison of leather and glue that I'd prepared for it. I sat down before approaching the luggage check-in and carefully glanced down at my feet. The seams were bulging, and a vague smell of dark Kerala hashish lingered over me. Would customs notice it? It looked so obvious to me, but there was no backing out now.

The whole situation became a whole lot tenser when I noticed the armed police officers. A civil war was raging through Sri Lanka and the Indians were on the alert for terrorists and arms trafficking. I hoped that Öde was paying attention and would let us through. Thank God we weren't alone when we approached customs. A group of much freakier looking hippies led the way and it turned out they had problems with their passports and visas. This kept customs distracted just long enough for us to flip-flop through. Again, Öde had sent angels to brush the path in front of us. I saw this as greater proof that I was doing the right thing; I was on the right path.

Once in Sri Lanka, we took our time to sell the merchandise as we were used to doing by now. In the next few weeks, we sold the hashish on the beach to Western tourists and hippies. We enjoyed beach life and the lush nature around us.

We found our way into the lobster-catching economy through a group of Austrian guys we met. The restaurants paid good money for fresh lobster and the reefs in front of the beaches were full of them. The Austrians had scuba diving tanks and a compressor to fill them with air. Raju, a Sinhalese guy, had a boat and he sailed us all out together at night to hunt. It was easy.

The sea was about ten to fifteen metres deep. We each went down individually with a flashlight. When I spotted a lobster, I shone the light in its eyes to paralyse it and with my other hand I grabbed its back and dragged it away in a sweeping movement. I had to be fast and deliberate. If I didn't catch it correctly, or if I was too slow, it would crawl backwards, piercing my hands with the row of sharp spines on its back.

I'll admit that this was a job that didn't really suit my vegetarian sensibilities, but at least I didn't eat the lobsters. It was good business, limited only by the time we could stay underwater. Raju's little boat always waited for us on the surface, bobbing along happily in the dark. Raju's job was to follow our underwater lights and make sure none of us were separated from the rest. We would dump our catch into the boat and from time to time move to different locations.

One day, Raju told us that he had an old scuba tank at home that some Austrians had left behind. He asked if we wanted to use it. The next morning, he brought it to our compressor so we could fill it up. From the tank's stamps, I noticed that it hadn't been tested for quite a while and decided to bring it to a diving club nearby where they could inspect the valve and the inside for rust and defects. Better safe than sorry! The people who operated the diving club were a friendly bunch who happily agreed to open the tank and check inside. I watched as a bemused look spread across the tank inspector's face.

"Is everything OK?" I asked, imagining what horrific rusty landscape lay inside the steel cylinder.

"Have a look yourself," the inspector replied with a strange look on his face.

The tank was filled to the brim with the highest quality grass and hashish I'd ever seen. A ripple of shock and a mixture of emotions swept through the room. There were about eight people present: me and another diver friend, Raju, the tank inspector, and a few other people from the diving club.

Let me be clear, grass was illegal in Sri Lanka and the law was enforced by long jail sentences. Along with this knowledge, another realisation rushed around the room: that amount of weed must be worth a lot of money. This realisation quickly led to an obvious question: who was the owner, or who was responsible for it at the very least?

Everyone in that room knew that this discovery couldn't be kept a secret. There were already too many people involved. Someone would surely alert the police who would then confiscate it, arrest everyone present and sell the dope through the local mafia. Greed and fear captivated the audience in the compressor room. It was a stalemate; whoever made the first move would lose. Unless I did something unexpected, that is. I needed to move fast.

I grabbed the tank, rushed outside, and threw it into the back of the car.

"I'm going straight to the police! Come. Now," I snapped at the wide-eyed diver and Raju as I rushed to start the engine.

"Are we really going to the police?" asked Raju in a hushed voice. "I really don't think that's a good idea. Anything could happen at the police station; they might not let you leave again."

"No, we're going straight to the beach and sailing out in your dingy. We're going to sink the tank to the bottom of the sea near one of the micro islands in front of the coast. Nobody will ever find it there. Before they've even had the chance to get a boat, it'll be safely out of reach, and we'll just be diving for lobsters like we do every night. Tomorrow we can figure out what we need to do."

And so, that's exactly what we did. When we returned to our rooms late that night, our nets filled with lobsters, the police were already waiting for us. We denied everything, and since they couldn't find any drugs on us, the case was closed. A few days later, we returned to our treasure and dragged it ashore a couple of beaches away, outside the jurisdiction of our local cops.

It was time for me to continue to Boracay and find Casper. It took a few flights to get to the neighbouring island, the last of which took place in a small four-seater plane. Before we could land, we were forced to fly over the airstrip twice. The first time was to chase away the playing kids, and the second time was to chase away the grazing cows. The arrivals/departure hall was a small bamboo hut with a hammock as its only furniture. From there, it was a short bicycle ride to the harbour, where a paraw (a canoe-shaped sailboat) left for the island of Boracay.

During my journey in the paraw I was unexpectedly hit with an intense vertigo, which was even stranger as I'm not usually scared of heights. The vertigo was triggered every time I looked overboard and saw the sea floor about fifteen metres below us. It was as if there was nothing between us and it. I could see the coral formations in crystal-clear detail and could almost count the grains of sand. We were sailing on an invisible layer of nothingness.

In an attempt to counteract the dizziness, I decided to only look ahead at the approaching island. A long white beach stretched out in front of us. The paraw drifted ashore and some passengers disembarked. The captain indicated that he would continue along the beach in a similar fashion. Boats were the only transport around the island. We sailed on and I wondered where I should get off to find Casper. I had no idea where he was staying on the island so when I saw that we were nearing the end of the beach, I got off the boat and hoped for the best.

It was the end of the afternoon; the sun was sinking towards the horizon and under some palm trees connected by hammocks was a little beach bar where a few locals and Westerners had gathered. I walked over and asked them if anyone knew Casper. Yes, they all knew him and knew exactly where his house was. It turned out that the talkative Dutchman was well known and liked by everyone. They were sad to tell me, however, that he'd just left for Tokyo.

"You probably crossed paths in the sky," someone commented. "Did you say you just arrived from India? Did you bring something to smoke?"

It was a typical beautiful Boracay sunset; a psychedelic sky with all kinds of changing colours in it, even green and purple. We got stoned, the people were friendly. I realised my mission had failed for now, but at the same time, I also realised that this was probably the best place in the world to fail in. Who knows, maybe taking the time to digest all the new information I'd absorbed from Ior the last few months was what my brain needed. Afterall, it had been exposed all day, every day to the Bock Saga that was filled with plenty of brain-upsetting information, not to mention the two to three parties a week that lasted all night and day and were soaked in LSD. Boracay seemed like the right place for now.

I should have known that my brain didn't have any intention to rest. I wanted to share the great news that I'd discovered by coincident with everybody. I talked to anyone who didn't walk away about our ancient heritage. About how people lived in the prehistory. About the Paradiset, the Paradise time, where all was great and in harmony. 'Her-moon-i' in Root language. Valhalla, Yggdrasil, the Wheel of Life and many more things. About the only creation story that was not religious and that had actual physical proof in the shape of golden bocks that we were going to dig up in the coming summer.

I don't think I converted anyone, but by repeating Ior's story, I was able to organise the many snowflakes of information in my head into structured strings of ideas. After all, that was what I'd come all the way to Boracay for in the first place.

I was doing well. Everything was working out. Since I left Berlin for the first time, a couple of years before, I'd been riding a wave of adventure and happiness. The universe had sent angels to dust off a golden path in front of me. I felt so positive and happy. I was involved in the greatest story mankind had ever known: the story of mankind itself. We were going to prove it too!

Everything in the Bock Saga was positive. When people finally realised this, we could all live like we did in Paradise time again. There is, after all, no practical reason not to. The minimum we would get from the excavation were three life-sized golden bocks. That would settle us financially, in the remote case that our monetary system wasn't abandoned in our new Paradise time.

I felt that Öde, or fate, had chosen me to play a part in it all. I was an unlikely choice, true, but that's just the way it was. There were so many coincidences that seemed meaningful. Like getting off the boat in Boracay at just the right spot. Like meeting Mr Yeah on that veranda in Baga beach and hearing about the 'movie' (I would never have gone to watch Ior's video if I'd known it was about some creation story!). Like coincidentally passing by Ior Bock's veranda. All these little events inevitably led to what was going to happen the coming summer. I was invincible and protected by the universe itself. I was flying through life like the paraw had flown over the invisible water.

Life in a paradise island like Boracay is cheap, but not entirely free. As time trickled by, my money trickled with it. I still had enough in my pocket to fly to Amsterdam, buy dope, and then fly on to Alaska for another season of dope selling and fishing on the high seas. I climbed onto the small private airplane to Manila, and after my usual stop in Amsterdam, I landed in Anchorage, Alaska, ten days later. I walked down the steps of the plane with loaded shoes. Somehow, I wasn't too worried about it this time round. Alaskan tarmac was much cooler than that in Sri Lanka, after all. When I reached customs, they asked me what the purpose of my visit was and how long I wanted to stay.

"I don't need a long visa, I'm not here to work. I'm just passing through on my way to Finland where I'll be digging up pre-Ice-Age golden bocks, all the proof needed to bring mankind back to paradise."

I just couldn't stop talking. The customs guy looked at me, stamped a six-month visa and told me to hurry up.

My shoes were heavy, but my step was light. I took another plane to Dutch Harbor and checked into a guest house. I was expecting a friend from Berlin who was also arriving from Amsterdam. We'd met in Boracay and had a lot in common. We had the same name, we'd both escaped urban Berlin and he was an adventurer just like me. Lastly, he'd also be loaded with hashish. The plan was to team up while selling the dope in Alaska.

It would be much safer if one of us handled the dope and the other handled the money. I waited a couple of days, but he didn't show up. I didn't know what had happened to him and could do nothing else than hope for the best. I decided that in the meantime, I should start hitting up the bars and selling. I was on a strict time schedule, having already been booked to work on one of the fishing ships. Plus, my Finnish adventure was drawing closer.

I had cut up the hashish into three-gram pieces and went from bar to bar selling them. At times it was quite scary as I had no idea who I would end up selling to. The American police was known to have undercover buyers. I couldn't sell my dope by keeping it a secret, however, and there's always a risk when entering a foreign market.

The option with the lowest risk was to find one person who you knew and trusted who would buy the whole lot. But such a person would then only pay half of what I was charging when I sold it in small quantities. I chose the fatalist way, knowing that Öde was on my side.

I hung around in bars, drinking beer, playing pool and selling hashish as much as possible. Money came pouring in and after ten days my friend Ronan finally arrived. I was glad he'd made it and hadn't been arrested as I feared he'd been. Unfortunately, he wouldn't be able to work on the same boat as me, as the crew was already complete.

Luckily, he was able to find another boat that was leaving in two weeks' time. That gave him enough days to sell some of his dope in the harbour city. I introduced him to all my clients, gave him my room in the guest house and boarded my ship.

Like the previous year, it was hard work, maybe too hard for a skinny tropical hippie with his head in the clouds. But it was manageable also thanks to the respect I received for selling hashish. When I got off the boat a few weeks later, one of the mates from another boat told me he'd heard that I'd been arrested for smuggling and selling drugs. Well, clearly, I hadn't.

"It must have been another Ronan then."

I went straight to the guest house, and they confirmed the story. From there, I rushed to the police station and to the jail. I was able to visit my friend Ronan. He told me that the authorities had already been after a German Ronan when he arrived in Dutch Harbor. When I'd left and another German Ronan appeared on the scene, selling exactly the same dope, they'd just presumed it was the same person.

What bad luck! I, on the other hand, had only just escaped his fate. He explained that he might get away with a light sentence of narcotics possession, as none of my clients had confessed to buying the hashish from him. But it was still a hairy situation, and if he was convicted for smuggling or selling, a long jail sentence loomed over him.

He told me that they hadn't found much on him because he'd hidden the majority on a small island close by. He then asked me to find it for him, sell it and give the money to a lawyer that could attempt to get him out on bail. He would then try to escape to Canada.

Thus, the plan was to find and sell more hashish to solve a problem caused by selling hashish in the first place. It sounded like a wild plan, and I was especially worried about the part I was supposed to play, considering the police had already been looking for a German Ronan.

It sounded like a lot of trouble. But what could I do? I certainly couldn't leave my friend in an Alaskan prison. With an indication of the vague location, I took the daily ferry to the island where the hashish was hidden.

The island was a mere dot on the map, with a small village on one side. It proved to be much larger, however, as I started to walk around it. The only indication Ronan had given me was that he had hidden his stash near a large nose-shaped boulder. The place was of course full of nose-shaped boulders.

I realised that all the boulders in the world looked like noses. I walked around from the early morning until night descended. I was hungry and thirsty and realised that I'd never find the god-damn hashish. I stopped walking and stood on a slightly elevated rocky plateau, overlooking the island and the beach, and watched the sun sinking towards the horizon for a while.

The last ferry was already approaching the village and I realised that I had to go back. As I stepped off the rock I'd been standing on, a gentle horizontal ray of sunshine lazily lingered on what looked like a flimsy bluish piece of plastic stuck under the rock.

It's always jarring to see plastic garbage in pristine natural places, and my surroundings were particularly beautiful in the golden light of dusk. Should I pick it up and dump it in a waste bin whenever I passed one? I knelt to pull it up from under the rock. I know you're not going to believe me, but I promise it's true. Out came the blue plastic bag and it was filled with hashish. Talking of coincidences.

During the next few days, I tried to sell the hashish as carefully as possible. I was paranoid that the police would catch and accuse me of all my previous sales as well. It seemed that luck was still on my side and when I'd collected all the money, I brought it to Ronan's lawyer. It didn't feel safe to stay in Alaska and anyway, there wasn't much more I could do for Ronan. I left for Anchorage and then made my way to Amsterdam. Sometime later when Ronan and I met again he told me what had happened after I left.

The lawyer was able to get him out on bail, but because he

was a foreigner, he was required to register at the police station every day. He was released on a Friday afternoon. As Dutch Harbor is just a small town without any crime or criminals so to speak, the police station closed over the weekend. The sheriffs were only available on request. So, the next time my friend could register again was on Monday afternoon. This gave him approximately seventy-two hours to escape the country and head to Canada.

With the last of his money, he rented a small private plane to Anchorage. Looking down over the clouds he finally felt free again. This feeling was rudely interrupted when dark fumes started clouding the cockpit, quickly accompanied by flames erupting from the engine located just in front of the cockpit. To Ronan's immense relief, the pilot didn't panic and managed to steer the burning plane to a small local airstrip.

He had contacted the local authorities on his way down, so the fire brigade, ambulance and police all greeted them as they landed. There was a lot of excitement and the police and airport authorities wanted to speak to Ronan to get his statement on the burning plane incident. God knows how, but Ronan managed to sneak off in the confusion and hide in a hangar where some workers were servicing a small plane. He convinced them to fly him to Anchorage.

Oof, a narrow escape. Although Ronan was now in Anchorage, he didn't have any money left for public transport and had to hitchhike to the Canadian border over 600 kilometres away. He needed to cross the border before the Alaskan police realised, he'd skipped bail and alerted the border patrol. A truck filled with frozen fish took him to the American border.

He passed the American border without a problem and arrived at the Canadian border with time to spare. There was just one problem. The patrol wouldn't allow him into the country because he didn't have enough money to buy a flight out. They didn't want to get stuck with a poor foreigner who would only end up costing the Canadian state money. Ronan's only option was to head back to the US, only a hundred metres away.

What to do. The only person he knew in Alaska was a guy he'd met earlier that year on a beach in Thailand who lived in Anchorage. With his last few coins, he phoned his friend, who was surprised to hear from Ronan and the strange situation he was in. Ronan begged to borrow $400, and luckily, the guy was willing to help. Now all that Ronan had to do was hitchhike back to Anchorage for 600 kilometres, grab the money and then head once more to the Canadian border.

He managed to arrive in Canada just before twelve noon on Monday and hitchhiked as quickly and as far away from the border as any truck driver could take him. Wisely, he's never set foot in the US again.

In the meantime, I'd arrived back in Amsterdam, where I met William again. We celebrated our adventures with champagne and big joints. I was rich now. I had ten thousand US dollars in my pocket. From here, I would go to Finland. Although I didn't really need the money now, I bought another supply of dope in Amsterdam.

As usual, I bought shoes and glue and packed it up well. In addition to this, I prepared 800 grams to swallow in little plastic wrappings. I'd decided that I would bring more than one and a half kilograms to Finland with me. I was sure that it would make a lot of money there.

I knew that I only needed money until we'd dug out the golden bock statues, thereby proving the Bock Saga true. The whole planet would then realise that our money-based society wasn't the right approach, and all money would become worthless.

Paradise time would replace the grim world we lived in now. Monetary slavery would stop; no one would have to be poor again. What a genius twist of fate that would be. After so many generations of poverty, we would be rich thanks to the abolition of money. It was clear that I had to spend my money before the Bock Saga, the new world doctrine, kicked in.

I arrived at Stockholm airport with a belly full of hashish nuggets and heavy shoes. Once again, everything went smoothly. I felt I was travelling on a magic carpet, floating on a magic cloud. I quickly sold all the nuggets in Stockholm and kept the shoes intact for the next leap to Finland. I met Mats, a regular at Ior's veranda. He'd stayed another two months in Goa listening to Ior's stories. Much had been added to the Bock Saga and Mats updated me.

Mats was a young and angry punk. He was so much of a punk that he didn't even bother to dress up as one. I was always on my guard in his vicinity. It's not like he'd ever actually done anything nasty to me, but I still felt unsafe around him. He was just a frightening guy, almost two metres tall with anger usually bubbling under the surface: a dormant volcano with boiling lava under his skin. I was always surprised that he had so much interest in the Bock Saga. I mean, it was a bit of an intellectual thing and also somewhat abstract with all its sound system talk. I could see how it could be viewed as a disrupting story, even maybe as upsetting in a cultural way, but certainly not nihilistic punk.

He proclaimed that he was ready to go up the barricades and defend the Bock Saga. He would take up arms to do so. I had no idea what he was talking about. Barricades? Defend? Defend what exactly? Against whom? Against all the evil capitalists and dictators in the world? Soon that would be all over, and Paradise time would come. Love would prevail.

I assumed this talk was fuelled by some early trauma brought about by having grown up in the schizophrenic society that Sweden was at the time. Everybody was so neat and nice and correct, yet when the alcohol flowed, all this good behaviour was quickly washed away. The moral correctness was a thin layer of lacquer, under which ferocious and savage heathen Vikings lived. That was their true nature. Mats was a Viking.

Early in spring, Mats had already been to Helsinki to visit Ior, who'd told him that what we would be looking for behind the Bock family estate was some old piece of wood that belonged to the family that had to be dug up. In addition, Mats explained the Alfarnas-Bete to me, the rhyme of the All-Father.

That was incredibly fascinating. It knitted the whole story together into a unified whole. It made so much sense. It was the heartbeat of the Bock Saga. That said, it still remained unclear to me what the piece of wood we would be digging for actually were. And this new information was different to what Ior had originally told us we'd be digging. What had happened to the golden Bock statues?

I was anxious to finally go to the scene where mankind had started its voyage through time. I was eager to see Valhalla and the great castle of Raseborg, the oldest building on the planet. I knew there was still much to be revealed within the Bock Saga.

I felt honoured to be one of the chosen few who would witness the unfolding of this next chapter in the great history of mankind. To be able to play a role in it all was more than I could ever have dreamed of. Only a few years ago, it looked like my future would amount to being stuck in a one-window apartment in East Berlin. Now I was travelling the world and would play a part in saving the world from dystopian, Orwellian greyness and changing it into paradise.

We took a flight from Stockholm to Helsinki instead of taking the cheaper train and ferry. There were less sniffer dogs in airports than there were in the train and ferry. Smuggling with the ferry was considered dangerous, as customs and the police had many hours to spend watching and checking everybody on board. Whereas at an airport, you arrived, went through security and that was that.

We arrived safely and took a taxi to Gumbostrand, where Ior's estate was located. From Helsinki's industrial modern airport, we drove into an endless homogeneous forest. Trees, trees, and more trees, until we reached the coast. In the summer haze, we saw a myriad of dreamy islands floating on a glassy sea. The tarmac road ended and became a dirt road. The driver refused to go any further. The price on the taximeter was already enormous.

"Hey, for that price you could buy a car in most countries! And all that to be just dropped off here in the middle of nowhere! How are we supposed to find where we need to go? How can we get anywhere from here?"

The driver told us not to worry and to pay the fare. He would drop us off at the Gumbostrand kiosk, a spot that in time would become one of my favourite places on Earth. The Gumbostrand kiosk was a local sell-everything shop that had cold beer, hot coffee, and sandwiches. We ordered one of each and sat down to adjust to the atmosphere around us.

The shop had a little terrace overlooking the Finnish gulf. The view could have been majestic if it wasn't for the handful of cute little islands each boasting its own quaint wooden house. Each house possessed a speed boat that was used to travel between the other islands or to reach the mainland, in which case the boats would be moored next to the kiosk. A lot of people were coming and going, but it was relatively quiet, as Finnish people generally don't talk a lot or make a lot of noise in the daytime.

We asked for directions to Ior's house but didn't get an answer. I thought that maybe the girl we'd asked didn't understand my English or Mats' Swedish. So, we sat back down and had a few more snacks. After a while, when we'd already made peace with the fact that we weren't going to get an answer, the girl behind the counter tapped my shoulder and gave us the following instructions.

"Walk up the dirt track for about twenty minutes and when you reach a large rock on your left, go through the forest to your right until you find the house."

Aha, that was easy. Mats, who lived in a Scandinavian country himself, explained:

"She needed to reflect on what we'd asked before responding. But that's just the way Scandinavians are. Sometimes you can ask a question and get the answer four days later, when you've already forgotten what you'd asked about in the first place."

We paid and I was again shocked by how expensive everything was. A couple of beers and sandwiches had cost the equivalent of a five-course meal in the Ritz in London. I hoped that Finland would be the first place to abolish money after we dug up the golden bocks and proved the Bock Saga true.

We set off through the atmospheric forest. Everything around us was alive in a fairy tale kind of way. The trees had faces, the undergrowth had a misty green colour to it and tiny blue flowers smiled up at us. Even the rocks were alive, I could feel their souls. I glanced at Mats to see if he was as spellbound as I was. The huge punky Viking walked beside me as if in a trance, clearly enchanted by the flowers and trees of the forest.

The magic dripped from the leaves and gathered in little streams that flowed in the same direction we were heading. Was it defying gravity and flowing up the hill? It was hard to tell. I could sense how close we were to one of the holiest places known to mankind. A lot had happened here, and we now understood why this had been the place where everything had started.

The hypnosis was broken, or at least altered, when we spotted two people struggling wildly in a pool of mud; the heads and body parts that we could distinguish were completely covered in mud. They were laughing and cursing at various entangled hoses and pipes that they were trying to connect to a water pump system.

I recognised those voices! It was Mr Yeah and Lola. After lots of 'Hellos (Hel-Oden)', they told us that they were preparing the site for the 24th of July, when the birthday celebration of Christina Victoria would take place and when we would finally dig up this mysterious piece of wood.

"And that's not all we'll be digging for. We're going to dig up the greatest treasure mankind has ever seen! Go to the house. Casper's there and he'll tell you all about it."

Lola

It was a place where you could easily imagine witches flying at night. We were surrounded by an enchanted forest, full of invisible creatures. I would kiss any frog I found; I was sure they were all princes. But at that moment, I was so dirty and covered in mud that not even a frog would kiss me.

After Xevi and I had gone our separate ways, I'd hooked up with Mr Yeah. He was a cool guy and good looking too. Quite different from the others. There are some that would call me promiscuous.

It's funny how a guy with many girls on the go is a hero, while a woman is labelled a slut. Well, I didn't have many guys, and I only ever loved one at a time. I just didn't want to marry any of them. In the Bock Saga, a woman chooses another man every time she has sex. That's what all those carnivals and festivals are for. I quite liked the sound of that. And the simple truth is that it was also convenient to hook up with a guy while travelling. You didn't get a moment of peace if you were a woman travelling alone to exotic places; the men were like hungry mosquitoes.

What I really didn't get was how Ronan always acted a little jealous when he first saw me with another man. It's not as if he'd have had any time to spend with me anyway! His whole life was devoted to the Bock Saga and how it was going to change the world. He really believed that if he could prove the Bock Saga true, everyone would once more return to paradise. If he really did want to live like a prehistoric Bock Saga man, he'd have to learn to respect the fact that I couldn't be possessed or owned. I am a woman, proud and free.

The way he talked about Öde also made me feel uneasy. It's as if he thought everything had already been decided by some great god in the sky. I was under the impression that there were no great gods in the Bock Saga, just a human 'All-Father'. Even if something like Öde existed, we little people would be too stupid to understand it. We could never know what this Öde was cooking up for us. Ronan was justifying himself within this greater perspective, like he was some sort of holy man. It's funny how he tried to transform normal everyday events into miracles of coincidence, which each served as further proof of the almighty Öde leading us in the direction of a new paradise. It made daily life so much more important.

I was just there to enjoy the adventure, one moment at a time. I was helping Mr Yeah clean out the pool of mud under which we would find an important piece of wood. I had no idea how a piece of wood could be this important, but I guess I'd find out soon. There was going to be a party too; *that* was exciting.

Ronan

We walked the short distance to the house. I had expected a grand estate, an aristocratic dwelling of large proportions. It was nothing of the kind. The word I'd use to describe it is charming. It consisted of a log cabin with a chimney that was surrounded by trees, and a field of about a hundred metres covered in flowers that swept down towards the sea.

On the shore was another cute log cabin where the boat lived. It was maybe not a lavishly rich place, but it certainly had atmosphere. The door was open, as were all the windows. We heard the sound of people working. On the veranda, we saw pots of paint and other building materials and tools. Casper came out of the house with a bucket full of brushes in his hands.

"Hey guys, welcome to Akanpesa, Akan's beach nest. Another name for it is Gumbo, Gumma's nest. 'Gumma' is the Root name for the Van word 'Aka'. Both are the title used for the retired Svan."

Casper wasn't shy to share his knowledge. Mats and Casper already knew each other, but this was the first time I'd met him. I'd travelled across the globe to meet Casper and finally, here in Gumbostrand, I'd found him. Casper wore a tie-dye t-shirt with colourful pyjama trousers and was completely covered in splashes of blue and red paint.

"We're preparing the house for the party. The Bock family bought the land 50 years ago. They moved this cabin here from another location. The family has owned the house itself for 400 years and it's stood in different locations around Finland until 1937. Ior wants it to look exactly the way it did when the family first bought this land. The wood is so strong that it could almost last forever. We're dealing with a family that thinks in millennia, not in years. Come inside and I'll show you around!"

We followed Casper eagerly inside. There was a hall, a living room, a large kitchen and some sleeping rooms, all positioned around a central fireplace and chimney. The house somehow seemed much bigger inside than it did outside.

"The winters in Finland can be seriously cold, but this house is built for them. The walls are made of oak tree logs, between them is horsehair. It's the best insulation there is. The chimney has several flues and even when only one of them is used, it stores so much energy that even in the coldest winter it keeps the whole house warm.

The food is cooked on the fire too. Look, here is the cast iron heater and oven. Every morning we make our own bread. I've painted the living room, or 'Sal', salon, in Russian Red and I used the same colour for the Bock 'kammare', the Bock's room. P Russian Blue for the Svan 'kammare', the personal space for the lady of the house. Green for 'moonkammare', which is the space for the children. Here on the wall are some portraits of Ior's grandparents."

Casper waved his hand towards a few old paintings and then stopped in front of a couple of heavy silver antique candelabras that were standing on the large stone shelf above the fireplace.

"Much of the antiques were lost two years ago. During the winter in which Ior first started to tell the Bock Saga in Goa, he had rented the house to a guy nicknamed Klepperachi. He and his young girlfriend were kleptomaniacs. They were stealing from houses in the area, most of which are the second homes of rich people in Helsinki. They stole a lot of antiques, art and other valuable stuff from these properties. They were caught when certain items showed up on the flea market in Helsinki; suddenly, expensive, museum-quality artwork was being sold for garage-sale prices."

"Klepperachi was caught, and they found a lot of the stolen stuff in Ior's house here in Gumbostrand. It was broadly discussed on the front page of the main newspaper in Helsinki, the Helsinki Raportti. Instead of finding out who'd lost what, the police decided to put an announcement in the Helsinki Raportti inviting anyone who'd had something stolen to Ior's house to pick up their belongings.

The police had no control over who took what and since Ior was in Goa, the locals decided to just grab what they wanted. Many cars and trailers full of stolen items, along with Ior's family possessions, left the premises under the 'watchful' eye of the police that day. A large part of the enormous Boxström art and antique collection was gone within an afternoon."

"Ior was probably the only Westerner in Goa who had access to a Western newspaper. He'd made a deal with someone at the newspaper office to have it sent to the Scandinavian embassy in New Delhi every day as part of diplomatic mail. From there, it was sent to poste restante in the Chapora post office. The newspaper arrived almost every day, but of course, since it was a long way from Helsinki, the news was already one month old when it got to Ior.

Great was the consternation one day on Ior's veranda when a newspaper arrived showing a photograph of his home on the front page with the headline: ROBBERY – BOCK FAMILY ES-TATE. A few weeks later, when Ior read the announcement in the newspaper inviting people to pick up their stolen goods from his home, it had already happened, and everything was gone."

"Apart from losing a great part of his family heritage, the whole situation really got to Ior. I know that he likes to complain about the politicians and the government, so do we all. But in reality, most of us feel safe with the authorities in Europe. Finland is governed by rule of law and not by individual despots, at least that's what we thought.

The fact that a police officer could give away all Ior's personal belongings in that way, and even advertise it in the national newspaper, well... that would make anyone feel unsafe. And what's worse is that this all happened during the same year as that burned monkey story. The scandals are piling up my friends."

I'd heard mention of the burned monkey scandal, but this was the first I'd heard of the tragic robbery. I looked around silently and tried to absorb my surroundings. Akanpesa looked like it belonged to another century; it was all classicisms. Nothing was electric or modern.

This backdrop was somehow not what I'd expected after the psychedelic setting of Goa and all the stoned freaks that had frequented Ior's veranda. The walls that hadn't been painted were covered with red traditional wallpaper and wooden panelling. The place was littered with antique pictures in embellished frames.

In Goa, Ior was always dressed in a less-than-formal loin cloth with a bare chest. He would only wear a t-shirt in the evening when it was cool. Here, there were portraits of his ancestors in old-fashioned stiff-collar dresses. The outside of the log cabin was romantic and in harmony with the surrounding nature; the inside was formal and static.

Casper hung the kettle over the wood fire in the living room. I rolled a joint. Casper didn't use drugs; he just smoked Indian beedis continuously. There was so much to talk about, I had so many questions. Casper started talking and didn't stop for many hours.

"Time and time again bishops and missionaries tried their utmost to convert the Scandinavians to Christianity. The Aser were afraid their Heartland in Odenma was under threat.

They had never been to war and were not planning to do so in the future either. They did react decisively however, by closing the most holy sites which had been part of the procreation system since the beginning of mankind.

The Lemminkäinen Temple and the entrance to the Bock family storehouse located in Akanpesa were shut and hidden with huge granite rocks. The interior of Castle Raseborg was hidden in the Offerlund. The plan was to leave them for a thousand years. After the last Akka of the Bock family would have died, the time would have come to open the temple again. It was planned for the 24th of July, the year 1987 AD. That is in a couple of days."

Lola

The next days were busy with the preparations for the coming party, as well as the excavation of the mysterious piece of wood. In the meantime, Casper had briefly explained what it was that we were looking for, and I felt like this new information was too big to grasp. In a way, it paralysed me. I didn't know what to do.

Mr Yeah knew what to do though, so I just followed his instructions. Together, we emptied out the water and mud that had formed a pool under the Etta Stupa. We moved countless wheelbarrows full of wet mud until we reached the granite bedrock bottom.

The Etta Stupa is a big rock with a vertical drop on one side and a slope on the other. After clearing away the mud that lay at the bottom of the drop, granite bedrock could be seen.

Ronan

That evening, Casper told us about the piece of wood that we were going to uncover on the 24th of July. The wood was actually a door, a gold-plated door. Under the Etta Stupa was the entrance to that golden door of the Lemminkäinen Temple. We knew that in the Bock Saga, Lemminkäinen was the person at the top of the procreation system in Paradise time, the All-Father of everyone on the planet. In this temple, Lemminkäinen exchanged 'offerings' with the so-called Rabi, who were all-fathers in the Ringlands outside Odenma.

"The Lemminkäinen Temple is the oldest temple on the planet and arguably the smallest, having been designed for only two people. It is literally a room in the bedrock. It has golden doors, and its walls and ceiling are also covered in gold. Back when it was still being used, the temple featured a golden divan under a golden Kupol ('dome').
The Lemminkäinen Temple was situated in the backyard of the estate where Ior Bock grew up. There was more, however. From the Lemminkäinen Temple, a corridor led towards the Bock family storehouse, also known as their treasure chambers."

I was happy to have finally met Casper. I'd travelled twice around the world to meet him, and it had been worth it. Any time I'd asked Ior a specific question about the Bock Saga, he'd always given me a monologue on a different subject than the one I'd asked about.
Ior seemed to have his own plan on what to tell whom and when. He was guided by ancient rules that had been handed down to him by experts in the oldest oral tradition on the planet. Casper, on the other hand, was an accessible euro-kid like me

and was happy to explain every detail he knew.

"The Bock family's treasure chambers are a conically shaped underground cavity which was created by centrifugal forces around the North Pole during the formation of the planet. During each Lemminkäinen's lifetime, a sal, or salon and two rooms were sculpted in the wall of this cavity. The treasures that had been sent from all over the world to Raseborg in appreciation to the boreal gods, were collected and brought to the sal by dragons (Drag-on, people carrying the treasures). In front of the entrance of his rooms, a life-sized golden statue of him as Lemminkäinen at the age of twenty-seven, was erected.

The storehouse was the Undervärlden, 'underworld', or 'wonderworld'. Countless generations created room after room, spiralling downwards following the conical shape of the cavity. The heathen people eventually reached rock bottom and then continued horizontally for some generations until it was impossible for them to create more additional chambers. This signalled the end of Paradise time with the First Ragnarök taking place, followed by the Altlandis, the Ice Age. The perpetual motion of the Wheel of Life came to a grinding halt and life on Earth changed dramatically.

There has been much speculation on the actual size of the storehouse. One theory goes as follows: if every Lemminkäinen of every generation had a room, and if, according to Ior Bock, there were more generations than people in modern-day Finland (circa 1987 AD) – which was about five million – there must be more than five million rooms in the storehouse. If each room is an average of two metres wide, there would be a path of 10,000,000 metres, or 10,000 kilometres on the inside of the conical cavity. The path with all the rooms would spiral down and even though each consecutive spiral would be larger and hold more rooms than the one above, there would still be a massive number of spiral turns indeed."

When Casper explained what we would find in the Bock family storehouse and how big it was, my mind was completely blown. I thought I had come here just for a party and to dig up a piece of wood that was somehow important for Ior's family. I now realised that Ior had given us just a sliver of the information that he had all along. The piece of wood was a door. The door was covered with gold leading to a temple of which the walls were covered with gold.

Behind the temple was the way to the largest cave of the planet. Many legends and mythologies around the world spoke vaguely about such a place in the north. But Ior was very specific. The entrance was just behind his house. I contained the accumulated treasures of all what mankind had produced in the very long period that was called Paradiset.

We were standing right on top of it. It was such a hard to believe outlandish concept, yet at the same time, it all sounded so logical. I believed every word. I didn't only believe it, I knew it. It was too logical not to be true. So much more logical and harmonious than the official stories from churches and scientists that we'd listened to all our lives. And I knew that we could soon prove it!

We were going to open the door to this temple, and from there, we would go through the corridor and see the greatest treasure that mankind had ever made. I was overwhelmed by the enormous magnitude of this information.

The most exhilarating and awe-inspiring part was that I would play a role in events that were much larger than myself and of a truly global scale. The entrance had been closed for a thousand years, and within a few days, some Goa freaks would open it again.

Casper

During the lead up to the magical day of the 24th of July 1987, more friends from Goa arrived. By coincidence, or maybe by Öde, there were exactly twenty-four people present the night before the celebration. Twelve beautiful girls dressed in hippie colours and twelve beach bums similarly dressed, all of whom were excited to be part of this magical gathering. Ior had also arrived, and we talked late into the night about what would happen and what we would do once the temple was open. Cliff compared our group to his flower of life paintings, with one circle in the middle and twenty-four around it.

Lola

We smoked many chillums and drank a lot of tea during that Finnish summer night that never got dark. We were all wizards and witches. We were beautiful and radiated energy from the sun that never sank below the horizon. When we were tired, we all slept together on the floor around the fireplace.

We felt part of a single organism that was big and strong and that had been there forever and would live until eternity and turn the world into paradise once again. We were the opposite of lonely and empty, which is how we'd all felt before arriving in Goa. We were going to jump together hand in hand into the greatest adventure mankind had ever experienced. We felt safe and complete, and we were so happy that the happiness flowed out of our ears, tears, and pores.

On the morning of the long awaited 24th of July 1987, we woke up and soon the room was filled with a chattering sound like that of hundreds of little birds. We were so positively excited. Casper made tea for everybody, and someone had gone out to buy cheese and bread from the Gumbostrand kiosk. We had our breakfast on the veranda, overlooking the Finnish gulf. The haze of the morning, which hid the myriad of little islands and rocks in front of us, slowly dissolved in the heat of the sun that walked slowly across the sky. The first joints were rolled, and their smoke followed the last tendrils of mist into the upper atmosphere.

Ronan

Ior had told us that the time to open the temple would be twelve noon. It was the time when the sun would be at the highest point towards the zenith. It was the time when Akka lifted her stick towards the sun in the Etta Stupa ritual. In pre-historic times, the rock next to the Etta Stupa had a sun dial on it that marked that exact moment.

Just before twelve, we walked together from the cabin towards the Etta Stupa. We kept so close together that we resembled a large millipede. Twelve girls and twelve boys and Ior Bock; we were about to witness a key moment in the history of mankind. From here on, everything would change radically. Paradise would come. We would prove that the Bock Saga and its mindset were true, logical and honest, which was actually the motto on the Bock family crest.

When we arrived at the spot, we spread out and sat on different rocks. Each rock had a name: Etta Stupa was the big and steep rock in the middle. To the right of the temple's entrance was the Auringonkellokivi, or 'clock stone', on the other side was Sibbo Berget, or Kypelli Vuori. From where we each sat, we could all see the slab of granite, approximately three by three metres in size, that lay central between the rocks.

Ior told us that the Bock Saga describes the situation as follows:

"First, there are 'sten slivor', the stone slabs. Behind these, a hallway leads to a 'water lock'. Then, we should find the golden doors to the left that are the entrance to the Lemminkäinen Temple. These lead to a corridor towards the Bock family treasure chamber, the conical-shaped cavity the top of which is right under the ancient North Pole. In addition to this, there should be two ventilation shafts that supply the treasure chambers with fresh air."

Chillums were lit as we sat looking at the large stone slab, wondering if we were about to experience an 'Open Sesame' moment. The sun travelled to the zenith, and nothing happened. The first questions were asked.

"Maybe because it's summertime, it'll happen an hour later?"

Yes, maybe. We waited another hour. Nothing happened.

"Maybe it's the wrong day?"

No, that was impossible, Ior assured us. It had to be now.

"Maybe we're supposed to dig the stone slabs out ourselves?"

Could this be? The moment of magic passed, and the first cracks of doubt appeared in the world vision that had glued our fates together. With these cracks, came the first jokes. But I knew in my heart that every word of the Bock Saga was true. It was just too logical not to be.

I looked Mr Yeah in the eyes. He was still a believer.

"It's not a matter of believing the Bock Saga for me, I simply understand it and know it's the truth!" he declared.

Casper, Cliff, and Ior all had the same expression in their eyes. But Mats was looking frantically from person to person.

"We've been cheated into this crazy story. Anyone who believes that a temple with golden doors will just suddenly materialise is crazy!"

This was exactly what all his friends at home had told him. He knew now they'd been right, and that they would take the piss out of him mercilessly for this. Mats looked at his friends and saw the same cracks of suspicion forming.

All the men were emotional, regardless of what they thought about the situation. The girls, however, took it in their stride. The Bock Saga is after all a male-oriented story full of dicks and pricks; that was how Ior had always presented it.

When he was asked to explain the female side of the story, he never went into any real detail. He always just said that it was similar for the ladies as it was for the men. Apart from a few little stories about Akka and Maija, he never elaborated further. So, it didn't really matter too much to the girls whether the story was true or not. Lola proposed to head back to the house for lunch. Everyone welcomed the idea, and we sauntered back. We all ate in silence, and the mood felt strange and confused.

What a stark difference from a few hours before. As we finished off our food, Lola stood up.

"Well, we're having a party tonight, right? We better start preparing for it!"

This was certainly something we all knew how to do. We'd had plenty of practice, after all. We spent the rest of the day painting the trees in fluorescent colours and setting up a sound system that consisted of many little sound systems borrowed from Finnish friends. That night, we had a great party and we danced for hours in the twilight of the Finnish summer. We paid our respect to Kristina Victoria. Like all great parties, it only came to a stop the next morning when the police arrived. We could have gone on forever.

The next day, those who wanted to continue putting effort into opening the temple gathered together to talk. A consensus was reached that the Bock Saga was true and not a fairy tale. It was now clear that we should stop treating it as such. The temple wasn't going to magically open on its own, we would have to do the heavy lifting ourselves. Yes, it was time to get practical. We walked to the site and looked again where this entrance to the temple could be exactly. It was granite all around. Mr. Yeah had brought a shovel en was poking around the bottom of the Etta Stupa where he and Lola had wheel barrelled out the mud and water. Ior had spoken about 'sten slivor', stone slabs.

"Look!" Mr. Yeah said, "This granite floor seems to have a rectangular crack around it."

I grabbed the shovel out of his hands and started shovelling the last remains of mud away. Around the cracks that Mr. Yeah had indicated, there was more mud. I got exited and began to dig it out. Lola rolled down the wheel barrel. The others got excited too. I got hot and took of my shirt. I dug deeper. Mr. Year and Casper were digging too with their bare hands. The shape of a granite rectangular stone slab became visible.

"It looks definitely man made!" I heard Lola say from above. She had climbed on top of the clock stone to get a better overview.

Some hours we worked like maniac ants to clear the stone slab. It measured about two and a half metres by one and a half. As more mud and earth from the sides of it disappeared into the wheel barrel, the shape became more pronounced. We could see that apart from it being flat and rectangular at the top, it had the same regular shape at the bottom. It was about a half metre thick. Under it appeared another similar stone.

We were so excited and happy. Ior had been right all along. Yesterday we had been so dumb to think that the temple would somehow excavate itself. No of course not. It was labour that was needed! Whatever the case may be: Soon the greatest treasure ever would be unearthed.

We walked back to the house to share the good news to our friends that were in various after-party modes. The news that we found the entrance set of another fresh party. People were cheering, there was music and dance.

We discussed the various ways in which we could lift out the stone slab. We soon realised that we would probably need to ask permission to the Museovirasto. They were after all the national Finnish Heritage Agency. Casper picked up the phone and asked them to lift the stones. They replied that they had no interest in doing so, but that we could do what we wanted; they didn't even care if we used dynamite to blast the stone away. They were convinced the Bock Saga was nonsense and we wouldn't succeed regardless of what we tried.

We decided that was actually good news. We didn't need this official scientific dust collectors dressed in suit and tie without any fantasy or flexibility in thinking. Öde had pointed to us to open the temple and we, the most unlikely group of Goa hippies, would exactly do that. Yippee!

I grabbed the phone and started calling people around the world to spread the good news. After I spoke to Goa friends who had gone home for the summer in their respective countries, being Japan, Australia, United States and so on, Casper warned me that the telephone bill would be out of our league.

"Just tell them to spread the news. We cannot pay for more calls. You just spend the amount of money for a business class ticket around the world."

"Don't you understand?" I told him happily, "Soon there will be no more money, no more debt, no more property. All that will be a laughable joke when the temple opens. It will be Paradise again. I cannot not spread the word that Paradise time is imminent!" I saw Casper looking worried. "Ok, just one more. I call Simon in Australia." I called Simon. He was in bed as it was in the middle of the night in Sidney. I told him that we found the temple and that he should come over immediately.

"I can't." He replied, "I am teaching in university in a couple of hours. My students need me."

"Simon, tomorrow there won't be a university anymore. It will be Paradise time. Get over here and help us digging!"

After the initial festive mood, we realised that we had some serious amount of heavy lifting in front of us. We calculated the stone slab's weight was at least four tons. There was no way that we could lift that out with muscle power. How those people had brought that stone there was a mystery. It was the same mystery as the pyramids and Stonehenge. We didn't have to solve that now. We just had to find a modern way of removing the stone and the one under it. We needed professional help.

We found a retired guy who'd been hacking through Finnish granite all over Finland and blasting rocks with dynamite while building the road system. He went by the applicable and prosaic name of Hakkolinen. He told us it would be far too expensive and risky to rent a crane and lift out the stone slab, especially since we had no idea how deep the stone went into the ground and how heavy it would be.

He proposed dynamite; so we bought dynamite. Hakkolinen drilled a deep dynamite-shaped hole in the stone with an enormous drill that violently spit dust around and chased away all the wildlife in the vicinity with its thunderous noise. From a distance, he exploded the dynamite.

When the dust had settled, we started to clear away the rubble with wheelbarrows. We drove them up the naturally shaped ramp and dumped the rubble next to the road. Under the pulverised stone slab, a second stone slab had appeared.

Again, Hakkolinen drilled a hole, inserted the dynamite, and exploded it. After clearing this new rubble, a third stone appeared. We repeated this process twice more. After clearing up the mess, we realised that the last explosion hadn't been into a granite slab, but into the bedrock. It meant we'd exploded one layer too many. We felt incredibly guilty, as Ior had often told us that the prehistoric Aser had never damaged or altered the bedrock, which was the body of Mother Earth.

We realised that from here on, we would have to excavate in a horizontal direction. We assumed that we'd find a door in the direction of Sibbo Berget, but this was a guess as there weren't a lot of clear instructions in the Bock Saga on this matter.

One evening, when everybody had already left the site, I was sitting alone at the bottom of the Etta Stupa absorbing the mystique of the place, when I discovered a straight horizontal organic clay groove at about two metres' height right under the Etta Stupa. I realised that under that enormous piece of rock was a fourth stone slab.

This one, however, wasn't lying flat in front of the entrance but was standing upright to form a kind of doorway. The door we'd been looking for was in a different direction than what we'd thought! This seemed like the most logical explanation. After long discussions with Ior, we decided to start digging this way instead.

Hakkolinen started drilling his usual hole. To his surprise, 120 centimetres into the hard granite, his drill suddenly hit something wet. It seemed that behind the slab of rock was some watery substance rather than more granite.

We were all extremely excited by this discovery. Could we finally be on the right tracks? Were we close to the temple that the Bock Saga described?

After the next explosion, we discovered that there was indeed some slushy material behind the now-blasted door-stone. We had a closer look at the wet material and touched it to feel its consistency. It seemed to be composed of ground granite (that Hakkolinen called 'rapakivi') mixed with some organic material and water. Its consistency was heavy, wet and mouldy. It resembled a dark variety of thick yogurt mixed with muesli. To our surprise, it hardened quickly; the whole wall of muesli and yogurt became rock hard within hours.

We didn't know what this was. Hakkolinen, who'd been blasting granite all his working life, had never seen anything like it. He was convinced that it wasn't a natural occurrence. In other words, it was manmade. It seemed that when the rapakivi and unknown organic material came into contact with the air and light, it hardened. We felt even more confident that the Bock Saga was true and had pointed us in the right direction.

What else could we do but drill holes in the now-hard wall of muesli? The drill spewed stones and dust as it twisted itself into the mountain. Soon we reached the wet muesli again. The holes the drill made into the muesli sagged and quickly disappeared. Hakkolinen had to drill a hole and immediately shove a stick of dynamite into it before it collapsed. It took a while, but eventually we managed to secure a couple of dynamite rods into the wall.

Hakkolinen hit the detonation button, but instead of the now-familiar *KABOOM*, all we heard was a wet, sticky sound. The hard part of the outer wall had come off in pieces of rock, while the substance behind it oozed out like melted ice cream. Within hours it had hardened again. What kind of tricks had these people laid on us a thousand years ago?

This work progressed slowly over several months. The days were getting shorter now, and the party crowd had long gone. Only the staunch believers were left: me, Casper, Mr Yeah, Cliff, Soma, GM and Andrew. All the girls had left. Ior was adamant that the temple had to be uncovered this year, although he wasn't often at the digging site. He was still working as a tour guide on Sveaborg and had not given up his formal life as we had.

I should probably introduce Andrew Higgins. He was one of the many eccentric people the Bock Saga had attracted. He'd studied as a lawyer but had never bothered to work as one. He came from one of those wealthy American families that were close to power. His father had been a financial lawyer for the White House during several administrations in the 50s and 60s. As a kid, Andrew had played in the oval office with the kids of secretaries of state and presidents. He told us how he'd played baseball on the White House lawn and how he and his friends had ventured into the secretive basement system below the main building. From a Bock Saga perspective: he was well connected. He joined the Bock Saga crew through Mr Yeah and Cliff in Hawaii and is probably one of the most egocentric people I've ever met.

Back at the temple site, our little group continued to make slow progress. To be honest, we were Goa hippies and not the best people for physical labour. We much preferred watching Hakkolinen, while coming up with ever more outlandish ideas on how to open the temple. And we smoked dope continuously, of course.

None of us had ever envisioned ourselves in a situation where we'd have to make decisions and organise dynamite explosions so as to open a pre-Ice-Age temple. We all had different ideas and opinions about everything we were doing. In hindsight, I think it's fair to say that none of us were really qualified enough for the task.

The only thing we did have in abundance was positive energy. We all wanted to do all we could to open the temple and change the world for the better. And there was nobody around to criticise or advise us. I can see how we might have looked extreme or fanatic to outsiders, but I think all we were was extremely dilettante, not fanatic. We were dedicated.

It was now towards the end of September. It was getting colder and rainier. The spot where we were blasting the stone slabs was filling up with water and mud again. And so was my mood. By this stage, I was flat out broke. I'd spent my entire fortune on dynamite and digging equipment. The winter was coming, and money or no money, there could be no digging during the Finnish winter.

Hakkolinen left. To my great astonishment, Ior also left for Goa with Soma. We now felt completely abandoned and alone. One by one, everyone else also started leaving. Casper went to Japan, Mr Yeah, Cliff and Andrew headed for Hawaii and GM left for Goa. I was the last one left in the now-silent house. I was scared I'd become stranded in Finland. I had to leave before the Finnish winter snowed me in. Mr Yeah had promised that he would pay me $5,000 if we hadn't found the temple by the end of the summer season. Thank God he kept his promise.

The gold dust that had covered my path for the last two years seemed to have blown away. Everything looked ragged and covered with normal dust now. I decided I needed some rest from the Bock Saga and thought that the best place to get this was in the most beautiful and peaceful island I'd ever known: Boracay. When I arrived, none of my usual friends were there, however, and with good reason. The typhoon season was still in full swing. I sat in a little bamboo hut for many days and nights, violently battered by the ferocious wind. The storm and rain easily pierced the walls that simply consisted of strips of bamboo. I sat shivering and lonely.

After the storms passed, the little island looked like one of those 'after-the-storm' scenes you see on the news: messy and chaotic. Luckily, the bamboo houses in Boracay were all built in a way that would allow them to withstand the most savage storms. There was no plastic around yet in those days. There were no streets, just footpaths and gardens and the beach, all of which were filled with fallen leaves and sticks and seaweed. The locals set out to clean their island. I was too depressed to do anything. I had to digest what had happened to me in the last year, what had happened in Finland and what the Bock Saga, or rather my belief in the Bock Saga, had done to me.

A couple of weeks later, some of the friends who'd been with me during the excavation arrived in Boracay. It was beautiful beach weather now. We rented little sailing boats with which we went on day trips to neighbouring uninhabited islands.

We were in paradise, but something had changed. We'd changed. We'd experienced something. GM, Malena, Casper, Mats and some other friends who knew the Bock Saga but hadn't been in Finland that summer were all there. We discussed what had happened endlessly and looked at it from every angle we could. We weren't virgins anymore, but we were still naïve, or at least some of us definitely were.

A multitude of feelings swarmed between us. There were strong doubts on the verity of the Bock Saga, the verity of Ior. Had he made up the whole story? It seemed too big a story to make up, especially if you considered the intricacy of the sound system. Had his mother and aunt made it up?

Maybe. The two little witches had been smart enough to do so. Was I angry at myself for being dumb enough to believe Ior and his thousand-year-old information on where the temple would be? A little, yes. And I was also angry at Ior for telling the story in such a convincing way and for letting us work like maniacs in the mud and rocks. And then he'd just left at the end of the season as if he'd had nothing to do with it!

We felt betrayed and abandoned. But what if the story was true, or at least partially true? Would we continue digging next year, or for many years after that? Everyone present had a different combination of each of these thoughts. Mats, GM, and

Malena didn't want anything more to do with the story. They didn't believe in it anymore and thought Ior had let everybody down when he'd left. They constantly made jokes about Casper and I and accused us of taking everything too seriously.

To be honest, I didn't know what to make of it all. To me, the Bock Saga was still a credible story. But the excavation was another thing altogether. And you couldn't deny that there were quite a lot of crazy people involved. The media aggravated the whole situation by constantly writing articles that didn't have even a trace of truth in them. I just wanted a break. The temple had been closed for 1,001 years now; it could surely wait another year.

I had other things on my mind anyway: sailing my little boat and partying at night. Suddenly, a Jewish princess named Tova came into my life. She was the most beautiful and pure girl I'd ever met. We fell in love immediately. She worked as a hostess in Japan like Casper's girlfriend, Susanne, and had come to Boracay on vacation. Because of her, I forgot what had happened the year before. She was an angel that came flying into my life. We lived a dream together in the pristine tropical paradise.

We got so lost in our dream that I forgot the golden rule of our lifestyle: make sure to always have enough money for a flight and a kilo of dope. But I cherished every second with Tova too much to interrupt our honeymoon for something as earthly as money.

I only realised what had happened when it was already too late. I was going to be stuck on Boracay and Tova was going to leave. But then my angel offered to lend me $3,000 that I could pay back a couple of months later, after a round of smuggling. I was surprised by her offer. She had worked hard to earn that money. We were very much in love, but we hadn't really known each other for that long.

I was terrified I'd destroy our bubble. If things went wrong, or even if things didn't go wrong, there was a risk that our dream wouldn't be pure anymore because of the stress and risk I would bring into our lives. I took her offer anyway. What other choice did I have?

With her money in my pocket, I travelled to Sagada in the north of the Philippines, where a strong strain of hashish grew. It was a dangerous place. The difference between the Philippines and most other South-East Asian countries is that the Philippines had been under the cultural influence of the Americans for a prolonged time; the most extrovert expression of this culture being the lethal combination of alcohol and guns. In Manila and Sagada, gun shots could be heard day and night. I bought my hashish in a shady bar. I paid and wanted to leave as quickly as possible.

"Have a beer with us," said the two heavily armed salespeople in a way that sounded more like a command than a suggestion. "Um... Yes, OK," was my rhetorical answer.

After a few beers, I finally left the bar and soon realised that my bag containing the hashish, my passport, ticket, and money had disappeared. You must be kidding me. My first thought was that it must have been the two salespeople, who were more like dangerous gangsters, let's be honest. Although I knew that the bar was probably not the best place to get into a fight, I had no choice but to head back and make my problem clear to the salespeople.

They were not amused, and an agitated stream of words in their language passed between them. At first, I assumed that I'd offended them and braced myself for the worse, but to my immense surprise, they genuinely seemed to want to solve my problem. One of the two told me not to worry. He explained that this bar was owned by the cops and that they would search and find my stuff. Stealing from cops or their clients was strictly forbidden. He offered me another beer and told me to wait.

A couple of beers later, police officers came into the bar with my belongings, including the hashish. They told me they'd found it in the house of the mother of a guy who'd left the bar while we'd been drinking our beer earlier. They apologised for the inconvenience and personally escorted me to my hotel. This was the first and last time in my life that cops went out of their way to protect me and even provided an escort to safeguard my hashish.

Once back in my hotel room, I prepared my usual shoes. This time, however, the shoes didn't look quite right. I'd put a large amount of hashish in their soles, and I worried that my feet were a bit too high up. I wore long trousers to try and hide this and glued an extra layer of imitation leather inside the shoes to make them look more professional. As a final precaution, I made sure one of the shoes had less hashish than the other. I thought that this would give me a 50/50 chance of passing a random check at security. When all was ready, I made my way to Manila.

There are many checks and hurdles to surpass in Manila airport before you can reach the safety of the plane. At one of these checks, two officers took me apart and searched me. The uniforms the officers wore symbolised the cruel treatment I'd be sure to receive if I was ever caught. I'd made sure to remove all traces of drug use and drug paraphernalia from my luggage. One of the officers asked me to stand up straight with my arms wide. He touched me everywhere and then started probing at my shoes. I was sweating all over.

"Take off that shoe," he ordered pointing at the shoe that contained the most hashish. I took it off and handed it to him. He took it in his hands, looked me straight in the eyes, smiled with only half his face and handed it back to me.

"OK, move on!"

In that terrifying moment, I'd been certain that my time had finally come. How could he have not figured out my trick? Or maybe he had and decided to let me go anyway? Maybe my path really was covered in gold dust. Maybe Öde still needed me to play a role in the Bock Saga. Could my luck with the police in Sagada also have been part of this plan? Unlikely, but still possible. Just as it's possible to win the lottery. I didn't know what had really happened or why. You can never be completely certain of what's really going on when in Asia. But I was ecstatic to leave the 'Wild East' unharmed. Half a day later, I arrived in Tokyo.

In Japan, I was able to sell my supply to the Yakuza who were happy to pay a great deal of cash for it. Within days, I was sipping champagne aboard a flight to Bangkok. From there, I went on to meet my angel on the island of Koh Phangan. We were so happy to be together again.

I'd brought a case of cassettes with the latest Goa-trance/techno music with me. I played it at a few parties. The music gave so much energy to the people on the dancefloor that they stayed up all night and danced until the sun peeked over the horizon. I felt that it wasn't too far-fetched to imagine a similar music used in prehistoric times during the rituals that the Bock Saga described.

The crowd was cheering, and I felt a new era was beginning, an era of positive energy, with or without an ancient temple! We had not yet been able to provide the world with proof that the Bock Saga was real, but at least I was able to give the world this ancient energy, the heartbeat of the universe!

I wanted to share the positivity I experienced through this newly invented style of music with the whole world. I was from Berlin, the walled city filled with fear. Maybe this positive dance music could bring down those walls. I still had friends who lived there, and I decided that I should spread some sunshine by bringing this new music to Europe.

The concept of making Goa-style parties in Europe was thus born while I sat under a palm tree with a beautiful princess at my side and loud music banging in our heads and a crowd going wild in front of us.

Before I brought the music to Europe, I had to first head back to Goa. Tova couldn't come with me because Israeli passport holders couldn't get a visa for India at that time. She went back to Japan instead. I never met her again. Even when I searched for her, I could never find her. Much later, I heard that after our affair she had committed herself to a monastery as a nun...

I arrived in Goa with Mats. The first thing he did was find Ior and yell at him for a couple of hours. He accused him of having abandoned his friends and the story he'd spent so much time promoting. He was completely fed up with Ior and informed him that he would have nothing more to do with either him or his Bock Saga. It had all been a dumb mistake and a waste of time.

I felt similarly, but I didn't blame Ior. He hadn't started telling his story and digging up the temple out of choice. He'd been put in this situation by his mother and aunt when they'd forced him to listen to the Bock Saga twenty years earlier. He'd never asked to be a guru; it had all just kind of happened to him.

Ior was often accused by outsiders of being the leader of a sect or some spiritual organisation. That had never been the case. Ior was just a normal human man who'd found himself in the position of being the only person left alive to know the prehistoric history of mankind. He'd never had a fixed strategy on how to proceed. All he'd ever wanted to do was tell his story to someone else and, if possible, find proof by opening up a temple and treasure chamber.

I understood all this, but I nevertheless felt the need to distance myself.

"Ior, I've had enough of this for now. I want to do other stuff like go to parties and organise parties to spread happiness on this planet. I won't be coming to your porch to listen to the Bock Saga anymore. Please leave me alone."

Casper

After leaving Hel that October in 1987, I went to Japan to meet Susanne. We went to Boracay on holiday together where we met our companions from the digging adventure. As you can imagine, the mood surrounding the Bock Saga and temple was not too thrilling. All that nervous, positive energy had leaked away into a pool of mud.

GM, Malena, and Mats no longer wanted to be involved. At best, they spent their time ridiculing the Bock Saga. At worst, their anger and belief that it had all been some scam concocted by the Bock family spilled over into rage.

After our holiday in Boracay, Susanne went back to Japan, and I flew to Hawaii on an invitation I'd received from Andrew. He organised a few gatherings with groups of people who were interested in hearing the Bock Saga, and I told Ior's story in a similar way to how he'd told it in Chapora in 1986. Another video was produced, this time filmed in the crater of the big Maui volcano.

With this new video in hand, I secured a deal with a film producer that was willing to pay three million US dollars up front to make a documentary on the Bock Saga and Ior. That money would buy us the opening of the temple, a total game changer.

When I arrived from Hawaii to Goa, I heard that Andrew had quarrelled with the film company, and they'd cancelled the deal. How could this have happened? For many years, we assumed that Andrew's legendary ego had destroyed the deal. Andrew had wanted to keep the rights to every expression of the Bock Saga. The filmmakers had to get his approval on every little thing they wanted to publish. We were convinced that he'd torpedoed our one chance to finance the opening of the temple. The whole Bock Saga group held a grudge against Andrew and his ego; some still do to this day.

Thirty years after the documentary debacle, William spoke to Andrew and agreed that he might've been right to cancel it. Making a movie's expensive, and the producers need to ensure it'll sell well. The filmmakers had wanted to change the Bock Saga here and there and leave out many parts that were considered taboo for the culturally sensitive American mind. Of course, it's impossible to change parts of the Bock Saga without changing its whole structure, just as you can't change laws of nature to please a religious organisation without compromising science as a whole.

But at the time, we felt that we'd missed a big chance to fund the opening of the temple. As part of his Bock Saga promotion, Andrew had sent letters to all the head of states around the world, including to the one in his native USA. In the spring of 1988, while we sat on Ior's veranda in Chapora talking about the Bock Saga as usual, a telegram arrived.

Ronald Reagan, the president of the USA, wanted to meet Ior Bock and have a sauna with him. What? Ior asked me to immediately renovate the antique sauna building next to the log cabin in Gumbostrand.

William

In the spring of 1988, Ronan seemed to have come to his senses again. He'd gone back to partying like he'd used to before this whole Bock Saga stuff. The Goa-trance music was changing by the season. It had become virtually only electronics now. Most of the lyrics were completely gone, which in my opinion was a good thing as no one really wants to hear melodramatic broken heart stories while tripping their heads off. Or worse, political stuff! The beats were getting faster. The whole music was being tuned to the Goa setting. We all loved it.

However, Ronan hadn't lost all his nervous energy. Even after the dramatic 'digging up a pre-Ice-Age temple to change the world' experience that had led to nothing, he still felt that it was his destiny to change the world. Now, he believed that he could do this through the Goa parties.

If you ask me, parties are made to be enjoyed, not to reach some political and philosophical goal or as a platform for preaching. Enjoy the moment, that's all. And these moments were getting better all the time as the parties got better. They were lasting longer too. They used to stop at dawn, but now they lasted until noon.

It was warm during the day, so the DJ would play slower, less energetic music when the sun spilled onto the dance floor. They thought that we couldn't handle the heat and that we were getting tired. We weren't. I loved it wild and fast at all times. If I got tired, I'd rest, drink water; If I got hot, I'd take a dip into the ocean. But when I was on the dance floor, all I desired was to lose myself in the loud, strong beats.

During this particular Goa season, Ronan had started talking about the 'perfect party'. He thought we should be the ones to organise it. It would start at sunset and last until the next sunset.

The perfect venue was found at the back of Vagator beach where a little stream flowed. This could be used to water the dusty dance floor. In addition, we would need to provide the public with shade during the daytime. This meant having to create some sort of sunshade apparatus that would cater for about 500 people. We would need good music that lasted for a full twenty-four hours, so we would need to ignore the complex DJ politics and steer clear from the common 'doing a friend a favour' attitude.

We decided that Mats, as the least social of our group, would be the least susceptible to any DJ attempts for favours, such as insisting to play at key moments of the party. The key moments, which are also often the best remembered ones, are of course sunset and sunrise when the energy on the dance floor surges.

I volunteered to make the sunshade. I knew it would probably be quite a difficult task, but at least it was only one task, and it meant that I wouldn't have to worry about all the other madness involved in organising a party in India. There were so many things to consider, like the police, baksheesh, and the locals, to name but a few.

Making a big shade, however, turned out to have its own complications. India had a closed economy, and all kinds of modern materials were not readily available, which meant my construction would have to be of the medieval kind.

Someone had once told Ronan that 'Vagator' meant 'bat' in English, so it seemed logical to him that the shade should be in the shape of a bat. That complicated things even further. After some thought, I envisioned a mathematical shape, like a wheel with spokes. I planned to only use half of the wheel shape and its centre would be high up in a palm tree. I'd make the spokes out of hemp ropes that reached down to the ground. Over these, I'd lay a giant bat-shaped cloth. A truly genius idea of geometric harmony, I thought, like the pyramids.

With a rudimentary drawing, I headed to the market in Mapusa. I bought an enormous amount of hemp rope and ordered a metal ring from the local blacksmith, which I would then tie the ropes to after having screwed it into the central palm tree. Then, I found a sewing shop and gave the owner my drawing and rough measurements for the fabric. I decided to use jute instead of light and colourful cotton so as to give the whole thing a prehistoric atmosphere. Lycra and nylons, which would have been even lighter and more colourful, were not yet available in India.

The sewer only had a non-electric sewing machine, as was the norm in India at the time. My vision would require hundreds of metres of stitching, after which, the enormous bat would need to be sewn onto the ropes. It was an enormous amount of work, and I had my doubts as to whether the skinny old Indian sewer with thick glasses was up to the task. But locals with their ancient technologies had surprised me with their ingenuity and persistence in the past by successfully completing what I thought would be impossible jobs. He told me it would be ready in a week.

When I came to pick up my sunshade, I found it folded into an enormous blob in front of his store. The deal I'd made with him and the supplier of the material and ropes had been based on the weight of the finished piece. Eight strong, skinny workers lifted the blob onto a scale. The weight was over 200 kilos.

I started to worry. I'd never once thought about the weight and how many kilos my central palm tree would be able to hold. After all, all that palm trees really are is a type of tall bamboo, which in turn is just a type of grass. How much weight could a blade of grass safely hold up?

I suddenly had the nightmarish vision of 500 tripping freaks trapped under a fallen medieval bat. I chased away the thought and decided to continue with my project regardless. I always had the option to cancel it if my doubts increased or if others strongly advised me against it. The workers lifted the blob onto a little truck and off we went to Vagator beach. There, they happily left me with the thing lying under my chosen palm tree.

If you've never had the pleasure of visiting Vagator beach, a short description might be useful. The ocean is to the west. The beach itself is a little bay, with rocks leading up to a mountain that stands about fifty metres high. All the way down this slope are steep terraces with palm trees.

Vagator is a perfect beach with fine sand to lie and to play on, and back then, it was filled with all kinds of freaks enjoying beach life. Along the beach's edge, at the base of the slope, were a few chai shops selling drinks and snacks, the roofs of which were made of woven palm leaves. Most of them provided palm-leaf-covered terraces where the freak population sat smoking their chillums, emitting enormous clouds of tobacco and hashish. The freaks here were mostly European with an over-representation of southern Europeans.

We had planned to have our party between the chai shops and the steep mountain behind them. Water oozed out of the rocks into a pool, and we presumed the water flowed underground through the beach towards the sea, as all water eventually does.

It was the start of March, and India was already warming up as it moved towards the summer period. It was noon, and I was already sweating in the sun as I stood next to the jute blob and my chosen palm tree. I had gone to the market early that morning to take advantage of the cooler temperatures, but it had all taken much longer than I'd anticipated and now it was hot, and I was sweating.

So. First thing first: how to raise the bat up the tree? I tried climbing up the palm tree imitating the technique I'd seen the coconut guys using countless times. It looked so easy, but it wasn't. I attempted it a few times, but the palm was too skinny, and the rings carved into the trunk were too irregular.

My actions soon caught the attention of a group of chillum-smoking Italians, who made no attempt to hide their laughter and idiotic remarks about my-less-than-impressive athletics. Luckily, a local coconut guy put me out of my misery by volunteering to help me for a small fee. Excellent.

He took the steel ring and a screwdriver with him and in a few seconds, he was up. He bolted the ring onto the top of the tree and came back down. I gave him the thick rope that was connected to the top of my bat. He climbed up once more and led the rope through another steel ring that was in turn connected to the main ring. He threw the loose slack back down towards me. In theory, if I now pulled the rope, the centre of the bat on its spokes would go up, allowing me to then secure the lower end of the rope-spokes to the ground with pegs before tying them to other palm trees in the vicinity. And *voila*, the bat would be up and ready for the party.

I started to pull the rope down to hoist the bat construction up. To my dismay (and great joy of my laughing spectators) instead of seeing my medieval bat rise gracefully to the sky, all

I was greeted with was a sad sagging of the palm tree. The bat was so heavy that its weight was bending the tree. My body was getting hotter from the exertion and so was my brain.

The coconut guy came once more to my rescue with a good idea. He was after all a palm-tree expert! We connected another rope to the ring in the tree and pulled it in the opposite direction, to force the tree into an upright position. It was like the mast of a sailing ship with rigging to counter the pulling forces of the wind in the sails. I hoped it was enough. I knew that once I'd attached all the ropes, the downward force on the palm's crown would increase. I'd chosen a strong tree, but would it be strong enough for my bat?

The two of us continued to struggle with the poor palm tree, which I imagine had had, up to that point, a good life with not much to worry about. As we concentrated on ropes and kilos of jute, while simultaneously trying to ignore the cynical and arrogant remarks coming from the very people Ronan insisted deserved the best party in the universe, a half-naked man came hurtling and screaming down the terraces of the Vagator mountain in our direction. In one hand, he was waving a large machete and in the other, a bottle filled with coconut feni.

This is one of the worst types of alcohol I've ever encountered in the world. It smells like benzene and is full of not only ethanol, but also methyl-alcohol, which is poisonous. The symptoms of this poisoning form a long list including blindness and erratic or aggressive behaviour, often leading up to delirium and severe organ damage. Many coconut guys drank it anyway, but their lifespan was shortened considerably because of this.

It was a frightening sight. The friendly coconut guy who'd been helping me translated what the angry, drunken, machete-waving man in front of us was yelling. It turned out that he was the owner of the palm tree we'd been tormenting. He demanded that we stop what we were doing immediately and provided him with adequate compensation for the damage we'd already done in bending and screwing a metal ring onto his beautiful palm tree. I hadn't even for one second stopped to consider whether the palm belonged to anyone. I'd been entirely focussed on the bat shade and the party and our holy mission of making freaks happy. The Italian spectators had now changed their tune and were shouting things along the lines of:

"Fuck the drunken guy! Chase him away!"

I realised that, as an entitled ex-colonial, I could indeed chase this man away, but that this wouldn't really be fair; it was, after all, his tree. And what if he refused to be chased away? That would put a damper on the 'perfect party atmosphere' and be a complete waste of my time. No, I decided to do what seemed to be the solution to most problems in poverty-stricken India: I offered the palm owner some money. At the end of the day, we weren't only damaging the serenity of his palm tree, but also inviting hundreds of freaks for a twenty-four-hour trip on his land without having asked permission.

I gave him a small (in my eyes) but substantial (in his eyes) sum, which the first coconut guy and my Italian audience thought was ridiculous. Now, I could finally turn my attention back to my bat.

My brain continued to boil in the heat of the day. Together with the two coconut guys, I continued to attempt hoisting the bat into the air. Our audience was not inclined to help whatsoever. Where were all the others that were supposed to be organising this perfect party?

As if she'd heard this internal plea, Lola came marching down the mountain. She looked fresh and strong. She rushed past me as if she didn't even know who I was, headed straight for the chai shop, and started cursing the Italian smokers in Spanish. You didn't need to be a linguist to understand what she was saying. She must have seen my struggle with the bat and the drama that had ensued, as well as the lack of support and abuse I'd received from them. She really went to town on them. It silenced the group, and they took off to the beach to play beach racket. Lola never even glanced at me.

"What a cool chick, but so unapproachable. I think that if she ever says something to me, I'll blush from ear to ear," I thought to myself.

The bat was now securely fixed to the top of the tree and the ropes hung down like the limbs of a dead octopus. I tied the spoke-ropes one by one as far from the tree as I could. I had envisioned a clean, geometrical, mathematical concept made from straight strong spokes unhindered by gravity and material flaws.

I hadn't realised that the hemp ropes would be a poor substitute for steel ropes and that the bat sewn on top of them would never stretch as beautifully as Lycra. We had to support the bat with sticks to ensure it would be high enough for people to stand under. It worked... but it certainly didn't look like a bat anymore. It made the whole space look like a prehistoric movie set. And that wasn't the worst of it.

The whole point had been to provide shade on the dance floor, some respite from the burning sun. But the jute was translucent, and the sun and heat that seeped through became trapped underneath it. Somehow, it even blocked the wind! Moreover, the bat exuded a permanent drizzle of dust that clung to your clothes.

Soon the sound system arrived, and a DJ booth was set up. To my immense surprise, everybody liked the weird blob that I'd built. Sure, nobody knew that it was supposed to be a bat, but then again, nobody knew that Vagator meant 'bat' in the first place. I was beginning to doubt whether it even did mean that. The party started at sunset. I was so tired that, instead of dancing, I sat myself outside the bat on a chai-shop mat and ordered chai and some food.

Lola walked up to the mat I was sitting on and appraised me with a judging eye before sitting down beside me. I tried to make some small talk, but I was shy; she was so beautiful and strong, and I felt so smelly and sweaty. I thanked her for the support she'd given me earlier that afternoon. My body felt weak and broken after the day's physical exertion, but as soon as Lola was close it became restless and nervous.

"Do you want to dance?" I asked.

I thought this could be my way out. We'd dance, after which I was sure she'd soon disappear into the crowd, and I could go home and get some sleep. So much for the perfect party.

"No way. Can't you hear what's playing? It's horrible," She was right. I have no idea who Mats had given the honour of playing the first set to, but it had been a poor choice.

"Maybe it'll get better later in the night," I replied.

"You look tired, are you sure you don't want to sleep for a few hours? It's your party after all. Shouldn't you enjoy it?"

"Sleep sounds pretty good to me."

"Let's go, you can sleep at my place. I'll even give you a massage to help you fall asleep."

I hoped the dust and sweat were enough to hide my glowing cheeks.

After a beautiful night, which even included a little sleep, I realised that it had been the perfect party; at least it had for Lola and me. We did eventually go back to the real party, as I needed to know whether my bat had survived the night. I was immensely relieved when I saw that everything had gone fine. We danced and partied the rest of the day, all beautiful and happy, enjoying the psychedelic, galactic, transcendental, spacy opera until the sun turned red and hit the horizon again. After the echoes of the last neurological psychonautic hallucinogenic soundwaves disintegrated into quantum particles, I joined a chillum circle made up of the party-organising crew.

"What a great party," Mats sighed. "It went by like a hypnotic dream."

"I loved the fluorescent sunlight filtering through the palm trees and the fluffy clouds above; the smell of body sweat mixed with incense and the sap of watermelon dripping from my mouth," Lola joined in as she sat down beside me.

We all agreed.

"I'm seriously spaced out," one of the DJs, Moon Juice, seemed to be sleep talking. "I mean, it was cerebral, mystical, a transpersonal configuration of merging fates into a constellation of zodiacally extrapolating infinity into time telescopy, if you know what I mean."

"A party for the history books," I remarked.

"Yes, but quickly forgotten," Ronan declared.

"What? Why?"

"Because we're going to make much better parties. I agree that it was great, but we can enhance the effects."

"When you say 'better', do you mean technically better?" I asked.

"Experience-wise, this was crystalline perfection," Mr Yeah smiled as he passed the chillum to his right.

"And if you want complicated effects, you'll have to head to Europe. There's not much more you can do here," I told Ronan.

"I've thought of this already. Amsterdam's the best place to try it. It's the most tolerant city I know," he replied.

"Foreigners always think that, but it's only because they

don't understand the language. I'm telling you; Amsterdam's not tolerant at all," I warned.

"How can you say it's not tolerant, if it's the only place on Earth where smoking dope is legal?"

"It's not legal. They just don't care enough to stop it from happening."

"Well, that makes it a tolerant place then."

"You can do anything you want in Amsterdam. The trick is not to bother anyone. The Amsterdam people are only tolerant if you don't disturb them."

"What about a psychedelic acid party?"

"As long as you don't keep half the city awake, like we do here, I guess you could probably get away with it."

"It'll be a whole different trip than what we have here, Ronan, with the whole money wheel thing to consider," Mr Yeah cut in.

"Why can't we just enjoy the life we have already? We party here and work there. There's nothing wrong with that," said Lola haughtily.

"Because we have the opportunity to introduce these fantastic parties to the Europeans and brighten their lives. We could even make a living from it!"

"It'll cost a lot of money..." I muttered, passing him the chillum.

"If we don't try, we'll never know," Ronan persisted. "It might solve our money problems and we might never have to smuggle dope again."

"Come on Ronan, you can't seriously be considering blemishing these beautiful pristine parties with money. You risk reducing them to a commercial trap," Mr Yeah warned, shaking his head gravely.

"No. We would never compromise beauty or psychedelics, that's the whole point. We're the good guys and we'll be doing the right thing!" There was no talking him out of it.

"I hope you're all in."

"What do the planets say?" Lola asked Moon Juice.

"Mundane astrology suggests a quadruplicity of Saturn dynasticity in combination with a cerebral stellium of Jupiter, which obviously enhances the Ptolemaic aspect of the interrogational hypsoma in Mercury. It's all very clear."

We all stared at him blankly.

"So... what you're saying is that the planets love parties?" Ronan grinned.

"Apollo and Aphrodite love parties," Lola whispered in my ear.

"Ok," I sighed. "I guess it's decided then. Let's organise a trance party in Amsterdam."

"This calls for another chillum!"

Casper

Ronald Reagan was set to meet his Russian counterpart, President Gorbachev, in Helsinki in the early summer of 1988. At the same time, he'd asked to meet Ior. The newspaper headlines read: 'Ronald Reagan to meet Father Christmas in Helsinki!' In the spring of 1988, I flew to Helsinki and started working on the sauna at the Bock family estate, as I'd done the year before on the house. The sauna was in reasonable condition, but it needed some love to bring it up to presidential level. It was hard to imagine Ronald Reagan coming to have a sauna here. He was a prude American, and I couldn't picture him being comfortable with other naked men in a damp room. But that was what the message had said, and it had later been confirmed by an American official from the embassy. They asked us to be discreet about where Reagan was to meet with Ior.

We also heard that it was the first lady, Nancy Reagan, who'd pushed her husband on the matter. She'd read one of the letters Andrew had sent the White House, that had included a rough summary of the Bock Saga. In it, he'd explained the mythological/historical story of how Lemminkäinen had fled to the north of Finland in the year 1050 AD, how he'd travelled in a sled pulled by reindeers, and how he'd then become known as Santa Claus. She was thrilled to meet Ior Bock, the current Santa Claus, whose ancestors had been Santa Claus before him and had lived in the Kola peninsula area.

She probably didn't understand much else about the Bock Saga, but the Santa Claus story was enough to grab her attention. That's how it is for most people who are interested in the Bock Saga. They hear parts of it, without really understanding the bigger picture, but then at some point, the story begins to make sense and invokes an 'Aha' moment. From there on, they're gripped. That's what had happened to me, to all my digging friends and it was possible that the same would happen to Nancy Reagan.

She always struck me as quite dim and completely out of touch with reality when she appeared on TV. She'd started the whole 'Drugs? Just say no!' campaign. As if just saying no could solve the complex socio-political relationship between people and drugs. Her campaign started the world-wide war on drugs that lasted decades, with hundred thousands of people losing their lives and millions spending their lives in jail. But by then, I also knew that the image delivered to the public by the media was often distorted.

Better meet Ronald and Nancy in person and reserve judgement until then, I thought. Nancy probably hadn't watched the Hawaii video of Ior telling the Bock Saga in full, or at all, and had just flashed on the Santa Claus part of Andrew's letter.

When all the work on the sauna was finished, we received a message informing us that the president and his wife would not be visiting after all. Some strings had been pulled by Nukke Mestari, the puppet master of Raportti Media and the Finnish government, who forbid any promotion of the scandal ridden Ior Bock and his disruptive Saga. Well, fine. We just went on with our business, lit the fire in the renovated sauna and enjoyed a sweaty evening with friends. A few Finnish newspapers that didn't belong to Raportti Media reported the headline: 'Ronald Reagan has been forbidden from meeting Father Christmas by the government of Finland!"

It was possible that Ronald and Nancy actually did discuss the Santa Claus story with Mr and Mrs Gorbachev, because after their meeting, the Russian Pravda requested information from us and published a few articles about the Lemminkäinen Temple. They were one of the few newspapers that reported the story as we had told it to them. For them, it was a matter of facts, rather than politics or emotion.

All these happenings weren't of great importance to us. What was important, was that we continued with the excavation that summer. To begin with, we needed to pump the melted snow and rain out of the hole in the ground under the Etta Stupa. This took a week. It was at this point that the deal with the American film company fell through. The Goa boys were broke. Ior asked an old friend of the family for help. This friend was the director of the Sibbo Sparbanken, a local bank that was part of a larger banking corporation. His name was Hans C. Andersen; the same name as the writer that had collected hundreds of fairy tales from northern Europe 150 years earlier. Hans Andersen and Ior sealed a deal by handshake, agreeing that the Sibbo Sparbanken would sponsor the excavation of the Lemminkäinen Temple.

Once the excavation was successful, there would be enough treasure to pay back the cost of the digging. The next day, it was in all the newspapers. Ior directed any curious journalists to me, and I sat with them on several occasions to explain the Bock Saga. I was used to the facts in the Bock Saga by that stage in my life, but it still baffled me how much of an emotional encounter it always was for Finnish souls.

Excerpt from the Bock Saga:

SANTA CLAUS
In the turbulence of the Third Ragnarök, the Bock family somehow managed to escape the wrath of the invaders. King Seppo and Queen Maija fled to Kajaani, 500 km north. It was a safe place. Surrounded by forests and swamps, it was too far and difficult for the Catholics to attack.

The father and mother of Lemminkäinen – Ukko and Akka – fled together with Lemminkäinen and the rest of the family, even further north to Korvatunturi in Lapland. One can still find it on the map; its main advantage being that it is extremely remote. There, they settled for the next 200 years.

Ukko, the All-Father, who previously used to travel around Odenma in a carriage pulled by eight bocks, was now seen getting around in a sled pulled by eight reindeer. Although the Catholics destroyed Hel and burned the rest of Odenma to the ground, the legend of 'Father Christmas' was very hard to uproot.

The stuff the reporters wrote down was usually a distorted version of what I'd told them. I do get it though, it is hard to believe a story of the dimensions and time frame of the Bock Saga, especially its description of the Bock family treasure chambers.

A description of an enormous conical-shaped space with all the accumulated treasures of mankind from before the Ice Age is like the description of the underworld in Egyptian and Greek mythologies.

Somehow, it was simply implausible for the Finnish press to believe that anything of that importance would ever have happened in a place like Finland. I guess that living in Finland during the 1980s and 1990s made such a thing quite hard to imagine, yes.

Yet again, strings were pulled by Nukke Mestari, and Hans Andersen was forced to change the deal he'd made with Ior. The bank would no longer sponsor the excavation but would finance it through a loan; Ior's estate would be the collateral. Ior signed the papers without much thought. He was convinced that there would be a result soon and everything would be financially secure.

A short while later, Hans Andersen lost his job as director and the new bank director transferred Ior's loan to another local bank, Alland Sparbanken. It was also a local bank, but because it was based in Allan (an island between Finland and Sweden) there was no real affinity between it and what was happening on the other side of the country.

In the meantime, Hakkolinen and his two helpers kept chomping away at the mountain. The work was slow. Hakkolinen was a strong guy, but not a sorcerer. There were many tonnes of granite, rapakivi and strange slush that needed to be removed from the hole. The bank loans were mainly meant to cover Hakkolinen's wage, the dynamite he used and the rent of the diggers.

It wasn't long before the Alland Sparbanken wanted their money back. The original deal with Hans Andersen had been that the money would only be paid back when the temple had been successfully opened. This turned out to be a fairy tale.

There was one way out. Ior had inherited two large Ehrensvärd paintings that were worth millions of dollars. He had planned to donate them to the National Museum, where they belonged, being national treasures. Apart from being a gifted painter, Ehrensvärd was also the architect of Sveaborg, the place where Ior worked as a tour guide. Now they came in handy.

We went to the art dealer Bukowski in Helsinki and offered

the paintings as collateral. We urgently needed $30,000 to pay off the bank loan, and to pay Hakkolinen for the rest of the season. Bukowski paid us that amount without a second thought. Oh, how dumb and naïve we were. We assumed that when the $30,000 was finished, we could go back to Bukowski and get some more. The paintings were so valuable, after all, and he could hang them for free in his shop and enjoy the status that accompanied such priceless assets. Ior and I had no idea about money matters and how the world turned in that respect.

The next time we approached Bukowski for money he said that he'd already given enough. We were in shock. We'd seen him as a friend, and we knew that the paintings were worth a lot more than the money we'd gotten for them. Later, he even cast doubt on the authenticity of the paintings. That was malicious. Anyway, that first $30,000 got us through that summer.

Ronan passed by a few times to sell his valuable sandals. He only visited Ior once in his town apartment and stayed with me in Gumbostrand. Although he remained aloof, he couldn't resist listening to the latest details of the Bock Saga I'd been absorbing from Ior since the previous October. Ior had continued to tell the Bock Saga to whomever was present. In return, Ronan told me about the Goa parties he and the others had been organising in Amsterdam.

Ronan

After the previous year's tumultuous summer, I'd fallen into a big dip. But my depression came to an end when I realised that I could receive and spread positive energy through the propagation of Goa-style parties. I realised that Goa was not the only setting where these therapeutic tripping parties could work. With William and Mats, I'd organised a fantastic prototype party in Vagator. We'd added many little details to enhance the whole experience. It had been a lot of work, but I was sure the party would go down in history.

I was more certain than ever that I could bring this style of party to Europe and decided Amsterdam was the perfect place to start. We had good contacts with the Balloon Company, who had their own village just outside Amsterdam. They'd been the 'studio audience' at the recording of the first Bock Saga video in Chapora, and they had a lot of experience in conscience-expanding experiments. Rudolf, the uncrowned mayor of the village, loved the idea of organising the party in the village church. What a perfect setting!

However, there were some doubts within the village as to whether such a large party was actually a good idea. They were afraid that their little village would be overrun by tripping heads, and that the music would attract the attention of the police. We sent William out on a diplomatic mission to persuade these doubters. After all, he spoke their language and knew their culture and sensitivities.

These diplomatic missions required William to endure tarot card readings with esoteric know-it-alls (William: "These goddamn cards can be read in any kind of way you want...") and to talk with farmers who hated anything and anybody from the outside, because 'nothing good comes from there anyway'. In the end, we got the required unanimous permission.

There were two Goa DJs involved in the project: Moon Juice from Australia and Sunscribe from Holland. Moon Juice's Japanese girlfriend, Akiko, created a trippy forest from the simplest materials available: cardboard boxes that she ripped apart and painted with fluorescent pigments. Lola, who was now William's girlfriend, painted like a maniac for a month to produce a fluorescent painting that was eighty metres long and covered all the walls. We'd turned the church into a psychedelic paradise!

We called our company 'The World Beat'. Our mission was to make the whole world beat. The deal we all agreed to was that everyone would pay an equal share of the costs up front. After the party, we would count what was left and share it out equally. Just a few days before the party, Moon Juice and Akiko told us that they weren't going to be financially involved anymore. That meant that William, Lola, and I would have to shoulder the entire financial burden.

What complicated matters further was that the concept of an all-night, acid, trance, techno party was unknown in Amsterdam at that point, making the party quite difficult to publicise. The people we were promoting the party to were very unclear on what it was that we were proposing. I decided that we needed to at least make it easier for the people of Amsterdam to travel to the village, which lay ten kilometres outside the main city. We rented a coach so that we could provide a free shuttle service that ran every hour. That drained our finances quite a bit.

The night of the party arrived, and we were completely exhausted from the effort it had taken to organise it. But as people started streaming in and the beats began their stomping crescendo, a new energy took hold of us. We could already tell that this event was going to be truly special. It was going to be the Woodstock of Goa trance; a first-man-on-the-moon experience.

Moon Juice and Sunscribe played perfectly, and the psychedelics dripped from the ceiling and walls. We were used to trippy parties in Goa, but this psychedelic environment had so many added dimensions, it was beyond what a person could imagine. The guests, who'd had no idea what to expect, were blown away. A new star had appeared on the firmament.

It was a beautiful night all round. That is, until Rudolf took several pieces of firewood from an enormous stockpile that had been collected to heat the church and all the houses of the village during the coming winter. The stockpile had the shape of a round pyramid and was about two floors high. Rudolf made a small bonfire with his logs, as was the custom at nightly events in the village.

Don't ask me how, but the great stockpile suddenly caught fire and soon the flames spewed higher than the church tower into the night sky. It radiated an intense heat, and all the tripping people ran out of the church in awe and fear. Within fifteen minutes, the fire brigade had arrived and saved the church from melting by spraying an avalanche of water over it. What a drama; what to do?

"Let's make the music louder," someone suggested.

Good idea! The dramatic and beautiful optical event had raised everyone's spirits and the huge group continued dancing in a psychedelic spiritual frenzy. Yes, this party had quite the impact! We had planned to continue until sometime the next morning, possibly noon, but like all good parties, it was stopped by the police in the early morning. It took William quite a lot of diplomatic effort to convince the police not to confiscate our sound system.

No one could deny that we'd set a great example for others to copy. Although, we did have to pay for about a hundred cubic metres of firewood and for the efforts of the fire brigade. All in all, we lost a lot of money. But we now knew that it was possible to organise a party of this kind! Sure, we still needed to fine-tune some of the details to avoid further bankruptcies, but that was to be expected.

William had had enough, however. He was broke. In later years, he proclaimed that the decision not to continue the party company 'The World Beat' was financially the most stupid decision he'd ever made. When we came back the following year after another Asian winter, a party company calling themselves the 'Beat Club' had filled the gap we'd left. They were doing parties every weekend in the various squat houses and warehouses in and around Amsterdam. They didn't bother with decorations. Music and drugs were their recipe. They made a huge amount of money and later evolved into a global party corporation that was sold to a hedge fund for $120 million.

I covered my debts in the usual way by buying hashish and sandals and flying to Helsinki. Later that season, I organised another party with other Goa friends in an Amsterdam squat called the 'Hemelvaart'. That was another great party. There were fewer costs this time and we once more used Lola's painting skills to decorate the venue.

This time, we made some money. Apart from the excitement of being at the forefront of a new, fast-evolving culture, I loved the idea of being able to earn a living by making other people happy and the world a better place. The definition of 'better' had become clearer to me since I'd learned about the Bock Saga. Generally speaking, 'better' was everything that resembled Paradise.

For William, 'better' was sharing his bed with Lola. I tried to explain to him that she was not a girl one could keep.

"Just enjoy the moment, and afterwards, enjoy the memories."

As I'd foreseen, the day came when she disappeared, and William was in tears. It took him a while to accept it all, and I think getting a new girlfriend helped.

Casper

The summer of 1988 had a quiet start. A few Americans, like Andrew, Cliff and Mr Yeah, continued listening to Ior by dividing their time between his town apartment and cabin in Akanpesa where the digging was still happening. Some friends from Goa visited, then left and then visited again. Some Scandinavian people also attached themselves to us. Ior followed the principle of: 'nobody invited, everybody welcome'. In this way, a growing number of people came to know the details of the Bock Saga. The Finnish general public continued to only know us through the constant stream of scandals we left in our wake.

Through the via-via group, a young photographer called Petri arrived at our door. He told us he'd heard of the Bock Saga and was interested. He'd listened to many hours of his friends talking about it, so he had a rough knowledge of the basic concepts. He asked if he could take pictures of us, the excavation of the Lemminkäinen Temple and the estate. Ior gave him permission to do as he pleased.

After he was done, he sat down with us to have tea and a talk. Ior asked him, as he always did with newcomers, what his grandfather's name was.

"Well," the photographer replied, "my grandfather has the same last name as I have, obviously. That name is Hellesvor."
Ior told him this was neither a Root name nor a Van name. It was a constructed name.

"What do you mean by constructed?"

There are two languages spoken in Finland. In the south of Finland, people speak Finnish-Swedish. In the Bock Saga, this is called Root and is spoken by the Aser, who lived in that area. Nowadays, for most non-Finnish-Swedish speaking people in Finland, who see the Swedes as colonial conquerors, this is the language of their former rulers. The other language in the Bock Saga is the Van language, made by the Aser for the rest of the planet. In modern times, this is called Finnish.

The Finnish nation has been independent from their former rulers Sweden and Russia for a hundred years now. Both these ruling nations had fought many wars against each other for Finland. Since independence, the Finnish language has been bit-by-bit replacing Finnish-Swedish as the main language and the language of bureaucracy. All the Finnish-speaking people who'd come from the forests after independence, felt like they were taking back their country by speaking Finnish. But as the Bock Saga explains, they never spoke Finnish in the first place. The exact opposite is true: the Swedes have the Finns from the south of Finland to thank for their language.

All this resulted in a situation, halfway through the 20th century, where people with Swedish-sounding names had less chances to advance in life than those with Finnish names. This, in turn, resulted in people with Swedish names changing their names to Finnish or German ones, or to non-descript names as was the case with our new friend Petri Hellesvor.

Petri was surprised to hear this and decided to ask his father, who was a university professor, if he knew more about it. After a couple weeks, Petri returned.

"I spoke with my father about the name change. My grandfather changed the name from Helström to Hellesvor sometime in the 1930s."

"Helström is actually a very old and aristocratic name in the Bock Saga. It means the stream from, or to, Hel. It is on the same level as Raström and Boxström," Ior explained.

"That's so exciting! I want to change the name back. Hellesvor is such an ugly name, and now I've found out it's also meaningless. I'm a Helström!"

"You should be careful with such things," Ior warned. "Sometimes, it brings nothing good to change it back."

"That's what my father said too. I had long arguments about it at home."

"You see, it creates disharmony."

But Petri was adamant that he wanted to change it.

"There can be all kinds of side effects that you can't foresee," Ior warned again. "Let it go, Petri. What's in a name anyway?"

Petri returned several times to Gumbostrand to enjoy our company and listen to the Bock Saga. He mentioned that he'd had screaming fights with his father, whose career also depended on the Finnish-sounding name.

It was difficult for us outsiders to understand what the big commotion was all about. But then again, there're many places in the world where competing tribes fight for control. That's what newspapers are full of everyday. We hadn't seen Petri for a while, when on one day there was a knock on the door.

"Open Up! It's the police!"

To our surprise it was a homicide squat. Petri had been murdered and there was strong suspicion that we'd had something to do with it. They told us that he'd been found cut up into pieces in a room in his apartment. In this room, he'd been growing weed under lamps, which was illegal. The pieces of the body had been packed into plastic bags, and this was what had brought the police to us.

This line of thought surprised us. They'd somehow made the connection between Petri's homicide and the story of the dead monkey, which had also been cut up and packed into plastic bags. There was also the fact that Petri had visited us several times.

What a far-fetched association! The burned monkey affair had really nothing to do with us, but the newspapers had been so full of that story two years previously and had made such a big deal connecting it with Ior Bock and pagan rituals. I really had no idea who'd murdered the talented photographer.

The only person I could think of as having had a motive was his father. Ior wasn't with us when the police came to Gumbostrand; he was in his town apartment, where he too was visited by the police. When I spoke with him on the phone later that evening, he'd had the same feeling about Petri's father as I'd had. But the case was never resolved.

The police had also been looking for a guy called Carry that had been marked as a suspect. Carry visited us frequently; he was a gypsy. He was also one of the 'via-via, nobody invited, everybody welcome' types. Carry divided his life equally in and out of jail. He was always involved in little crimes like stealing, fraud, and all other kinds of little manipulations of the truth. But anytime he was around, he was always sympathetic, charming, and helpful. He provided a local anything-you-need services.

The usual situation that arose involved one of us giving him money to buy dope, tools, food, or alcohol, after which he would leave and not show up again for a considerable amount of time. We spent more time waiting for Carry to deliver our desired objects than we spent with him.

When he returned, he always had an unbelievably complicated story that explained exactly how it was that he'd surfed the waves of danger, or fought some conspiracy, all in the name of our required item, which he promised he would bring soon. And if he did then produce the item, it always ended up being more expensive than it had been initially. He always tried to make you feel lucky to be in his company.

Ior had known his father, who'd been killed in one of the many vendettas of the gypsy families in Finland. According to gypsy tradition, the murder of a father had to be avenged by the son, and in this case that was Carry. This particular vendetta had already cost the lives of many gypsies over several generations and there was no end in sight.

Carry was afraid, because he knew that if the revenge was carried out, he would then be the subject of the next step in the vendetta. He knew that even in jail he wouldn't be safe. But it was his family destiny and he'd have to eventually comply. One night, he even tried to steal dynamite from our store. His plan was all too obvious, however, and he was caught by an angry Hakkolinen, who called the cops. He was then arrested by the police, who were not at all charmed by the dynamite-stealing, vendetta gypsy story.

Carry's shady dealings and the fact that he'd often associated himself with our group at Gumbostrand, made him an obvious suspect within Petri's case in the police's eyes. However, he just wasn't to be found. The police never thought to look for him in jail, which is where he turned out to be. But by that point, he'd already been acquitted.

As you can imagine, the Raportti Media newspapers revelled in yet another opportunity to write about an 'Ior-related' scandal. And they did, for weeks to come. They connected the story with many later-retracted suspicions, as they always did. They embellished the murder story and connected it to Ior, plastic bags, paganistic burned monkeys, the production of weed and dynamite-stealing gypsies. They of course later forgot to mention that Ior had been cleared of the whole case. Again, Ior was at the heart of a scandal that had nothing to do with him. And there was nothing we could do about it.

While the Scandinavian media demonised Ior and cast a sinister light onto his Bock Saga, there were a few people who were quietly interested in him but preferred to stay out of the limelight. They were the monarchs of Norway, Sweden and Denmark. They were curious about what the Bock Saga said about their past, their ancestry and their former role in society.

They had access to a lot more information than the average civilian had and could connect the dots. The monarchs shared a lot of knowledge about the past within their families, knowledge that was not always shared with the commoners.

The king of Norway, especially, took time every year to visit Ior and request his presence as his personal 18th century tour guide during self-organised tours of Sveaborg. The truth was that during these tours, which often also involved other royal members, it wasn't 18th century history that was discussed, but the so-called prehistory outlined in the Bock Saga. Sveaborg was the location of Valhalla, Asgord and Hel. No journalists were invited to these events. Not that you could even call them such. From the outside, it just looked like a group of friends walking around a historical attraction while enjoying pleasant conversation.

Apart from Ronan and the royals, there were other people who also frequently visited Hel and Gumbostrand. It became common knowledge within the Goa group that Finland was a good place to sell hashish. More and more frequently, friends that were interested in the Bock Saga passed by and brought a kilo of dope to sell.

Wessel was one of them. He passed by with increasing amounts of hashish. The weird, six-foot-tall monster of Frankenstein lookalike had already joined the group the previous year and had returned this summer too. He always seemed to walk with his head lost in a dark cloud. He had a gruff heavy voice and always wore a dark expression in his deep-set inky eyes.

Being in the same room as him was like starring in a monster movie.

He spoke a lot about all kinds of conspiracy theories, all of which he linked to extremely precise numbers. I think he believed something was true if a precise number could be linked to it. I guess that's why everyone started calling him '2.2'. That was his approximate height in metres.

Out of everyone who joined the Bock Saga group, he looked the most satanic, but in reality, he really wasn't that evil. Sure, he did lie and cheat Ronan out of money one time, but that was about it. There were people within the via-via group that happily bought the hashish for extremely high prices. Cash on delivery. As well as being the centre of Bock Saga activity, Ior's household soon also became a dope-dealing centre. People came to view the estate, and especially the living room with its roaring fire, as a sanctuary for hashish smoking.

Let's not forget that it was highly illegal to smuggle, own and use any kind of drugs in Europe at that time. The laws in Finland were the same. Before our group had arrived, drugs had never been a problem in Finland; they were seen as an American problem, or maybe a Chinese one.

The Finnish population had the impression that nothing ever happened in Finland, which was mostly true, and there were no signs of the local youth using drugs. This view started to slowly change when officials or journalists were welcomed by hazy clouds of exotic smelling dope when they visited the Bock family estate.

Smoking cannabis was allowed within the logic of the Bock Saga. People had always smoked dope in history. Hashish is a natural product. The Bock Saga made a strict distinction between nature and concentrated nature. Hashish, mushrooms, wine, beer and all other kinds of herbs were natural. They were considered good. Concentrated substances such as heroin, cocaine, MDMA, other chemicals and strong liquor were not approved of.

According to the Bock Saga, this had been the understanding and rule of thumb since the first people on the planet were born. In modern times, however, the rule of law thought differently, and a lot of propaganda was created to enforce this idea. Those who didn't listen went to jail. People that were not from Goa or the via-via group were shocked at what they saw in Gumbostrand. They spoke about it at home and at work, and soon the news spread that the pagans had drug rituals. Illegal drug rituals, that is.

Some might have spotted the dark clouds forming high in the sky over the Akanpesa house, but if they did, they didn't act on it. The Akanpesa house made us feel safe, we felt we were being protected by laws that were ancient and just. The estate in Gumbostrand was a sanctuary that had been founded by the holiest people on the planet during a time were everything was right in the world. This time was called Paradiset.

Nothing could happen to us. And anyway, we were all on the brink of proving the Bock Saga, of opening the temple; a new world order and a new way of thinking, which was the oldest way of thinking, would prevail. And we were all making money from the hashish, and we were all stoned. All except me. I was never stoned, and I took note of the foreigners coming in with ever larger amounts of hashish. Unlike them, I spoke the local language and I understood the sensitivities of this society; it was clear to me that this could not go on forever.

I knew that the people in the neighbourhood who led normal lives and went to work every day would start asking questions. How can these freaky looking people who are doing nothing visible to earn money live in this way? How can they fly all over the world, go to India and not work there either? They thought that you had to be extremely wealthy to live like us.

But we didn't look wealthy at all. Maybe colourful, in our ragged hippie outfits, but certainly not wealthy. Eyebrows were raised. Something smelled fishy; although, what they were smelling wasn't fish but the big clouds of hashish that drifted from Ior's house.

Everyone in our house felt so safe that they even used the house phone to make their dope deals. I was worried. If there was one phone line in the whole of Finland that was being tapped, it was going to be ours. My only hope was Andrew. He constantly used the phone line to call all around the world; each conversation lasted hours and created a mighty phone bill. I hoped that these endless conversations would make monitoring our phone line too tedious a task, and the dope-related conversations would in this way be missed. It was wishful thinking on my part.

Of all the parts of the day, the evenings in Akanpesa seemed to last the longest. It didn't really get dark at night during the northern summer. Thinking about it now, this made it the shortest part of the day. Anyway, we experienced it as evening and each of our evenings usually followed the same formula. After temperatures dropped in the afternoon, we all gathered inside around the fireplace, the glowing coal of which kept the super-sized teapot warm. One by one, we fell asleep on the cushions scattered around the floor. At some point, someone would wake up and start the fire again for the tea. It was an evening like so many others and Andrew was performing a monologue on the landline phone. "Hey, watch that phone bill!" I warned him.

"Sssh! I'm on the line to Japan, this is super important."

Andrew waved away my interruption and continued directing his barrage of words towards the other side of the planet. Sitting comfortably in front of the fire, Mr Yeah was experimenting with the Root language.

"'Ma' means land. If you mirror it horizontally, you get 'Wa'. 'Wa' is the opposite of land: water. 'MaMa' means mother. Hence, 'WaWa' should be the opposite of mother. What would that be?"

Everyone else present was only listening with half an ear, while watching Mr Yeah with half an eye. The room was filled with smoke. Not the usual smoke of hashish, however, *that* had finished a while ago, and we were all broke. We'd given Carry our last money days before, and he'd predictably vanished.

"'WaWa' in Root is 'VaVa'. That means double Vaner. When you look at it from the Aser's point of view, it's not 'mother' or the generation before you, but the generation *below*: Vaner," Wessel replied.

"Yeah, it must be that," Mr Yeah mumbled, lost in thought.

"'Pa' is 'Asernas Polen', the pole of the Aser people. In this same line of thinking, 'PaPa' is your father and 'dada' is mirrored horizontally and means the boys from the generation below."

"What a bunch of nonsense. You're just making this all up," scoffed Cliff, who'd been silent in the corner all evening.

"We're just exploring," Mr Yeah replied. "I'm just trying to apply the laws of Root and extrapolating–"

"Extrapolating? You don't even know what that means!" Cliff interrupted him.

"True, but I might find out through the Root language system."

"I'll help you," Cliff mocked, "'Blah Blah' mirrored horizontally is still 'Blah Blah'. And that's been the case since Frei and Freia!"

"Hey guys, quit it," Ronan jumped in. "We've got more serious things on our mind than 'WaWa' and 'Blah Blah'. We ran out of dope days ago. Nobody's doing anything about it."

"Something will come up. It always does," Mr Yeah smiled.

An excited looking head popped up outside the window.

"Knock knock. Open up, it's me!"

"Hey, it's Hal!"

We all recognised the shiny bald head with popping eyes and a laughing face. I unlocked the door, it slammed open, and Hal came racing in.

"I made it!" he proclaimed, arms spread wide as if to receive a standing ovation.

"Great!" said Ronan.

"Great is exactly what I am!"

Confused eyes tried to follow his hands to understand what he was getting at.

"I came by car from Amsterdam this time and it's loaded with hashish," he said, grinning wildly.

Cheers of excitement and jumps of happiness filled the room.

"I need help getting it out. It's kind of technical, it requires cutting steel."

"Maybe it's more sensible doing it tomorrow in the daytime. We don't want to keep our neighbours awake with noisy steelworks unloading hashish in the middle of the night."

"No, we want to smoke joints now!" The little crowd cried.

"Don't worry we'll be safe about it. And it makes more sense to do it now, so that we can hide the bulk of it in the woods tonight, away from the house."

"How much did you bring?" Ronan asked.

"A lot. I broke the Akanpesa record of smuggling. It's more than all the others brought together this year."

I sighed deeply. Everybody else was happy and cheering. No,

not everybody. Mr Yeah poked at the coals with a steel trident, a dark expression on his face. Cliff had returned to his corner and made himself invisible. Everybody went outside to help Hal rescue the dope. Amidst the hullabaloo, Carry suddenly appeared. He had a story to tell, as usual, but nobody was listening. So, he just sat down by the fire and drank tea. Mr Yeah gave me a pointed look that I interpreted along the lines of:

"Look who's appeared just as the hashish problem's been solved."

Two hours later, Hal and the boys returned triumphantly holding an enormous bag of hashish. Hal took one kilo out and gave it to me.

"That's for the household kitty."

He then gave me another kilo.

"And that's for the household to smoke."

It was extremely generous. Most people didn't even bring two kilos to sell, let alone to give them away as a gift. One kilo would be sufficient to cover the whole household's costs for two months. The other kilo would last about the same amount of time, maybe a little less, depending on how many people came to visit.

"Can you call some of the Finnish buyers tomorrow?" Hal asked me.

"Ow, Ow, Ow. Why's it always me?"

"They trust you, and you speak their language."

"It's fine, it's fine. I just like complaining."

Hal then loaded a large backpack with the rest of his stash and started heading for the woods to find a good hiding place. I remember thinking that he looked like an overloaded camel. The boys only had eyes for the dope scattered over the table and were busy rolling joints and chatting about the quality of different strains.

Mr Yeah, who'd been quietly watching the scene, stood up, trident in hand.

"Now listen everybody! You've all lost it. Have you forgotten why we came to the end of the world here in Finland in the first place? We're not here to be dope dealers! We're here to open the Lemminkäinen Temple!"

The room fell silent. All we could hear was Andrew's endless chattering on the phone.

"Hey you, Mr Important. Are you listening to me?" Mr Yeah fired at Andrew. "This includes you too. You come here, sell kilo after kilo, and never give anything for the household. Then you leave with suitcases full of money and come again with new kilos of dope. You make Casper sell your stuff; Casper, who doesn't smoke, and has never wanted anything to do with the business. Casper's only here to open the temple. You're all steering towards disaster and can't even see that."

"Chill out, Mr Yeah. I'm in the middle of a very important conversation with people from Brazil. Whatever your point is, it can wait til tomorrow."

Mr Yeah exploded in anger. He charged towards Andrew, and Ronan jumped in between them just in time.

"Stop guys, let's talk it over. There's no need for violence."

"Tell Mr Nutcase to fuck off!" yelled Andrew. "He's screwing up my meeting. It might be thanks to this very conversation that we're able to open the temple. These are rich people I'm talking to, and they're seriously interested in helping us out. If the temple doesn't open, it's because of him!"

Mr Yeah exploded again and threw the trident with great force and precision towards Andrew, who was only just fast enough to dodge the deadly projectile. Mr Yeah took two steps towards Andrew, who backed away quickly. Mr Yeah then lifted the phone off the floor, ripped the cable out with a roar and threw the whole thing in the fire. He picked the trident back up and positioned himself in front of the fire like a Helvetian guard, making sure no one interrupted the softening of the plastic phone. There was complete silence in the room, broken only by the flames crackling at the plastic. The next time Mr Yeah turned to look, the phone had melted into a black blob.

"If you want to deal dope, then go to Amsterdam, New York, Chicago, Tokyo or somewhere else, just not here. Is that clear? This is one of the holiest places in the world. All you guys are doing is talking shit and making money. Or worse, letting Casper make money for you. It's vampire money. If you come from Goa or Amsterdam and you bring some dope to smoke, you share it with your friends here. But if you want to make money, then go somewhere else. This is the home of the Lemminkäinen Temple and kilos of hashish will not open it."

Hal walked into the silent room.

"What's the hap? What's with all the long faces? Look at all the dope I brought! Cheer up, won't you."

Mr Yeah quietly explained his point of view once more.

"I understand, man. I promise this is the last time."

I looked up at this. Anytime I heard the words 'it's the last time' they were either completely untrue, or something was about to go terribly wrong. Well, whatever. It was time for a cup of tea and some sleep.

The next morning, we were rudely awoken by a screaming Hal.

"All the dope's gone! I hid it in the forest and now it's all gone. This is a disaster!"

I made a fire and put the kettle on it. Here comes the next drama, I thought to myself. Hall asked me to return the two kilos he'd given me; then he quickly gave them back and asked me to sell them for him to cover some of his costs. He left a hundred grams for the household and didn't contribute any money to our kitty. Unsurprisingly, Carry was nowhere to be seen.

Part of me was happy that the phone had turned into a black plastic blob. There was too much going on over that phone, and it was still unclear who would pay the monthly bills that often reached the thousands. The downside of losing the phone, however, was that I lost contact with Ior.

He lived about twenty-five kilometres away in the centre of Helsinki, which was a two-hour walk or a half an hour drive. Ior and I would often check in and consult with each other over the phone about our plans and to decide who we would or wouldn't speak to.

The foreigners in Gumbostrand lived their lives away from Finnish society. They didn't speak the language. Ior and I did, however, and we were still trying to properly introduce the Bock Saga to Finland. We realised that this was our best bet to opening the temple. Money, energy and logistical help were needed, and if these were going to come from anywhere, it would be from Finland, not from the dope-smoking, smuggling and dealing freak-heads in front of the fire in Gumbostrand, even if they were the only ones who kept the fire burning.

Losing the phone further isolated our group and made the social dynamics even more turbulent. There were many strong characters in that house whose egos increasingly spun out of control. The house became more and more like a mental asylum, and this attracted even stranger people who started treating it as such.

I missed Ior. There was madness brewing in Gumbostrand and there were no forces to control it. There were no girls either to keep things civilised. I spent my time sweeping and cleaning the place, making sure there was always hot tea available and trying my best to diffuse any conflicts that arose. I took all the remaining antiquities to the attic to protect them from raging freaks.

About ten to fifteen men slept on the floor around the fire each night. Some stayed up late, some woke up early. It was becoming too crowded, and this couldn't go on for much longer. I thanked the gods when the summer drew to a close and nothing really bad had happened yet.

Autumn finally came. It was cold and rainy, and the Goa birds left for the south. Ior was getting ready to leave too. Hakkolinen had made a lot of progress, but in the end, he'd been forced to stop due to lack of money. I started preparing the estate for the winter. One morning, there was a knock on the door.

"What's the next headache now?" I wondered as I opened the door.

"Hi, my name's Maya Dahlgren and I'm from the *Hufvud-stadsbladet*. I'd love to interview you."

God, not another one of these snakes, I thought. But this snake did look friendlier than the rest.

"OK, come on in."

Maya turned out to be just as friendly and honest as she looked. We sat by the fire, drank tea and had a long talk that afternoon. She asked me a hundred questions, and I told her about the Bock Saga and the digging and how it all came to an end because of the approaching winter and lack of money. After hearing my story, she offered to help.

"I think that we should contact a friend of mine who's the director of Lemminkäinen Group. I think he'd be very interested to know about this excavation, especially since the temple has the same name as his company. He might even sponsor your operation, you never know. His name is Henki Penti; I'll introduce you."

I was surprised. I'd heard of Lemminkäinen Group, of course. Everyone who spent more than three days in Finland knew the name. It was all over the place. The group was by far the largest construction company in Finland. They built roads, underground systems and lots of big buildings. Even our own Hakkolinen had worked for them at one point.

Maya contacted Henki Penti, and it turned out that he was indeed interested. Although Ior came from his same social circle, he'd never gotten to know him personally. The two men met and immediately clicked. They came from similar backgrounds; both had grown up in important families who'd laid out life plans for them before they'd even been born. Both had grown up with a mountain of responsibilities and expectations.

Ior gave Henki all the video and audio material we had on the Bock Saga. Henki had already booked a holiday to the Maldives with his wife and was leaving the next day. His wife later told us that he'd stayed inside their holiday bungalow for the entire trip, just watching and listening to the tapes. Henki understood the Bock Saga at once and fell in love with it. Yes, he did want to sponsor the excavation. He would do this after the winter had passed. The large, rich Lemminkäinen Group would excavate the Lemminkäinen Temple. It was a gift from Öde.

Perfect. Now, I could finally take a break and clear my head. I left for Japan, and Ior left with Soma for Goa.

Ronan

After an intense summer during which I'd made a living by organising psychedelic parties in an attempt to steer our global culture into a joyful direction, I needed some rest. I'd done some hashish runs in between all the frantic activity and had enough to buy a ticket to Goa where I planned to settle down for a while. In my high-octane, high-heartbeat life, 'settling down' simply meant not boarding a plane for a few months. I found a house for rent in a Goan village called Baden. It was a little outside the centre of the freak mayhem and beach chaos, and that was just what I needed. Everything was still accessible by motorbike, of course.

Driving a motorbike in Goa in those years was a romantic experience. There were far more chickens and goats on the road than mechanised traffic. The light, from early morning until sunset, tinged the landscape in magic. My motorbike became a flying carpet, which I used to fly to Mapusa and back on multiple occasions, buying paint, tools and building materials and ordering cushions for the veranda.

The house was more of a ruin than a house, but I could see its potential. All it needed was the roof to be repaired, along with some whitewashing, floor polishing and gardening, and it would turn into a cute little palace. It had a large veranda and large garden. I spent every hour of daylight during the following three months working on my new home.

I had lots of ideas on how to use the light in the morning and how to filter the burning sunshine through the foliage during the hotter parts of the day. I spent less time at the beach and didn't visit Ior, even though I knew he was close by in his house in Chapora. The psychedelic parties, of which there were many that season, became my only social life. There, I often saw the other Bock Saga friends. Mr. Yeah, Andrew and several others regularly visited Ior to listen to the Bock Saga. Ior was still adamant that the temple could be opened at any moment, and I was told that his Bock Saga was ever expanding. Sure, I was still interested, but it was no longer my life.

One day while I was out in my garden pruning a bush of *aboli* flowers, two motorbikes pulled up to my house. It was Soma and Nag, Ior's two helpers, and mister Bock himself on the back of one of their bikes. He invited himself onto my veranda, settled onto some cushions and straightened his now guru-length beard. I stood speechless, pruning shears in hand.

"Do you have any tea?" Ior asked as if his sudden apparition was the most normal thing in the world.

"Sure, Ior," I replied, matching his intonation.

We drank tea together and talked about mundane things as you would with a family member you hadn't seen in a while. It felt so familiar. We'd experienced things and emotions together; we had an undeniable bond and he felt like family. After we'd caught up with each other's news, Ior brought up the Bock Saga.

"Is the Bock Saga still alive in your head?" he asked.

"Yes, it is."

Ior smiled and we talked about Bock Saga trivialities. But I knew he had me then. He returned to my veranda the next day and every day after that. And because he came, other friends also came, and with them came more people that wanted to listen to Ior tell his Bock Saga. Soon, my veranda and the shade of the banyan tree in my garden became the Bock Saga meeting place. It took a while for me to accept this, but yes, I can't deny that I was listening eagerly too.

Winter 1989

Chandrakhan owned a chai shop on Vagator beach and had seen a lot of strange behaviour in his life. He'd grown up amongst Christians, Hindus and hippies. This day was like any other during the Goan party season. Semi-naked hippies played beach racket along the stretch of beach in front of his chai shop. Some were swimming in the sea, while others ate fruits offered and cut by the colourfully dressed fruit-ladies.

Tribal kids from a neighbouring state, dressed extravagantly in their culture's most colourful garments, played a glass-shatteringly shrill flute and were accompanied by a petite bull-calf who was just as extravagantly dressed as they were. They walked up and down the beach asking for money. Their trick was to play continuously on their flute until their victim surrendered and threw a few coins at them. This was all that was needed to persuade them to move on to the next group of hippies a little further along the beach. The few Rupees they collected were enough to keep them returning every day.

At both ends of the beach, some Indian tourists who'd come to Goa from afar to see naked white girls gathered and drank beer. They were too shy to talk to anyone, but they could x-ray a person with their intense staring eyes. I really do believe that they could actually see through people's clothes. Maybe even through to their flesh and bones.

Within the chai shop, life was simple and predictable. The hippies ordered chai, double chai, lemon tea, bhaji and pakora. Each of these items had a corresponding hand signal, so language was never an issue. In fact, it was such a non-issue that very little was said within the chai shop.

Big clouds of chillum smoke floated through the chai shop unhindered by windows or doors, of which there weren't any.

The continuous smoking of chillums meant that everybody was always stoned, which also added to the lack of conversation. Every now and then, a holy cow walked into the chai shop and tried to eat the palm leaves that formed its roof or to snatch some food from the table. Chandrakhan would then make a lot of noise and wave a bamboo stick in the air to chase the cow away.

Ior Bock entered the chai shop and sat down on the far side, opposite the entrance. People looked up in interest. He was already quite well known in Goa by this point. He ordered a chai and stroked his long beard. Some hippies invited him to share the chillum that was going round, which he accepted. After the coughing was over and the clouds had drifted towards the beach, they asked him a few questions about his strange Bock Saga.

Ior had fallen into a period during which he refused to discuss the Bock Saga with anyone. Well, almost anyone. He continued to share his knowledge with a select group of friends, which included Cliff, Soma, Mr Yeah, Casper and me. He felt that this was enough. It wasn't his role to constantly repeat the same basic principles of the Bock Saga, and he hated discussing it with non-believers who often aggressively forced their arguments onto him.

Worse were the staunch believers of conspiracies such as UFOs flown around by lizard brained aliens who sank Atlantis or other such beliefs, who felt the need to attack Ior's story with vigour. Although Ior felt it was his responsibility to share the Bock Saga with the world, it wasn't his job to constantly defend it and convert people into believers. So sometimes, he would try to put people off.

This was exactly what happened in Chandrakhan's chai shop on that warm hazy Goan day when the group of hippies asked him about the Bock Saga. Ior quietly set a naked foot on his lap, tore of a toenail, and ate it noisily. Then he started to clean his ear. With a long nail he scooped out a lump of yellowish-brown wax and showed it to the people around him.

Chandrakhan registered everything and smiled. In the silence Ior's body language was loud and clear. The rest of the lazy day unfolded without any incidents. As predicted, the sun set in the Indian Ocean on time and the beach emptied.

William

Spring 1989

The Vondelpark was a meeting place for Goa travellers in Amsterdam. There, by the statue of Vondel, you could find travellers from all over the world. Back then, there was no internet or other means of establishing contact with fellow travellers other than frequenting these types of places.

This connection node was only known to Goa travellers. It functioned a bit like the famous bar at the flea market in Anjuna, Goa. There were other places like this scattered around the world, and if you'd been to Goa, you always knew where to find likeminded people. The statue was also a great place for travelling freaks to hear news of what had happened to people that year, as well as hearing about new opportunities and dangers on the road.

I walked in the spring sunshine pushing a stroller in which my three-month-old daughter was sleeping. From a distance, I could see the big clouds of chillum smoke rising from under the statue. My friends had returned. After lots of greetings and hugs, we discussed what had happened to whom and all our own narrow escapes in our smuggling adventures.

My daughter had woken up, and as she crawled around in the grass under the statue, business was discussed. I was considered a 'trusted local' by most of the people who gathered here. And that I was. I had access to the so-called 'kantoortjes', the Dutch wholesale trading houses where anything from kilos to shiploads of hashish were traded. I could offer a service and I needed the income. I never smuggled anything myself. It was too dangerous, and I was now a caretaker and provider for my daughter.

Her mama was sweet and beautiful, but also dysfunctional in just about everything, including taking care of babies and making money. She believed that all these things should, and would, be provided to her by the universe. That was me, Mr Universe. And thus, with the little one in my arms, I bought and sold hashish in Amsterdam that summer. Because of my international contacts, I earned a place on the big chessboard of the hashish trade. I treated it as a game of strategy and as a serious profession.

I know that it might not have looked that professional carrying boxes in and out of warehouses and cars with a baby in my arms, but there wasn't much more I could do about that. I had no place where I could leave my daughter during the day. There were no functional grandparents. Looking back, I now realise that I could've brought her to a kindergarten. But back then, that never even crossed my mind. I was too preoccupied with being both a papa and a mama and believed that she would only be safe with me.

The freaks who arrived in Amsterdam from India and didn't want to travel any further with their Indian hashish sold it through me. Some of them would then buy some cheaper quality hashish in Amsterdam to sell in some other European country. Gangsters and heavy criminals never got a foothold in this market, as the product that was being traded and the culture of its users were just too peaceful.

Over the years, more and more people came to Amsterdam from India, sold their high-quality dope there and then bought a lower quality to sell in Finland, so as to make a maximum profit. Ronan was one of the first to do this, but soon more and more freaks started making the same the trip to Hel. I was often invited to join them and visit the excavation of which I'd already heard so much about by this stage. I decided to finally take them up on the offer at the end of that summer.

Casper

I came back from Asia in the spring of 89. I'd been to Japan and Boracay. Oh, it was so beautiful there and so quiet. I'd had a wonderful time with my girlfriend, Susanne. My mind was serene, and my body was full of energy from having been surrounded by nature for so long.

As soon as I arrived back in Helsinki, I was bombarded by Swedish newspaper headlines full of Ior Bock bashing. Mestari and his Raportti Media group were really going for it this time. They described Ior as a satanic cult leader who brainwashed his followers with his dangerous Bock Saga. The campaign was spread out over different newspapers, each with a slightly different point of view, but all with the same conclusion: the Bock Saga is evil, and everything and everybody that has anything to do with it is also evil or a victim turned evil!

"Wow. These people really do have strong emotions. At least, we're being taken seriously. What a pity that they want to destroy us instead of helping us reveal Finland's history," I thought.

By this point, I'd become accustomed to hysterical newspaper headlines, but this attack made me feel uneasy. It made me feel like we needed to watch our step. Like we had enemies. All of this over a creation story and an archaeological excavation! What a strange place Finland is.

It didn't take long for the first scandal to hit us. Two boys were caught masturbating together. They'd told their parents that wanking was good and that it was the Bock Saga that said so. The mother of the youngest boy immediately went to the police. Because the youngest of the two boys was a minor of just seventeen, while the other boy was eighteen and therefore considered an adult, it suddenly turned into an underage sexual abuse case. The authorities took this very seriously. The older boy was prosecuted for paedophilia and sent to jail.

The two boys had never actually had sex together, they'd never even touched, but this didn't seem to matter. The parents of the older boy sided with the parents of the younger one. The police related the story to the newspapers and... you've guessed it! Ior was in the headlines once again. He'd never met either of the boys and had no idea how they'd come up with the idea to wank together. In Ior's opinion, it was just a case of puberty and nothing to do with the Bock Saga.

The older boy was released from jail six months later. When he stepped out into the bright summer sunlight, 600 boys were there waiting to greet him. Without knowing it, he'd become a cult hero. A cacophony of yells was being directed at his parents who'd come to pick him up. Well, it was an easy choice for him to make. His parents had after all helped cause the whole mess. Without looking back, he joined the group and headed to a nearby forest where the whole bunch held a wanking ritual. This gave the newspapers further ammunition. Ior and I had been swept into yet another stream of events that we truly had nothing to do with.

During the summer of 1989, as had become customary, Ior stayed in the town apartment with his Goanese helpers Soma and Nag, while I stayed in the estate in Akanpesa next to the Lemminkäinen Temple. Henki Penti kept his word and started working at the temple excavation. On the first day, a long convoy of trucks cleared the piles of rubble that had been left from the previous years' efforts.

Up to that point we'd just been dumping everything outside the entrance of the temple. Henki Penti's team then built a fence around the perimeter and took various other measures to ensure their usual safety standards were met. After that was done, Hakkolinen took charge. He immediately started drilling, and it wasn't long before we heard the first dynamite explosion.

Over the next few weeks, the first friends from Goa started arriving with their heavy sandals, beach rackets and specially prepared bags. They came from everywhere on the planet, but each of them passed through Amsterdam first. Most stayed only a short while.

The problem was that life in Finland was so prohibitively expensive that it didn't take long before all their smuggling money was spent. Not on champagne or caviar, mind you. No, it would be spent on bread and peanut butter sandwiches. Only the real Saga-heads stayed longer. As well as the usual crowd, some new people appeared on the scene: the Germans; the friendly freaks Shavas and Ulven.

Ronan

I often visited Ior's apartment to listen to him tell the Bock Saga. I was joined by Mr Yeah and Casper on many occasions. No matter what time it was when we knocked on Ior's door, we were always welcome. It was a small apartment, like most are in Helsinki. It was the Svedlin family company owned by Ior's stepfather who'd built most of the houses and apartment buildings in that area. The Svedlin company had enormous concrete businesses that built boring suburban cityscapes all over Scandinavia and Russia. A concrete box for every family. Ior jokingly called this part of his family history the 'Box Saga'.

We sat in his apartment with Soma and Nag and others who dropped by. There was usually at least one other person from the via-via group present. The Bock Saga was ever expanding. Ior had gone into intricate detail explaining the Offer-Ring system and the Wheel of Life. There were so many words in English and Swedish that he explained to us from a Bock Saga perspective.

Weeks went by and he discussed one word a day. Apart from talking, Ior was smoking continuous Indian beedies and joints and chillums. The place was thick with smoke clouds and resounded with the sound of his coughing. When he started a coughing fit, it was sure to last a long time. The coughing broke record after record in the decibel scale. The windows trembled. It interrupted the conversation and made it hard to sit close to him for long. Poor Soma and Nag had to put up with these fits all day, every day. I don't know how they did it.

Ior told us that this was going to be the year we would finally open the temple. He'd said the same thing the previous year and the year before that. We had our doubts, but it anyway remained our biggest wish. Ior also told us not to make any long-lasting obligations, so that when the temple opened, we'd be available to spread the story. He didn't want us to start a business or have a mortgage. He also told us that the Bock Saga specified that a man needed to be at least 180cm tall to have children. None of the core Saga-heads were that tall. Since there were seven of us in the core group, we compared ourselves to the seven dwarfs digging in the mountain for treasure. Ior, of course, was Snow White.

This procreation rule was bad news for our girlfriends, as it was clear they could never have children with us if we followed Ior's advice. We were too short, and we anyway should be dedicating ourselves to the Bock Saga and remaining available for the responsibilities that came with that.

There were some who saw this as somewhat sect-like, and I can understand how it could appear as so. From the outside, it might seem like Ior was telling us how to live our life. But since a central part of the Bock Saga focussed on procreation and the benefits of following its system, this was hard to avoid. In any case, the Bock Saga was so important to us that we accepted all of it.

When Henki Penti's Lemminkäinen Company first started supporting the excavation, Ior became stricter with all his followers, but especially so with his Goanese helpers. He told them that they shouldn't be making any long-lasting obligations outside of the Bock Saga, such as starting their own chai shop or restaurant in Goa. He didn't want the Bock Saga to only be a white man's story. Although the centre of the story is based in Helsinki, its beginning stems back to Paradise time where everyone looked mostly like Indians do now.

Apart from this, Ior had noticed that Indians found learning the second central language of the Bock Saga (Van/Finnish) easy. To understand the language is to understand the Bock Saga. Furthermore, his Indian helpers had found it much easier to grasp the concepts laid out in the Bock Saga, as they'd been brought up in the only living mythology left on the planet: Hinduism. Hindu festivals are enormous and those who celebrate them often go into a trance-like state. For the Hindus, it's not just about belief, but about taking part in the harmony of the universe. In Christianity, the pantheon was replaced by saints and the holy family who turned into a god in the sky, a holy ghost and a son nailed to a cross. Ior thought it was crucial that when the temple opened, Indians would also take part in presenting the Bock Saga to the world.

Back in Gumbostrand, we always had much to discuss. There was a lot of new Bock Saga information that we needed to get straight in our heads. We learned about the Wheel of Life, the sound system and so on.

The Bock Saga isn't a story that can be fully grasped simply by listening to it. No, it's a story that has to sink in, it's a way of thinking. Others called it a brainwash. But to us, everything that we'd learned in school was a brainwash and the Bock Saga was an enlightenment and clarification of the world around us. Suddenly, everything made sense. The whole Bock Saga was based on easy-to-understand facts rather than vague mystical religious beliefs.

That's why we wanted the temple to open so badly. It would prove to the world that the Bock Saga was true. And if everyone understood our common past and how we'd lived for aeons peacefully and sustainably on our shared planet, then we could maybe make better decisions for our future.

William

I don't believe the Bock Saga could ever really change the world. Even if it was proven true and the temple was opened, it still wouldn't make a difference. Imagine you lived in Saudi Arabia and one morning you opened your newspaper and saw an article that claimed a prehistoric temple had been discovered that explained all our ancient history.

Do you think you'd really pay much notice to it? – that the streets would suddenly run wild with people embracing freedom? Do you think the traders on Wall Street would get up, leave their desks and head for the beach? No. None of this would happen. And anyway, why is the opening of the temple really that important?

Surely, if the Bock Saga truly is as significant and important as the Saga-heads claim it to be, it should be possible to convince people of its validity simply by exposing them to it. After all, the Bock Saga followers were all able to grasp its significance simply by listening to it; they constantly claimed that they didn't require any proof as confirmation of its truth.

They believed in the Bock Saga so much that it was no longer 'belief' but 'understanding'. Did they think the rest of the world was too stupid to understand it as they did? Or maybe, they were so desperate to open the temple because deep down they *did* need that proof, that confirmation.

Whatever the case, I talked to enough Saga-heads to realise that one of the real driving forces behind the excavation was the excitement of treasure hunting, the excitement at the thought of being the first to enter the underworld and walk amongst countless prehistoric treasures. I do get it. I just hope they realise that the real treasure is the Bock Saga itself. If I were them, I would put all my energy into recording the Bock Saga and spreading its information to the world, or at least the part of the world that matters. That's what I would do if I were them, but I'm not them.

Ronan

The constant opposition from the Finnish media and the Museovirasto frustrated us greatly. We were trying to show them their own heritage, and the only thing they did in return was to ridicule the Bock Saga and demonise and discredit our characters and lifestyle. The Museovirasto ensured that there was no way for us to excavate the golden bocks. They even went as far as actively obfuscating facts and hiding objects that could possibly support or prove the Bock Saga.

We got impatient and restless. Lemminkäinen Company was working hard. Almost every day we heard explosions coming from under the Etta Stupa. Bobcats were roaring and trucks rumbled past loaded with granite rubble. They went deeper and deeper into the mountain. We had no idea how far we were from a result. It could happen at any moment, or it could happen in five years' time. We just kept on waiting; there was absolutely nothing else we could do.

Sitting around all day with Mr Yeah, Andrew and the rest of the Saga-heads and fruitcakes was starting to get old. We were all getting on each other's nerves. We spent hours and days and nights talking and speculating about all kinds of Bock Saga intricacies. We drank tea, ate bread and cheese and smoked dope. That was it. I decided I needed to try something different to get to some sort of result.

I'd heard a lot about the three golden bocks, about how they'd been buried around the same time that the temple had been closed, a thousand years or so ago. They'd been buried under two oak trees that Ior had pointed out in a place called the Offerlund. It was obviously a place where ritual offering had been performed in heathen times.

My idea was to go to this place with a metal detector and

see if I could get a reading that would prove the existence of heavy metal objects buried underground. If I could prove that something was buried there, maybe we could start an excavation more easily. I decided to ask the owner of the land for permission to carry out a non-invasive test. All I wanted to do was walk around the land with a high-tech machine and see if it went *bleep*.

It just so happened that the land was owned by the church of Snappertuna. Soma, Mr Yeah and I approached the minister and asked for his permission. It really wasn't that big a deal. If the minister had some goodwill, he would grant us access and help with our archaeological research. It turned out that the minister had no real say in the matter, however, and simply told us to speak to the National Forest Preservation who took care of the place and the whole area around it. Ok, easy.

We made an appointment with their office, and after speaking to various people, we were referred back to the church. So, we visited the minister once more, and he referred us to the bishop. After weeks of referrals, we finally had some form of approval. We even found out from the minister's wife that the church records mentioned the golden bocks! She told us that local stories spoke of these hidden statues, but it was unclear where they were buried. That wasn't a problem for us as we knew exactly where to find them.

In the via-via group, there were two brothers from Denmark who were Bock Saga fanatics. Yes, I can call them that. There was a difference between their fanaticism and my fanaticism. I had an intellectual hunger and a burning desire for knowledge to make the world a better place. These two brothers, who'd visited Akanpesa often over the last two years, were chaotic madmen. You could see it in their eyes. They were madmen, but they also owned a metal detector company. They'd offered to investigate the Offerlund for just the cost of petrol and the ferries to get there.

We'd tried to make an appointment with them over the phone a few times already, but they'd always cancelled at the last moment. Finally, it seemed they really would make the trip. Soma, Mr Yeah and I waited at the location where we'd decided to meet. It was within walking distance from the Offerlund. The brothers finally arrived two hours late. As they disembarked their vehicle, they spoke incoherently about things that nobody understood.

When they finished unloading the equipment from the truck and screwing it all together, they realised that the main, most sensitive machine wasn't working. It turned out that they'd forgotten to bring a vital part and now the whole machine couldn't function. It was a three-day trip back to pick the part up.

This knowledge increased the Danish scientists' heartbeats and a larger and faster stream of incoherency flowed from them. This was coupled with a large amount of undeliberate and inefficient movement of unrelated body parts. Soma, Mr Yeah and I watched quietly.

Oh, why could things never be normal, we asked each other with silent stares. I know we were freaks, living a life that couldn't be described as normal, but why did we always end up attracting even freakier people than us, people who were actually insane?

The two Danish brothers had one smaller working device, which was finally assembled. We walked with this towards the oak trees and scanned the area for metal objects. No *bleep*. We really needed a bigger machine. We realised that searching for metal in ground that contained heavy granite stones and an abundance of clay with a high metal content was not going to be easy.

The brothers felt guilty that they'd let us down and were almost in tears. They'd failed to prove the Bock Saga, which according to them was all that they lived for. We told them to chill out and take it easy, but they left in a more chaotic state than what they'd arrived in.

Later we heard that the younger of the two brothers had killed himself and had mentioned the shame and despair he'd felt that day as one of the causes of his depression. We felt terrible. I mean, the Bock Saga's important, but not important enough to die for. He could've come again on another day with the right equipment. But it's hard to understand a depressed mind.

We also heard that because the brothers came from an important family in Denmark, the newspapers had gotten hold of the story and connected the Bock Saga to yet another death. We shrugged it off again, but I tell you, we never got used to all the disasters that followed us and how the media portrayed them.

Casper

The Berlin wall had fallen and suddenly the enormous Russian country was open to us. Many people came to western Europe from the East to enjoy our wealth and freedom. A group of Goa hippies got together and decided to give the Eastern people the gifts of positive thinking, colourful lives and Goa-trance music. They found a big bus, dressed themselves in their most extravagant, fluorescent outfits and left for Russia.

The bus set off from London and filled up along the way with DJs and party people who all wanted to share their happiness with their brothers and sisters from dark, fun-deprived Eastern Europe. The bus passed through Amsterdam, of course, and more psychedelic people got on board along with plenty of psychedelics. They headed north-east to Germany where they took a boat to Sweden. From there, they continued to Finland, making parties all along the way.

There were generators on the bus's roof that provided electricity for the large sound system, loudspeakers and fluorescent lights all used to psychedelicise their surroundings. The psychedelic caravan arrived in Akanpesa just before midsummer.

We knew that they were coming, of course, and it was a happy reunion. We'd announced a big party through the via-via group and suddenly hundreds of Finnish, Swedish, Danish, German, Russian, you name it, people were camping in our garden. There were also some 200 people from our Bock Saga group. We danced all day and all night around the bus with the latest Goa-trance music from the hottest Goa DJs blasting out of the loudspeakers. There was little difference between day and night in the north around midsummer. It was never dark. As the estate was by the sea, we were able to swim like we did in Goa parties. It was fantastic and we were all so happy.

Suddenly, a police boat came from the sea in the middle of the bright night.

"Oh, no, already!?" I thought to myself, knowing that this was the usual way parties came to an end in this world.

The police disembarked and asked who the responsible person was.

"Uhm... Hmm... Responsible?"

Wrong question. The thought of getting an official permission for the party hadn't even crossed our mind. We'd informed all the neighbours in the area, and they were ok with it. It was normal to have parties on midsummer. It's such an important event that the whole Scandinavian economy comes to a standstill for a couple of days. The two policemen were sent to me. That was ok; I was probably the only one on the premises that was not tripping on LSD or mushrooms.

I expected them to stop the party for some reason or another, and I hoped they wouldn't confiscate the sound system. To my big surprise, they told me they'd found a small boat out at sea with some foreigners in it that were apparently completely lost. Because we had a reputation of welcoming anyone to our estate, they asked if we could take care of these people as well.

"That's all?" I asked, relieved. "Sure, no problem. Where are they?"

Behind the police boat was a small dingy that I hadn't noticed before. In it were four extremely beautiful blond Scandinavian-looking girls. They were so beautiful; I suddenly became shy. Not everybody had that same reaction though, and the girls were immediately welcomed by the party crowd. I told the police that we would take good care of them. The girls loved partying and danced all night long.

In the end, the party was stopped by the police, of course. If it hadn't been, it would still be going today, as a fairy tale narrator might say. The girls stayed with us a few days longer and added to the general atmosphere of happiness that the party had evoked. After a few long sleeps, the bus of fairies went on to St. Petersburg and beyond, taking the girls with them. They had many adventures in that unknown country. But that's another story for another time.

The party had been really great, but now we were more broke

than ever. The work on the temple went on and on and on. Every day there were new blasts of dynamite. *Boom*! We responded with a 'Boom' of our own that we yelled when we lit each new chillum. There was more Bock Saga talk and strange discussions, while frustrations mounted as some people, especially the Americans, grew ever more impatient. Ior had promised them it would all happen this year, but so far, all we'd found were more rocks and there seemed no end in sight.

If you put a group of people together in relative isolation, it's unsurprising that social and mental processes start fermenting into weird behaviour. If they're weird people to begin with, this happens at an exponential rate.

If the main topic of conversation and interest is the Bock Saga, things can deteriorate very quickly indeed. Add to this a persistent dire financial situation resulting in empty refrigerators and you've got the story of Akanpesa. The clouds of weirdness condensed into thick sticky weirdness that dripped off the walls and turned, from time to time, into hailstones of weirdness.

Stranger people came to Gumbostrand and were encapsulated by the 'nobody invited, everybody welcome' mantra. This was Ior's mantra, not mine. But I'd taken it upon myself to have some kind of responsibility for the house and the household. The people that came with hashish had to donate some money to the household purse, so we could buy tea, wood, and food.

Finland was so expensive that this money evaporated quickly, and we were soon poor as rats again. Some people came without money and expected to be fed. For instance, we suddenly had a sleeper in the house that had come from Germany on a small moped. We soon found out that he originally lived in Frankfurt in an apartment with his mother and a three-metre-long crocodile whose favourite spot was the bathtub. Somehow a newspaper got hold of this story too, and we were off again on another media carousel ride...

William

Autumn 1989

I was curious to see what my friends had been up to in Finland. I'd already heard a lot about it over the last few years. I'd met Ior in Goa twice and both times he'd asked me if I knew who my ancestors were. My family has been documented since the 16th century. I thought that this was a long time but compared to the time scale in the Bock Saga, it's merely a flutter of a fly's wings. I wondered if my aristocratic family was somehow linked to the Bock family in Hel. It was hard to say. If anything, my family was probably closer to the Jarl caste in the Bock Saga. This was the highest caste in the Ringlands, but lower than the core Bock family.

Aah, I didn't like thinking about these things. They brought back the burden of all those family responsibilities I'd only just escaped from. Later in life I realised that 'family-karma', 'caste' or whatever you want to call it was hard to escape.

But on that afternoon sitting on Ior's veranda, I didn't want to discuss this sort of stuff any further. I didn't want to enter his sphere of influence. I preferred to continue my party and beach life enjoying the happiness I'd finally found and avoided wasting time and energy on such serious matters.

Anyway, I'd heard about the chronic money shortage in Gumbostrand and the enormous demand for hashish. I didn't want to smuggle illegal things into Finland, so I went to the Amsterdam market and bought a car-full of food. There was fresh food, peanut butter, cornflakes, and lots of other things I thought my friends would like. Shopping finished, I drove my bursting car up to Lübeck, the harbour in Germany, where the ferry to Helsinki departed from.

The next day I found my way to Gumbostrand. There were

about twelve guys living together in a large log cabin. This was the first time I'd met Andrew Higgins, Ulven and some of the other Saga-heads. I knew Ronan, Casper, Mr Yeah, Hal and Wessel from Goa. It was very much a male-dominated household. There was nothing romantic about the hut, it looked more like an on-site building than anything else, and everyone was smoking continuously.

The garden was neglected and beautiful, overgrown with yellow turnip flowers, sloping down to a small private beach. Next to the house was a sauna, which was also a log cabin. After the initial greetings and hugs, chillum, and tea, we went into the sauna. I was amazed at how this pre-mechanical technology worked so well; it was roasting inside the place! Afterwards, we ran naked into the sea. Then, the guys showed me the excavation behind the cabin.

Under a large granite rock, hidden between other rocks and trees was the dark hole of a cave. It sloped down into the mountain. Ronan, Mr Yeah and Casper pointed out the Etta Stupa, clock stone and the Sibbo Berget. There was granite rubble everywhere and various machines lay about the place. Inside the cave, it was dark and moist. They showed me where the four stone slabs had been, which had been blasted by the first dynamite. They showed me in which direction they thought they should be digging.

There was much speculation based solely on a few inconclusive words from Ior Bock, who really didn't have much of a mathematical mind. They were following the roof of the cave, which formed the bottom of the great granite rocks above. It was not clear how deep they should dig, but they were sure that sooner or later they'd find the golden door on the left side.

There was endless speculation on how and where the water lock would be discovered. Everybody acknowledged that they didn't really know anything for certain and that the only way forward was to keep on digging without destroying the bedrock.

To me, it wasn't clear whether the entrance was manmade. It was granite rock. It could very well be natural; or it could have been made yesterday or a million years previously. I understood the excitement and the urge to dig, as well as their burning curiosity for what lay behind the golden doors.

Later that night, I asked my friends what would happen if the temple finally opened. Casper took a deep breath and started his explanation.

"According to the Bock Saga, the opening of the temple needs to happen on the 24th of July. Every important event that happened within the Bock Saga happened on this date. If we find the golden door on any other day, we'll just have to wait until the 24th of July to enter the temple. This would work in our favour, as it would give us time to prepare for the great events that will inevitably follow. Once it is the right day, we'll enter the temple naked, as was the custom before the ice time. This isn't really a problem for us anyway, as we're used to sitting naked in the sauna and all of us have spent a lot of time on beaches where everybody's naked."

"Nobody's ever entered the temple with clothes on and we don't intend to change this custom. We go in bare, and since we're many, we'll be 'bare-bare', or 'barbarians' you could say. The whole group will go inside together. And by the whole group I mean anyone who's contributed to opening the temple by carrying stones or by sitting with us by the fire at Akanpesa. Altogether, that's probably a few hundred people. We won't take anything out of the temple.

The Lemminkäinen Temple is small, just one little room with a divan. From there, a corridor extends towards the Bock family treasure chambers, also known as the storehouse. The Bock Saga explains what we can expect to find inside, but not much about how to get to the entrance itself. A lot of people in this area know about the Lemminkäinen Temple, but relatively few have heard about the Bock family treasure chambers. They both share the same entrance, just behind our house."

"After passing through the Lemminkäinen Temple and finding the entrance to the treasure chambers beyond it, a corridor continues underground in the direction of the North Pole. This corridor stretches twenty kilometres and leads into the chambers themselves. The tricky part is that the Bock Saga describes two ventilation shafts that supply fresh air to the underground rooms, but we still have no way of knowing whether these are still open and working.

We'll need the help of specialists who can analyse the air to ensure there is enough oxygen and no presence of other harmful gases. It'll be quite a technical operation. If it really is twenty kilometres to the chambers, it will take us about a day to walk the distance. Once we've managed this, the chambers themselves are described as being massive in size.

But really, we have no idea what we'll find exactly. Are there going to be rails and some form of functioning train? Will it be pitch dark, or will there somehow be some form of light? Is there a possibility we could get lost inside? We need to be prepared for all eventualities."

"The storehouse hasn't been used since the beginning of the Ice Age. That's 50 million, 10 thousand and two years ago. The chambers were ready by the end of Paradise time. Everything had been prepared by the Bock family; everything imaginable. They knew their era would end many generations before it did. The plan to reveal the storehouse to us already existed then. They had all the time in the world to prepare for the chambers' closing one thousand years ago and its eventual reopening. In the Altlandis time, the Ice Age, they didn't produce any new chambers. The storehouse is entirely a product of our forbearers from Paradise time. A chamber was created for every new generation during this time.

Ior's mother told him that there were more generations than there were people in Finland at that time; that's about four million. And she told him that the surface of the storehouse, the bottom of this enormous cavity is bigger than Odenma with a diameter of 250 kilometres. Can you imagine how huge that is?"

"At the beginning of each chamber is a life-size statue in gold of the then-living Lemminkäinen at the age of twenty-seven. Inside the chamber are two rooms filled with the treasures received by Ra and Maja in Raseborg during his reign. In addition, each chamber had a saloon with a table, which could be used to inspect the treasures. They probably also left messages for us in there. I don't know, it's all speculation, but it would make sense if they did."

"All the chambers are placed in a spiral along the walls of the witch-hat shaped cavity. This spiral wound deep down into the void. With over four million chambers, each about two metres wide, this forms a very long spiral. The top of the cavity is under the former North Pole that was situated on the island Odens Ö, just in front of what is now Helsinki. Thus, the Earth's axis went vertically through the middle of the storehouse. The shortest route from the first chamber to the last isn't down the spiral path along the wall of the cavity but down this axis. Our ancestors must have had some way of doing this, maybe some elevator system.

"When we go down into the storehouse, we'll count how many chambers there are. We'll then know exactly how many generations Paradise lasted for. We'll know what was made for each Bock during Paradise time. The last chamber in the spiral gangway belongs to the last Lemminkäinen who lived just before the First Ragnarök ended Paradise time. At the top of the spiral is the first chamber, where we can find the statue of the first ever Lemminkäinen.

His personal name was Frei, the first man on the planet. It should be there. We'll know when the first man lived, what he left for us and what message he had for us, his offspring. We'll know what he looked like."

"And through the proof of photographs and our witness accounts, we'll finally be heard, and we'll spread the Bock Saga and change the world. Once our recordings of the temple and treasure chambers are shared with the public, there'll inevitably be a lot of questions. All the answers to these questions can be found within the Root alphabet. We'll explain it to everyone; the alphabet, the All-Father's Beten, the rhyme of the All-Father."

"Everything will become clear after we enter the storehouse. It's the largest encyclopaedia to have ever existed. It'll take a few generations to completely understand it all. If the Museovirasto lay their hands on it, it'll take forever. The storehouse is made by people with a great knowledge of nature and of themselves. They were naked; they were in direct contact with the world around them.

The people in the Museovirasto wear a suit and tie; they could never properly understand anything from heathen times. Their clothes are too protective and uncomfortable. Their ties are tied around their necks too tightly. Their minds are too closed to take in new information; they will just relate everything they see to things their so-called scientific colleagues wrote down long ago and repeated enough times to convince everyone they're true.

Repeating that the Earth is flat never made it any flatter. They're like a bunch of geese honking as loudly as they can, searching for a common sound and prevailing in the noise until this happens. And when this consensus appears, they call it scientific truth."

"When we see the golden doors, it will be impossible to keep them secret for long, but we'll have at least a few hours or a day to explore our discovery. We want to take pictures so that we can share them with the world. We have to do this before the Museovirasto comes and closes it off to the general public for the foreseeable future. We really don't trust them with this. Until now, they've sabotaged everything to do with the Bock Saga. We must be able to share the knowledge before they can put a lid on it."

Casper stopped to pour himself some more tea.

My mind was spinning. That was a lot of information, and I knew there was so much more to follow. I had trouble digesting it all and placing it into a coherent story that would give me an overview of the Bock Saga. I proposed taking a trip through Finland and visiting all the sites that played a key role in the Bock Saga. Everybody thought that this was a great idea and we decided that the most practical approach was to divide it up into day trips. Every day, we could visit one of the sites and hear the corresponding part of the Bock Saga. In the evening, we would return to Akanpesa.

But first, we would have a night out in the town! After all, we were people who spent most of our time partying with each other. After dark, four guys and I jumped into my Mercedes and drove off to Helsinki. We knew that even just a couple of drinks would cost us an arm and a leg, but at that moment we didn't care. Maybe someone had just arrived with another load of hashish. I forget what it was. But anyway, the guys all thought they deserved a treat after being isolated for so long in Akanpesa.

I drove the car easily through the Helsinki evening. It was dark, and the streetlights illuminated the drizzle making the city look like a black-and-white film noir. We were heading in the direction of the city centre where we knew we'd find the Helsinki bars. Five guys, all from Goa, all stoned. Ronan had rolled a huge joint that was filling the car with heavy clouds of smoke. Suddenly, a flashing light from the car in front signalled us to stop.

"Police, stop!"

"OK guys, play it cool," I muttered as I felt the car tense.
The police vehicle slowed down and came to a standstill forcing me to do the same. Before I could wind down the window to talk to the officer, all four doors were flung open, and we were pulled out roughly by the policemen.

"Oh god," I thought. "We're five Goa psychedelic-heads. We're bound to have drugs on us. I just hope nobody was stupid enough to throw them out in my car. Otherwise, it'll be solely my problem."

Hal had been sitting in the middle of the back seat, so he hadn't been pulled out with the rest of us. Within seconds, he'd jumped out onto the pavement of his own accord and started pulling off his jumper and sweater over his head. He stumbled around like a madman fumbling with the garments in the heavy drizzle and dim glow of the streetlight. We all stood staring at the bizarre sight in front of us. As soon as he managed to free himself, he threw his clothes dramatically to the ground, flung out his arms wide and with wild eyes he thundered:

"What in god's hell is going on here?!"

His unexpected actions surprised everyone and brought smiles to his friends' faces. The policemen were less impressed, and two of them jumped onto Hal to constrain him. He didn't put up a fight, to their continued surprise and meagrely complied with their orders. This was when the interrogation started.

We were divided up and each of us were asked the same questions:

"What's your name! What's your nationality! In which country are you registered!"

"My name's Casper, I'm American and I live in Japan."

"My name's Ronan, I'm German and I live in Bangkok."

"My name's Hal, I'm American and I live in Nepal."

"My name's Mr Yeah, I'm English and I live in Hawaii"

I noticed that my friends' answers hadn't brought much satisfaction to our interrogators.

"Whose car is this?!"

I raised my hand.

"And you!? Are you from Mars and live in Disneyland?!?"

"No sir. My name is William, I'm Canadian and I live in Indonesia."

Although it was amusing, I knew that our chosen answers wouldn't set us free. I think that in most countries, cops would call it a day in hearing us list all those countries and just choose to put us all in jail and sort out the mess on the following day. But not here. In the drab rain, where our innocent group was by this point soaking wet, the police started to strip-search us.

At the same time, four cops started searching my car, inspecting everything they could stick their fingers into. They knocked on metal, hoping to find a sound that would reveal the secret stash. A cop arrived with a toolbox and started to take the car apart. Each screw was removed, as was the back seat, the spare wheel, the inside of the doors, the bumpers, the engine hood and the air and oil filters. Each was inspected closely by the now greasy fingers. Inside the car, the carpets and the glove compartment were thoroughly examined and taken out. The front chairs and the rear mirror were also removed. Underneath the car, the bottom plates and other technical parts were unscrewed and checked.

This went on for a long time. Eventually, the policemen realised that there was no contraband to be found and started to put the car back together again in great disappointment. This proved an even harder task than taking it apart and took even longer. In the meantime, the other policemen continued to search through our clothes, shoes, underwear and even our hair. To my immense surprise, they found no hashish on either me or my friends, and we were allowed to go. The cops mumbled angrily that they knew our type and something about 'next time'. We were wise enough not to answer back and got into the car. I drove off and could see that my friends were feeling just as shaky as I was. After a moment of silence, I asked:

"Didn't you guys have any dope on you?"

"Oh, yes...!!" came four replies, and everyone told me where they'd hidden their stash and why the cops hadn't found it. Only Hal had had too large a piece on him to hide (about twenty-five grams), so when he'd jumped out of the car and pulled his t-shirt and jumper over his head, he'd had to swallow it.

"I ate the whole piece in one go. I think I'm going to be very stoned soon guys..."

"We'll look after you, don't worry!" we reassured him as the car filled with laughter.

"Hey Ronan, what did you do with that joint we were smoking when they stopped us?" I asked as I suddenly remembered he'd been holding it.

"Uh, nothing, William."

"So, where is it then?"

"It's still in the ashtray."

"But they turned the car inside out! How could they not have found it?"

"No idea," laughed Ronan. "Can I light it back up?"

We thought it was the funniest thing, and Ronan claimed that we were all protected by Öde. We were doing important work for the world, for the Bock Saga, we couldn't be caught by the cops. Nobody saw it as a last warning.

We all had a great night in Helsinki. We didn't care about money, even though a beer cost the same price as a bottle of champagne anywhere else in Europe, but what the heck? My friends kept insisting that soon all money would anyway be abolished, and we would be rich. Rich in some form or another, anyway. And yes, Hal got very stoned that night, but he handled it like a knight.

The next day, we went to visit Porvoo, just one hour from Akanpesa. In the Bock Saga it was called 'Trojaborg'. It was the place of the first ever labyrinth.

Excerpt from the Bock Saga:

The difference between a labyrinth and a maze is that a maze is designed as a 'puzzle' in which one must find the exit, whereas a labyrinth was designed according to the pattern of a specific dance. Dancing rituals were performed to select the next generation of mothers.

The day after that, we went to Raseborg, the oldest building in the world. And the following day, we spent a whole day on Odens Ö, the place where it all began. The boys were happy to be doing something other than hibernating and isolating in a dark room in front of the fire, alone with their pent-up intellectual energy threatening to burst through the windows.

For me, it was nice to spend time with my friends, be away from home for a few days and get to know the Bock Saga a little better, although I still had no intention of submerging myself into the thick atmosphere that had surrounded it since the day the temple hadn't opened in 1987.

We were happy on those golden days, but I noticed that my friends were growing increasingly impatient with the story. They needed a result so badly. Result, result, result. I heard that word so often. 'Result' only had one meaning and that was opening the temple. Everyone's mindset was fixed on that one aim. I'm not a psychologist, but to me it was near obsessive.

Casper

Justin was a Canadian guy we'd met in Goa at some party or other. A friendly trippy head, who wasn't much out of the ordinary for Goa standards. He'd heard about the Bock Saga from Mr Yeah and Ronan in a chai shop and had even spent a few afternoons on the veranda in Chapora with Ior. At the beginning of autumn in 1989, he decided to pay us a visit in Helsinki.

He'd heard talk of the crazy drug prices in Finland and had decided, like so many others, to take advantage of this. Thus, he made a stopover in Amsterdam and bought a leaf of paper trips, containing 500 LSD tabs, to bring with him. He then took the train to Copenhagen and the boat to Sweden, another train to Stockholm and from there, a boat to Turku in Finland. This was a lot of stops, but it was the cheapest way to get over to Finland and had the added benefit of allowing him to discover Scandinavia along the way. He'd also heard reports that we were poor and had little to eat in Akanpesa. So, he decided to try and help us out.

At the breakfast buffet on the last ferry to Finland, he stuffed his pockets full of food, intending to bring this to Akanpesa as a gift. He even went as far as raiding the kitchen, filling his bags with packets of cheese and sausages. This was noticed and, of course, considered theft. He was turned over to the on-board customs for some not-too-serious moral preaching. The customs asked him the usual questions:

"Who are you, where are you going, and how long are you staying?"

Justin told them he was going to visit Ior and gave them his address. And that was when they found the LSD. To them, it was clear, Justin must have been delivering the LSD to Ior. Predictably, the newspapers later described it as extremely dangerous LSD.

Later that day, the police knocked on the door of Ior's town apartment, arrested Ior, who was drinking tea and smoking dope with some listeners and arrested them too. At the same moment, the police burst into Akanpesa and arrested everyone there as well. They had already been focussing on us for some time and had been waiting for a good opportunity to intervene, and this was it. They'd been listening to our phone line and knew who our Finnish friends were. All around Helsinki there were knocks on doors and arrests. Game over.

I was locked up in isolation. I'd gone from being a free-flying bird to a bird in a cage. A cage without windows. I could feel the panic rising from deep inside. My soul screamed a primordial 'Help!' It couldn't be, it was unfair, it was horrible, and it was... Quiet. They just left me there to simmer. How long? I've no idea. A minute lasted an hour, which lasted a day.

I lost all feeling of time. There was no natural light and so no real indication of whether it was day or night. A large stark light indicated daytime, and a dimmer bulb indicated night. The guards used these lights to mess with my natural rhythms and knock me out of balance. They even played with mealtimes. It produced an awful jetlag feeling. But I was no stranger to jetlag. The cell was both empty and dirty at the same time. There was nothing to do but worry about what my friends might be saying and what the police already knew. What would become of the temple and the Bock Saga now? After a long time, I managed to get some sleep and the worries, anger and frustrations started to subside. My life in that cell then became a long blur. I tried to pass the time in meditation: just trying to empty my mind; no attachments, no expectations.

As more time passed me by, I realised that in a strange way I was kind of glad that the madness had ended. My prison cell was the antithesis to the life I'd been leading before the bust. There was nothing, and a lot of it. No more screaming Americans throwing furniture around the room. No more psychotic cretins coming up with ever-stranger ideas and plans. No more Museovirasto with their idiotic denials. No more dynamite exploding constantly by my ear. No more newspapers. Well... I'm sure they were keeping busy.

I accepted my situation and was able to get more sleep. I had no idea if I'd stay here for days, months or years. Öde would decide, I had no say in that anymore. After another while, I stopped waking up fully from my sleep. There was nothing to wake up for. I knew every inch of my cell walls and ceiling by now, and the food was certainly not something that I needed to wake up for. Every possible thought I could've had about my situation had already crossed my mind and been polished smooth at least a thousand times.

Then the endlessness ended. I had a visitor: Inspector Kant from the Helsinki drug police. He asked me countless questions about drugs and drug smuggling and drug dealing. I told him I didn't know about those things. I didn't take any drugs. Inspector Kant scoffed at this claim. Did I think I could fool him, convince him that this was the case? That was a ludicrous idea. Whether I took drugs or not, he knew I was a central player in this great drug smuggling ring. A wicked conspiracy to flood Finland and its naïve youths with enormous quantities of dangerous, psychosis-inducing, addictive drugs.

"You know all the foreigners! You know all the Finns! You know both languages and you're from Amsterdam! You think I don't know that *you're* the spider in the web?"

The next day I appeared in front of a judge whose job it was to decide if I had to stay another month in provisional detention or if I could walk free. Inspector Kant's opinion was clear. But my lawyer informed the judge that this was all it was: an opinion. All the twenty-six other detainees had unanimously declared that Mr Casper neither smoked nor used any other drug, nor had he been involved in any other drug-related activity. In addition to this, no drugs had been found in his possession and there had been no other indications that Mr Casper had anything to do with drug dealing, smuggling or possession.

The prosecutor and the inspector warned the judge that if I was released and new facts then came to light, it would be too late to prosecute me. I was a foreigner, so I could just leave the country and disappear. The bird would fly! Besides, could Mr Casper provide any other evidence to explain how he'd been able to live in Finland all this time and fly around the world without any financial worries?

They tried their best, but the judge decided I was free to go.

I couldn't believe my ears. Inspector Kant and the prosecutor fumed. Twenty minutes later, I was on the street. I stood blinking in the light, wondering what I should do. The door of the building opened behind me, making me jump. Lo and behold, there were Shavas and Ulven looking as dazed as I felt. What should we do now?

"Let's first get the fuck out of here, before they change their mind!" said Shavas. "My car's in Akanpesa, I want to pick it up."

We took the bus to Gumbostrand. As we walked towards the house, we passed the excavation site. The drilling and dynamite explosions had stopped. The big machines were gone and there were no trucks in sight. No explanation was needed, it was clear Henki Penti didn't want to be associated with drug dealing hippies and had left the sinking ship.

It was understandable. And it was all our fault, after all. We'd screwed that up ourselves. I feared the worst for the house, imagining scenes of devastation from frantic police searches. As we entered the building, it took me a moment to recognise the place. I hadn't seen the house so clean and tidy since before the Kristina Victoria party in 1987, when I'd renovated and painted the entire house. Two years of hosting ten-to-twenty freaks and crazy people a night had changed the atmosphere in the house. Just before we'd been arrested, the house had felt worn out, dark, sleazy and depressing. Now it smelled fresh, and the sunshine danced through the open windows. Flowers spread their colours on the table. Lola sat by the fire.

"Hi guys, want some tea?"

She told us that she'd visited the house the day after the bust and was surprised to find it empty. She went to the neighbour, who'd told her what she'd seen. The neighbour also gave her a spare key. Lola phoned Ior's town apartment, but there was no reply. She thought the best thing she could do was to clean the house, just in case the police came back to look for more evidence. After a few days, she travelled into Helsinki and learned that a lot of people had been arrested. Some foreigners had been lucky enough to have left Finland just a few days before the raid.

Andrew had left for Hawaii with a suitcase filled to the brim with hashish money just two days before the bust. The police had noticed that the main telephone user in Akanpesa had vanished at the right moment. There was a lot of media attention and Andrew even got his own headline in a national newspaper: 'It's not clear if Andrew Higgins smuggled tonnes, or tens of tonnes, of drugs into Finland'.

What was clear was that he wouldn't be coming back any time soon. Hal had also just left after having sold a carload of dope in Finland. Ronan had been lucky too. They wouldn't be returning either. All the Finnish people were still in jail, including Ior. The police had finally nailed him. The newspapers gloated smugly: 'In the end there's no escape from justice!'

Shavas, Ulven and I franticly scrambled for a plan to get Ior out of jail. Of course, he was innocent. But they'd found fifty-thousand Finnish Marks hidden in his piano, a Canadian was arrested on his way to Ior's residence with 500 LSD tabs in his pocket and they'd found an additional twenty grams of hashish in the pockets of Ior's friends in his apartment. This all needed to be rectified and explained.

Nobody in the world would testify that Ior had ever bought, sold, or smuggled drugs, because he hadn't. The money in the piano was from the sale of the apartment that had belonged to his aunt and mother. The banks could confirm that. All that left was the hashish, and this wouldn't be a matter of life and death. Sure, it didn't look great that everyone in Ior's circle had been affiliated with drug dealings, but this still didn't make *him* a criminal.

Shavas and Ulven came up with a master plan:

"If we can prove the Bock Saga is true, then everything that Ior has claimed becomes credible. Instead of focussing on digging in Akanpesa, we could go to Kajaani in the north, where, according to the Bock Saga, a golden bock is buried under the water well of the castle. We don't have to actually dig this up, as this would require consent from the god damn Museovirasto, but we could prove its existence with a metal detector.

We know a high-tech company in Germany that can supply us with the right equipment. If we prove that the bock is there, the Museovirasto will be forced to dig it up and keep their obligation to the nation of Finland. The appearance of this golden bock will produce such shockwaves throughout the national consciousness that they will have to acknowledge Ior's Saga. Hashish would probably be legalised immediately. They'll be forced to release him immediately," explained Ulven.

"And the great thing is that if we find something, we'll finally have our own confirmation of the Bock Saga. If we don't, we'll know it's all been some crazy dream of Ior's, and we'll be free of it for good. It's that simple. If I'm being honest, I don't expect to find anything. If that's the case, I'll bid adieu to you all and catch you on a sunny beach or at some crazy party somewhere in Goa," smiled Shavas.

"It's that simple, huh? Nothing's ever been simple when the Bock Saga's involved," I thought, realising that everything we'd ever tried to do had had the opposite result to what we'd hoped. But why not? Even if this extremely unlikely and naïve plan went wrong somehow, the worst that could happen is that Ulven and Shavas will have wasted their money on a fruitless scan. The only negative outcome I could envision was that the whole thing just led to nothing. I was getting used to nothing by this point.

"Ok, let's just go for it."

Shavas and Ulven began the preparations to leave for Germany by car and ferry. I hitched a ride with them to Helsinki where I wanted to visit Ior's apartment, for which I had a key. I also wanted to visit some of the girlfriends of the Finnish men in jail to hear how bad our situation was. Before driving to the harbour, Shavas made a quick detour to the police station to pick up his driving licence. He drove into the underground parking and both him and Ulven jumped out.

"I'll wait here for you," I murmured, trying to make myself as small as possible in the back seat, while cursing the situation.

At the reception, Shavas was immediately recognised and led to the desk of Inspector Kant.

"Wait right there, I'll get it for you. By the way, where's your friend Casper?"

Shavas mumbled something incomprehensible in Plattdeutsch and looked at Kant blankly. A few minutes went by, and Kant eventually returned with Shavas' driving licence.

"Now get the fuck out of Finland. If I see you again, I'll throw you straight back in prison and this time there'll be no way out. Am I clear?"

"Yes sir, that's very clear."

When Shavas returned to his car in the garage, it also became clear to him that as Kant had been shouting his warning, I'd been arrested again. The police had seen me on one of their cameras entering the parking garage on the back seat of Shavas's car and had arrested me without a second thought. One hour later, Shavas and Ulven were on the ferry to Germany, and I was in a police cell again. Denial, anger, negotiation, depression, acceptance...

Ronan

I'd left Finland for Amsterdam just before the bust. I racked my brains trying to understand why Öde had saved me. I should've been in jail too. I'd made the trip to Helsinki many times with sandals, beach rackets and bags full of hashish. I was just as much to blame for the disaster as the other smugglers.

The fact that the bust happened in the first place, didn't surprise me at all. We'd been so open about our dealings. We'd been dressed in such an eye-catching colourful way. When we walked as a group through Helsinki, every head turned towards us. We emitted psychedelic rays. People talked about us. They knew we were hanging out in Goa in the winter and not working from nine to five in Finland either. It had been just a matter of time.

But why was I not in jail with the others? I couldn't let the thought go. The only reason I could think of was that Öde had other plans for me. The reason I'd left for Holland just before the raid was to set up another Goa-trance party. Was this the reason that Öde had let me off the hook?

Did Öde want me to continue spreading happiness around the planet by organising psychedelic parties? Were the parties somehow key to creating the open mindedness needed for the acceptance of the Bock Saga? Whatever the reason, I felt confident that I must have a role to play in the world-changing events to come. I could think of no other reason why Öde would save me in this way.

During this time, Hal had made his way to Amsterdam as well. He was lucky to have left Helsinki in time, but he had a Finnish girlfriend who'd been arrested with the others. As time passed and more people turned their secrets over to Inspector Kant, the police started to connect all the dots.

They knew that Hal and his girl had brought a lot of hashish to Finland. Hal decided to take all the blame. He somehow negotiated a deal with Inspector Kant that involved a confession from Hal, on the condition that the statement would be taken in Holland rather than Finland. Kant was prepared to travel to the centre of international drug trade: Amsterdam.

I thought it was very brave of Hal to agree to this. Either brave or stupid, that is. Was Kant really to be trusted? It would be so easy to collaborate with the Dutch police and set Hal up. And Hal had American nationality. What was stopping Kant from contacting the American drug enforcement? If they became involved, Hal would no longer be safe anywhere on the planet, including Amsterdam.

And if Kant decided to break their deal, Hal might never even know it had happened. He could just be happily going about his business when 'bad luck' caught up with him in a more problematic place like India, Singapore or even the US. He would then have to serve serious time.

It turned out that Kant had another reason to come to Amsterdam. He finished the interview with Hal, which exonerated his girlfriend. After that, he asked Hal to give him a tour of the city. He was especially interested in the red-light district that was a bustling place at the time.

He'd never even dreamed that something like that could exist. He also wanted to be shown where drugs were bought and sold. Hal showed him everything, and Inspector Kant stayed in Amsterdam for longer than a week. He couldn't get enough of it. His life completely changed, but that's another story.

Casper

I found myself once more in a dank nothingness. This time, however, I was certain that my luck had run out. In my head was the monumental Bock Saga, around me were concrete walls and outside my cell was an enormous machinery that worked tirelessly day and night to extract drug confessions from me and the others.

Kant had sunk his teeth into the case and refused to let go until he saw some serious convictions. He'd made that painfully clear. He moved from cell to cell listening to what everybody had to say, comparing these stories to each other, and then sharing them, often in a slightly twisted format, to the others in custody.

He didn't have to wait long for a crack to appear in the wall of silence. With that amount of people in custody, it was inevitable for someone to eventually start talking and, in so doing, implicate one or more of the others. Yes, the first to crack was Wessel, the German pseudo-number cracker and self-acclaimed genius. The others quickly followed suit. Except for Mr Yeah. He kept his lips sealed:

"Why confess? Let them produce the evidence. It's their job, not ours."

You all know the game; it's been played countless times around the world in hundreds of different variations. Innumerable books and films have depicted the now too familiar interrogation and confession scenes. To cut a long story short: we all received a prison sentence of one to two years. It could be worse.

Only, it did get worse. In prison, I was given the choice of sharing my cell with either Wessel, Frankenstein's monster, or Mr Yeah, who was in a constant rage. I told them I'd much prefer to be alone. Let the two madmen live together. But this wasn't an option. They were afraid that Mr Yeah's anger might pose a threat to Wessel's wellbeing, who had, after all, snitched on Mr Yeah and the others. Out of respect for Mr Yeah, who insisted on remaining alone, I chose Wessel.

Every day we were released from our concrete box into another concrete box on the roof of the prison to get some air. The roof concrete box had bars instead of a ceiling and was our only chance of seeing the sky. I soon discovered that, from time to time, Mr Yeah was held in an adjacent roof box.

And so, in the freezing cold Finnish winter, with snow falling around us, Mr Yeah and I were able to shout through the concrete wall at each other and have conversations. Mr Yeah was allowed a visit from Shavas and Ulven who told him what had happened outside the prison walls. It was in this way that I heard little by little what had happened to Shavas and Ulven in Kajaani.

Shavas and Ulven went to Germany on the day of Casper's second arrest. They were terrified the same would happen to them and took inspector Kant's advice literally. One hour later, they were on the ferry to Germany. There, they contacted the high-tech, sub-earth-radar-sonar-metal-detector company and convinced them to carry out a scan at the castle of Kajaani to check whether the golden bock was buried there under the old water well. They asked the company to acquire permission from the Museovirasto who owned the castle.

Ulven had prepared a professional presentation with drawings of the local area and all kinds of other technical details using a letter head from this respectable company. To everyone's surprise, Museovirasto agreed to a non-invasive scan of the castle. Two weeks later, the 'Wheeled Ashtray', as Shavas' car was called, drove off the ferry from Germany into Helsinki. There were no cops to greet him, thank heavens. Before driving to Kajaani, Shavas and Ulven decided to pass by Ior's town apartment to see if there was anyone there who could fill them in on the ongoing drug-bust situation.

As they were ringing the doorbell, Ior, Soma and Nag waltzed down the street towards them. Everyone was shocked to bump into each other in this way. Ior and his two Indian friends had just been released from the police station and were psychologically exhausted from having suffocated for two months in prison, in a constant state of uncertainty and stress.

"Well, this settles it!" Shavas proclaimed. "This is proof from Öde. Get your asses in the car and we'll drive like a whirlwind to Kajaani." He quickly explained the situation to Ior and the Indians and told them the scan had been scheduled for the following morning. A successful scan would prove the Bock Saga at once!

"Ior, you must come with us! Only you really know that location of the golden bock. If you come with us, we won't have to worry about whether or not we've looked in the right place. Only then can we really prove the Bock Saga beyond a doubt!" Shavas didn't think it worth mentioning that the whole point of the plan had originally been to get the man in front of him out of jail...

Ior, Soma and Nag were bone-tired, but they just couldn't resist Shavas' energetic plea. The only compromise Ior demanded was a chance to change into a fresh shirt, as he'd been wearing the same shirt for over two months now. He ran upstairs, cursed the police who'd ransacked his apartment for drugs and money leaving an indescribable mess, grabbed a fresh shirt and ran back down the stairs. Everybody got into the Wheeled Ashtray, lit cigarettes, and joints and – whoosh – they hurtled towards Kajaani, 600 kilometres to the north.

It was a long drive, but the group arrived on time early the next morning. The German scientists (Shavas called them 'the nerds') were already waiting at the entrance of the castle. I can only imagine what name 'the nerds' assigned to them behind our backs, the ragged, strange-herb smoking, psychedelically dressed, incoherently speaking weirdos they had as clients. They kept their faces neutral in front of the well-paying customers, however. Ior showed them to the courtyard.

According to the Bock Saga, the golden bock was buried in the bottom of the water well in the middle of the courtyard. The well no longer existed, but there was a clear indication on the stone surface of where the round hole had been filled in.

The Germans took their task seriously and walked up and down with their machinery scanning the entire area. Then, they continued throughout the ruin on the tiny island and scanned the whole place. They finished in three hours, packed their machines into a rented truck, explained that the results would be ready in a couple of days and said goodbye.

The Bock Saga gang drank coffee, more coffee and smoked a few packs of cigarettes, then got into the Wheeled Ashtray and drove back. No one knew what the outcome was going to be. I'll let you imagine what the conversations during this return journey were like, especially since more than half the passengers had just spent a second sleepless night after two months of prison. Late that night, the bunch arrived back in Helsinki exhausted and slept in the mess the police had left in Ior's apartment.

After a comatose sleep, Shavas and Ulven, who weren't tempted to tickle Öde anymore than necessary, left with the first ferry to Germany. A couple of days later, Shavas called Ior.
"WE HAVE A RESULT!"

My heart jumped. I gasped for breath. My legs melted and I laid my tired body on the floor face up. Through the steel bars of the ceiling, fluffy snowflakes twirled down and kissed my face. Oden itself was congratulating me.

The last few years I had been in a hostile environment for so long. Every single day we had to fight our way through to prove the Bock Saga. No help came from the traditional society that dominated our lives. Its culmination being locked up in a concrete box. And now suddenly this fight came to an end. We have made it. Everything we had done was true and just and made sense. I felt like being in paradise.

The scan had detected a heavy metal object on the spot where Ior had said the golden bock was buried. The Bock Saga was really true and everyone in the world could acknowledge that as a fact. My trust and year-long solidarity, along with the suffering and patience, had all been worth it. It was true that the Bock Saga attracted weird and crazy people, but it was now clearer than ever that the Bock Saga itself wasn't the problem. The result proved it was all true. I could even tolerate Wessel for a while.

It seemed logical to me that this result left the Museovirasto with no choice but to dig up the golden bock. I was sure that the procedure could be done in no more than a few hours. After that, the other golden bocks in the Offerlund could also be dug up and then the temple and the storehouse.

And after that? We could finally reveal the Bock Saga fully to the public. It would be accepted and studied by serious people, and it would go from being considered as madness to normality. And when everybody had listened to the Bock Saga and finally understood it, then we'd see our history in a different light, and with that, our possible future. A lot of decisions that people (important and influential people) make every day would change dramatically. OK, but first thing first. Museovirasto needed to finally fulfil their role as a historical institution.

Of course, the most logical thing didn't happen. I knew by this point that I wasn't involved in a logical story. What did happen was so bizarre that it was also unpredictable. Bizarre and unpredictable were so far the only constant factors that accompanied our quest in the Bock Saga.

The Museovirasto flatly refused to dig up the golden box that was seen by the German high-tech machine. Shavas and Ulven wrote pleading letters to the president of Finland, to the parliament, to all kinds of ministries, universities, and anyone of influence they could think of.

Eventually, they were granted a meeting with the institute director of the Museovirasto, Gardberg. Yep, the one who didn't like the Bock Saga, who didn't like Ior Bock, and who only liked scientific reports written by his cronies that didn't contain anything about the Swedish language or Swedish people and certainly not anything that claimed to have happened more than a thousand years in the past. According to him, that was the year that the first Homo sapiens came to Finland.

Then came the day that Shavas and Ulven paid me a visit. They told me how this episode with the Museovirasto and the golden bocks had ended.

Shavas and Ulven entered a baroque office filled with old dusty books and antique ornaments. Despite the light that came in through the high windows, everything was in shadows.

"Welcome gentlemen. Please enlighten me as to why you want to excavate in our Kajaani castle?"

"We don't want to excavate anything; we want you to do it," snapped Shavas.

Director Gardberg was not used to being addressed in this way. His adrenalin gland tightened a little and his eyes widened slightly.

"Well, gentlemen, why's that the case?"

Our friends explained, pleaded, showed him the scan results. Director Gardberg was like his office, old and dusty. Shavas and Ulven were light shining in from the outside, but they couldn't pierce through the shadows in his head. After twenty minutes, Gardberg interrupted them.

"Stop, I can't listen to this anymore. You've seen too many Indiana Jones movies. Do you think I don't read the papers? You're just brainwashed followers of LSD-guru Ior Bock! Everything you've just told me is absolute nonsense. There's nothing below the courtyard of the Kajaani castle. What you see in the scan is just some steel pen left over in the construction of the castle."

Shavas couldn't hold himself back.

"Are you blind or something?" he yelled. "I've just shown you a scan result from the leading metal detection company in the world! Are you accusing them of being LSD-guru followers too? Maybe your problem is that you can't get anything in your brain that hasn't been written down in some dusty book a few centuries ago. You can't tell a newspaper story from clean and hard facts!

All we want to do is introduce Finnish mythology and history to the Finnish people, yet everyone treats us like drug addicts. We have science on our side here. Elementary physics, not some misty belief system, which is what you seem to live in! You should be ashamed of yourself, withholding the truth of your own history from your fellow country folk! You're paid by them to uncover their past."

"In neighbouring Russia, your colleagues have dug up artefacts that are over 8,000 years old. The same goes for your neighbours in Sweden, in Germany and in the Baltic states. But according to your 'scientific feeling', in the centre of all that activity 8,000 years ago, nobody set foot in Finland and not one single thing happened here. How can you sleep at night? Do you take sleeping pills so you don't have to think about what might have happened here before a thousand years ago? Do you take tranquilisers during the day to trick yourself into believing that nothing ever happened in Finland? Who's the one on drugs here? And you accuse us of not being able to see the truth because of substance abuse? What the hell are you on, to live like that? What do you tell your children when they ask you about your work?"

The distanced and superior attitude of director Gardberg visibly crumbled under this barrage of words. Nobody had ever talked to him like that. It was possible that he'd talked to others in this 'I know everything, because I'm a scientist and the director of supreme knowledge in this country' style, but these foreigners were not in the least impressed by him. They couldn't care less that he was the authority of the monolithic Museovirasto, whose words were carved in stone even more than those of the Bishop of Finland.

"Well... Even if it wasn't all nonsense, we don't have money to excavate into the courtyard of the castle."

Shavas and Ulven stared incredulously at the now deflated man in front of them.

"That's your excuse?! We'll pay for it then!" thundered Shavas. "How much could it possibly cost?"

"Around fifty thousand marks," Gardberg replied.

This was an enormous amount of money considering all they needed to do was dig a hole several metres into the ground. It was extortion.

"It's a deal then. You'll hear from us soon."

With this, the two Germans hurried out of the office before Gardberg could get a hold of himself and return to his former authority.

Ulven and Shavas drove back to Ior's apartment and filled him in on their half victory.

"They've agreed to excavate, but we'll have to pay for it ourselves. It's a mountain of money that we don't have and will never be able to scramble together."

Ior asked how much they wanted.

"Fifty thousand."

"No problem, I've got it," Ior smiled.

Everyone looked up at him in disbelief.

"I mean it! Just this morning the police returned the fifty thousand that they'd confiscated during the bust. They've checked with the bank who confirmed everything was in order and the money really was from the sale of my auntie's apartment. They couldn't find any traces of drugs on it, so they were forced to give it back. There's only one slight problem. In the process of testing for drugs, they used a chemical that turned the blue 100-mark notes into pink."

"Well, we can just head to the bank and change them back into regular notes. Then we can pay this bunch of thieves for the excavation," Shavas said excitedly.

"No, we're going to do no such thing. It was blue money; it was tested for being black money and now it's pink. That's exactly how the Museovirasto will receive it. They must accept. It's been given out by the bank of Finland. They have no choice in the matter," was Ior's reply.

"Let's celebrate then! The Museovirasto will dig up the golden bock, Gardberg will be responsible for proving the Bock Saga true, and we'll make all this happen with pink money."

Ior sat down, lit a joint and sipped his tea in celebration, indicating that the discussion was finished and there was nothing left to say on the matter.

Within a few hours, Shavas and Ulven returned to the Museovirasto with a big bag of pink money. It wouldn't enhance their credibility, but so what? As long as the Museovirasto accepted it, and dug up the golden bock, it would be a victory. And they did accept it! They even wrote out a receipt for the money. And so, it came to be that a few freaky foreigners paid for the excavation of artefacts in an attempt to reveal Finland's heritage to its own people. What a humiliation for the proud nation. Or at least this is what should've happened. But of course, it wasn't what happened.

A few weeks after accepting the pink cash, Museovirasto sent a friendly note that stated they had reconsidered the whole deal and wouldn't be carrying out the excavation after all; they claimed that the chance of finding something was less than zero. They politely asked which bank account they should return the fifty thousand to. We were back to square one...

This blatant betrayal sparked various demonstrations from the via-via group, who joined forces with around two hundred locals and baptised themselves 'the diggers for truth'. They set off to excavate the golden bock armed with spades. Alas, when they arrived at the spot, the ground was frozen stiff; digging was impossible. They decided to come back in a warmer season, but when they returned some months later in even greater numbers, they found that the Museovirasto had taken measures to protect the ancient ground. They had placed a one and a half metre thick slab of reinforced concrete over the spot where the old water well had been, preventing any digging.

The opposite of what we tried to accomplish always ended up happening.

We were seen by the public through the eyes of the hostile media: terrible people because we dressed funny and smoked joints. Everything we ever told journalists was published as its exact opposite. There're countless examples of this.

We learned throughout the years that if things came from outside our group, we could react on them, without a worry. If we had an idea ourselves, on the other hand, and took the initiative, cars would drive into canyons and people would fall dead. Strange things happened around us, and strange people were attracted to us.

We didn't know how to handle this. We tried not to take it personally, but sometimes we did, and we carried the weight of the Bock Saga on our shoulders and were convinced we were somehow responsible for it all. We would've preferred to leave that responsibility with the people who'd lived at its core since the dawn of mankind: the Bock family.

We started to attribute the increasingly strange events of coincidence and fate to Öde. We did this to create space between us and what happened.

I realised that we would never succeed with unlimited optimism alone. The jail time we'd been given had not helped in matters, and we very much felt like we'd hit a wall. That we had stumbled upon the history of mankind had seemed unlikely to us at first, but not impossible. We now realised that the impossible part was involving the rest of the world in the story.

Raportti Media and the Museovirasto were formidable opponents who appeared at a time when we hadn't even realised we had opponents in the first place. And of course, it's undeniable that we were our own opponents as well. All the illegal smuggling had made us vulnerable, and the crazy stories had only given us headaches and a bad reputation. We weren't political people; we just wanted to open a temple. But we'd come to realise that there was no escaping the political roots that had dug their way into our story.

Lola

There was no way I was going to let those knuckleheads come back into the house in Akanpesa and undo all my hard work. Someone had to make a stand and, as usual, it ended up being me. I rounded them up and made my position clear.

"You guys are always fighting. You're fighting amongst each other. You're fighting against the Museovirasto and Raportti Media. You're fighting to scramble enough money to live on. You act as if you're in a chess game where the only goal is to kill your enemy's king. Chess, Shah, Czar, it all means the same to me. It's a male game and you only ever talk about male subjects. As a kid I used to play a female game. In Spanish it's called 'juego de damas'; in English it's called checkers. *This* game focuses on all the pieces and the whole board. This is what you guys are missing: a female touch and a greater overview of the playing field. You've got to get more practical.

If your main pursuit really is to open that bloody temple, then why are you allowing all these idiots who've never even held a shovel in their hands to sleep on our floor and eat from our fridge? This is not the salvation army, nor is it a free hotel. Kick them all out!"

Casper

When I got out of jail, I needed a break to ground myself, to analyse what had happened to me and to our group, and to decide what we should do next, if anything at all. To my surprise, Akanpesa had become the perfect place for introspection. Whereas before it had been more like a mental institution, where people ran in and out continuously and anything could happen at any time, now it had become an oasis.

The reigns of the household were firmly in the hands of Lola and the other girls who had set strict rules. The men had their own quarters, which they had to clean every day. The girls had their Svan room, which was off limits to us. The men had to chop wood for the fire in the living room and the sauna.

The Americans and their violent fights were gone. There were no gypsies, psychos or drug dealers. The place was clean, and everybody was clean in body and soul. Every day a home cooked meal was made with real ingredients from nearby farms. The whole house filled with the most wonderful smells that announced each meal, and only the girls were allowed in the kitchen. While they were cooking, the men had to clean the house, which was the only way they would be allowed an evening meal. We'd feel so guilty if we didn't perform our tasks with devotion, since the girls were working so hard and putting so much effort and love into their work. So, we made sure we completed our work as perfectly as possible. It was an enjoyable time. The garden was full of flowers and the windows welcomed in the crisp, fresh Finnish air. The sun seemed to always be shining.

When the days shortened, I left for Goa. There, I had a quiet time. Ior was telling the Bock Saga every day in a chai shop in Chapora, and Ronan, Mr Yeah, Shavas, Ulven, and some Scandinavians attended regularly. It was the golden age of the Goa-trance parties, so we divided our time between Bock Saga, party and beach. Everything was as it had been before my time in jail.

Ronan

My path was clearer than ever. Öde had made sure to keep me safe from all the drug drama in Finland, and Shiva, the god of dope smoking, was working alongside to protect me as I made trip after trip with my stomach, sandals and beach rackets full of hashish. It was all for the greater good: to buy time to spend with Ior and listen to more of his Bock Saga. Time and time again, I found myself in sticky situations and managed to escape without a scratch.

Like the time I shared a train compartment with a middle-aged Dutch housewife who was smuggling white powder from Amsterdam to Milan. Customs and police were all over the train when they found the neat little packets in her suitcase. Sniffer dogs swarmed the carriages and came heart-stoppingly close to finding the hashish hidden in my shoes. But the fact remained that they didn't find it.

The police also missed the stash of dope I'd expertly hidden under the floorboards of a van I drove from Amsterdam to Italy on another occasion. Sure, that was partly because of how skilfully I'd hidden it, but the change in weather that had expanded the floorboards and melted the glue I'd used to seal away the hashish made it a very close call. I really have no idea how the police dog missed that one. Actually, I do. The dream team of Öde and Shiva had my back. My path was clear.

Casper

It was generally believed, or at least hoped, that the Indian god Shiva would take care of us. He was a blue god that smoked chillums and every time we lit one, it was our way of praying to Him. In return, He guided us through the restrictive regime the authorities put on smoking. In other words, it was a common belief that if you smoked enough dope, nothing bad could happen to you. I thought that this was a dangerous presupposition. I was more a believer in the laws of chance, which could be calculated, and I preferred the tactic of working hard and paying attention to the little details that often ended up making the biggest difference.

There were so many adventure stories filled with examples of how luck and coincidence had saved the day, however, that many easily believed in Shiva's guiding hand. Besides, the unlucky ones who hadn't felt this guiding touch were usually not around to tell their side of the story. I don't think you'll find it hard to believe, but Ronan was amongst the firm believers in Shiva's protection. After all, the underlying concept was quite like that of Öde. I'm certain that Ronan had smoked more than his fair share for safe passage, but it turned out Shiva had another fate in store for him.

I was in Goa enjoying the pleasures of life when I got word that Ronan had been arrested in Panipat in the north of India for drug smuggling. What sad news! The minimum punishment for this crime was ten years. Usually, there was a way to bribe yourself out of this situation, but time was of the essence.

When you were caught, you needed to immediately bribe the policemen who'd caught you. If that wasn't possible and you were brought to the police station, you'd have to bribe all the police there too. As soon as the case was registered, everything became much more difficult as more and more people became involved in the case. Once the judge resided over the case, it became too large a bribe for most people to afford. If the media got wind of the investigation, it was game over. The authorities would never allow themselves to lose face. If this was the situation, the best thing to do was to confess and start the process as soon as possible in the hope of somehow getting free afterwards. This was only really a viable option for stupid but rich people.

I'd heard of court cases where the defendant had claimed that they'd been set up by a corrupt police system. This was also a stupid route to take. An accusation of this kind was viewed as an insult to the Indian society, even if everybody in the courtroom knew the statement was true. The Indian authorities didn't like disharmony. They felt pain deep in their hearts when such claims were made. Even though the judges were independent, they would never publicly stand against their own justice system.

Thus, it was madness to allow yourself to get to this stage in the process, and if that's where you found yourself, it was usually the result of a long string of stupidities. What made things worse was that it took about two and a half years for the trial to even begin, and it could then drag on for years after that. Until a verdict was reached, you'd be stuck in jail, whether you were guilty or not. There was a bail system in place, but the Indian judges were reluctant to extend this to foreigners. They knew that a foreigner could easily escape the country or, if they weren't smart or rich enough for that, could quickly disappear within India.

Some of Ronan's worried friends, along with some admiring girls, had discussed the case while smoking chillums and had concluded that Ronan's chances of freedom were extremely slim and that he had only one real chance of avoiding the ten-year jail sentence. I had to travel to Panipat and rescue him.

To be honest, I was quite surprised to hear that I'd been singled out as the best person for the task, as I hadn't had much experience with the authorities other than having been in jail myself. I'd never been on a diplomatic mission or accomplished any sort of large organisational feat, for that matter. The closest I'd come was being involved in party planning, but even then, I'd never had anything to do with the permissions side of things. After some deliberation, I agreed that I'd give it a try. Ronan's friends held a collection that paid for the trip, with enough left over to also pay for the bail and potential bribes.

I went to Mapusa market and purchased some formal wear. If I was going to do this, I was going to do it properly. That night, I pondered on how I'd carry out the job. I looked up Panipat in *Lonely Planet*, which was the travelling Bible of India. The book showed me where it was: far north of Goa and Delhi and just south of the Himalayas. The first comment in the chapter read: 'Definitely the city with the most flies in India. Walking should be done with a closed mouth.' It was far away and a horrible place. Off I went anyway.

I arrived after a few days of travelling. Yes, it did indeed have a lot of flies, I could now vouch for that. It looked like a dusty town from a Spaghetti Western movie. There was a bus station, some government buildings, and a collection of shacks. There were no cowboys but lots of cows, holy cows at that.

The people didn't look Western at all, but were dressed in saris, lungis, and turbans. Soon, I found the local police station. There, I asked if anyone knew where Ronan was and if they knew what had happened the day he was arrested. The police-man who arrested Ronan happened to be working and explained the story in detail.

Policeman

That day, I was strolling over to the bus station when I saw a man dressed in what I would describe as poor people clothes. He had long hair, which I assumed meant he had no money for a barber, and he carried an expensive-looking Western-style bag. He stood out and was clearly not from around here. Only local buses stop in Panipat, so I suspected that the strange man might be planning to stay in the area and was thus worth a closer inspection.

I remembered that two years earlier a similar-looking man had been stopped at a bus station and had been found to be carrying illegal drugs. I decided to investigate and asked the man for his ID. I thought I'd just shake the tree a little and see what fruit fell out.

The man reacted in a very unfriendly, impatient, and almost aggressive manner. This set off alarm bells in my head as these were clearly the signs of someone who had something to hide. I asked if I could check his bag.

I was slightly nervous myself as I'm not used to dealing with foreigners. They're rich and therefore influential. How else can foreigners travel abroad and pay for airplane tickets, hotels, and food? Here in Panipat no one's rich enough to make such a trip. And even if one had that sort of money, they wouldn't dare go so far away from home alone. This man was clearly confident and influential. That's why it was so strange that he was dressed like a poor man. But I thought that this was perhaps a decoy, or just a foreign custom that I would never understand. I found about two kilos of charas in his bag. I told him that this was a serious crime, and he could go to jail for a long time for it. I told him that everything could be settled there and then with a fine, however, but I'd need to also confiscate the contraband, of course. Imagine if he was caught again at the next bus station and it got out that he'd already paid me for the crime. That's why I didn't want to give the charas back to him. And of course, confiscating it would allow me to sell the drugs myself.

Instead of taking me up on my offer, the man lectured me on the benefits of smoking charas. He told me that the Lord Shiva himself smoked charas and that Shiva would protect him. I informed him that it wasn't a matter of good or bad, but of the law. It might be true that Lord Shiva smoked charas, but he was above the law.

Charas was forbidden to the people on Earth in India and Lord Shiva didn't protect criminals. He didn't want to listen; he didn't want to settle there and then either, so I had to take him to the police station. Here, he just repeated what he'd said earlier, and the local judge sent him to prison to wait for his trial. This will take place in two years' time.

William

I found myself grinding my teeth. How could Ronan have been so stupid? It sounded like the policeman had been reasonable and would have gladly settled for a bribe. Why in the world would Ronan not take that offer? It was beyond me. I learned that the prison was fifty kilometres to the north of Panipat, in a town called Ambala. It was already late in the day, but I decided to get a taxi to Ambala, find a hotel and sleep. I wanted to be as fresh as possible the next morning for my visit to the jail.

When I opened my window to let in the early morning rays, I saw Ambala in the daylight. It was an exact copy of Panipat. Next to the bus station, I found a small but bustling market and within it a place that could wash and iron my clothes.

While I was waiting for the clothes to be cleaned, I had a breakfast of honey and fruits and a chai. The good thing about India, I thought, was that even in the bleakest of places you could always find deliciously intense-tasting Indian food served with hot chai. With the sugars rushing through me, my body and mind slowly started to wake up.

I contemplated what the best way to approach the situation would be. So far, it looked terrible. Ronan had been caught and had done everything in his power to worsen the situation. I knew that without spending millions it would be nigh impossible to get him out of this place.

Over the last few years, the Goan police had increased their bribe demands dramatically. This was due to international pressure placed on them by the US who insisted they do something about the drug problem they had amongst foreigners. In some cases, bribing had been impossible, and hippies were serving long jail sentences in horrible dungeons. Any jail in India was worse than a slum in Calcutta. I tried not to focus on these glum details as I made my way to see Ronan.

The jail looked like a medieval castle but not of the romantic baroque kind where the princess falls in love with the prince. No, this dreary building looked more like the lair of an evil baron; I wouldn't have been surprised to see a kidnapped princess waving for help from one of its towers. The four high towers were connected to each other by windowless walls, and the entire building only seemed to have one entrance.

I knocked on the door. It opened. I saw moustached guards with rifles. I told them who I'd come to see, and after a first refusal ("Prisoners can only have one visitor per month and visiting permission must be applied for beforehand") and my first of many pleas ("I've come from the other side of the planet, please make an exception"), I was told to wait until the correct papers were prepared.

This gave me extra time to flesh out my plan and decide on the best tactic to take. My mind went blank. I told myself that improvisation would just have to do for now, at least until I understood the situation fully.

One thing I did decide on, however, was how I would play my role. I was going to be somewhat friendly, slightly charming with a touch of colonial superiority, completely non-offensive and fully respectful of the guards' authority. I would portray myself as belonging to the same ruling class as them, albeit a smidge above, which would allow me to apply added pressure if necessary.

It was a subtle balance, but I realised that I would never win through bullying and raw power. My only experience of power play was from my occasional games of chess, but I was able to also draw from the knowledge that my ancestors had ruled a large country in their time. Persuasion and leadership were in my blood, I repeated to myself nervously.

As I waited for the admission documents, one of the guards told me he'd spoken to Ronan just the day before. The guard had been curious to know what Europe was like and whether its people really were rich enough to afford plane tickets that took them all over the world.

He told me that Ronan only wanted to talk about the benefits of smoking charas and his disdain at the Indian laws that forbid it. It seemed that he'd been ranting about this to anyone who'd listen. And it got worse. He'd also started telling the guards and other prisoners about the Bock Saga. Everyone unanimously agreed that both story and man were incredibly strange.

I was escorted into the bowels of the castle through an open courtyard filled with chained men washing clothes. The further we went, the darker it became. We passed many barred rooms bursting with prisoners who looked at us with big round eyes. After many twists and turns, stairs and hidden doors, we finally arrived at a much emptier cell to the rest. Ronan, who'd been crouching in a corner, jumped up in enormous surprise. I asked the guard if we could speak in private. My request was granted. That was the second little privilege I'd received that day. Things were going well.

"You look smart," Ronan appraised.

"You look pretty shitty," I replied. "Tell me what happened."

"I travelled to Manali high up in the Himalayas, and from there, I hiked through the mountains for a couple of days until I reached a small farm where the famous charas is produced. I worked with the farmer and his family for a few weeks on the steep fields surrounded by the majestic mountains. We produced around two kilograms of first grade charas. With my bag full of black, sticky treasure, I walked back to Manali and took several local buses in the direction of Delhi-"

"Spare me the details of the trip itself and get to the important bit, you idiot!" I snapped at him.

It turned out that Ronan had decided not to take the direct interstate bus in the hope of avoiding police roadblocks. I couldn't deny the logic in this decision. The political situation in the north of India was tense; the Sikhs were fighting for independence and the Muslims in Kashmir wanted to become part of Pakistan.

In addition to this turmoil, the police had realised that large numbers of hippie travellers often travelled to Manali to purchase drugs. The police also realised that these travellers often had rich families and friends who were willing to pay large ransoms. The route quickly became a profitable destination for the police force who saw the hippy smugglers as roaming lottery tickets.

And so, this was how a smug Ronan happened to be waiting for a local bus at the dusty bus station in Panipat when the police officer approached him and asked to search his bag.

"I didn't expect to be searched! It was such a quiet little town. No foreigners ever came through there; I was sure I'd be safe." The rest of Ronan's story was surprisingly similar to what I'd been told by the policeman who'd arrested him.

"Did you really refuse to pay the guy when he gave you the chance of avoiding a ten-year jail sentence? What on Earth were you thinking?!"

"He wanted to keep my charas. I'm on a mission from Shiva, William, I know that he'll protect me! We're going to change the world. We'll open the temple and make the world a happy place by spreading charas and Goa-trance parties. We'll finally break free from this never-ending ice age. The world is dark, it's our task to bring the light."

"The Ice Age finished over 9,000 years ago, you dumbass."

"No, there's still ice in the North Pole."

"So what? You're in jail. Can't you see that Shiva hasn't protected you? Please can you snap out of it and get practical? I came all this way to save your ass. From now on, you must do as I say. My name is Shiva now, OK? First of all, you're going to stop ranting about how great it is to smoke charas. Why on Earth do you think you can change the laws of this enormous country through words alone? The law is fixed, understand? And for god's sake, stop talking about the Bock Saga! There's a high chance you'll offend everyone around you in ways you don't even understand. They're all Hindus, Sikhs and whatever else. They already have a belief system; they don't need yours. From now on, you're going to insist that you're innocent without contradicting the police version of events."

"But how? They're contradicting stories."

"Never contradict the police. The court case will be in two years at the earliest. Many additional facts can play a role between now and then, maybe the policeman changes his mind. Maybe you plead insanity. It wouldn't take much to convince them of that with all the crap you've been saying."

I left him. His, or should I say 'our', chances were dim. He'd done the exact opposite of what he'd wanted to achieve. Back at the jail office, I asked to see the director. I was informed that he was at home, in the beautiful house right next door to the jail. I walked over to the large colonial building that stood in the shadow of two big leafy trees. Bright bougainvillea climbed the walls and a large porch framed by tall pillars welcomed me as I drew closer. A couple of deck chairs sat lazily on the porch and a large marble table filled the rest of the space. It was a friendly place and in total contrast with the jail beside it.

I was let in by servants who wore the same uniforms as the jail wardens. It turned out that the director had time for me, plenty of time. After some friendly small talk, during which I was just as charming, gentle, and colonial as I'd planned to be, he invited me to have lunch on his porch. We sat at the marble table, and plate after plate of delicious food was served. It felt like we were two colonial rulers. I warmed to my role, and I could see he very much enjoyed his.

He looked and acted like Mussolini did during his better days. I'm not political, and in daily life, I'm tolerant to anyone who's nice to me. Where I draw the line is with Nazis. I can't be certain whether the director was a Nazi, as we didn't talk about politics, but he certainly looked like one. He'd never spoken to a foreigner outside of his prison and was curious to do so. He wanted to know about life outside India. Like most Indians, he was full of prejudice that had been fed to him by the media, but he was surprisingly open and listened to every word I spoke.

He then talked about his own life. In his Mussolini-like, self-congratulating manner, he told me how good he was to his prisoners. He pointed at two cows that were grazing between his house and the jail.

"I bought these cows for my prisoners so they can have milk in their chai."

I couldn't see how the two skinny cows could ever produce enough milk for the many hundreds of prisoners, but I wisely thought better than to point this out to my host.

"Of course, I still apply for the government yearly milk allowance. The cows feed themselves and now the allowance goes into my own pocket," he confided to me.

Was he trying to prove how smart and practical he was? I wondered if this confidentiality came from the feeling of trust I was building between us or from a certainty that he was untouchable. It was probably both.

"The prisoners are like my children, and I am father to all of them."

"Reminds me of the All-father," I thought silently.

"I want them all to be healthy and happy and everything I do is to accomplish this. It's not easy. Many are troubled minds. That's why they're criminals."

"Do you think that maybe some were just very poor and hungry and simply wanted to feed themselves and their family, and that this is what led them to commit a crime?" I suggested. "I mean, is it possible that they are also victims in some sort of way?"

"Yes, they're victims too. They suffer from a disease that makes them antisocial. There's no other reason. That's why I see the sentence they're given as an opportunity to cure them rather than a form of revenge," he argued with a doctorly expression.

"Cure?" I thought, thinking of the gloomy medieval cells I'd seen a few hours earlier. "How do you cure them?"

"I show them justice and teach them harmony. We live our lives together in there. We grow old together. When you live as part of my family, you become enlightened through me," he explained benevolently, raising both hands upwards.

"Does this approach work?" I asked, truly interested now.

"For most of them, yes. Some remain antisocial, however. We apply other methods to cure this. We're very modern here and use psychological therapy."

"Is there a psychologist in the prison?"

"I am the psychologist," said Mussolini. "And the guards apply the therapy."

"What kind of therapy are we talking here?"

"Bamboo sticks and whips work best. We do it in the courtyard when everybody's present. That has the best effect. It greatly enhances the harmonic glue of our prison family. It teaches them good and bad. They learn a lot from it."

"Yes, very psychological," I nodded, inwardly vowing to remain on this side of those bars.

"They must learn that the good of the whole family is more important than that of the individual."

The harmony he was describing would be called 'order' in the West. Through my democratic Western sensibilities, I recognised him a despot of the worst kind. He saw himself as a god doing godly things for the good of the universe. I'd never spoken to a despot before; I'd only ever experienced one through propaganda movies. To meet one, sit on the porch of his house and have a prolonged lunch together was an eye opener. In the gentle breeze of the afternoon, surrounded by bees drinking greedily from the bougainvillea, it couldn't be clearer that being a director of a jail in India was infinitely better than being one of its prisoners.

I had to remind myself that I hadn't come here to have a conversation about right and wrong but to get my friend out of jail. This thought sat patiently in my mind as the director and I spent an enjoyable afternoon living like colonial rulers, both talking about our respective 'kingdoms'. We were becoming friends, and in this friendly atmosphere, he confirmed the story about Ronan that I'd already heard from the policeman.

I told him I was a friend of Ronan's family and that they'd sent me here to find out what had happened. I told him it was inconceivable that Ronan had smuggled drugs, that he'd never touched drugs in his life, and that there had clearly been a mis-understanding. Ronan had probably just gone mad. That was the only way to explain all that had happened. We both agreed that, at the very least, he was certainly talking like a madman. The thought of asking the director to exclude Ronan from his 'psychological therapies' did cross my mind, but I didn't want to use the goodwill points I'd gathered so far on a favour of this kind.

"Do you have any other foreigners in your jail?" I asked as the afternoon drew to a close.

With a troubled face he confided: "No, not anymore. But two years ago, I did."

"Was he set free?"

"No, he killed himself," the director told me sadly, as if talking about a lost son.

"Why was that?" I pressed on.

"The man couldn't live with the idea of being without his family and the life of a solitary foreigner was too harsh for him."

He then explained that all the prisoners were kept alive by their families. These families lived in shacks outside the jail and provided the prisoners with food. Without a family, it was hard to survive; it was impossible on jail food alone. He told me that

I must convince Ronan's family to come and live here to keep him alive.

I smelled a tactical advantage.

"I think Ronan will suffer the same fate as your last foreigner," I told him, shaking my head in visible sorrow.

Mussolini looked alarmed.

"It would be impossible for his family to live here, and without them, he will surely die of some disease or by suicide. He would just simply miss them too much," I persisted.

I could see all the consequences of another foreigner's death flash before the director's eyes.

"It wouldn't look good for the Indian government and certainly not for me, if all the foreigners held prisoner here died." He hadn't realised the significance of this until that moment.

"Exactly."

I could see the panic creep into his cheeks as they lost their warm glow.

"Can you please advise me on how to solve this problem and get Ronan safely home to his family? I believe that such a solution would bring the greatest harmony to everyone involved."
The director nodded distractedly and informed me that Ronan would be transported to the court in Panipat in three days' time where a judge would decide the conditions of his detention for the next six months. That would be the moment where fate could change.

"Go to Panipat. Your chances are slim, but I can't see any other way."

He offered I stay for dinner, but I thought it wise not to overdo things and left. I hoped that the director's fear of another foreign suicide in his prison would somehow work in Ronan's favour. It was hard to say.

The next day, I visited the courthouse in Panipat. The building was a mixture of colonial and Maharaja-style architecture. Like many buildings in India, it reflected both grandeur and a stark lack of maintenance. It consisted of a walled-in compound with a tower at each corner topped with a pointed dome supported by elegant pillars. Under each dome stood a fierce heavily moustached guard. Similar guards also stood at the monumental gate. They asked me for my name and purpose. I told them who I was and that I'd come from Europe to speak to the head judge.

I was bluffing, but apparently being a foreigner in a place that never saw any, opened doors. I was let into the courtyard. The scene in front of me was something out of a movie. Shackled prisoners chained in rows were being marched through a gate on the other side of the courtyard. Guards, prisoners, lawyers, and judges, all dressed for the occasion, were scattered everywhere. Some bustled to and fro, while others waited in position. I was led into the main building up a colossal staircase where a set of large wooden doors opened in front of me. I entered the courtroom. Antique, worn-out wooden benches lined the room, opposite which stood a stage with a heavy mahogany table. Behind this, on a highchair covered in wooden carvings, sat the judge. The whole scene radiated power.

The judge spotted me immediately and signalled with the smallest movement of an eyebrow for me to sit down and be silent. I sat opposite his stage and watched the proceedings of the court. One after another, the prisoners were led in front of him. The judge listened to the prosecutor and lawyers before giving a verdict.

The whole process proceeded swiftly, and I couldn't help but wonder why each case had to wait two years before being heard. But this wasn't for me to judge, especially since I'd only seen a fraction of the entire operation. And anyway, it wasn't important for me. What was important was that this judge emanated a whole other level of power than my friend Mussolini. I was witnessing Stalin sending prisoners to Siberia.

After deciding the fate of a hundred or so people, he took a break. With a movement of his index finger, he beckoned me to the side room where he was retreating to. I stood up and made my way over, aware that I was being followed by numerous inquisitive eyes. I opened the monumental door and entered the room.

There sat the judge, alone on a couch with a cup of chai in his hand. He gestured with his eyes for me to sit down. How was I going to find a common ground with this man? I needed to strike a conversation to discover whether we had any similar interests. I needed to small talk. Only in this way would I be able to sense him, figure out what made him tick and use this knowledge to free Ronan. But it was very clear that this judge was the master of the situation at hand. Nothing in his demeanour hinted that he would treat me any differently to the rest of the world. Except of course, he'd already done so through the act of inviting me into his chambers.

"Well, what do you want?" he asked. I realised just how little time I had at my disposal. At any given moment he was going to stand up, head back into the courtroom and continue with his life. There was no time for friendship, connection, or small talk. I got straight to the point.

"The day after tomorrow Mr Ronan will appear before you. He has been accused of drug possession. I am here on his behalf as I am worried about his future and wellbeing."

"I've heard about this case."

"Mr Ronan is a well-respected man in our society. It's impossible to conceive that he'd be implicated in a case related to drug smuggling. He does not need the money and has never used drugs in his life. His wife and children are missing him dearly."

"The police report was clear. Do you think the arrest was unjust?"

"I spoke to the policeman, and I do not doubt him. What's clear to me is that this must be a terrible misunderstanding."

"What's been misunderstood?"

"I believe that Mr Ronan had a moment of temporary insanity. There's no other way to explain it."

"The police found drugs in his bag. Mr Ronan did not deny these were his. He even pleaded guilty for the general use of drugs."

"This only further proves my point. A sane person would never have said such things in this sort of situation. I know that by the law of India, a crime has been committed. But the circumstances remain unclear. Mr Ronan would suffer a great deal in jail. There's no family to take care of him, as they live too far away. Although I realise the seriousness of the crime, I want to stress the fact that there were no victims apart from Mr Ronan himself. In a robbery or violent crime, there's always a victim. Here, the only victim is Mr Ronan. I believe it would be most harmonious for the state of India and everyone involved to release him on the condition that he will never return to this place."

"When he appears before me after tomorrow, I will not be judging his innocence or guilt, but whether he will be granted bail."

"I understand, Your Honour. The court case itself will not begin for another two and a half years' time and will last for an additional year, if not longer. Mr Ronan should be provided with the opportunity to be granted bail, surely?"

"Well, most people are indeed released on bail. But there is too much risk involved in granting bail to Mr Ronan as he's a foreigner and could easily escape the country."

"Your Honour, please could you explain to me how it is that people are able to afford such an expensive bail? It's something I've never understood."

"Most of them can't afford it. A bail bond is used as a guarantee and is usually either a sum of money or property. If the accused doesn't show up in court, the guarantor will lose his bail bond. The guarantor is generally either the head of a family, the mayor of a village or an employer."

"Thank you, I'd never realised this before."

At that moment, on the far end of the couch where the honourable judge was sat, a little mouse appeared. It sniffed around for a moment and then climbed to the back of the coach. I saw it from the corner of my eye but tried to ignore it as much as possible. I needed to remain concentrated on the conversation at hand. Besides, the judge might be embarrassed to have the mouse pointed out to him.

The judge continued in his explanation of the Indian bail system and the little creature crept ever closer. It got to the point where I started to think that I would have to say something after all. The judge would soon spot the mouse and wonder why I hadn't acted. But I found that I couldn't say a word. The mouse crept closer still and was now only a few centimetres away from the judge's head. It carefully stepped onto the collar of his black robe, crossed the judge's shoulder, sniffed his neck and continued on its path. I couldn't believe my eyes. If it hadn't looked so real, I would have thought it a hallucination, especially since the judge appeared to remain oblivious to its presence.

The fearless mouse gave me a boost of confidence. I took it as a sign from the gods. They were showing me that even a powerful judge could be walked over by a mouse.

"I visited the jail where they're keeping Mr Ronan yesterday. I heard that another foreigner was arrested two years ago for similar charges. Do you know the case?"

"Yes, drugs were found on him at the bus station. He appeared here in court, but the case against him was never finished."

"He committed suicide. He could not accept a life so far away from his home. He was alone. Even though the court case against him wasn't finished, in a way he was given a death penalty. This sentence is worse than the sentence he'd have been given if he'd been proven guilty. Imagine how it would look if Mr Ronan, who is formally innocent until the verdict, also committed suicide due to the circumstances forced upon him. I shudder to think."

Then came the punch line:

"If such an outcome could be foreseen, which we have just proven it can, this horrible eventuality would bring terrible karma onto the justice system."

For the first time, I saw a hint of emotion behind the judge's eyes. I asked again whether there was a way of releasing Ronan on bail. The judge sat silently for a moment, and then told me to find a lawyer. I asked if he could recommend one. He told me that this would be inappropriate as it was his duty to remain neutral. I told him I understood this, but that as a foreigner, I would be most grateful for some informal help. Maybe he knew someone who could advise me. He nodded and rang a bell. A servant entered the room and received some instructions in Hindi. The judge told me to follow him.

I thanked the judge for his time. Somehow, I had the feeling that against all the odds, my task of getting Ronan out of jail had shifted from impossible to merely unlikely, and this was considering that he'd been caught red-handed and fully confessed to his crime! I followed the court servant out of the courthouse, across the courtyard and out of one of the gates.

The servant led me silently to a what looked like a marketplace that operated under a patchwork of rags not too dissimilar to the bat sunshade I'd designed for the party. As we drew closer, I realised that this was indeed a market, it was a market for lawyers. Under the uneven shade, there were at least a hundred lawyers each with their own desk, typist and secretary. The lawyers were dressed in old-fashioned striped tailcoats and the typists were dressed in traditional Indian wear, with long beards, long shirts and turbans. They sat on the floor with type-writers in front of them, hammering away.

The amount of paper was staggering. Metre-high stacks piled around them. It was a cacophony of typing with a continuous buzz of flies in the background.

The servant brought me to two similar-looking lawyers who were drinking tea and studying some papers. I could tell they were surprised to see us, even though they tried to hide it.

I stayed silent so that the servant could deliver whatever message the judge may have given to him. Only a few words were exchanged. I'd hoped for more... There was still a chance that the words that had been spoken were important ones. I understood a little Hindi, mostly just formalities and greetings, but couldn't pick out any recognisable words. I took this as a sign that something meaningful had been said.

To cut a long story short: I discovered that the two lawyers were twin brothers and the proverbial sleazebags that lawyers are often accused of being. They liked to get paid a lot and up front. But I must say, in their defence, they took things seriously and produced an impressive amount of paper.

"It's absolutely imperative that Mr Ronan is released on bail. If not, he'll die."

"Why would he die?"

"He has no one to take care of him in jail and he'll miss his family too much. He's a family man, you see."

"We'll do our best, but foreigners are generally never released on bail. Do you understand that?"

"Can we find someone respectable enough to act as guarantor for him?"

"That's going to be very difficult."

It proved impossible. It was my attempt to avoid paying the full bail sum myself. In recent years, the expected sum had increased from $1,000 to $50,000 in some cases. The authorities had clocked on to the fact that it didn't matter what bail was set at, a foreigner on trial would always try to escape the country.

I still had some of the money that Ronan's friends had collected. After the travel expenses and the fee for the lawyers, there was about $4,000 left. It all boiled down to whether the judge would allow bail to be set and, if so, what amount he chose to charge us.

The day of the trial came, and I waited with my pair of lawyers for Ronan to arrive. He finally appeared sitting on the back of a bicycle rickshaw with one other prisoner and a guard. As the three men dismounted, I saw that they were each shackled to the other via a chunky chain. The whole situation felt absurd. I couldn't help but think how easy it would be for the two prisoners to overpower their guard.

I asked the chained prison guard if it was ok for me and Ronan to go outside the court compound and eat some food together. He agreed to this on the condition that he and the other prisoner came too. It turned out he couldn't have left us go alone anyway as he didn't have the keys to the locks. So, our ragtag group sat together for lunch. The two lawyers and I, dressed in suits, sat on one side of a table. Ronan, the guard, and the other prisoner sat in their corresponding uniforms, all shackled together, on the other side. I ordered food for everyone. Again, seeing the guard outnumbered in that way, I felt the urge to run for freedom. I controlled myself.

It would have been stupid to attempt an escape. It was their country and there was only one road that went through the town. It would take a single phone call to alert the next town and we'd be caught. Besides, the whole situation wasn't even really my problem. I was already free. Why would I risk a lengthy prison sentence to free my idiot friend? It wasn't like I was married to him. But the temptation remained.

I talked to Ronan about the case. I told him what and what not to say. I forbid him from making any wisecracks or philosophical lectures. I told him that if he wanted Shiva to save him, he should give Shiva a chance. After lunch, we returned to the courthouse and took our positions. The judge gave me no sign of recognition, which I took as a good omen. A lot of words were exchanged between the prosecutor and our lawyers, all in Hindi of course. All I could do was wait for the judge's verdict. It finally came:

"I am setting the bail bond at $3,000, effective immediately."

Bingo. I went to the cashier and paid. I was impatient now and pressured the clerks to hurry their paperwork. I wanted to leave immediately before anyone could change their mind. The lawyers told me to relax. I told them I couldn't.

"Well, just pretend to relax then. You're not helping."

After about twenty teeth-grinding minutes, Ronan emerged, unshackled. I asked them for some papers that stated his release and was handed a flimsy, handwritten piece of paper that didn't look too convincing. Once outside, the lawyers told me that the judge had set the bail that high because he believed that we didn't have the money to pay for it. The judge had been surprised when I'd produced the cash. A lucky escape then!

We needed to get the hell out of there. One of the bail conditions was registering at the courthouse regularly, the next required registration being in twenty-four hours' time. By then, we needed to be far away. I solemnly promised the lawyers that we'd see them at the courthouse the following day and then got straight into a taxi for Delhi. It was a long and hard journey. There were fire-lit roadblocks every twenty-five kilometres or so. We had to bribe our way through each one because Ronan didn't have a passport. My plan was to get him to Delhi where he could get a fake passport and fly to Europe.

But Ronan insisted that he needed to meet his girlfriend in Goa and attend some unfinished business. I told him his girl could come to Delhi, but he wouldn't listen. He insisted on having it his way.

"Don't give me that Shiva crap again," I snapped.

"But don't you see, William? I was right, Shiva and Öde did save me. How else would I be free now?"

"You're not free! You're on bail, and if you don't register tomorrow, you'll be on all kinds of wanted lists. I set you free, not Shiva."

"Shiva and Öde sent you."

I swear I could've killed him, but instead I got him on a plane from Delhi to Goa without ID. I felt like I did a pretty good job overall. Back in Goa, we had little contact. This surprised me considering I'd saved his ass. I'd spent weeks in a city famous for its hordes of flies for him. I'd expected at least a 'thank you'. But Ronan seemed to take it all for granted. While I was saving Ronan, his girlfriend had stayed in my house and, according to the locals, had had an affair with some German guy. At least he'd had the decency to leave my house before we got back, which spared me any additional problems. The German lover even ended up lending Ronan his passport so that Ronan could leave the country. The German simply reported the passport stolen after Ronan had left to be issued a temporary one from the embassy.

I should have guessed, but was still surprised to find out that Ronan, on a 'stolen' passport and with the knowledge that he was probably on a wanted list somewhere, still managed to smuggle a kilo of charas with him when he left India. Hail Shiva and Öde.

More like madness and money, I thought. The whole story left me with mixed feelings. I'd expected some respect and eternal gratefulness and was silently insulted that I hadn't received either. On the other hand, I was proud that I'd accomplished something that had seemed impossible. I felt there was some deep undefined power in me. A power that had maybe been passed down to me – either by upbringing or DNA – through my ancestors. It wasn't until quite a bit later that I heard about Ronan's adventure out of India.

Ronan bought the cheapest flight from New Delhi to Amsterdam, which happened to be from Aeroflot, the Russian state airliner. It went via Moscow. Now, as we've discussed before, the Dutch customs didn't really care whether someone smuggled drugs into their country. What was much more important to them was that that person had enough money to sojourn in Holland. They had a strict rule that, on arrival, you needed to have a minimum of 250 Dutch guilders in your pocket, which was about $130. If you couldn't prove you had this minimum requirement, they'd simply send you back on the plane you'd arrived on.

For Ronan, who only had enough money for a train ticket to Berlin, this spelled trouble. He tried to explain that he'd only be in Holland for two more hours, but the customs were inexorable. Eight hours after arriving in Holland, he found himself back in the transit section of Moscow airport.

The Russian customs found it highly suspicious that a European hadn't been allowed into another European county and put Ronan in a cell. It didn't take long for them to find the illegal drugs he was carrying. The Russians were not as lenient as the

Dutch when it came to drugs and sentenced him to five years in a Siberian prison. There was no convincing me to go and save his ass this time round, not in Siberia!

The story sent chills down our spines. Siberia is probably the closest thing to hell hippies like us could imagine. The realisation that this could happen to one of our group made me feel like a *slow* antelope suddenly realising there are lions hiding behind the grass. On the other hand, how can you be so *stupid* as to fly to 'safe' Amsterdam via Moscow? Ronan wasn't a slow antelope; he was a stupid one.

If you did decide to smuggle drugs, you needed to treat every part of it as if it were a serious job or preferably even an art form, something that is an essential part of the Goa freaks lifestyle demanding both attention and opportunistic wit. To treat the risks involved as trivial and believe they can be mitigated by smoking chillum after chillum in Shiva's honour, is stupid.

One year later, Ronan got lucky again when there was a prisoner swap between Russia and Germany in which he was included. He told me that the Russians never found out that he'd escaped East Berlin some years earlier. If they had, he'd have spent the rest of his life in Siberia. Ronan was keeping Öde incredibly busy.

Ronan

When I got back from Siberia, I found out that Casper had resettled in Akanpesa. I wanted to visit him, with some hashish below deck, of course. I did feel a little paranoid this time, as I knew that my name had cropped up on multiple occasions when the Bock Saga group had been interrogated for the drug bust. I'd escaped that mayhem just a few days before it started, and I really hoped I wasn't on the Finnish police wanted list. To fight my growing fear, I took a Valium before the flight from Amsterdam to Helsinki. I went to the airport, passed through all the security checks, and fell asleep at the gate. I missed the plane.

When I woke up, the plane was long gone and had already landed in Helsinki. The only thing I could think to do was buy a train ticket. It was going to be a lengthy trip, which included a long boat ride. Before going to the train station, I went to the pharmacy to buy constipation pills.

My stomach was full of hard little balls of wrapped hashish, and I needed to make sure it would stay there for the next sixty hours. It was a horrible journey. My stomach was rock hard. I didn't let myself eat during the entire trip. I felt incredibly hungry and full at the same time, and due to the stress of the situation, I endured excruciating cramps. When I finally arrived in Akanpesa a few days later, I was exhausted.

My next challenge was to get rid of the balls in my stomach. I drank diarrhoea-inducing tea that introduced a whole new level of pain. What's more, the little balls didn't come out all at once. I must have dashed for the toilet at least fifty times that day and they still weren't all out. I had counted the balls before I'd swallowed them and knew that what goes in must come out, but I couldn't have guessed that it would take more than a week for everything to leave my bowels. As you can imagine, a week and three days travel in my stomach had not enhanced the quality of the product either.

It was horrible, and I felt dirty inside and out. Throughout the years, I'd accumulated a big debt to Öde. Statistically, I knew it was impossible to continue forever one narrow escape after another. And I could see that Öde was sending me serious warning signs. I realised that I'd reached the end of my smuggling career. I headed to Goa to plot my next moves.

William

A big party was planned for the 17th of January in Goa to celebrate Ior's 50th birthday. Ronan was the main organiser and put
all his energy and creativity to work, as only he could do. It was
to be an extravaganza, even for Goan standards. Ior's Goanese
helpers had already flown back to Goa earlier that month, and
Ior would arrive on the day of the party.

With the help of his local network, Soma oversaw sorting out
all the necessary arrangements to ensure not only total police
tolerance, but also full protection. He would impose clear reg-
ulations that would specify who ran the bar, taxis and gambling gangs, as well as who would supply the sound system and
other such logistically and financially sensitive matters. Who
had control over what within the Indian network of locals had
always been a bit hazy to us foreigners, and we were never too
sure where all the baksheesh we paid for peace of mind ended
up. We did have a feeling that half the money we usually paid
wasn't necessary, but experience had proven that being stingy
didn't work either.

We assumed that since Soma was one of our own, he'd be able
to find a middle ground and make sure all was well arranged.
Sure, he'd put some of the money in his own pocket without
telling us, but if this ensured a successful party, it couldn't even
be called corruption.

The hype for the party had been building for weeks, and the
anticipation was hitting high frequencies. A famous party organiser once said that the energy you put into the preparation of
a party can always be felt during the event itself. Thus, the more
people that help with decoration, show elements and general
logistics, the more fantastically energetic your party will be.

All the major Goa DJs were involved and had been collecting and saving their most exhilarating tracks especially for this night. Ronan went about creating his fantasies, as if the concept of a budget didn't exist.

The chosen party grounds were inland, far from the sea and next to a jungely bush of enormous prehistoric-looking bamboos. Ronan made an imposing entrance that led from the parking area to the party grounds, lined on both sides by large shields that bore the Bock family crest: a keyhole with the words 'Logic, Honesty and Truth'.

This personalised touch was a major deviation from the Goa party norm where individuals were seldom glorified and where even symbols were generally avoided. Only the most general, nonspecific, non-personal symbols were used, like those found in astrology, for instance. A reference to a family or a person was completely out of the ordinary.

But Ronan saw it as appropriate due to the great importance of the Bock Saga and the role of the Bock family within it. Ior later told us that he'd actually felt quite awkward about it. Even though the Bock family had been an important and long-lasting caretaker of the human race, for Ior it had always also been an incredibly personal part of his identity.

The entrance led to the main area where antique mango trees dominated the landscape. They spread their ancient arms over the dance floor to protect the sweaty dancers from the sun. A group of ladies who came from at least twelve different countries were painting the mango leaves in trippy fluorescent patterns.

The colours and markings would help transport us to another world where the laws of nature were different to those we experienced normally, or at least were made up of elements that a sober mind could never have noticed or perhaps had forgotten. The paint on the leathery surface of the leaves created strange chaotic patterns that a psychedelic mind would easily recognise as an expression of alien mathematics.

The centrepiece of the party, which was also going to act as the main special effect, was an oversized sculpture of a straw bock, which is traditionally used as decoration during Scandinavian Christmases. Its shoulders were about two and a half metres above the pedestal on which it stood, and its horns reached a further 150 centimetres above that. It was a proud-looking bock made from a steel frame that had been welded together for the occasion and which was hidden under the mass of straw tied onto it.

The plan was that, at four o'clock in the morning when the party was in full swing, the bock statue would be set on fire from each of its four legs simultaneously. The fire would burn upwards toward the body and head and would finally reach the horns. These had been filled with fireworks. Loud explosions would fill the air, and flashes of colour would light up the sky.

Usually, such strong optical and audible displays caused the dance floor to explode with energy, bursting into a climatic amalgam of jumps, flic-flacs and raw screams of joy. Everyone who'd seen the straw monument was excited in the anticipation of this spectacle.

There were other unrelated and more worldly anticipations in the air as well. Thousands of kilometres away, between India and Europe, the Americans had responded to the Iraq attack on Kuwait and assigned themselves the role of 'white knight' and pledged to free the little country. The preliminary moves had already been made, and a full-blown propaganda programme bombarded the media day and night both in the East and in the West. A grand rocket attack on Bagdad was imminent and everyone in the world held their breath. Because of these tensions, less people had travelled to Goa that year. The hardcore party squad that travelled to Goa every year had still made it, of course.

Ior had booked a flight that was scheduled to arrive the day of the party. Luckily, it didn't get cancelled like many other flights had been. However, since the daily flights had been reduced down into a weekly schedule, the airline had chosen a larger airplane, which happened to be full.

Somehow, Raportti Media had found out that Ior was leaving for Goa and heading to a drug-crazed party for his 50th birthday. The story was in all the newspapers. It was even on the front page of the newspaper that was being handed out on the plane Ior was sat on. A large photograph of his head dominated the page.

Soon after take-off, the news that Ior was sitting on board amongst the economy-class passengers nonetheless, flew round the plane from person to person. It seemed strange that a personality like Ior who was so often depicted by the Finnish media as an eccentric, jet-setting, drug-guzzling, satanic-sect leader would be travelling with commoners. Of course, the reality was that Ior was a simple storyteller flying on the cheapest ticket he could find.

It seemed that the newspaper article's apocalyptic tone hadn't had its intended effect on the tourists, businesspeople and travellers aboard this particular flight; on the contrary, passengers started approaching Ior and asking him where the party would be and if it was an open guestlist.

Were there hotels in the area too? Was it difficult to get there? The group of interested passengers gravitated towards Ior and grew larger and larger until their weight started to affect the plane's balance. The pilot picked up on this and asked the flight attendant what was going on.

"There's a popular celebrity on board and a lot of our passengers have gathered around him asking questions, sir."

"What sort of questions?"

"Something about a party. I think it's meant to be tonight in Goa, there's talk that there'll be drugs involved, at least that's what I read in the paper."

"Sounds good. Can you tell everyone to return to their seats and ask this celebrity to come into the cockpit, please?"

"Yes sir."

Ior was brought to the cockpit and asked the same questions again. He told the pilot that the party was being organised for his 50th birthday and that everyone was welcome.

"Instead of answering each person's questions individually, can you just announce the details on the intercom, please? It'll save us any additional disruption."

And so, Ior announced his birthday party to hundreds of Scandinavians and told them they were all welcome to the psychedelic Goa-trance party that evening. Free entrance for all and cheap food and drink. All extras and details to be discussed on arrival.

"Be welcome!"

After landing, the pilots organised a large bus that transported everyone who wanted to the party. And so, that evening, many white, respectable people witnessed an event that would've normally only been attended by the inside 'know-your-party' elite.

Lola

I remember arriving at the party and parking my motorbike amongst the taxi drivers, alcohol sellers and vendors of all things imaginable. There was a lot of feverish action. The place looked like a Fellini-on-acid movie. I passed the rows of shields and entered a world that existed in a different reality. The paint on the mango trees worked well in the black light. It created a transmorphing, quantum-energised, multi-dimensional, astro-soul, psychedelic flowerscape. Just outside the sheltering arms of the mango trees stood the stout bock, overlooking the dance floor.

I took an LSD trip and danced. I loved the ritual of stomping out my anger, frustrations and fear into the dusty dance floor. The long, deep, dark night was designed for conquering my demons, and I took no prisoners. I knew that after my sweaty fight to the fast and constant beat, the dance floor my battlefield, I would enjoy the happiness of the coming morning. The first sun rays just below the horizon would herald the fact that we were in Goa and all around us was paradise and ecstasy. We'd be happy and dance forever, loving and kissing one another as exotic fragrances engulfed us in a spiritual dream.

William

But for now, the music was still loud and fast. It was trippy body music. The disco, slightly melancholic Italo sounds were draped upon hard computer drums. It was a nonstop trance into the darkness of the night, entering unknown lands with unknown people while exploring unknown landscapes, and ruled by emperors that changed the laws of nature on a whim. Nothing was certain, except the stomping beats. We marched like Roman legions into Germanic forests, where no one ever returned from in recognisable shapes.

Lola

After an indeterminate amount of time had passed, I took a break and plummeted onto the mat of my favourite chai lady. She made me a chai and gave me a homemade cookie. Close by, I could see the crowd on the dance floor going berserk. Yes, it was a great night! William sat down beside me. Together, we noticed that the group of white tourists that Ior had invited looked pink in the bright lights of the party. Most of them looked slightly bewildered.

"Well, I think that's pretty normal for a Goa-trance party initiation," I pointed out.

I could see that some of the Finnish tourists had turned to alcohol as a stabiliser and were swaying around the dance floor. In the background, I could hear a little transistor radio playing. I realised that it was the chai lady's radio and as I tuned in, I could hear that it wasn't music that was playing, but a continuous stream of news in Hindi and English. It was discussing the growing war tensions and speculating when the Americans would hit Bagdad. I certainly didn't want to listen to the news while tripping so I tried to ignore the small voices flowing from the mat. I hated wars. I'd heard some of my family's horrible Second World War stories and that was enough.

Suddenly there was fire.

"Ah, Ronan must have lit the bock," William informed me. I saw the flames playing around the four legs and then expanding into a blaze when the fires reached each other. The whole body soon became an enormous fireball, and the head was engulfed in flames. Out of the flames, the shape of the sturdy horns rose into the sky. Suddenly, there was an explosion of firecrackers as the soaring flames reached their mark and flares and rockets flew in all directions. Everyone gathered around the blazing pyre and leaped in a savage volcanic ritualistic dance.

William and I stood up in excitement to get a better view of the spectacle. Next to us, the chai lady also stood up grasping her little radio in her hand. A look of shock and bewilderment danced across her face in the flickering light. From the radio, an agitated voice was giving a live account of the first bombs that were raining on Bagdad at that very moment. The city was ablaze. Hundreds of buildings were being blasted to rubble and countless people were burning to their death.

All three of us stood speechless listening to the horror that was happening in that historical city that was so distant from us yet felt so close through the speakers of that little radio. At the same time, the music in the party went from wild to ecstatic.

As the feverish voice of the radio host gave its live report, we watched the large bock, a symbol that represents the devil to many in the world, burn. As the fire raged on, its flames licking the sky and rockets whizzing above the heads of wild-eyed screaming dancers, the head of the bock started to slowly tilt backwards until it was looking straight up into the sky.

The chai lady, William and I stood watching it in bewilderment, our eyes, and mouths wide open in astonishment. The burning bock looked into the black sky above it, lit by a trillion sparks and stars, as if crying in desperation. I could almost hear its cry:

"Spare us from the orgy of greed and cruelty that spreads death and destruction wherever it reaches. I beg you, spare me from another useless war and the vast suffering it will bring..."

William

How did it all end, I hear you ask? Well, the war between societies had already been going on for a few thousand years and is still raging in several parts of the planet now. No end's in sight. If I could make a suggestion to the generations after me it would be this: if there's a war and you're requested to fight for whatever reason, don't do it! There's no winning in wars, at least not for common people. They're dangerous places to be.

And the party? Well, like most good parties, it ended when the police got involved. Ronan and Soma had put a lot of effort into paying the police to ignore calls asking for it to be stopped. It had involved a lot of money. Some thought they'd paid the Mapusa police too much and that the Panaji police had gotten jealous, but later we found out that this hadn't been the case.

Through the machinations of the Raportti Media, word had been sent to Delhi that a large airplane filled with international drugs traffickers was on its way to hold a drug party. They informed the Delhi police that the whole story had been in international newspapers. If India wanted to be regarded as a modern country with a rule of law instead of a rule of chaos, then it was their duty to do something about this party. Delhi instructed the head of police of the Goan state capital, Panaji, to put a stop to this party if he valued his job and that baksheesh should not be accepted on this occasion. They warned that India was being watched by the international press and various governments, so there was no room for leniency.

The Panaji police took this message seriously and sent a considerable police force to find the party. Although Goa parties were never advertised, they were also not very difficult to find due to the general racket they produced. It took the police a few hours to locate the party and to direct their forces to the location. When they arrived in the early morning light, they smashed the whole place up. They destroyed the sound system, puncturing the loudspeakers with sticks. They smashed up the DJ booth and all its electronics. They beat up everyone they saw.

Most people, like me and Lola, ran away as soon as they arrived. There were so many of them. From a distance, hidden in a rice field, we watched their trail of destruction. The group of pink tourists had no idea what was going on and didn't know how to react. They were helpless prey frozen on the spot, mouths gawking at the stick-wielding men in uniforms. They were beaten up badly and many were arrested for being there and for drug possession. It didn't matter that none of them had drugs on them or that they'd never taken any drugs in their lives, for that matter.

And all the while, as this violent excess played before our eyes, bombs continued to fall on Bagdad. If I believed in astrology, I'd say there must've been a heavy constellation in the sky that night. Maybe that's what the straw bock had been looking at as it cried to the stars while spewing firework rockets.

And what happened after that? There was a severe diplomatic row between Finland and India. Finland couldn't accept that a group of peaceful tourists had been beaten up without plausible reason. Behind the curtains of diplomacy, the Indians argued that it was the Scandinavians in the first place who had caused a row and had forced the Indians to stop the party.

The Finnish diplomats argued that this might indeed be true, but it was the Finnish media, not the government that had done so. On that argument, the Indians replied that the Finnish government should have better grip over their media. The Finnish explained that Finland had the pleasure of free press. The Indians then pointed out that the free press seemed to have more of a say and influence on Finnish society than the official government. Both sides agreed on the following:

All tourist flights between Goa and Finland would be stopped for the foreseeable future. The war had discouraged Goan tourism. There are plenty of beach destinations much closer to Finland. After the war, when the whole case was forgotten, the Goa flights would be resumed. All other flights to Indian destinations, like for instance to the Taj Mahal, would continue and those tourists would be protected by the Indian tourist police.

The arrested tourists in Goa would be flown home as soon as possible. Until then, they'd stay at five-star hotels, all expenses paid. The hotels were empty anyway.

The Raportti Media, who'd caused the whole drama in the first place, directed the blame at Ior. They sold a lot of newspapers over the following days with headlines that included words such as: Ior Bock, drugs, crazed hippies, LSD, smuggling, police and arrested. The usual stuff. Anyone who'd been involved and everyone who'd read the news could confirm this portrayal of Ior and no world views were shattered.

I still feel sorry for the people who'd been beaten up that night and the people who'd died in the fire storm in Bagdad. And I will never forget that moment when the bock tilted its head backwards towards the sky.

Oh, and if you're wondering why the head of the bock tilted in that way, I found out later that the steel bar that connected the body of the bock with the top-heavy head had melted. That was all. Laws of nature and all that jazz. No witchcraft involved.

Ronan

Casper, some of the via-via group and I had taken the day off. We all crowded into my camper van, the old but tireless Bedford, and headed to Raseborg. In the old castle was a 'festspiel' with theatre shows. It was a nice, quiet, and enjoyable event. After that, we grabbed a bite to eat nearby in Snappertuna and discussed the digging progress with our 'via-via' friends.

The wild-looking Vikings from Norway had taken up the mantle and were chomping away at the mountain. The familiar sound of dynamite explosions was once more a daily event. We discussed the admirable tolerance of the locals living nearby. Already for five years now, they'd endured the noise, and until now, there had been only mild complaints about the nuisance.

Next, we passed by the church of Snappertuna to pay our respects to Ior's ancestors who'd been buried in its garden. There in the garden, under the mighty arms of the Yggdrasil, rested the former generations of the Boxström and Raström families, who'd steered the Bock Saga through the winds of time. However, when we arrived, there was no shadow on the graves, for the Yggdrasil was gone.

Vicar of Snappertuna church

Yes, I cut down the tree. It was just a tree. A tree that caused trouble. People constantly kept coming here to watch it grow. They walked all over the graves as if there's no respect left in the world. This has always been a quiet place and that's how it should remain. Let the souls buried here rest; they have the right to do so. That tree wasn't the Yggdrasil. That's just a folk story. The tree in paradise was an apple tree, everybody knows that. Well anyway, it's all over now. I told them to tell their friends they weren't to come here anymore.

Ronan

We were all in shock. No one spoke the whole way back to Akanpesa. That evening, we sat in silence around the wood fire. A storm brewed outside, and the dark sky threatened heavy rain. We sat together drinking tea, the same thoughts going through each of our heads. The most holy relic in the Bock Saga had been cut down by some ignorant idiot. Or was it part of some great conspiracy by the puppet masters of Raportti and Museovirasto? Or both? We could feel the sting of the blow on our faces.

Everything we stood for and had made our life work was being negated and trampled on. Why, oh, why? It wasn't fair. Not believing in the Bock Saga was maybe stupid in our eyes, but not a deadly sin. To actively undermine our work was a challenge, but to destroy the holy sites of the Bock Saga was just one step too far.

After dinner, Casper took the stage.

"It all started with that book Ior was given by the Shah of Persia in Teheran in 1975. We must find that book. I must go to Ior in his townhouse and ask him what happened to that bottle. This whole thing started with Aladdin's lamp. 'All-addin'. We all must 'add in'. Then we must pass it on."

It wasn't the first time that Casper had spoken about things nobody understood. The Bock Saga had so many twists and turns and Casper's knowledge and understanding of it was unsurpassed. Whatever he said was always fully accepted, and not understanding him meant that you still had more to learn. I imagine it was the same with Einstein and his pupils.

Casper asked me to warm up my Bedford parked outside. I ran through the rain and woke the engine before going back inside to collect my papers, coat and, of course, Casper. Back inside the house I could hear Casper repeating his Aladdin lamp and

Teheran book story. It sounded like rambling. That was also possible. Although Casper was usually the most together person in the house, he could sometimes go on and on about a subject, repeating himself several times.

It somehow sounded different this time. He seemed completely focussed on this one thing, or should I say two things. Book-lamp, book-lamp, book-lamp. I didn't know what to make of it and just complied with his wish to see Ior. I hoped that Ior could make sense of what he was talking about, or at least quiet him down. Together we walked outside towards the van, and I opened the door for Casper.

A big cloud of smoke emerged. Flames too! The engine was on fire! I ran inside the house and grabbed a fire extinguisher, spraying its contents in the general direction of the engine. I kept on spraying, but the white powder wasn't reaching the centre of the fire.

I realised that I had to open the hood of the van. I went inside the cabin with my eyes and mouth closed, found the lever in the thick, wild, black clouds and pulled it. The hood sprung open. I sprayed the engine, and black clouds mixed with white clouds as the whole van sizzled down. The engine was destroyed.

"Well, Öde prevented us from going anywhere, it seems," I said looking disappointedly at my burned-out engine. All at once, I realised the many things I would now need to do to bring my beloved van back to life; it was the materialistic centrepiece of how I organised my life during that time. It seemed that Casper had also had a revelation of some sort and was mumbling to himself.

"Yes, you're right; I have to do this on my own."
He ran inside the house and grabbed a poncho, threw it over his head and ran off into the night.

"See you later, I'm going to 'add all in'!"
Before anyone could say or do anything, Casper had disappeared amongst the trees. We didn't see him again for a couple of weeks and became quite worried.

Casper

I ran off into the rain. I felt hot and cold at the same time. Bright lights flashed in my eyes and all around me was darkness. I knew everything and nothing. I was nothing and everything. The night passed me in a blur, but I remember every detail sharply. I ran and ran, and I knew where I needed to go.

I had to go north, to Kajaani. I ran straight through the woods. All the trees looked the same, but I knew which direction to send my feet in. It was silent in the woods as I ran over the wet moss. Every now and then, I heard the cracking of a little branch pulverising under my feet. When I stopped running, I started marching like the soldier I'd never been. In my head, I could hear a Goa-trance song over and over: 'some are clever, some naïve, everything's relative. Einstein, check, check the time, time'.

I felt intensely sad. Not for myself, not even that much for Ior, but for all the generations of Boxström and Raström who'd gone through the ordeal of keeping the Bock Saga alive in secrecy. Imagine how heavy it must have been to know where humanity came from, where it was leading and not being able to share this knowledge with your friends.

Everything your family ever did and would do is always only viewed from the context of the Bock Saga. And this has been going on since the beginning of mankind. Your fate is decided before you're born, as is that of your children. Can you imagine the loneliness? Can you imagine not only spending your youth, twenty years of it, silently listening to the monumental story, but then also having to transfer this onto your own children hoping it will stick in their brains? The inconsolable knowledge that you're condemning your children to that same loneliness, and that this needs to be done for some greater good that's beyond you and beyond them. Imagine thousands of years of sacrifice.

After the onslaught the family suffered a thousand years ago, where the whole extended family and our birth ground were rooted out and destroyed, the family had had to flee and live in one of the most inhospitable areas on the planet, without once complaining.

And now, finally, at the crescendo of it all, after everything that had been sacrificed, at the very moment that had been awaited by so many generations, when the Bock Saga was to be finally revealed and the temple opened uncovering the work of these ancestors, all we had to show was an almost inaudible implosion of energy, our energy, disappearing into a little black hole of indifference and mediocrity. Revealing the Bock Saga, so far, had been the anti-climax of the aeon. And now, the Ygg-drasil had been cut down to emphasise the utter indifference of the Finnish people towards their heritage.

I marched and ran like a madman. I didn't sleep and I didn't eat. I occasionally stopped to drink from little streams that I passed and sometimes had to wade through. I had an inner compass that told me to go north to Kajaani. A couple of days later, I arrived in the early morning. I'd walked over 500 kilo-metres. I went straight to the castle and into the local office of the Museovirasto. I talked, I pleaded, I drowned them in a tsu-nami of words.

"Take responsibility for digging up the golden bock! Don't deny who you are! You can't be sure that the bock doesn't exist. The scan showed it! You can only know for sure by digging in that spot."

I went on and on and on. Then it got dark again. I had no money and no food and no place to sleep. I didn't care. I realised that I needed to settle this with higher authorities. I decided to go to Helsinki to the 'big boss'. To the relief of the people in the castle, I left.

I went to the police station and asked if I could stay the night. They saw my situation and gave me a cell to sleep in. A locked cell. They even gave me food. In hindsight, I'm grateful that they didn't take me to a mental asylum. I certainly wouldn't have stood out amongst the other patients. In the morning, they initially wanted to kick me out onto the street.

When I started rambling again about golden bocks and the Bock Saga, they realised that they would rather ensure I didn't remain in their city. They gave me breakfast, bought me a train ticket to Helsinki and escorted me to the train station. They asked the ticket collector to make sure I didn't get off the train until it reached the destination and made him promise to call them immediately if I escaped.

During the next weeks, I went to the president's palace, to the parliament, to the ministry of education, the ministry of culture, to the head office of the Museovirasto, to the bishop, to the mayor, to every place I could think of going to plead my case. I never met the president, ministers, and the bishop. Their secretaries and security prevented it. I looked and acted too strangely. I was in a feverish dream-state.

I didn't meet Ior or any of the other Saga friends either. This was my own journey. I didn't eat or sleep and I sped around with more energy than an atomic rocket. Once more on foot, I walked to Raseborg, to the Offerlund, to the vicar who cut the Yggdrasil, to all kinds of official places in that area.

This episode lasted about four weeks, until I bumped into someone from the via-via group on the street. I told him a story about Aladdin's lamp and how I 'added all in'.

"Aladdin Sane," he told me. "A lad insane."

He'd heard that I'd gone bananas and thought it better that I left the country before something nasty happened to me. Sooner or later, I risked disappearing into a mental institution, from where I'd struggle to leave. These institutions were known for applying very strong drug therapies to newcomers to ensure they complied with the house rules.

After that, I'd probably be more or less brain dead and at their mercy forever. If I wasn't imprisoned in an institution, I'd maybe have an accident of some kind; perhaps someone would get into a fight with me and stab me, or maybe I'd be hit by a car. He brought me to Turku harbour and bought me a ticket to Stockholm.

I just let it happen. I was still in my fever dream-state when the ferry arrived in Stockholm. I saw everything as if through a kaleidoscope of constant flashing lights. All my thoughts and words ran at high speed.

When I stepped off the ship and my feet touched the Swedish

concrete quay, I suddenly calmed down. My heartbeat returned to a normal speed. I could see straight again. I realised just what sort of state I'd been in over the last month. I suddenly felt incredibly tired. I could no longer carry the weight of the world on my shoulders; I couldn't even carry my own skinny body anymore.

I sat down on the side of the pavement and realised I smelled awful. I hadn't washed myself in weeks. No wonder the president and all the others had refused to receive me. My clothes were torn from walking through the forest. I looked like a caveman. And what I realised above all was that I was hungry. No, not just hungry, enormously hungry. I'd hardly eaten anything the last month and needed to remedy this as soon as possible.

I still didn't have any money, but at least I realised that I could ask friends for help. My good friends GM and Malena lived within walking distance. I could hardly lift my feet; I was so tired and weak. Burning through the last of my reserves, I stumbled to their flat. Nobody was home.

I collapsed in front of their door, and that's where Malena found me when she came home that evening. She gave me food, a shower and a bed. When I woke up, I ate again and went back to sleep. I stayed with them for a few weeks to strengthen my body and mind.

Malena and GM both had steady jobs in Stockholm. They'd been part of the around-the-world-travelling-freaks-who-loved-beaches-parties-and-smuggling group. We'd spent time together in the Philippines, Goa, and Japan, amongst other places. They had also been part of the magic twenty-four who'd witnessed the anticlimactic temple opening ceremony in Akanpesa on the 24th of July 1987.

After that first season of Bock Saga drama, they'd left. We were still friends, but they were no longer involved in the Bock Saga. They were always making fun of me, Ior and the temple, and just didn't believe that the Bock Saga had any importance. In the beginning, this had made me doubt myself, because Malena, being Swedish and having Swedish as her mother tongue, should have been able to recognise the validity of it all. But she didn't and refused to spend any more time on it. She wanted to get on with her life. It had probably been a good decision. Look at how our ways had diverged.

I had spent the last few years eating bread and cheese, surrounded by madmen and in jail, the whole time pursuing an impossible goal. I had flipped out and found myself lying mentally and physically exhausted in front of Malena's door, with no money, no house, and no future. Meanwhile, she and GM had organised themselves. They had jobs that were interesting, meaningful, secure, and financially pleasant. They had a beautiful apartment in the centre of Stockholm and their life was predictable, enjoyable, and healthy.

I wanted all these things too. I wanted rest, predictability, stability. And I no longer wanted all the things that came with the Bock Saga. I wanted to go home. It was now possible because recently the Dutch government had pardoned everybody who had illegally evaded the military service. The Cold War was over since the Berlin wall had fallen.

I was free to go back. I took the train, boat, and more trains until I was in my hometown station. From there, I walked to my parent's house with all my belongings in a little bag and rang the doorbell. The door opened and there stood my mother.

"It's been a long time since I last saw you, son."

"Yes, mum, I'm back. I don't know where to go or what to do. Can I stay here for a while?"

She let me in with a wise old lady look on her face. I spent the next day telling my parents everything I had experienced since I'd left home for good. They were happy that I was back and could tell that I'd grown up. They particularly appreciated how open I was with them about all my smuggling adventures and the crazy stuff surrounding the Saga.

Although it was nice to be back with my parents, I found myself spiralling into a deep identity crisis. I'd abandoned the Bock Saga mission, along with the lifestyle and friends that came with it. I felt empty. The next news I got came from Tokyo. My girlfriend, Susanne, ended our relationship. She wanted to be with someone who lived closer to her and shared her same desire for children. She'd found someone who fit the bill and they were both going to move to Australia and settle down there.

Was settling down the new avant-garde thing to do? Or was it just that we were growing old and boring? I didn't know. I didn't know anything anymore. Who even was I? What was my purpose on this planet and what should I do next? I felt unbelievably confused.

Ronan

At the beginning of 1995, Ior was invited by the organisers of the 'Magisk Uke' to do a presentation of the Bock Saga. The event was to be held in the prestigious Rockefeller Music Hall in Oslo, Norway, during the summer of 1995. The event organisers' idea was to provide a platform for the exchange of alternative thinking, philosophies, and lifestyles.

There was a general feeling amongst the organisers that our civilisation needed some fresh ideas. The public domain and intellectual space were dominated by monopolistic schools of thought. All our world problems were seen as economic, and all the solutions were searched for within technology.

Norway was a rich country, so when a few voices of doubt started to emerge, they soon found each other and eventually culminated in Magisk Uke. Apart from Ior, various other philosophers, yogis and traditional tribal speakers had been invited to share their way of thinking.

There was some deliberation over who would go, where the group would stay and who would pay for the transport and other expenses. In the end, it was decided that Ior would take the stage accompanied by three of his students. Ior asked, then pleaded, for Casper to be one of these students.

Although Casper had distanced himself from the group over the last few years, he eventually agreed. The other two were going to be Soma, who would tell the story as seen from the perspective of a Hindu, and me. Mr Yeah felt left out and invited himself along. We agreed on the condition that he wouldn't speak about the Bock Saga itself but focus on the ongoing excavation of the temple in Gumbostrand.

Shannon of Norway had volunteered to host us all and had gotten ample budget to do so. And so, we all arrived at her spacious mansion located near the Rockefeller Music Hall via different means of transport and each from different points of departure. Most of the group took a plane or train, but I drove my Bedford van. When I arrived, Ior, Mr Yeah, Soma and Casper were already there. Shannon was baking a cake in the oven and the whole house smelled like a nostalgic dream.

How Ior had envisioned our group spending our old-age days was beginning to materialise. We sat in luxurious surroundings delighted that an official institution had finally asked us to talk about the Bock Saga. Up to this point, we'd had to peddle our story from door to door, enduring the indifference we received in return. Our present situation was how we envisaged our future: travelling around the world on invitation, telling our story and being compensated with free transport, food, and accommodation. This was the pension we longed for and felt we deserved after the last few years' hard work and struggle. This is what we wanted the rest of our lives to look like. We saw ourselves as university scientists and professors.

We were welcomed by Shannon and felt happy to meet each other again in such comfortable surroundings. The via-via group from Finland and the via-via groups from Sweden and Norway who'd been actively digging over the last few years were also happy to see us finally enter the realm of official recognition and decided to support us.

This group of about twenty-five people invited themselves into Shannon's house and settled there. Very swiftly, Shannon found her house overrun with dope-smoking Vikings who attacked her orderly household and raided her fridge. She panicked and eventually freaked out. She threw the whole group out onto the street and included us in the eviction.

Even before the Rockefeller show had started, our entry into the realm of normal, common people had abruptly ended with Shannon's banishment. I had a tipi on the roof of my Bedford that I used during my European festival tours. I set this up in the Rockefeller Music Hall gardens and we all moved in. The tipi was quite big, made to hold a small family as well as some kitchenware and a wood fire in the centre.

Now we shared it with the group, which consisted of about twenty-five long-haired Saga-heads. I asked the Vikings for some carpets to cover the floor, as it was still cold in Norway. They brought me reindeer skins. What a lovely gesture! At least that's what we thought until the smell hit us. These weren't skins you bought in a souvenir shop with long, soft hair and a smooth underside. No, these were hardcore, Lapland reindeer skins. On the outside, the hair was hard and prickly. On the inside, they hadn't been treated or cured, but merely skinned. The fat inside the skin hadn't been removed either, as per ancient tradition. It greased the grass floor of the park and stank of dead animal. Intensely so. The skins were warm, however, so we endured the smell and sat crammed together on the prickly, greasy, smelly skins.

We were happy with our lodgings even though they were drastically different to the luxury of Shannon's house. The day before the event was due to start, we sat in the tipi smoking fat joints and watching the smoke rise out of the central hole. Drifting in from the closed fabric door came an irritating didgeridoo noise that vibrated the tent. To our surprise, it was Shannon of Norway who sat outside our tipi blowing furiously into the long tube. She still looked a little crazed as she produced the horrible, distorted sounds and refused to stop.

Casper and I exchanged a look. We both recognised the situation. As soon as things seemed to settle and start moving in the right direction, someone around us would flip out and shatter the fragile tranquillity we'd worked so hard to create. There was nothing we could do, and we knew that at any moment someone would most likely do something unpredictably weird that would work against our interests.

The Magisk Uke, the 'Magic Week', consisted of numerous esoteric presentations and speeches given by contemporary thinkers who had something new to add, something different from the mainstream media. Bock Saga sessions were scheduled on four consecutive evenings. These sessions would be enhanced by a yoga show during which some of the via-via group would perform exercises described in the Bock Saga.

On the first night, a naked Ior appeared on stage, sat down, sipped his tea, lit a beedi and introduced the other speakers. Casper, Soma, and I sat next to each other, naked, illuminated by a few candles. Ior explained what the Bock Saga was to the audience and gave them a short overview of the story. He then handed over to Casper who roughly explained what life was like during Paradise time.

On the following night, I was first to speak. I'd been given the task of talking about Altlandis, which is the Ice Age that followed the Paradise time. I remember getting lost in my own story at one point and having no clue what I'd been saying or what I'd been planning to say next. My mind went blank, and I sat there speechless. The hall was very quiet and darkish. There I was, sitting naked on stage behind my candle feeling completely lost.

"Hmm, where was I?" I mumbled to myself, feeling my cheeks burn.

A hundred eyes looked at me in anticipation. Suddenly, a deep voice from somewhere in the crowd answered me.

"You were talking about the Bock Saga!"

This broke the spell, and I was able to continue my story.

On the third night, it was Soma's turn. He talked about mythology in general and made some comparisons between the Bock Saga and Hindu mythology. He'd prepared many examples of rituals and words that were similar in both mythologies. The fourth night hadn't really been planned, but we had agreed that Mr Yeah would take centre stage and discuss the temple excavation project. He was supposed to steer clear of the Bock Saga itself.

Mr Yeah was, and still is, a gifted speaker who's able to tell a clear story and make difficult concepts appear easy. On that night, he didn't limit himself to his designated subject but spoke about all kinds of world consequences that the temple opening would bring. He then talked in detail about the function of the temple in prehistoric times and all kinds of other Bock Saga-related subjects. Although he did receive praise for his speaking skills, he also got a lot of shit from our group for not having stayed on the agreed subject and for having gone directly against our wishes.

Mr Yeah felt misunderstood. Mr Yeah felt underestimated. Mr Yeah felt excluded. Mr Yeah felt betrayed. Mr Yeah felt unloved. Mr Yeah felt insulted. Mr Yeah was pissed off. Hurt feelings and anger raced through his brain. He'd once been told by a Native American that the worst insult you could give another person was to shit in front of the entrance of their tipi.

And so, ears fuming, eyes burning and throat puffing, he squatted in front of my tipi in the damp Norwegian dawn. He contracted his bowels and laid a classic-looking turd by the door of the tent. It was hot compared to the crisp morning air and sat steaming fumes into the tipi. Mr Yeah gave it one last satisfied look, feeling that justice had been served, and left.

As the Magisk Uke came to an end, we gathered our thoughts and reflected on how things had gone. Although our smooth stay in Norway had been somewhat disturbed by our eviction from Shannon of Norway's house, the greasy reindeer skins, and the pungent steaming turd, we still felt energised by the successful performances that we'd all given. We decided to celebrate this accomplishment in the town centre with a few beers. We even allowed Shannon to join us, with the solemn promise that she wouldn't bring that damned didgeridoo. A row of old cars, with the Bedford closing the caravan, drove into the centre of Oslo. We all found parking spaces and headed to a bar. We spent a glorious night toasting our victory.

When Soma, Casper, Ior and I returned to my van in the early morning, we discovered that someone had broken a window. Moments later, we found that all our valuables had been stolen. All our bank cards, hashish, money, and passports were gone. All except Soma's Indian passport. The thief had removed it from his bag but then had discarded it on the van floor. All of us looked at each other and suddenly knew who the culprit was: Mr Yeah.

Mr Yeah had been so pissed off that he'd disappeared that morning without a trace, except for the turd he'd generously left behind. It was clear. We cursed him and discussed what we would do to him when we saw him again. He was probably already far away, on a plane in the sky somewhere. With the wind whistling thorough the broken window, we drove back to the Rockefeller Music Hall. We decided we'd nap for a few hours and then each go our separate ways again.

When we arrived, parked the van and opened the door of the tipi, lo and behold, there was Mr Yeah sleeping like an innocent baby. We all realised our dark thoughts had been completely misplaced. Mr Yeah would never have stolen from us. Never.

It didn't matter how pissed off he was. He was a friend; one of the few real friends we'd made in the world. We felt incredibly guilty about our huge and dumb mistake. We all jumped on the sleeping man and hugged him. He woke up, having no idea what was going on, tried to curse us, and finally accepted our affection, letting the love of friendship between knights of the Bock Saga flow. Then he smiled and said:

"Now go make me some coffee, you god-damned idiots!"

Shavas

My anger had been bubbling within me for a while, and one day it came exploding out of me. I confronted Ior and let my feelings flow freely.

"You sit here telling your story, but what's your actual role in the whole thing? You sit here, smoke all day, and tell pre-Ice-Age stories. But what's the point? What's your ambition?"

"I'm only here to tell the Bock Saga."

"Ok then. You tell your story, then what?"

"Then other people listen to it."

"And then what?"

"By telling the story, energy will be created that will open the Lemminkäinen Temple and the Bock family treasure chambers."

"And then what?"

"And then the temple will do the rest."

"And what does the rest consist of?"

"You'll see."

"What will I see?"

"The Lemminkäinen Temple and the Bock family treasure chambers are an exact reflection and embodiment of the Bock Saga."

"Fuck you, get the fuck out of my life and out of my head with your fucking stories! I've had enough of bocks, Zen masters and people who thinks they have all the answers. You're all mind fuckers! I've had it with this shit. I'm done. I don't want to have anything to do with drugs and drug smuggling again. You sit here, looking so innocent, as if you've got nothing to do with the madness you leave in your wake.

People have gone to jail; lives have been destroyed. People have gone crazy and all you do is hide behind your words. 'All

I'm doing is telling a story'. Bullshit. You forbid us from having girlfriends and kids and demand that we dedicate all our time to you and your precious Bock Saga. We're forced to buy that time by smuggling dope, since we're so unlucky and poor that we can't even afford a lottery ticket."

"I went to jail for you, and I only just managed to escape a lengthy sentence. The police aren't crazy, you know. They know what we're doing and are certain that we must be running a global drug trafficking network. And you know what? They're not wrong. Their only mistake is that they picture us as rich gangsters rolling in cash with private planes and fancy cars. They don't realise just how poor and miserable we are. All we eat is bread and peanut butter.

It's only a matter of time before they lock us up for life. I've had enough of gurus and wise men. And I've had enough of all drugs and anything to do with them. I'm leaving and never coming back. I'm going to dedicate my life to things that I like and that I'm good at, and that's organising and decorating parties."

Ronan

Since I'd quit the smuggling life, I had to find another way to sustain myself and make time to be with Ior and listen to the Bock Saga. After thinking about it for a long time, I came up with the following plan: in the summer, I would travel through Europe along the Goa-trance festival trail, where I would set up a shop from my Bedford van and sell silk prints. In the autumn, I'd drive to Berlin, where I had a small workshop. I'd work from there for three months making new prints.

This would involve drawing designs, transferring these designs to silk screens and the elaborate work of dying each print individually with several layers of ink. All my designs were references to scenes, symbols, and concepts from the Bock Saga.

When I first started learning about the Bock Saga, I blasted anyone who didn't run away with my knowledge. I was like a Jehovah's Witness, so full of the story. Now my manner of expression was a subtler one. Through my prints, I felt that I could spread the Bock Saga on a subconscious level. I could marinate the public with concepts and symbols from the Bock Saga. And the silk prints sold well!

After three months in Berlin printing silk, I would then fly to Goa for another three months. I always brought a few suitcases of printed silk with me to sell at the Wednesday flea market. In Goa, I divided my time between the market, beach and parties; however, the majority of my time was still spent sitting on Ior's veranda listening to the Bock Saga.

The story went into more and more intricate detail about life, rituals and how these are expressed within the Root language. Every day, Ior would sit on his veranda drinking tea and smoking chillums from morning to dusk. His process involved choosing a word, dissecting it into sounds and then making all kinds of cross references to other words in different languages.

Then at the end of the season, in what was always an unexpected way, Ior would pull together all the knowledge that had been discussed into one new concept. This concept would then always appear to us as a crystal-clear, logical, and inevitable truth. It was beautiful how the logic of the sound system and the order of the universe and our human cultures, regardless of where or when they came from, fit together in such harmony.

I'm tempted to give some examples, but they would be meaningless without the backbone of the sound system. That's the whole point of listening to the Bock Saga year after year; it's a twenty-year story.

Lola

All men are the same! All they think about are dicks and pricks, mostly their own. And when they do think about women, all they dream about are overflowing vases of lady juice. The Bock Saga's a man's fantasy.

I remember once attending a Bock Saga listening session that Ior had agreed to do with a group of us girls. He said he would explain the female side of the Bock Saga to us. Normally, he didn't have much to say about this side of things, but he decided he'd reveal it to us. We were curious and a little apprehensive as we sat down in the candlelight holding our cups of tea.

What he ended up telling us was that the female structure of the Offer-Ring system was like that of the men and that we could figure it out for ourselves. Nothing new there. Then he told us a story about how men in prehistory used to have sex with chickens. The whole lecture focussed on men's weird sexual activities and how they never had normal fucking sex with women, or other men, for that part. Ok, we get the point. If that's what sex was like in Paradise time, I prefer modern times.

Ior also told us that a man needed to be at least six foot tall to have children. After the session was over, I was convinced more than ever: even if they were sixteen foot tall, I'd never have a child with this group of guys. I preferred to find a man who'd love his children above all else, rather than find one who smoked dope all day and daydreamed about some fairy tale. The entire experience was more than disappointing.

Ronan

A wide variety of people came to us through the via-via group. Since we abided by the 'nobody invited, everybody welcome' principle, we had little influence over who sat with us around the fire in Akanpesa. There were the quiet listening intellectuals who had inwardly tuned personalities. These individuals were used to churning their thoughts around in their heads endlessly until they were threadbare and worn out, at which point they'd come to us for a fresh input of ideas that they could then think over until these too were scratched to the bone.

There were also plenty of nice 'normal' people who, after hearing about the temple, wanted to help and do something about the whole situation. They approached us with all kinds of digging solutions that usually ran aground due to the prohibitively expensive digging equipment and the fact that Finnish society seemed to simply reject the Bock Saga.

What everyone in the via-via group had in common was that they liked to smoke hashish, or at least they could tolerate the dense clouds that filled the living room in Akanpesa. They also needed to remain immune to the media onslaught on Ior and everyone associated with him. A subgroup that lived within the via-via group were the slightly unstable 'mentals' who were predisposed to an insatiable hunger for attention and psychedelic drugs.

Kertu belonged to that group. He had sat with us at the fire in Akanpesa and had been to Goa twice. I'm not a psychologist and find it hard to describe his mind and actions in an understandable and logical way. The fact is that he could absorb fragments of the Bock Saga and spit them out again as unrecognisable madness. We had attracted people like this before and knew that as soon as he started to identify with characters from the Bock Saga, we'd be in trouble.

On Kertu's second visit to Goa, he'd been seen taking LSD in huge quantities at parties and restaurants. People kept their distance from him. He talked about stranger and stranger things that even the highly tolerant Goan population started to regard as bizarre. He was lonely and felt rejected. Sometimes he sat for hours talking softly to himself.

Occasionally, he'd show his other side and rave madly at everyone around him with a special emphasis on Ior. He would run around the village of Chapora screaming insults and accusing Ior of all sorts of imaginary things. As was the custom, the locals tied him to the pole in the middle of the village and gave him a bamboo massage. This technique is designed to bring a person back to their senses, but it didn't help Kertu much. He became a classic Goa flip-out.

The party season ended in March and most foreigners left Goa for more hospitable places or for their home countries to earn enough money to return there the following year. Some foreigners who had their roots deep in the Goanese soil stayed for the summer and the rainy season as did the flip-outs who'd overstayed their visas and ran out of money. Some sold their passports; some hardly knew where they were.

That was Kertu's situation. The ashram in Vagator that had taken care of such cases in previous years, no longer existed. The details of what happened to Kertu at the beginning of the rainy season are lost. What we do know is the report from the Bombay police that he arrived in Bombay from Goa under police escort and that they accommodated him in one of their gloomy prison cells for a few days until the Swedish/Finnish embassy paid a ticket for a direct flight to Helsinki. Kertu's resistance to this extradition was overcome with an elephant-dose of Valium. He arrived in the airport of his hometown just in time for the great midsummer celebrations.

There was no one there to pick him up. He had no money for a bus ticket into town and even if he'd had it, he had no home to go to. He stuck out his thumb and hitched from the airport into Helsinki. There, he visited various friends, but being in such a dazed and confused condition, nobody wanted him to hang around for very long. He visited a bar where some of the via-via group met regularly.

According to testimonies, this is where he heard that the Kajaani representative of the Museovirasto, Mr Kirrkko, had stated that as long as Ior Bock was alive, Museovirasto would refuse to excavate the golden bocks. Or maybe what Mr Kirrkko had said was that they wouldn't excavate the golden bocks in Ior's lifetime, or something along those lines.

From then on, Kertu started rambling on about how Ior was the devil and responsible for the temple remaining closed. At one point, he visited his mother who was bewildered to see her son in such a state. She was glad to see him leave quickly. It's probably from there, in his childhood room, that he picked up the 'puukko', a hunting knife.

That evening, Valto and Ior sat together in Ior's apartment discussing the English translation of the Finnish book they'd produced together, *Bockin Perheen Saaga*. They sat on the floor of a candlelit room. Ior had made tea with a gas burner. His financial situation was already so dire that the electricity had been cut off. This was the reason why the electric doorbell wasn't working either, which in turn was the reason why he received less visitors during that period.

Ior's apartment was on the second floor and anyone who wanted to visit him knew which window to throw pebbles at to get his attention. As the electric buzzer wasn't working either, Ior would then throw down his apartment keys allowing the person to open the downstairs door.

Ior and Valto heard a pebble hit the window, then another, followed by a whole handful. Ior opened the window and saw Kertu gesticulating wildly below. Ior recognised the state which Kertu was in and told him he didn't have time for a visit. He should go somewhere else.

"But I have the solution to everything!" Kertu screamed, starting a whole rant of gibberish directed at Ior's window.

"No, not now!" Ior insisted, closing the window, and turning back to Valto. "In Goa he spread bad rumours about me and acted in an aggressive manner towards me. Now he claims to know the solution to everything. Why do I attract these kinds of nutcases? Let's just get on with our project."

They both turned their attention back to their translation

and quickly forgot about the incident. Approximately twenty minutes later, they were interrupted once more, but this time it was by a distressed voice coming from the landing. As they looked up from their papers, they heard something scraping and clinking at the apartment door. Ior slowly got to his feet and made his way to the hall to see what was happening. Just as he reached the door, it was violently knocked in to reveal a wild-eyed Kertu brandishing a blade that glistened in the dim light of the hallway.

"Ah! there you are, you devil! This will decide it all! You're the only reason the temple hasn't opened, but I can change that now."

All it took was a simple thrust of Kertu's hand. The knife slid in. Then out, then in, then out, then in again. Ior fell heavily to the floor. Kertu fled the house, bleeding knife in hand. It was at this point that Valto, having heard Kertu's garbled screams, ran into the hallway. He found Ior in an expanding pool of blood. Frantically, Valto tried to find the wounds so he could press on them to stop the bleeding. He could feel Ior still breathing but the amount of blood that was gathering told a different story.

Valto's mind raced as he calculated the best course of action. There was just so much blood. Hands trembling, he realised he needed to call an ambulance immediately. Pressing on the wounds wasn't going to do much good. Within five minutes, the ambulance had arrived in the street below.

Valto scrambled around for the damned key and threw it from the window to the waiting paramedics below. As he watched his friend being rushed down the staircase, he couldn't help but wonder whether it would be the last time he would see him. The blood left behind congealed slowly in the flickering candlelight.

After the incident, Kertu had gone straight to the centre of Helsinki and was seen dancing on a billiard table proudly proclaiming:

"I killed the devil! I killed the devil!"

It isn't surprising that the police had been called considering his clothes were blood stained and he was still clutching the glistening knife. Besides, bad news travels quickly, and the news of Ior's stabbing didn't take long to arrive into Helsinki. Kertu was swiftly arrested.

Ior just barely survived, but the attack left him paraplegic. Kertu was brought to court but not convicted to a jail sentence as his lawyers pleaded that he had been 'temporarily insane' during the attack. The judge found that there was no proof of premeditated attempted murder, even though, on the day of the attack, Kertu had proclaimed that he was going to kill Ior. The judge concluded that Kertu was too insane for premeditation and assigned him to a mental asylum. Even I must admit that Kertu's reason for attacking Ior did sound pretty insane:

"Yes, I wanted to kill Ior. I wanted to kill him because the Museovirasto told me that they wouldn't dig up the golden bocks in Kajaani while he was alive. By killing him, I've cleared the way for the excavation. Ior was what was stopping the Bock Saga from being proven true."

Casper

During the years leading up to the attack, I'd had less and less contact with Ior. It wasn't that I no longer liked him or the Bock Saga, but since my flip-out, I'd chosen to focus on my own mental sanity. The Bock Saga had proven to be not just a nice story, but a dominant force in my life.

I couldn't take it lightly anymore. I found it difficult to accept the insanity of a society that just refused to learn about their past. And I could no longer accept all the insane people the Bock Saga attracted. I'd had enough; it had all been too much. I just lived my life in Holland as a carpenter, enjoying the pleasures of having a normal job, a normal house, and a normal life.

I had made an exception when attending the Magisk Uke in Oslo. It had been nice but confirmed to me that it was impossible to be involved in the Bock Saga without weirdness going on. Afterwards I had occasional contact with Ior and the guys, but I tried not to solely live for the Bock Saga anymore.

Then the news of the attack reached me. It shook me to the core. I cancelled everything and took the first train to Helsinki. I wasn't the only one to do so. All the hardcore Saga-heads were there. Ior was in a miserable condition, but his mind remained positive. He seemed to be recovering reasonably well, but he couldn't walk anymore and that changed everything.

Ior was now confined to his apartment. To get to anywhere other than the toilet was a big logistical operation. He needed to be carried everywhere by his helpers. He didn't own a car, so other means of transport had to be arranged. At the beginning, to everyone's surprise, Ior remained optimistic and joyful. He simply accepted his fate. As long as there was something to smoke and tea to drink, all was fine. Because the Finnish insurance paid for his helpers, he was never alone. They slept with him in his apartment, made food and kept the household in order.

He tried to do exercises to regain his strength and try to reactivate his nervous system in an attempt to restore some muscle movement. But this required an immense amount of will power; it didn't come naturally. Although he'd done a lot of yoga and dance exercises in his life, he'd never been consistent with these after he first started to tell the Bock Saga.

In October, he travelled to Goa as usual. It wasn't easy to get him there. All his friends got together to help, both in Finland and in Goa. Every morning, he was carried to a local chai shop where he would sit all day, drink tea, smoke joints and talk about the Bock Saga to whomever was around, which were not many at that point in time.

Ior used to be an outgoing person, a socialite, a traveller, a theatre-show man. When he started to tell the Bock Saga in 1984, this all changed. He grew a beard and he stopped doing his yoga practice. He stopped taking care of his body. He hardly brushed his teeth and only went to the dentist if the pain became unbearable. He stopped eating healthily. He kept himself alive mainly through bread and cheese in Europe and bread and beans in India. He neglected the maintenance of his apartment. Since 1984, the apartment hadn't been renovated once.

Ior also neglected his financial situation. Digging was expensive. After selling his mother and aunt's apartment there wasn't much left of his capital. He'd chosen not to be the heir of all the family industries and there were no hidden trust funds set up for him. He was slowly becoming poorer and poorer. After his time spent in prison, there were no more windfalls.

Bills that arrived at the townhouse apartment were put in a pile behind the curtain. Unfortunately, these types of problem don't tend to go away on their own, although Ior had hoped that they would as soon as the temple had opened. But the temple didn't open, and the bills accumulated behind the curtain. At some point during that Goa season, Ior received the news that his debts in Finland had grown so much that there would be an auction of his properties.

As I think you'll agree by now, the world works in strange ways. Remember Aatos and his LSD-induced flip-out in 1984? Well, it just so happened that the policeman who'd been assigned his case had somehow managed to position himself as the auctioneer in charge of Ior's property. After Aatos arrived in his hands, this policeman had dedicated himself to studying the effects of LSD on the psyche.

He'd never tried the drug himself, of course, but had studied the occasional case of LSD flip-out that encountered the police. All the people who'd had good LSD experiences and hadn't encountered the police were never accounted for in his studies. But the man firmly believed that he was now a specialist in the matter. There was one clear thing that most of his subjects had in common: their lives had in some way been intertwined with that of Ior Bock.

Exactly how and why he managed to appoint himself as auctioneer is still unclear to me, but he did a fantastic job at selling everything. Even though the auctioneer's friends bought most of the items at a price far below the market value, this still yielded much more money than was required to settle Ior's debts.

The debts were not that great, consisting mainly of old utility bills that had accumulated interest. Overall, the sum owed amounted to several thousand Euros. The estate in Gumbostrand was situated at a prime location, where all the rich Helsinkians loved to show off their wealthy mansions. The town apartment was in the centre of Helsinki and was worth a lot of money too. In addition to this, the town apartment was filled with antiques that were regarded as invaluable national heritage. Some artefacts were from the time the Bock family returned from the north to settle in south Finland, around 1250 AD. Where the excess money raised by the auction ended up, remains a mystery, but I think I would be able to make an educated guess...

Ior learned about his expropriation sitting at the chai shop in Chapora, smoking his morning joint.

"I lost my legs, and now I've lost my home. All that's left is my Finnish passport."

I think that this might be the moment when a shift happened in Ior's mind. He started to feel that since he'd now finished telling the Bock Saga, the universe no longer needed him and that this was the reason he'd lost his legs and property. He'd played his role and now it was time to leave the stage. He'd given all he had to fulfil his duty of bringing the Bock Saga out of the confinement of his family.

Apart from a bohemian group of outsiders who had plenty of time but little money to give, nobody had shown any interest. Ior believed that Öde had decided his fate. Before he'd started telling the Bock Saga, he'd had no idea that everything would become so dramatic, that opening the temple in modern times would prove to be much harder than closing it a thousand years ago.

After all the twists of fate and strange happenings over the last twenty to twenty-five years, nothing was unimaginable anymore. It seemed that Öde's final plan was for him to lose everything, and Ior really did feel like he'd lost it all. There seemed to be no merit in fighting against greater forces. He'd basically given up.

In the spring, Ior made the long trip home. He was appointed a simple social housing apartment in a suburb of Helsinki. The street name was 'Dragonsvägen'. The 'dragon' was the symbol of the Offer-Ring system going up to Hel. The end of his journey had brought him to the end of the offering. He felt he'd offered everything he had for the Bock Saga. On the first day that he'd started telling the Bock Saga, he'd lost his girlfriend, Cecile. He then lost his job, his social life in Helsinki. He lost his health, his legs and now all his material possessions.

He resumed his life on the two-square-metre mattress within the four walls of his new apartment. After the attack, all digging and other Bock Saga activity had stopped. The Norwegians, who'd been the most recent diggers, went home. The English translation of Ior's book was put on hold indefinitely.

The via-via group was in big disarray. They were in shock that one of their own had tried to kill Ior. They had thought that all evil would come from outside of the group, but it hadn't. Could the attack have been prevented? During the auction, Valto and his partner had managed to buy the land of the Lemminkäinen Temple. This meant that in the future, they would still be able to continue the digging. But for now, everything simply ground to a halt.

Shavas

After I'd said goodbye to Ior and departed for good, he'd made several attempts to pull me back in. He'd been a few times in Berlin and had invited me to join him and the others at some Oslo event. Any time we were both in Goa, he would always reach out to me. Although I did still like Ior, I knew we could never have a friendship without the Bock Saga being involved and all the consequences that came with that. Ior and the Bock Saga were one thing and could never be separated from each other.

In 1999, five years after I left the Bock Saga group, I met him in Somadillo's chai shop in Goa. It was a nice experience. We made peace with one another, but I still refused to go back to that old lifestyle. I swore that I wouldn't, but in the end, that's exactly what happened. I started to listen to his stories again. This time round, everything made more sense than it had before. He explained so many intricate details.

Later that year, he was stabbed. He couldn't move anymore, and it meant that I would need to go to him if I wanted to see him. He wasn't going anywhere. Visiting Ior became a routine, like going to a restaurant where you know your favourite meal will always be on the menu. In this case, it was my brain that needed the nourishment.

Although Ior was now only focussing on the small details of the Bock Saga, these pulled the whole story together into one giant tapestry. I knew the rough outlines of the Bock Saga, having listened to Ior for a couple of years already. But now he went deeper and deeper into the sounds and their meanings and the connections between each of these meanings.

During the first ten years of his telling, he'd laid out the neurological plan for the brain, if you'll allow me the analogy, and now he was explaining all the connections between the synapses and what these combined connections could do and mean. Yes, we, the listeners, felt like Bock Saga neurologists.

Now I could see why Ior had proclaimed that the heterosexual system had condemned our planet. Since the system had been implemented by the religions of Krishna and Christ, amongst others, the planet had become overpopulated. It's still impossible to even discuss our world's population problem and possible solutions without clashing with every religious leader and being called a Nazi. I believe that there's a way to create a selective system of some sort that outlines who should have children and with whom, without being a Nazi, or without enforcing the Chinese one-child policy. From the perspective of the Bock Saga, the heterosexual system is the biggest mistake in history and should be one of the easiest to solve. And there's a big chance that, by solving this, the human race would also solve most of its other problems too.

The whole subject is totally taboo, however. By telling the Bock Saga without telling people how to live, we hope to at least show people how such a system has worked in the past, what an alternative possibility could look like. Until now, not many people have been interested in the Bock Saga, but this might change once we open the temple.

Excerpt from the Bock Saga:

It is impossible to foresee whether we will be one family again or whether we will merely live together as distant cousins. But we could choose to live in harmony on our 'Pale Blue Dot', or 'Blek blå punkt'. Maybe a future generation of 'illiterate linguists' can shed more light on this matter.

Ronan

Not much happened during the following years. The existing situation just progressed. It got harder and harder for Ior to do anything. For him to move from Helsinki to Goa once a year, and to then make the same trip back six months later, was not only physically a tour de force, but almost impossible without money or the possibility to earn some. Our group of friends organised a collection for Ior every year to pay for his ticket and expenses during these trips.

I led my silk-printing lifestyle and only saw Ior the three months when I was in Goa. I saw him there every day during this time and listened to him explain one word a day. Things became more difficult for him every year. At a certain point, he started taking cortisone pills to curtail the infections in his body. These made him swell up like a Ganesh statue. It became more difficult to lift him in and out of cars.

His strength decreased and he could no longer go to the toilet independently. The only physical exercise he was getting was from his daily coughing fits. When he felt a cough coming, he'd inhale deeply, grind his bronchi stiffly together, and cause a sub-sonic thunder that reminded me of the sound an airplane makes when it breaks the sound barrier. He'd throw around mucous, saliva and bits of joints, as well as other stuff you'd find in a whale's stomach. I think that, although they didn't sound healthy, these coughs kept him fit.

In later years, his deteriorating physical situation started to eat away at his confidence. I remember one time, when we finally arrived in his Chapora residence after a long and strenuous journey from Helsinki, the first thing he asked was who would take him home six months later and how he'd ever make that trip again.

This was so unlike him. He'd always been so carefree. He'd always believed that the universe or Öde would provide what was needed and would solve all problems in time. Now, he was no longer sure whether Öde was on his side. But he kept on doing what he believed was his responsibility.

Back in Helsinki, only Shavas, Ulven and a few others from the via-via group continued to pass by occasionally. Akanpesa, that had always been the centre of activity and omni-directional energy, now lay desolate. The tunnel that had been dug deep into the mountain towards the entrance of the legendary Lemminkäinen Temple filled up with melted snow. Ior's energy, as well as the energy of the whole Saga-heads group, was like a wilted rose. The petals hung limply, before falling into the wet, muddy earth and disappearing into nothingness.

This wasn't like after the Third Ragnarök when the kingdom of the roses had overgrown and lay waiting for a kiss to wake it up. No, this was the end of something. It was the end of the great Bock family that had been with us since the dawn of mankind and had guided us through the storms of time. Ior was the last of the Bock family lineage and his life spirit was like a dying candle flickering in the wind.

Ior had many different helpers in those years. They came and went. They were Swedish, Finnish and Goanese. Most of them really were professionals, who tried to make Ior's life bearable. It wasn't an easy job. They had to share the small social apartment in Finland with Ior, who smoked continuously and talked day and night about the intricate details of this prehistoric Saga. It was clearly not a job that anyone could do. And clearly not a job anyone could do for a long time.

Ior always had two helpers, so apart from living with Ior, each helper also needed to share their living space with another person. And they might want to have a life of their own too. Taking care of Ior gave the helpers an income, but it was hard to maintain a social life, impossible to have girlfriends or children themselves. Forget hobbies and studies. Taking care of Ior was a lifestyle.

During the last few years there was Abji. He was one of Ior's favourites. To this day, I've never heard anyone say anything bad about him. He was like an angel. He was from a Goanese fishing village and had got the job through a cousin. He loved sports. He hadn't had much education, but he somehow managed to learn to speak passable Finnish in a few months' time. That was something that most of us European foreigners had never been capable of doing. He was the ideal helper. He always listened to the Bock Saga, but never talked.

At a certain moment, his cousin, who was the other helper at the time, had a medical complication and couldn't work anymore. This cousin appointed another cousin to work with Abji and Ior. As is the case so many times in India, this kind of decision wasn't made in a practical or meritocratic style, but in a complicated social style, where relative importance and standing was calculated by caste, age and through many other factors that can seem incomprehensible to outsiders.

In this way, Milesh was appointed helper companion to Abji. The contrast between the two couldn't have been greater. Physically, Abji was strong and tall, the perfect athlete. It was important that the two helpers were approximately of the same height to carry Ior around. If one was smaller, Ior wouldn't be level and the smaller helper would have to bear most of his weight. Milesh was not only smaller, but also physically weaker. Their lifestyles and interests were also totally different. Abji loved sports. He went running in the park and made friends with other athletes in Helsinki.

Milesh went out to get drunk and loved putting any powder he could find up his nose. He only took the job for the money and simply couldn't put any love into it. He just wasn't a loving person. I've never heard anyone say anything good about Milesh. And he resented the Bock Saga.

Ior wanted to get rid of him, but that wasn't easy. The social rules in India are strong. But at least he was only temporary and would be replaced when the first cousin returned. Once a year, both helpers were given a month's leave. Milesh returned home to Goa, the Finnish insurance company paying for his flight, and bought a house with a mortgage. Because of these new monthly payments, he couldn't afford to lose his job as Ior's helper. The situation grew tenser still, as Milesh let down both Abji and Ior on several occasions. Drinking was more important.

The alcohol and drugs combined with the long, dark Finnish winters chipped away at Milesh's mind. He disappeared more and more often into the city. He slept at strange hours. He often talked to himself.

"Oh, oh, where have we seen this before..." Ior thought to himself.

On one of these long nights, Milesh was roaming the streets of the dark and snow-covered Helsinki when he bumped into a Finnish guy dressed in a Hindu outfit. They decided to go for a drink together. The Finnish guy turned out to be Kertu and they soon discovered that they both knew Ior and the Bock Saga. They discussed Ior's stabbing a few years earlier.

Milesh was curious about what had happened to Kertu, who had stabbed Ior after all. To Milesh's surprise, Kertu told him that he'd not gone to jail, but had been sent to a mental asylum instead. Mental asylums in Finland were more like sanatoria and a far cry from the concept that Milesh had of jail, which was a gangster and insect-ridden horror movie where the only winners were cholera and typhus survivors. Kertu told him he'd already been released because the doctors declared him cured and mentally fit to live in Finnish society. These were all new concepts to Milesh. In India, if you killed someone, you'd probably be killed by the victim's family or the police before you'd even seen a judge. If you did make it to a judge, your fate would probably be even worse.

After Kertu had been released, he'd had nowhere to go. Nobody wanted to hang out with him, and no one wanted to give him a job, with one exception: the people who believe there's good in every person, the Hare Krishnas. Kertu now lived with them and dedicated his life to karma yoga. This is a yoga exercise designed to clean away your bad karma. In practice, it means working in the kitchen and cleaning the floors and toilets. But that didn't matter. What mattered was that Kertu was welcome there.

Milesh and Kertu had a long conversation. I don't really know what was discussed that night. All I know is that Abji confirmed later that the conversation left Milesh in a state of great excitement. This excitement didn't diminish over the days that followed. On the contrary, it lingered and grew stronger. Milesh got a strange look in his eyes. It was as if he was taking in more photons and impressions than usual, and his brain was having to work overtime to process all the extra information. This extra effort made his body hot and sweaty, even though it was cold in the cheap social apartment on the Dragonswegen.

When you live together in such a small space without separate sleeping rooms, you don't need to like one another to know each other well. You smell each other, you hear each other's breathing, and you sense each other's being. Not on an intellectual level, but on an animalistic one. The three men had already been sleeping side by side on the small living room floor for one and a half years. Abji saw his cousin change and wondered what was happening to him. It made him worry. Was his soul being taken over by some demon? He didn't like leaving Ior alone with him anymore. The situation in the little apartment went from tense to overwrought. Ior could feel it too.

Casper

On the 22nd of October 2010, I was driving through the Black Forest in Germany when my mobile rang, and I saw that it was Ior's number. I remember feeling quite surprised as Ior never phoned me. It must be important. I pulled the car over to the side of the road and answered.

"Hi Casper, how are you? I just want to check that you know everything."

"Everything of what?"

"Everything of the Bock Saga!"

"Well, I remember everything you've told me, except, of course, for the things I've forgotten. No, I'm only joking. You repeated everything to me so many times, and I've then repeated them myself to others and discussed them endlessly with Ronan and the rest of the group. Why are you asking me this? Are you OK?"

"I just want to check whether you still know everything."
He then went through a verbal checklist of many of the concepts in the Bock Saga.

"Do you know the Offer-Ring system, the procreation system, the sound system, the caste system?"

He asked me many detailed questions about each of these concepts. He then went on to check whether I knew hundreds of Root and Van words, their meanings, their place within the sound system and their connection to each other.

"There is one thing that you promised on many occasions to tell us about, but never did."

"What was that?"

"Your aunt Kristina Victoria. You told us she was very important to the family, but you never told us why and what she did that was so important. Maybe now's a good moment?"

"Yes, it's the perfect moment. Kristina is the name of her function within the family. 'Krist' comes from the Root word 'Krisis'. It means a big disruptive change. For example, both Jesus Christ and Krishna were disruptive figures in their societies. It was with their arrival that the king systems ended and monogamous marriage within an individual's own caste was introduced."

"I see. Are you able tell me now what it was that Kristina did that was so disruptive?"

"Her task in life was to guide the Bock family to extinction. The plan laid out by Gubben-Noah just after the Ice Age foresaw this event. Kristina's role was to ensure that I was born so that I could tell the Bock Saga to the outside world, and that there would be no new babies in the Bock family after me."

"I don't quite see why that was so disruptive."

"Don't you see? From now on, the human race will have to live without the family that created them. According to Gubben-Noah's plan, the human race would by this point have been developed enough to live without us. We provided All-Fathers through the ages. You and I know that this is now over. Those times will never return. Do not wait for a messiah or anyone from the heavens; we will not come back. The human race will have to go on alone from here."

"Are we developed enough now? Are we strong enough?"

"I don't know. It doesn't look good. But it's not up to me, I just followed the plan the same way Kristina did."

"What did Aunt Kristina have to say about it all?"

"She said that her second name was Victoria. Its meaning is easy to guess. She said she lived up to that name. So, I guess you guys might have a chance. You know what you must do, don't you?"

"Open the temple, you mean?"

"Exactly."

The phone call lasted more than two hours. In the back of my head, I was wondering why this sudden conversation was taking place. It was completely out of the ordinary. Twelve hours later, I got another phone call from Helsinki with the message that Ior had been stabbed to death.

It was early on the 23rd of October 2010 in the Ior's apartment in Dragonswegen, Helsinki. Abji was in the kitchen preparing breakfast like any other day. It was the weekend, but for Ior and Abji all days were the same. Suddenly, Abji heard screaming. He recognised the voice as that of his cousin Milesh.

"I will kill you! You're the devil!"

Then came the sound of things falling, probably books. Abji jumped towards the living room and saw Ior lying in a pool of blood, Milesh standing over him stabbing and stabbing into the already lifeless body. Milesh saw Abji and ran towards him knife still in hand, while what was left of Ior flushed over the carpet floor. Abji ran into the bathroom and locked the door. Milesh tried to open the door with the knife and by kicking it repeatedly. Being made of cheap double-sided plywood, the door started changing shape. With one hand, Abji managed to get his mobile out of his pocket and dial the emergency number. Someone immediately answered.

"Police, police, come quick! Someone's been killed and now he's trying to kill me too! Come to this address!"

In the meantime, Milesh continued to kick the door and scream: "I killed the devil! I killed the devil! I killed the devil!"

When the police arrived in full strength only a few minutes later, Milesh was sitting quietly by Ior's body. There was blood everywhere. The bread knife was lying between Milesh and Ior.

"The killer's in the bathroom, I locked him up," Milesh told the officers.

The police asked for the bathroom door to be opened. Abji, trembling all over, opened the door and was immediately arrested.

"I didn't do it!" he cried. "It was him!" Abji frantically pointed in Milesh's direction.

Milesh remained quiet, ice cold and denied everything.

"I'll give a statement at the police station."

When they all arrived at the police station, it soon became clear who the real culprit was. Milesh was covered with blood and Abji hadn't been near the body. Still, it took three weeks for the police to release Abji. They wanted to know if there was more to the case than devil-killing. Was there drug trafficking, satanic rites and so on involved too? Abji told them all he knew, which is what I've told you.

In the courtroom, Milesh knew what strategy to take. Although there were many facts to the contrary, the judge decided the following: Milesh had been 'temporarily insane'. He was extradited to India to recover, and all travel costs were covered by the Finnish government. Three months after the murder, he was home. From the insurance company compensation he received for losing his job in such a tragic way, he bought a restaurant in Goa. As far as I know, the restaurant's still running reasonably successfully and Milesh is happily married. He refused to comment on the events that happened the morning of the 23rd of October.

After Ior's death, came his funeral. He was buried, not under the ancient Yggdrasil, as he'd envisioned once, but next to its stump. Almost everybody that had ever been involved in the Bock Saga was present that day. The group was in great disarray. We no longer knew where to direct our energy. It was the end of digging and all other efforts.

We realised that we would never again get new Bock Saga information. Ior had been the sole source, and this had now been irrevocably cut. There was also a realisation of just how explosive the story of the Bock Saga was and the potential dangers it brought. The general feeling was to distance ourselves from it as much as possible for a while. Let the dust settle and see. Maybe, just maybe, after a few years we'd be able to re-accept the responsibility and start digging again. It was clear that quiet times lay ahead, everybody going their own separate way and leading their own lives.

And that's exactly what we did, but Raportti Media had other plans. They fuelled a media blitz where they argued that Ior was not the son of Rhea Boxström, but an adopted child. Therefore, his bloodline didn't belong to that of the mythological ancestors he'd claimed to descend from. This proved that he was a liar and that the Bock Saga was merely a nonsensical fantastical story that had been invented by an adopted nobody in an attempt to become a somebody. They produced lots of proof and legal papers that backed their accusations.

Ior had always been aware of the existence of these papers and had warned me on various occasions that something like this would eventually happen. The truth was that Ior was the son of Rhea and her father Victor Boxström. The husband of Rhea, Svedlin, couldn't have children, it was medically impossible and a well-known fact. Thus, the only accepted way for Rhea to have a child in those days was through legal adoption. That's why papers were forged stating that a cleaning lady in the area was Ior's birth mother and had given him up for adoption. The story they told people was that a German Nazi officer had left her pregnant during the dark days of the war.

I've seen all the papers. It doesn't matter now anyway. Everybody involved in the scandal's dead. I believe my old friend Ior, the man I knew better than anyone else in the world. I didn't want to get into the whole thing anymore. Raportti Media will always come up with something new that discredits Ior and the Bock Saga. All I wanted to do was leave to an island far away in the ocean. I didn't want any access to the internet or a phone. I told everyone not to contact or try to find me. I needed some time.

Excerpt from the Bock Saga:

Ior Bock said he could not reveal the entire Bock Saga to us. Instead, he gave us the key – the Root alphabet with its sounds and meanings – to unlock it for ourselves. According to him, to figure it all out was an 'Ord lek, tanke lek, sällskap lek', which means 'word games, mind games, parlour games'.

Epilogue

William

The years passed and we all got older. One year, we decided to visit the temple, or at least the digging location, one more time now that we were all still alive. It was midsummer's day and we stood at the entrance of the temple, just under the Etta Stupa. Ronan finds it difficult to travel now but had made it anyway. He had some organ troubles and there were tubes sticking out of his belly. Casper was in a better condition but had the habitual coughing fits of a heavy smoker. He had to take care not to overexert himself because of his high blood pressure. Lola was a bit wobbly on her feet, but apart from having gathered additional wrinkles, she was relatively fine. I walked with a stick. All my sporting activity and accompanying accidents had made my knees weak, and every step that was not absolutely horizontal was painful. Shavas and Ulven seemed fit but carried their own maladies under their skins.

We were waiting for Mr Yeah to arrive from the airport. We'd heard that his flight from Hawaii had already landed. A taxi arrived and Mr Yeah jumped out. A lot of hugs and laughs ensued. We looked at each other. We'd been young hippies once and now we were old hippies. We wore the same colourful, rainbow, tie-dyed and fractal designs, but our bodies were worn out, our hair grey, white, or gone. Long beards had grown. We never thought that we'd really grow old, but that's what had happened.

"Come on," said Casper. "Get your walking sticks and rollators and let's walk up the Sibbo Berget. We can collect some wood for a fire and make tea, roll a joint and see what happens, like we did in the old days."

Everyone agreed and soon we were sitting on top of the little hill under which the famous Lemminkäinen Temple was supposedly located.

"So, who would've thought that almost half a century later we'd still be sitting here on top of a hidden temple?" Mr Yeah asked, leaning back on his arms. "This thing should've been opened the very first year we arrived here. The golden bocks should've been dug up soon after, if not before. It's all because of that damned Bishop and the idiots at the Museovirasto. So much wasted time!"

"On the other hand," Ronan pointed out. "We wouldn't have been prepared for what would've engulfed us if the temple had opened that day."

"Are you guys any better prepared now?" I asked.

"No, but at least we know the whole story now. We know the full Wheel of Life and the workings of the sound system that are the concealed backbones of the Bock Saga. We didn't have that in our brains in 1987," answered Casper.

"Anyway, there wouldn't be much left for us to do if the temple and storehouse opened now," Ronan mused.

I interrupted the moment of silence that followed with another question.

"Imagine that the golden doors of the Lemminkäinen Temple have been excavated and you've got the door handle in your hand. The door's opening, what do you do? I mean in that very moment."

"Well, firstly I'd have to make sure it's the 24th of July, as that's the designated day for entering the temple. If it's not the 24th, we'd have to wait until it is. Ior had a bunch of brass lanterns with candles that we'd use to light our way. Then, we'd undress and go in completely naked and marvel at what lies within," Casper answered decisively.

"And I suppose I'll just stand outside and keep the media, politicians and police at bay, making sure you lot have a good time inside. Why would I be allowed in? I'm a woman after all! Oh yes, we woman are so respected, but that doesn't change the fact that we should anyway be excluded from anything that matters," Lola said bitterly.

Ronan countered quickly: "Oh, Lola. We discussed this so many times throughout the 80s and 90s. Before the temple and the storehouse were closed a thousand years ago, only men were allowed inside. The temple was only made for Lemminkäinen and a Rabi. Ukko died inside the storehouse. Thus, the argument was made that even back then women weren't allowed inside out of respect to the tradition of the elders. I know that this is hard to hear and that the women in our group always struggled to accept it. You've gone through the whole journey and experienced every drama just as much as we have. But should we allow you in just because we live in so-called democratic times? Should we not respect the ways of the elders who created the place and created our whole human race? Akka, the holiest lady on the planet, made her Etta Stupa just outside the entrance, and in the history of mankind she never entered the temple and storehouse, not even once. It's not an easy decision."

Lola turned to look directly at Ronan. "The Bock Saga has been criticised for being a story without love or friendship. It's all rules and formalities. And it's true. There's no love. Paradise time is over, and maybe it wasn't as fantastic as it's been painted to be. And besides, the temple and storehouse don't have their original functions anymore. Their only function now is to educate the living people on this planet about what life used to look like. But apparently, according to you, we women don't need to be educated. At least that's what you guys decided when you opted to exclude women from entering the temple."

"Lola's definitely got a point there," nodded Mr Yeah.

"Ior was very clear: no women allowed!" retorted Ronan, a sharper edge creeping into his voice.

"Well, if Ior was so smart and all-knowing, then why has the temple not been opened yet?" Lola asked, glaring at Ronan.

"He was smart and all-knowing, just not about digging. His focus was always the Bock Saga, you know this."

"Uh-uh, sure. Well, what happens if you lot are all old and sick and rotting in some hospital bed, and I'm the only one left who's still strong. What happens if I'm the one who opens the temple?"

"That's up to Öde to decide."

"Aha! So now it's Öde who decides and not you?"

"Stop it kids! Enough. No more fighting on what might be our last meeting," I scolded them both.

Ronan and Lola settled back down, and we sat in silence for a few minutes.

"The biggest mystery that remains, in my opinion, is how on Earth the temple still hasn't been excavated. I mean, the Bock family were connected to the crème de la crème of money in Finland. Ior's stepfather was a Svedlin, the owner of one of the biggest companies in Finland. Surely, the Bock family, who were known for carefully thinking everything through, sometimes for millennia, would have known that digging was going to be expensive," I wondered out loud for what felt like the thousandth time.

"I know what you mean," said Mr Yeah. "In the decades that we've been struggling with this thing, the Svedlin family have built an entire subway system under Helsinki."

"You're right. But Ior always believed that the Bock Saga should be the thing that provides the energy needed to open the temple. And for a while, it really did look like that would be enough, especially when Henki Penti's company got involved. It's such a pity that we screwed up so badly with all that smuggling business. I know that Ior never explicitly told us to smuggle, but he didn't mind that we did either. And he did ask us to remain available and avoid getting jobs and other obligations," said Casper with a troubled look on his face.

"He liked that you guys always brought him free dope to smoke as well," muttered Lola.

"He did."

"But the Bock Saga energy didn't open the temple in the end. I think that in any other country, everything would've been sorted within a few short years. If this were Holland, there'd be dozens of five-star hotels already built here, and probably around each of the other Bock Saga sites as well. There'd be Bock Saga tours and everything," I insisted.

"Probably. But here in Finland we still suffer from the fight between the Root-speaking people and the Van/Finnish-speaking people who see Root as the language of the Swedish rulers. The Museovirasto is the exponent of the Van people," Shavas pointed out as he got up to fill his cup with more tea.

"There were plenty of influential people on our side as well though. The king of Norway, the minister of foreign affairs of Finland, even the former prime minister," said Ronan.

"But none of them helped to open the temple. If the King of Holland ordered something to be excavated, it would get done and quickly too! There'd be no Museovirasto strong enough to stop it," I pressed on. "Another thing that's never been clear to me is the role that Raportti Media has had in all this. They keep popping up throughout the story and sabotaged everything you did. They just seemed to cook up one scandal after another."

"That took so much energy from us. We always did try to ignore them, but the whole situation damaged a lot of people. It damaged us. We tried to do something good, but were only ever portrayed as criminals, idiots or worse," sighed Ulven.

"I feel damaged too," muttered Ronan. "If I hadn't given all my time and money to the Bock Saga, and if I hadn't always remained available for Ior, I could've used my life and talent for my own good. The majority of the people I know own houses and have some money saved up for retirement. I have none of that. I even gave up my romantic relationships for the Bock Saga. I had no family because of it. We were supposed to be available, always, because the temple could be opened at any moment, and then we would be needed. I would've loved to have had children and grandchildren."

"That's the first time I've heard of this!" laughed Lola. "Would you have loved to have had kids with me?"

We all laughed at the look on Ronan's face, and I couldn't help adding:

"Lola, without the Bock Saga, you'd have had children with the lot of us!"

"One big happy family," Lola smiled. "You missed your chance, guys! What could be more Bock Saga style than that?"

"I never committed to anything bigger than a couple of silk prints," continued Ronan. "It wasn't an easy choice, but I never let my own interests prevail over the Bock Saga."

"Isn't that the definition of fanaticism?" I asked.

"I don't think so," he answered. "Sure, I made everything in life secondary to the Bock Saga, but it didn't feel like fanaticism. It was just a matter of priority."

"I did the same as Ronan, but I don't see myself as fanatic either," agreed Casper. "I just had nothing more important to do. I did distance myself from the madness after my flip-out, but I always viewed that madness as separate from the Bock Saga itself. For me, the story is larger than any one person. It's logical and simply a matter of fact. It's only the persistent chaos and crazy people the Bock Saga seems to attract that I reject. If you regard the Bock Saga as a true story, which I do, it would be lunacy to turn your back on it. But yes, it has cost me too. I spent a lot of time in places doing things that I'd have done very differently were it not for the Bock Saga. No regrets though. It was never boring, and I got to see the world, meet lots of people and make good friends, most of whom are still my friends today. And here we are, still alive."

Casper looked round at us and smiled.

"I also gave my life to the Bock Saga," Mr Yeah told us, setting his cup down and poking the fire with a stick. "It became the most important thing from the moment I heard about it. I spent my whole life listening to the Bock Saga, and when I wasn't listening, I was telling other people about it. I agree with you, Casper, I don't regret what we lived through, but I also suffered a lot from it. Oh, actually! I do regret one thing."

"What's that? I'm curious now," asked Lola, a glint in her eye.

"I regret telling Wessel about the Bock Saga. It was because of what he spilled to the police that we all ended up in jail for as long as we did."

"He's definitely the largest idiot of all, at least in centimetres!" laughed Lola.

We sat staring at the fire as it licked the air around it. I soaked in the sense of calm that I'd come to recognise from this place. It seemed like only yesterday that these very friends of mine had brought me here for the first time. Mr Yeah cleared his throat, pulling me out of my reverie.

"Anyway, over the last few years I've been making YouTube videos with Alexei with all that I've left to give. I've now put everything I know into words. I hope that the videos attract some people to the Bock Saga. In any case, there's nothing more I think I can do. And that means I don't have to be available anymore. I can die with a quiet feeling now. We've been waiting for half a century for this temple to open; I don't see it happening during my lifetime anymore. I'm sure it will happen, but I'll be long gone by then."

"I feel the same way, Mr Yeah. What about you Casper?" asked Ronan.

"You guys are probably right."

There was one more thing that had always niggled at me.

"What does 'Ior' actually mean in Root anyway?"

"The name Ior is a title, not a personal name. It is the title of the last member of the Bock family. Like the first human born of another human, the son of Frei and Freia, Ior's parents were meant to be brother and sister. Ior was supposed to be born out of Rafael and Rhea. Because Rafael died prematurely, the only male left to create an Ior was Rhea's father," Casper explained.

"Ok, but what does the name or title 'Ior' actually mean within the Root language?" Shavas asked patiently.

"Ior means i-oden-ra. These are the basic concepts of the Bock Saga. You all know that." Ronan replied.

"It is also one-zero-R. In mathematics R is any real number." Ulven added.

"It's funny, Ior used to joke that only the Vatican bank and the donkey from Winnie the Pooh were called Ior," Mr Yeah chuckled.

"I believe that the meaning of his name is associated with 'lillior' which is the plural of lily. It's also the flower he put on his mother's grave. Frei – Fresior, Valkuria – Valkurior," Ronan said.

"Does adding 'ior' to a word make it plural then?" asked Mr Yeah looking a little perplexed.

"No, not plural. It is in relation to the two flowers called 'Lillior'," clarified Casper.

"This Root language makes me crazy! Every time you try to find a regularity, it turns out to be something different," lamented Mr Yeah.

"In English, many words end in 'ior', like 'superior' for instance. But in itself, it's I, O and R. 'I-Oden-Ra', in the rays of Oden. Or it's 'Ra-Oden-I'. 'ROI', like royal. But there are many endings with 'ior', and they don't always make that word plural, like 'superior'," explained Casper.

"Superior. 'Sup' is something liquid that you eat," joined in Ronan.

"What makes this particular soup superior?" I chuckled. "I still don't get what 'ior' in 'superior' is meant to mean?"

"You should know by now what kind of soup we're talking about if the Bock Saga's involved. It's always the same: dicks, pricks and sperm," retorted Lola in her usual tone.

Ronan ignored her and continued with the line of thought.

"There're lots of words that end in 'ior', like 'interior', 'junior' and so on."

"Hmm... I think that those are words ending in 'or', some of which have 'ior' at the end. 'Or' comes from the Root word 'jöra', which means to make. Some examples are: 'author', 'vendor', 'mirror' and 'anchor'. It's the same in French, where the ending is 'eur'. French is a form of high-caste Root. It's clear if you're not reading it. It has a much finer way of expressing than the more boorish German, Dutch, and English languages," observed Casper.

"French is superior so to speak... Well, they do make the best soup!" smiled Ronan.

"I disagree," interjected Lola. "I think that French is the boorish language. They just refuse to pronounce the last few letters of a word, just like the dialect of most peasants around the world."

This wasn't leading anywhere. I tried once more with my question.

"Ok, but I still don't understand what 'Ior' means. Do any of you know?"

"Did I ever tell you about Ior's dream island?" interrupted Casper.

"No, tell us!"

"After we finally reached a result in opening the Temple, Ior had hoped to settle on his own little island at the end of the archipelago. It would be a red granite island with two small hills on it that would be connected to each other by glass walls that formed a house. He wanted the granite to keep its natural shape, as was the tradition in the old Aser culture, but he wanted to polish it until it was a beautiful shiny red. The house would have a similar function to the Winter Palace in St. Petersburg, where all the Russian dukes and governors stayed for three month each year. Ior planned to spend three month a year in his own glass winter palace, with its floors of polished red granite and soft bear skins positioned around a central fireplace. Through the glass walls, he could look over the sea and he'd be able to see any boats that approached. The roof of his house would be made of wood with grass growing over it. It would be his own private space where he could hold a conversation in the knowledge that no stray ears would be listening in. He would no longer receive unexpected visitors, unlike what had been happening for all those years in Helsinki and Akanpesa. All conversations would be held in Root, and everyone present would listen in silence. When he wasn't residing on the island, he'd be travelling around on invitation telling the Bock Saga."

"That's a beautifully poetic fantasy. Pity he never got that far," sighed Lola.

"Oh, by the way, since we're talking about houses," exclaimed Ronan suddenly. "Do you remember that policeman who over-saw Aatos' case and who later auctioned Ior's property while he was paraplegic in Goa? Well, years after he'd sold all of Ior's property, it came to light that he'd put all the excess money into his own pockets. It was a considerable sum. He was convicted for fraud and, as the judge put it, could now spend the next five years in jail studying the psychological effects of greed on the decision-making part of the brain. In the end, Ior never saw a penny of the money that had been stolen from him."

"I'd heard about that," nodded Casper. "That's not all. Do you remember the policeman who'd put that announcement in the newspaper inviting anyone who'd had their valuables stolen to come collect them from Ior's house in Akanpesa? So much of Ior's antiques went missing that day and there was nothing Ior could do as he was in Goa at the time. Well, I found out a while ago that that very policeman was arrested and convicted for several corruption cases, this being one of them. They discov-ered various Boxström antiques in his possession. I mean, none of this brought all those antiques back, but it at least gave us a sense of justice."

"And we were always seen as the bad guys," snorted Ronan.

"I know. Since we're gossiping about old enemies," continued Casper looking pleased. "Inspector Kant, who led the investiga-tion in the drug case against us, just got arrested for running a 27-year-long smuggling operation. When he busted us in 1992, he got to know everyone in Finland who was in the dealing and smuggling game; he even made contacts for wholesale drugs supply in Amsterdam through Hal! When the Finnish dealers got out of jail some years later, he started a smuggling racket of his own. He used the Amsterdam contacts and smuggled and sold tonnes of drugs, from hashish to cocaine to MDMA. He did well for himself until his retirement last year. His replacement is a young enthusiastic straight-edge guy who uncovered the whole scheme. The new inspector busted everyone involved. Detective Kant had gotten away with it for twenty-seven years but couldn't control his replacement."

"Maybe detective Kant was as straight edged as his replacement when he busted you guys. Maybe his replacement will start his own drug scheme and run it for twenty-seven years now," I grinned.

"Yes, and then get caught by his replacement!"

"Unless drugs are legal by then."

"Or the temple's open and there's no police anymore."

"Not even temple police?" laughed Lola.

We sat again in each other's company, each of us lost in our own thoughts, when I suddenly remembered what I'd been so excited to tell my friends about.

"Hey, Casper. Do you remember when the Yggdrasil was cut down by the vicar in Snappertuna?"

"How could I forget! That's what triggered my entire flip-out."

"Well, I have some good news. I met Ulven a few months ago, and he told me that he'd managed to take a clipping of a shoot from the original roots. He managed to do it some years ago during Ior's funeral."

"Yes, I grew the shoot into a bonsai tree and had kept it in my house since then. I contacted William a while ago to tell me that I was moving house and was looking for a more permanent place for the tree. I asked William if he knew a place in Holland that had a reasonable chance of remaining unchanged for a couple of generations," Ulven explained.

"Initially, I told him such places don't exist in Holland, but then I remembered that my family has a mausoleum. It's part of an ancient manor. Enormous old oak trees grow on its grounds and there's a columbarium where the urns are kept. Contrary to other similar burial places in Europe, this one has no Christian symbols in it. The only symbol I could find is a snake biting its tail, the symbol of the Wheel of Life: Ouroboros. I've planted the Yggdrasil there."

"Öde," smiled Ronan.

Casper

It was probably going to be our last meeting together in that place. We'd gotten old. We used to jump in and out of airplanes like it was the easiest thing in the world. Now travelling had become a whole logistical enterprise. We'd planned to have one last supper in Helsinki before each of us returned to our own countries. We decided to step down the mountain and give the excavation one last look. We entered it in silence. It went about fifty metres into the granite bedrock.

Everything was dark ahead of us, but we knew the place by heart. The place was filled with memories, the memories of our lives. Everything we'd done in our lives had revolved around this place and its promises. We'd brought little flashlights that helped us find the way. Not that we could get lost, it was a 'straight on' kind of cave. We stood for a while staring at the dark granite walls, wishing we could see through them at the temple's hidden secrets. Surely, we couldn't be far from those elusive doors. We'd dug so deep! But the granite walls didn't listen to our silent pleas, they just stood there as they always had. We'd done enough now. Half a century of blisters on our hands and on our souls was enough.

"Come on, let's go!" someone said.
"It's enough, nothing will change anytime soon..."
We slowly walked up the ramp side by side.
"Where shall we eat tonight?" Ronan asked.
"The Thai on the harbour used to be great!" Mr Yeah replied.
"Not anymore. The new owner is cutting expenses. All the ingredients are bought frozen and are precooked, or so I hear," Shaven said.
"The Argentine?" I proposed.

"Nah, they don't have a lot for vegetarians," Shaven dismissed.

"There's that yoga place that has great south Indian food. Cheap and the best," Ulven said.

"No worry, rice and curry!" Lola said smiling.

We all agreed on that.

As the little group walked slowly up the slope littered with granite rubble and talked about their dinner plans, Lola picked up a rock and threw it into the cave's entrance as a last goodbye. She then turned and followed the others up towards the car. None of them noticed the domino sequence of rocks rolling down the slope that knocked over a vertical rock, which in turn fell over another piece of rock that was sticking out levering down on it. For a few moments, everything was silent. Then something softly rumbled. Stones and dust and rocks fell down deep inside the dark cave. Suddenly, the soft reddish yellow of gold shone faintly in the dark.

THE END

"Oden is a ring."
"Oden is everything."
"Oden has always been."
"And Oden will always be."
"Oden is the sun."

348

Printed in Great Britain
by Amazon